AF489755

Lark
Colar
Petaki
Basik
Icar
Mossarai
Niverly
Masai
The Aori Plains
Belara
The Rift
Retrai
Olyan

Also by

<u>The Sea of Flames Duology</u>
Sea of Flames
The Great Dragon

Please by aware

King Assassin is an adult fantasy book containing potentially traumatic scenes/themes such as depression, insomnia, and violence. There is also mention of past rape, necrophilia, and an attempted assault made upon the main character. If any of these things are potentially harmful to you, please take care.

You are not made of only your mistakes.

Contents

King Assassin

Anneliese Peters

Chapter One

THE CORONATION WAS CANCELED halfway through the ceremony when an arrow flew into the heart of the dear future king. Even a Fae couldn't heal from something like that, and while Kit had been caught almost instantly with an imminent, looming execution, she couldn't have cared less. Not then.

She was grateful to the humans for attacking the castle when they did and, in turn, for saving her life, but she wouldn't have minded dying either. It hadn't been her intention, but it was always a possibility. Now, too many things were different, and Kit often thought it might've been better if the humans had attacked just an hour later. After her execution.

The arrow taunted her so many months later. It hung on her wall like a sick decoration just above her fireplace. The arrow that killed someone. The arrow that started a revolution. The arrow that still had remnants of Fae blood on it. It hung on its hooks, and nearly every day, Kit reached up to take it down, but that wouldn't have been acceptable, so it stayed.

It flew through the back of her mind as she walked down the hall of a grand castle. She could feel it against her hands, finding it far more distracting than usual. Perhaps it had something to do with Aspen's latest accusation—that she wouldn't befriend a Fae. It had come up at their spring, a place that had once been a safe haven. It was yet another thing now marked by what she'd done.

Would you be friends with one? Aspen had asked. Kit didn't have an answer. She *couldn't* be friends with a Fae, not after what she did. And still, she tried to defend herself. Still, he had no reason to believe her. He'd wanted her to agree with him when he said that the orphans he looked after shouldn't be allowed to befriend a Fae boy. But if she did agree, what would that make her? The monster everyone believed her to be?

"King Assassin!" A guard on her left shouted. Kit lifted her head and smiled halfheartedly. Most of the time they simply wanted to be right that they spotted her—their hero. Some wished to have a conversation, but Kit kept walking before she could be intruded upon.

She reached her hand into her pocket. Her thumb circled a necklace, one that had once belonged to someone else. The smooth medallion calmed her slowly as the arrows at her back shifted with every step, reminding her how much she used to find comfort in the sound.

Kit made it to the castle's main hall. Sunlight filtered down from the row of small round windows above her, and a bird cawed as it flapped its small wings through the air. The ceiling was high, and because this had once been a Fae castle many animals were given sanctuary in the great stone walls. The Crowns—Mali most of all—had ordered that all holes and cracks that animals could get through were to be sealed. There had been a public outcry when *rat catchers* were called to work in the castle. It had resulted in a small riot, one that ended in the deaths of twelve humans and fifteen Fae.

Followed by six more, who were executed for inciting the riot.

A guard appeared very suddenly, having popped out of an open doorway. She looked around quickly and her eyes widened when she spotted Kit. She cleared her throat and smiled strangely. "Good afternoon," she said. Kit paused a few steps away from her.

"Are you lost?" Kit asked. She looked through the door the guard had come out of. Inside was a simple room with hardly any features in it. If Kit had to guess, she'd say it was one of the old Fae greeting rooms. There were six or seven spaced around the castle that Fae used to go to for private meetings. Kit then looked at the guard, suddenly despising herself for considering her to be a Fae in disguise. The guard in front of her didn't quite look like everyone else. There was a striking beauty to her, something so common among Fae, and if she had pointed ears they'd be easily hidden beneath the thick curls on her head. The tawny color of her skin wasn't common in Calar, but Kit couldn't say much about that—her skin color wasn't common, either.

"I believe so," the guard admitted. "I've only just started, and I know my directions; I just think I've walked around too many times."

"Do you need help?"

The guard hesitated, but if she wanted to keep her job she'd have to take the aid Kit was offering. "I'm supposed to be in West Ball, and I know I'm on the west side of the castle—"

"This is the east side, actually," Kit corrected. The guard's broad shoulders slumped. "Come on, I'm headed in that direction," she said. Kit began walking and the guard moved in step with her. "Why haven't you found another guard? They're all over."

She glanced away, her head turned to the left. "Embarrassment," she finally said.

Kit said, "I doubt any of them know what they're doing, either." She looked around as they stepped onto a rough blue carpet that stretched along the hall. Their footsteps softened. "The Crowns appointed so many of you, it's hard to see how any of you could keep up with yourselves."

"You believe there are too many castle guards?" She asked.

Kit shrugged. "I don't believe a single Fae would attack right now, and I believe that having so many of you that don't know what you're doing is far more dangerous than only having a few well-trained guards. No offense."

"I don't take any," she said. The guard was silent momentarily, and Kit made eye contact with a servant carrying a laundry basket. He grinned brightly at her, and Kit returned it but did not allow it to go further than that. She kept walking, not looking back at the man. "Can I ask you something?" The guard finally asked.

"I suppose," Kit said. They moved up a single step to a part of the hall with many more windows. To their right Kit could now see into the gardens, where a few men were working on tearing down a statue of Crius the Great—the first Fae King and the first Fae to be blessed with wings by nature. He had ropes wrapped around him and tools were being banged against him until down he went, landing hard on the stone pathway below him.

Kit looked away quickly. She only vaguely wondered who'd they be replacing Crius with.

"Do you think King Assassin lives here?" The guard asked.

Kit snorted. "No," she said, "I just come here for the horses." The guard stopped, so Kit did as well. "I have rooms upstairs, but I prefer living in my apartment in the city."

"You're her?" The guard asked. She looked Kit up and down. "But you're so..."

Kit wasn't entirely sure what she was going to say. So young, so small, so this, so that. "I'm Kit," she said and stuck her hand out. "Khatri."

The guard reached out and shook slowly. "King Assassin—uh, Kit Khatri, sorry. I'm Ralyn Cara," she said faintly, "sorry, I just... wasn't expecting it to be you."

"The arrows didn't give me away?" Kit asked with a small laugh. Ralyn flashed a perfectly white smile—no pointed teeth to be seen. She looked at the arrows for a few seconds before Kit began to walk again and she picked up her pace to follow. "I'm only ever in the castle to see Jassin, otherwise I'm going to the stables."

"Crown Jassin Gillhan?" Ralyn asked. Kit nodded. Jassin was just upstairs, probably bent over a few stacks of parchment trying to make sense of the kingdom again. "I haven't seen him yet. I heard he keeps mostly to himself, is that true?"

Kit said, "he's not one for company, no." Except for hers. Jassin always did his best to make time for Kit, even when he was at his busiest. "Here," Kit stopped again, this time at the base of marble stairs she would climb to reach Jassin's study. She pointed to a heavy oak door that would lead to a ballroom no one used but was, apparently, easily broken into. "There's West Ball. They're probably going to shift rotation soon, so I'd get in there before you lose your job."

Ralyn nodded. She took a step backward as Kit began walking up the stairs. "Hey, Kit?" Ralyn said. Kit looked back. "Thanks for killing that prince."

She could only smile. Kit turned away, climbing the stairs just a little faster. They wrapped around to the second floor, and Kit took them two at a time toward the top. She rubbed beneath her eye and kept close to the wall, avoiding the shining sun coming through the windows.

Many lined this hall, and one was open across from Jassin's study. Kit went over to it quietly.

"—losing land," a Crown said from the study behind her. Kit glanced back before pulling the window shut. "And now there are reports of us losing land to disease."

"It could be a fluke," another Crown—Nolen—said. He sounded angry, but Kit was sure that was his normal tone. Nolen was usually in an angry state. He'd been second to Jassin in the revolution that usurped the Fae Throne and had never liked Kit in the slightest. She could easily recall all the times he tried dismissing her whenever she sat in on their rebel meetings to listen to what they had to say.

"Or," Mali said, "nature is doing as was written."

Kit's brow furrowed. She faced the door to Jassin's study. Jassin spoke for the first time. "It could be either," he said in his normal appeasing tone, "but I for one won't risk anything. We should have Boisin go out and start a fire to kill the diseased crop. Tell him to keep it away from the forest otherwise no one will believe a Fae is burning down our food supply."

"Like in Lark?" Mali remarked.

Nolen replied, "that was *not* my mistake."

They began to bicker.

Kit usually loved it when the two of them butt heads. She and Aspen were certain they were secretly in love and had sex frequently, but now it wasn't very funny. Not when they were talking about disease and blaming Fae for burning down what fed the whole kingdom.

Footsteps echoed on the marble steps and Kit rushed forward. She pulled open the door to Jassin's study before she could be caught snooping, stopping at once when the two bickering Crowns paused to stare at her. "Did I interrupt something?" Kit asked.

"Kitali," Jassin said happily. He straightened from his bent-over position. "*Kit*, sorry. Of course you haven't interrupted anything." Nolen looked prepared to disagree, but Jassin moved around the table they were gathered around to pull Kit inside. His space was ample, yet cramped. It was full of tables and chairs that he'd either made or collected, making it a maze to walk through to get from one stack of parchment to the next.

"I was hoping to eat with you," Kit said. She passed Mali, the only female Crown out of the three of them. She'd fought for her position. When it came to appointing those who would lead Olyan, Nolen and Jassin were two obvious choices, but Mali had been voted in. She won her small election by just two votes. Kit had been one. She was a tall woman, towering over both men she worked with, and had very, very small lips. It was difficult to know when she was frowning or smiling.

"Nolen, will you speak to Boisin for me?" Jassin asked. Nolen nodded curtly and left without a goodbye. He sneered at Kit when Jassin wasn't looking, and Mali followed him out with a pinch to her thin, pale lips. "Did you go hunting today?" Jassin asked.

"What?" Kit looked up at him. What would've been a plain of sun-kissed skin was cracked with age like the earth of a desert in the western kingdoms. The cracks deepened when he smiled at her. "Oh, no." She pulled her quiver and bow off her back and set them aside as she said, "Aspen and I were at the spring."

"Ah," he said. Jassin went to pull a cord on the wall that would call a servant to the study. Kit looked over at the arrows once before she sat on the table he'd been leaning against. She picked up a document all three Crowns had signed, squinting to read something about taxing for Fae magic use. Jassin took it from her and set it aside before she could try to read any more. "How have you been?" He asked. Jassin stood in front of her and moved her thick, damp hair over her shoulders.

She grimaced. "Jassin, would you be friends with a Fae?"

He shifted his feet and Kit looked up at him. "What sort of question is that?"

"It's just..." Kit took a deep breath. "Aspen is taking care of these two orphans before the city finds a place for them, and one of them has befriended a Fae boy. Aspen doesn't want her anywhere near him because of what he is, but I don't see the problem. We argued and he asked if I would be friends with a Fae, but I can't. Would you? Now that things are different."

Jassin considered this, looking off and around his room. "Things aren't that different, Kit," he said, "you'd know better than anyone."

Her chest burned with an old ache. Kit looked away from him at the arrows she'd placed on one of his many chairs. She was famous for them. It was probably the most unexpected thing about the whole ordeal—how big of a pedestal the Crowns put her on. Shortly after the arrow was presented to her they'd done so much more than make her a figure for the humans to worship and the Fae to hate. They'd torn down a statue of Crius the Great in Calar's main square and replaced it with one of her. They'd put her likeness on the currency. "I want things to be different," she admitted.

"They will be," Jassin said gently, "these things take time."

She nodded once, tearing her eyes away from the simple weapon she'd been given. A knock came to the door and Jassin left her to answer it, telling some servant that they'd like a meal sent up for them.

Kit rubbed beneath both eyes and looked over at Jassin. He was on his way to a desk on the other side of the room. "How's being a Crown going?" She asked, as she often did. He smiled at their little inside joke as he pulled one of his favorite chairs out from beneath the desk and dragged it over to her.

"It's been stressful these past few days," he said. Jassin sat and began moving papers out of the way for when their meal arrived. "There was an uprising near Niverly that I've been trying to sort out," he said, and Kit tried not to react to hearing the name. *Niverly.* Jassin shifted more pages before he said, "I'll never forget finding you there."

She looked at him. Kit would never forget it either, but she doubted her perspective of that day was the same as his. Of the raid in Icar. Of the attack in Niverly. Of afterward.

"And I'll never regret taking you in, you know that, don't you?" He asked. Kit nodded carefully. She smiled, though it was half-hearted, and looked away from him.

Chapter Two

KIT'S APARTMENT WAS DARK when she arrived home. It was small, one with just a front room attached to a kitchen and a bedroom just big enough for her bed. It was covered in books and messes that she had no desire to clean up. Kit fumbled for candles to light around the space before walking toward her favorite chair. It was in the center of the room, the thing she gravitated toward more than her bed or anything in her kitchen. She put her hand on the back of it and looked at the arrow on the wall. It was the only one left to taunt her. The others had been left at the castle and her old quiver collected too much dust in the corner to be noticeable.

Her mind spun with things she didn't want to think about. Kit didn't want to consider Jassin doing more harm than good. She didn't want to believe he was covering things up and blaming Fae for destroying land, but she remembered the fire in Lark. The farms were in the north, they weren't on very well-traveled trade routes and hardly ever got traffic, but they provided goods for the kingdom. Six months ago a fire had started that killed acres and acres of barley, oats, and other grain stalks. The Fae had been blamed for it instantly. Most people were convinced, and everyone else was confused. They could believe a Fae would burn down crops, especially because Lark was a human town, but a forest had burned down with it.

No Fae would risk harming a forest just for some oats. It was completely against their nature to do that kind of harm. That was an evil left only to humans.

A familiar ache settled in her head as she backed up a step. Her gaze fell on the arrow. She wanted to break it. To throw it into a river and let it disappear along with all the nightmares surrounding it. But then she saw Jassin's face. The proud look in his eyes the day he presented it to her. *You did it,* he had said, *you saved us.* Saved who? Suddenly it felt as if all she'd done was put humans in power so they could blame the Fae for their wrongdoing.

She squeezed her eyes shut for a few seconds and headed to the door. It couldn't be like that—the Crowns would make things *better*. That was the whole point.

When on the street, Kit found herself wishing she had the comfort of her bow. Never once had she enjoyed using it as a weapon, but to have it on her back brought a sense of security she did not feel walking on the street alone. She pulled her jacket tighter around her torso to fight the coming winter's chill. Calar was not asleep late at night, though she wished it to be. Kit couldn't stand that aspect of living in the city—no one ever slept. There weren't even just a few hours in the early morning that no one was around.

She walked over the cobblestone street and kicked a rock every few steps. People passed by her. Kit moved away from the lights of shops to avoid being spotted.

The stone went flying, hitting the boot of someone ahead of her. She looked up. A Fae. "I apologize," Kit said calmly, "I wasn't paying attention." He bent and picked up the rock. "I didn't mean to hit you."

He looked at her closer and recognition shone on his face with the shining light of a tavern. "King Assassin," he said.

"Kit," she corrected, though she knew she'd never escape the name unless she fled the city.

The Fae raised a brow. "Kit?"

"That's me," she nodded, "Kit."

"But you are King Assassin," he tossed the rock into the air and caught it easily. Kit wondered if he was going to throw it at her. "Don't like the title?" The rock twisted and turned in his hand. He then suggested, "maybe you shouldn't have murdered the prince then." He tossed it up again. Her brow furrowed and she looked away from him altogether. No—no, maybe she didn't like the name, but killing the prince was right. She'd gotten her revenge. That was what she'd wanted. Kit just didn't want the attention or the prized arrow. She wanted peace.

She nodded carefully. "Have a good night," she said as she moved around him.

"You aren't going to kill me?" The Fae asked.

When she glanced back, he chucked the rock at her. Kit managed to raise her arm to block her face and her jacket kept her skin from being cut, but it didn't do anything to stop her ears from ringing with the laughs of the Fae and those watching.

She walked until she couldn't hear them, then quickened her pace, desperate to get off the streets. There was a stabbing pain in her left forearm from the strong throw. It would've hit her face, that was for sure, and it would've cut her.

No one had ever thrown a rock at her before.

Kit made it to the gate without any more interruptions, though her neck tingled as if someone was right behind her waiting to scare her. She reached back to rub beneath her hair. The guard made mild conversation, telling her that his children wanted to take up archery to be just like her. Kit only laughed a little before being allowed inside the castle walls. She tried not to picture children running around with weapons, laughing because their hero had used them to murder a prince.

She went through the front door to the main hall, then turned right like she did so often. Kit thought of nature as she walked. How much the Fae were connected to it. She knew that the Fae Kings had wanted to keep connected to the earth despite their stone castle, so they painted stars on the towers and grew vines on the walls. They painted flowers on the steps Kit climbed to reach Jassin's study and allowed animals to roam the carpeted halls.

Kit wasn't sure what she intended to do when she arrived in the hall. She wanted to know what the lost land and the taxes truly meant, but would she stoop to the point of spying on the man who saved her life?

"—what with how much time she spends in here with you," the voice of Nolen said. Kit paused. Light and shadows came from the sliver in the door to Jassin's study. "She didn't mention anything about overhearing us speaking?"

She stopped next to the door. Jassin said, "no, but I'm sure she heard it and she'll come asking eventually," and Nolen laughed. Jassin sighed slowly. "I almost wish I had let her leave when she wanted to. She wouldn't be so curious if I never convinced her to stay." He sighed. "Can't ask questions if you don't know what's happening."

"You know we needed someone to draw attention away from the Crowns," Nolen told him, "and to take the fall if we were unsuccessful in taking the city."

Kit's hand flew to her mouth.

"I'm glad we were successful," she heard Jassin mumble. Kit backed up and hit the wall with her shoulder, her eyes wide.

"And if we weren't?" Nolen asked. She imagined them drinking, sitting across from each other with empty plates, papers, and bottles of wine between them as they discussed King Assassin. "Would you mourn King Assassin?"

Was he nodding? Did he shake his head? "For a time."

Kit sunk down the wall and hugged her knees with one arm. For a time? How long was just a time?

"And what of her questioning Fae friendships?"

"There's nothing we can do about that," Jassin said. He might've shrugged. Kit imagined him shrugging. "Perhaps we just need to redirect her."

Nolen hummed and was silent for a moment. Kit tightened her hold on her legs as he said, "or stage something to remind her of that hate."

Her eyes widened even further.

"Next time she goes hunting?"

"That won't be for a while," Jassin said. Jassin? Jassin agreed? Kit pressed her hand hard against her face and felt tears reach her eyes. "We might need something sooner." She attempted to hide a sharp intake of breath. She closed her eyes as their conversation turned. They discussed the fire now. It would be a successful cover-up. Kit leaned to the side, removing her hand from around her legs and pressing it against the ground for support.

The sound of a chair creaking as Jassin said he was headed to bed caused her to run. Kit didn't stop. She ran and ran, hardly breathing when she had to wait for the gate to be opened once again. The guards had rotated while she'd been inside, so she didn't have to converse with the new one. Kit just kept going.

She slammed into someone and groaned, grabbing her shoulder tight.

Ralyn spun to her. "Watch it—oh, Kit." Recognition floated in her eyes and her anger dissipated. "Are you all right?" She asked. Something was in her eyes—a flash of concern unbefitting an acquaintance.

Kit swallowed. "I'm fine," she insisted. She glanced over at the castle but said nothing else.

"Are you sure?" Ralyn asked rather than continuing to walk where she'd been headed. Kit nodded. She kept aware of her surroundings. The last thing she needed was to run into another Fae. "You look like you've been crying," she said.

Kit wiped her eyes. "I'm sure," she said, "very sure." Ralyn moved closer, and Kit looked her over. Without the uniform, she still had a muscular build. Yes, she would make a good guard if she knew which direction was west.

"I'll walk you home," she said gently. Kit wasn't sure if that was what she wanted—then again, Ralyn seemed genuine. Couldn't she make a friend? She nodded, and Ralyn smiled. Kit began moving in that direction.

It wasn't a long walk. Kit stopped at her building. "This is me," she said.

"Oh," Ralyn looked at the building, her head slowly turning toward the castle. "Easy access," she muttered. Kit swallowed. She hadn't thought of it that way before. "Well, it was good to see you," she said, but she didn't walk away again.

Kit looked at her carefully. *Make a friend that isn't Aspen,* she told herself. "Would you like to come up?"

She asked, motioning to the building. Ralyn smiled and nodded. She followed Kit through the front door.

Chapter Three

RALYN SURVEYED HER SPACE and Kit grew increasingly self-conscious—not of how small it was but of how messy it was. She wasn't a clean sort of person, and that meant that in the small front room, clothes were scattered around, as were blankets, stacks of books, and dishes. The kitchen to the left was worse. Kit hadn't washed anything in ages. She rinsed and reused.

"Do you read often?" Ralyn motioned to a stack by Kit's favorite chair. She made her way toward it.

Kit went to the kitchen with a cringe on her face. "Honestly," she said, "I don't. I've never actually read any of these books, I just use them to get people to stop talking to me." Ralyn laughed as she picked one up. "You are more than welcome to borrow any," she offered when Ralyn began reading the first page of one.

"If you aren't so attached," she said.

"I'm not remotely attached," Kit replied.

She'd never been one for reading. Her hatred for books did not stem from her lack of love for stories—stories were one thing, *reading* was another—but from the fact that she couldn't read fluently. Letters mixed up. Words escaped her mind as if they'd run away from sentences.

Kit began setting everything up for tea, unsure of what to do. It had been ages since she last cleaned and had anyone other than Aspen in her home. "Would you like some tea?"

Ralyn looked over. "Yes, thank you." She walked further into the room and sat in Kit's favorite cushioned chair. "I love reading," she said. Kit thought she would continue talking about books she liked, but she paused for some time. Kit braved looking over, wondering if she'd become so absorbed in the book that she forgot where she was. "Is that it?" Ralyn asked, though. "The arrow that killed the prince..." She stood, her attention no longer on the book she'd set on the uneven-legged table that Jassin had made Kit years ago. She didn't look back when it slid off and hit the ground. "I heard it was given to you," she said.

Kit nodded despite her not looking. She put her kettle over a fire. "A prize for King Assassin," she muttered, leaning against the center island that took up all the space in her kitchen. It was what she hated most about her apartment. There was plenty of counter space already; why did they add more in the middle of the room?

"Sounds like you aren't fond of this either," her voice quieted. Kit watched her stand directly in front of the fireplace where the arrow hung. Her head was tilted up and she stared at it.

"I'm not particularly fond of any weapon," Kit said, "except my bow, that was a gift. But an arrow is an arrow."

She said, "this isn't just any arrow, though. This is an arrow with the blood of kings on it." Kit stood off the island as Ralyn got to her toes and moved as close to the arrow as possible.

"What are you doing?" Kit asked.

Ralyn stepped back. "Just curious," she said, "I didn't realize you'd mind."

"I don't mind, you were just staring at it like it was going to jump out and dance because of some king magic," she said with a small laugh. Kit went back to preparing tea.

"Can I hold it?" The question was soft. Her nerves rang out like a wet cloth.

"No," she said, "it's spelled to the wall."

Ralyn looked at it. "So no one can take it off?"

"Only the person who put it there originally," Kit said. She looked at the kettle, wishing it would boil faster. She waited for Ralyn to ask who had put it there, but she didn't, and it somehow made a bit of weight fall from her already heavy shoulders.

Ralyn turned away from the arrow and joined Kit in the kitchen. "So, how long have you lived here?"

"A few years," she said. Kit dug around in the cabinet she kept her food in and found a day-old roll of bread to split with her.

"Was it hard before? Living with more Fae than humans?" Ralyn leaned on the island and took her half of the loaf. She ripped off a bite.

Kit said, "not really. This close to the castle were more of the regular snobs than anything else—human or Fae—but I think it's different everywhere. I get robbed on the street less here, but I've been spit on more in this area."

"Why do you live so close then?"

Now, she hesitated. "Jassin, one of the Crowns," she said. Kit thought of what Ralyn had said before about it being easy access. Kit knew the area well; she knew the escape routes and could navigate the streets better than if she lived on the edge of town where the rent was cheaper.

Ralyn nodded and took another bite of the roll. "Must be easy now with a lot of the Fae leaving the kingdom."

"I got a rock thrown at me today," she said. Kit could no longer go anywhere without being recognized because the Crowns presented her with that arrow and ensured everyone knew she was King Assassin. The name followed her on the streets, in shops, in the market.

Draw attention away from the Crowns.

Was it a setup? The idea replaced the weight Ralyn had just relieved.

Her hand trembled as she poured the hot water over some tea leaves. She stirred an obscene amount of sugar into her cup and gave Ralyn the other, then went to sit on the lumpy chair so Ralyn could have the better one. They drank in silence, and all the while, Kit wondered if she'd been manipulated. She'd been lied to for sure, but she knew Jassin. Jassin wouldn't set her up.

There had to be some explanation for it. For all of it. She was reading too far into things.

Chapter Four

RALYN WAS GONE WHEN Kit woke up in the middle of the night despite her having fallen asleep on the chair like Kit so often did. A nightmare rocked through her head, bouncing around with voices and terrible thoughts. Tingles flew over her skin as she sat up and looked around. The blanket Ralyn used was folded nicely, and her cup was washed. It was now the only spotless thing in Kit's kitchen. There was also a note thanking her for the tea and the book. She'd borrow it, that was all.

Kit sat in her favorite chair and stared at her old bow in the corner of the room. The one she'd had for years. It was times like these when she wanted to shoot something. Nothing living, but specific spots on trees or pinecones. Kit had always been a good shot. It was her talent, the only natural form of magic humans had that wasn't simple spell casting. Like Fae had blessings, humans had talents. And Kit's was aim. She could shoot with near-perfect accuracy every time. Now, she itched to take her bow and a dusty quiver into the woods. Just for a little while. What would be the harm? Aside from the looming threat of the

Crown's attack on her. Kit sat in her chair with her arms wrapped around her legs until the sun rose, considering exactly what they could mean for her. Were they going to pay a Fae to hurt her or someone else?

She paced as the sun's rays slowly lit her apartment. Things couldn't be planned that quickly, could they? She could still go out for a while, then hide in her room for weeks. Now was not the time for that, though. Now was the time for arrows and woods.

She wiped her face and she readied herself. Kit looked at her tired reflection as she braided her hair behind her head. There was little life in her eyes, yet she couldn't think of a way to help it. Her usually warm russet-toned skin had lost some of its color and her cheeks were sunken. Jassin had told her once that she looked like her mother. The picture of her in Kit's mind was preserved at forty-four years old. She had a deep, dark color to her skin and thick hair that usually cascaded down her back. Her brows were always perfectly shaped on her head and her eyes were framed with beautiful lashes. She always had such a lovely smile on her soft lips. It took everything in Kit not to think of what her mother would say to her now, with how little she looked like herself—let alone the woman who raised her.

Kit ignored her face and grabbed her bow and the old quiver. She set off struggling to get her jacket on with her hands full and breathed in the cold morning air. Calar was a city nestled between mountains and mornings so late in the year were shrouded in blankets of chill. Kit sniffed, pulled her ratty braid out from beneath her jacket, and then fit her quiver over her shoulder. Old excitement trickled through her tired system.

Her feet moved her to the woods, her eyes scanning what was before her. No Fae yet. Maybe there wouldn't be an attack at all. Perhaps they thought better of it, that Kit was allowed to be curious and sympathetic. She'd only wondered if Jassin would befriend a Fae for the sake of children—a boy, who happened to have pointed ears, and an orphan who deserved friendship wherever she could find it. That was all it was. Kit just didn't want a child to be hated by her best friend simply for being a Fae.

And she didn't want to be hated by them.

They always would, though. And Kit could live with that; it just hurt to think about it.

She saw the trees in front of her. They were a muted green, brightening with the morning sun. Kit could already feel the calm sureness of pulling her string back and letting an arrow fly off toward a target.

A scream made her stop. Kit stood still. The scream was followed by a cry of pain in such a familiar voice a chill ran down her spine.

She turned around and went back the way she came. It had to be someone else. Or something else. Yet a circle of people had gathered, and a crowd was forming. Kit moved forward and pushed past people. Fae and humans struggled to watch a fight. They were all equal when someone was getting beat. Entertainment brought species together.

Kit shoved past a large man and caught sight of red hair. She moved faster. Someone said *King Assassin* and suddenly she didn't have to push anymore. Maybe they saw the arrows and knew. Kit saw two little girls holding each other—the twins—and Aspen. He was limp and being held up by two Fae. A third was punching him. With each slam of a fist against his face more blood dropped to the ground at his knees.

"Stop!" Kit shouted. Her voice cracked weakly. She broke through the line and grabbed the elbow of the Fae that was punching Aspen, only to be punched herself. Kit stumbled backward and hit a Fae, who shoved her forward. She landed on her hands and knees, her bow at her side. Kit blinked dizzily and her eyes watered.

Aspen said her name before he cried out with another punch. Blood sprayed the ground. Kit grabbed an arrow from her quiver. This must've been the attack. It had to have been. To make her hate them all over again and to make them hate her even more. Here she was, King Assassin, holding an arrow notched to her old bow about to fire it.

She just had to pick which Fae. Her gut churned with the thought as she stood. "Stop it," she said as evenly as she could manage. The circle of onlookers widened slightly, giving her room to step back. Bows weren't meant for close quarters, which put her in danger. She'd only have one shot before her life was at risk alongside Aspen. "Let him go," she ordered.

"Going to kill us?" The Fae throwing the punches asked. He had silver hair and a sick look on his face. He was also thin, most likely someone who lived on the streets like the twins.

"What's one more Fae?" Kit asked him. She hated herself for saying it.

He stepped toward her. Kit flinched. The Fae was taller than she was. He looked like he could snap her in half, even with how thin he was. "You look afraid," he taunted. She gripped her bow tighter, and his smile grew. Behind him, Aspen's head hung low. "Are you sure you can do it—"

Kit let go of the bowstring. Her arrow flew a short distance and struck the Fae in the neck. He stumbled further than she had and hit the ground harder. Blood pooled in the street, and the two other Fae dropped Aspen as quickly as a hot coal. Kit's bow clattered to the ground, and she went for Aspen. Someone spit on her as she grabbed his swollen, bleeding face.

"Aspen?" She asked him. He blinked slowly.

"You're bleeding," he mumbled, reaching up for her cheek. He missed and his hand got stuck in the strands of her hair. "Thanks for the rescue," he said faintly. Her brows furrowed as his hand dropped and he fell unconscious. Kit wiped blood off her face, and the twins came forward. They were both crying. Nessa wrapped her little arms around her sister and sobbed. A man they both seemed familiar with came over, followed by another carrying a wooden board. They set it down and the first man, someone around the age of Jassin, said, "thank you. I thought they were going to kill him."

"Did he do something or..." She didn't finish.

"They just attacked him," the man said, and they lifted Aspen onto the board. Kit stayed on her knees for a moment as they carried him to a healer, her gaze slowly moving toward the dead body of the silver-haired Fae. He was being taken care of as well. Some nature rite was being done over his body and his eyes were covered in a leaf of some kind. Kit looked away, ashamed. She'd just killed someone. Again.

Water splashed onto her legs, mixed with red. She cringed as she stood and collected her soaked bow. People watched. She wondered how they saw her. A twenty-three-year-old girl and a killer—did they see that or just King Assassin? Did King Assassin come before everything else?

She went in the direction Aspen had been taken, and people moved so they wouldn't touch her.

Chapter Five

IT TOOK HALF A day for Aspen to wake. Kit stayed with him the entire time. She sat in an old chair and hugged her legs, waiting for him to move. When he did, she wasn't sure if it was real. Aspen groaned and reached up to touch his face. Part of it was covered in a bandage from a large gash that ran down the right side of his pale face. It covered the space from his temple to just above his lip. Kit wasn't sure how it happened so quickly, but she was sure it would scar.

"Are you all right?" He asked with a faint grunt.

"Me?" She stood. Kit went over to him. He was looking at her, one eye swollen shut and purple. "What a stupid question."

He smiled, winced, and she sat in the chair closest to him. The room was small, with a bed pressed against a stone wall. There was a thin table above it full of different physician's instruments and another table behind her where the door was. "How'd you get us out of that terrible situation?" He asked. He was trying to be light—maybe he saw what she did.

"I killed one of them," she told him quietly. He said nothing. "And his blood is still on my pants. I can smell it." She looked down at her hands, itching to put one in her pocket, but the necklace wasn't there. She'd left it in the chair she should've been lying in. Her brow furrowed, and a knot formed in her throat. "I killed him," Kit repeated, her voice a whisper.

Aspen took her hand. "Come here," he pulled, grunting painfully as he shifted to the side and lifted the blanket. Kit sobbed and crawled next to him, curling into his side. "It'll be all right," he said.

"I'm sorry," she said, choking on her spit. She coughed and pressed her face into his strong shoulder. Aspen pulled her closer, and she realized she was probably hurting him, but she didn't want to move away. "I'm sorry."

"You did nothing," he said gently, "you're all right."

It made her cry harder. It had to have been her fault. If what the man said was true, the attack was unprovoked. Aspen was most likely on his way to see her when it happened and they attacked to get to Kit. That made it her fault.

"I'll get a nice scar out of it, anyway," he said. His voice was rasped, usually an indicator that he was falling back asleep. Aspen was hot—feverish—and she stayed still to soak in the warmth of his bare skin. She wondered when the bruises would form on his body. If he broke anything. If Jassin ordered the attack.

Kit was glad to sleep, and it came with no . Aspen was there, talking to someone, and she listened to his heartbeat. The hum in his chest. His breathing. He was alive, but would they have killed him? Would they have beaten him to death in the street if she hadn't turned back? "I love you," she whispered to him. He gave her a tight squeeze, and she went to sleep.

***

Aspen snored. Loud. And it sounded worse now that he was injured.

She sat up and uncurled herself from him. Kit rubbed her eyes. A single candle was lit in the small room and night reflected around them. She grunted and climbed out of bed, stretching slowly. It couldn't have been that late, but she doubted she'd get to sleep again.

"Come back," Aspen said, and she turned. "Just lay with me."

"Wouldn't you be more comfortable with the whole bed?" She asked.

He grunted. "Take your damn shoes off, unbraid your hair, and lay with me."

She rolled her eyes and did as she was told, tucking herself back into the blankets. "Satisfied?"

"You're my best friend," he said. She craned her neck to look at him. His eyes were closed, but he didn't look peaceful. She imagined Aspen wasn't used to lying broken this way. He was strong and no Fae challenged him the way they did other humans. "And I know killing that Fae was hard, but thank you for doing it."

Her eyes moved away from him. "You're welcome," she whispered. She hated killing more than anything else. She thought her killing would end with the prince, and now she'd taken two lives. "How are you feeling?"

"The physician says I have a few broken ribs and I got lucky with my eye. So far it looks like I'll still be able to see when it heals," Aspen explained, "so I'm all right, Kitali."

"I will punch a bruise," she warned. He chuckled.

"Why don't you like being called Kitali?" He asked, knowing she wouldn't answer. It was connected to her necklace, to the reason she killed the Crown Prince, and it made her want to cry every time she thought about it. Now, after so many years of them being friends, Aspen asked it to be ironic. He was curious, but he never pushed her. Only Jassin called her Kitali, and that was on occasion. The name was gone from her life, replaced by Kit—and now pushed even further down by the overbearing name *King Assassin.*

She breathed in deeply and adjusted, moving her arm over his chest so she could pull on his straight red hair. "You're all right?" She asked.

"I'm all right," he confirmed. "And I love you, too."

What if she told him about the attack and the Crowns? Would he hate her for it? Blame her? "What were you doing on the street?" She asked, "the sun had hardly risen."

"I was going to surprise you," he said. Aspen let out a short breath and said, "I had your favorite sweet cakes. I was going to take you up on the roof and tell you Nessa called me her big brother yesterday."

"Congratulations," she poked his neck a few times, "big brother."

He chuckled again. "It was when I saw her with the Fae kid I was telling you about at the spring. His name is Reno, and he's this short orphan who's missing an ear and has a limp. Nessa introduced me as her big brother."

"And the Fae?"

"He seems harmless enough," Aspen mumbled and shifted uncomfortably. "Smells awful and I think he has fleas, so I told Nessa that she wasn't allowed to hug him until he had a proper bath."

She lifted her head. "Did you let a Fae into your home?"

"Gave him soap and a blanket." For some reason, he sounded almost ashamed of his actions. Could taking care of a child be so terrible? He was doing it with two girls—human ones, sure, but they were still children. "I thought it would make you happy," he said.

She kissed his cheek. "Better than the cakes," Kit told him. He reached up and touched her cheek before she could lay back down. "What?" She blinked quickly.

"He hurt you," Aspen said. His thumb brushed over a bruise and what must've been a cut.

"It's all right," she said, "no stitches... it doesn't hurt." She took his hand and pulled it away. "I'm just as all right as you are."

Aspen sighed and nodded. He pulled her back down and she closed her eyes against his chest.

Chapter Six

SHE DIDN'T KNOW WHO was knocking on her door, but she didn't want to answer. Aspen was asleep on his stomach in her bed, snoring, and she was attempting to organize her clothes to be washed like he told her to. There was currently a pile in the middle of her living room when she grabbed a knife and unlocked the door, peering through the crack. A smile appeared on her face. "Ralyn," she said and opened the door wider.

"Got you something," she said. Ralyn held up a tin of tea with a Fae inscription. Kit took it, moving over so she could come in. "Doing your laundry?"

"I hate cleaning," Kit muttered as she smelled the tea. Flowers were on the label with a list of ingredients in Travesta, the Fae's common tongue. "Aspen's in the bedroom," she said. Kit had limited experience translating flowers and leaves from the Fae to the human language. The most she got was lavender, some root, and chamomile. The last one was easy. Kit and the humans spelled it *chamomile* and the Fae said *chamomeel.*

"Aspen?"

"My best friend," Kit said. She shut her door again and entered the kitchen to put the kettle on. "He was attacked by Fae a few days ago and whatever medication he was given has him sleeping most of the time." She checked the boil on her favorite dented pot and went to chop the carrots she bought the day before. Ralyn leaned on the counter on the other side of the island and smelled sage drying against the wall. "Do you like rabbit stew?" Kit asked her. "I think I'm making too much for two people."

Ralyn watched her dump the carrots into the pot. "If I'm not the one cooking it. And no salt for me," she said. Kit grabbed the dead rabbit and she laughed, "what's the face for?"

She positioned her knife, cringing as she began to skin it. "I hate this part," she said. Kit tried not to gag as innards slid out of the dead thing and Ralyn laughed at her again. She went around the counter, washed her hands, and took the knife and rabbit away from Kit.

"I heard what you did," she said. Kit moved out of the way. "In that attack."

She looked away, leaning against the island. "I'm sure everyone did," she said.

"Are you all right with it?"

"I don't like killing and I just..." Kit trailed off and sighed. She went to prepare tea, focused on trying to find something to do with her hands. "I thought that maybe I wouldn't have to anymore after the prince was dead."

She glanced over. "That was the first time you killed someone since the prince?"

"I wish I wasn't in this stupid city," she muttered, drying her washed hands. Kit poured the hot water over the new Fae tea leaves. "I wish I had left, I wish I had never taken that stupid arrow, I—"

Ralyn nodded a little. "If you could go back knowing everything you know now," she began, stopping what she was doing to look at Kit. "Would you still kill him?"

She stared. Kit opened her mouth, unsure of what she'd say. She didn't get to answer, though, because a grunt came from her bedroom and Aspen's heavy feet shuffled out. He rubbed his face and pushed his red hair back from his eyes. "Who's this?" He asked.

"Ralyn Cara," Kit answered, "we met in the castle. She's a guard."

He smiled a little. "Did she convince you to skin the rabbit for her?" He asked with a chuckle. He came up to the counter and stole Kit's just-made cup of tea, drinking it down. "Gods, you use too much sugar," he said.

"Stop drinking it, then," she replied. Kit took the cup from him and poured another. She then looked at his eye. It was still swollen, but there was a slit, so it was open ever so slightly. He still couldn't completely see out of it, but it was promising. His stitches were clean and precise. The hope was that the scar would be minimal.

"Never," he smiled, then faced Ralyn. "You work as a guard? Sounds awful."

She stared at them but breathed a laugh and returned to the rabbit. "I can't say it's perfect, but it's better than unemployment."

"I'm lucky my boss is human," he motioned to his face, "he's giving me time to heal with pay."

She nodded. "What do you do?"

"I build homes," he answered. "Renovate some, keep inns looking nice. It's not where I wish I ended up, but I'll take what I can get."

Kit said, "you should hear him sing." She moved closer to the two of them. "It's so beautiful, even his humming—" Aspen nudged her with his shoulder, and Kit shoved him back, not caring that he groaned. She crossed her arms. "He won't pursue it even though the Crowns would pay for a voice like that."

"Really?" Ralyn asked.

"Mali loves music," she looked at Aspen seriously, "and appreciates the arts. She'd say yes if you auditioned for her to sing at her next party."

He rolled his eyes, "only because I know you and she knows that."

"What does that matter if it gets you a job doing what you love?" She asked, but he was done with the conversation. They'd had it a few times. He didn't want any favors from Kit and her connection to the new rulers.

Aspen sighed. "Where are you from, Ralyn?" He asked her to shut Kit down.

"Up north," she motioned with a bloody hand.

Kit perked up. "Near Lark?"

She raised a brow, "no, closer to the mountains than that. Why was Lark the first place you thought of?"

"It's as far up as I could think to go," she shrugged.

Ralyn nodded, then looked at Aspen. "And you? Where are you from?"

"Born and raised in Calar," he said proudly. She nodded, looking him over. Perhaps she was trying to see how much he'd experienced and how much he hated. If she were a Fae, he would be the last person she wanted to befriend. She looked at Kit. "Same as him?"

"No, I came from Niverly," she answered.

They both quieted. Ralyn went back to the rabbit. She was trimming it, something Kit could've done, but she was doing a much better job. Ralyn got as much off the bones as possible. She slid the trimmed meat into the stew.

Niverly was such a conversation killer. Anytime someone mentioned it, everything paused. No one liked discussing a tragedy, but now Kit wondered what Ralyn thought. If she was a Fae, her perspective of the attack might've been different. Still, Kit had met Fae who were just as horrified about what happened as everyone else. Would Ralyn feel the same? Knowing where Kit came from, would her perspective change?

Chapter Seven

IT WAS DIFFICULT NOT to picture Jassin telling a group of Fae to beat her best friend in the street. Giving them money, saying one of them might die—but how did they know Aspen would be there so early? And where were the cakes he told Kit about? She hadn't seen any on the street and doubted anyone would take them. And Aspen would've defended himself, yet she hadn't seen any wounds on the Fae, just on him.

When she looked at Aspen from where he sat on her floor, she imagined him there, nodding to Crown Jassin and Crown Nolen, accepting money for the twins and his family and waiting to be attacked. Then him lying to her about the cakes and the boy and being called a big brother. Would he do that? He could've just been in the wrong place at the wrong time.

Jassin called an attack on her best friend to get her to hate Fae again; that was certain. If Kit didn't know—hadn't heard him—would she hate them like they wanted? Would she brush off the Fae orphan and say they all ended up like the males who attacked Aspen and it would all go back to normal? King Assassin would stop trying to sympathize with Fae. She would stop caring about peace. She would realize that things would never be different or better.

Aspen left with a kiss on her head, and she breathed deeply as she watched him leave. The door clicked shut. Ralyn slurped the probably tasteless broth, and Kit looked at her. She was sitting with her legs crossed on Kit's favorite chair while Kit was again stuck on the lumpy seat. "Do you think things could be better than they are now?" She asked quietly. Ralyn lowered the bowl from her mouth, a little struck by the question.

"Better how?"

She said, "better like I didn't feel the need to kill a Fae to stop him from killing my best friend in the street for seemingly no reason. Do you think things could be better than that, or are we all going to keep spinning in the same hateful circle where people die and no one ever feels safe, no matter who's ruling?"

Ralyn was quiet, just looking at her. "I don't know," she admitted softly. "What do you think?"

Her eyes went to her bowl, where she mashed a carrot into the side. "I think that I didn't want to kill that male. And I wish I didn't have to."

"What if you didn't have to?" Her brows furrowed, her head tilted slightly to the side.

"Then I'm a murderer," Kit said. She went to dump her stew back into the pot and rinse her bowl. She washed it and scrubbed at the wood until Ralyn was beside her, setting her bowl on the counter.

Ralyn said, "you did it in defense of your friend." Kit closed her eyes. "Kit, you did what you thought you had to."

"But what if I didn't have to?" She asked weakly. She picked up another bowl that should've been washed long ago. It gave her something to do and something to look at instead of the person on her right. She could feel Ralyn's brown eyes on her, and she wondered if the potentially pointy ears under her hair could hear her heart beating rapidly.

"I don't think it's that simple."

"I'm King Assassin," she said. Kit set the bowl aside and grabbed a teacup. "Killing is in the description."

There was another beat of silence before Ralyn said, "but you aren't just King Assassin. You're Kit. The girl that hates reading but pretends she loves it so people will leave her alone. She's really good at chopping vegetables—" Kit laughed a little. "—and she hates skinning rabbits."

"I don't even like killing animals," she whispered. She wiped her hands on her pants and turned, returning to her little sitting room and picking up three books tied with string. "These are the ones that most people recommend to me. Apparently they're the best ones out right now. One of them is signed by the author."

She took them. Ralyn looked at the spines. "Which one do you recommend first? In your *expert* opinion."

"The middle one has sex scenes," she nodded to the stack, "I went through the book to find them."

Ralyn bit her lower lip awkwardly and said, "I'm not really... into that sort of stuff. I like the romance, but I'm not a sex person. In literature or life."

"Oh, then..." Kit took the stack back and untied it. She took the middle book out and went to the stack behind her favorite chair. "This one is about these two girls who fall in love," she held it up, "or this one is just friends." Kit grabbed another. She slid a third out of the stack, and it toppled over. "This one is about a girl who's like a ball of light or something and she learns to be human."

Ralyn smiled warmly as she took the books. "Thank you, Kit. I really appreciate it." She then looked Kit up and down and took a deep breath. "Sometimes we have to kill," she said in a gentle tone, "but it doesn't mean we have to like it. I doubt the Fae would've stopped."

Would Jassin have told them to keep going? Not to stop until one of them was dead? "I suppose," Kit said.

"I should be going. I'm on night duty today. Thanks for the stew."

"Would you like to take some for dinner as well?" Kit looked at the kitchen.

Ralyn looked as well. "I don't think I can take a bowl."

"Oh, I have a lidded one Jassin made me," she said. Kit went to the kitchen and pulled the bowl from a cabinet. "I use it when I want to go on longer hunts. Sometimes I just have meat, but I can also put stew in it if I don't jostle it too much."

Ralyn raised her eyebrow at the bowl. Kit thought she might refuse, wondering if her stew was disgusting, but she nodded with a smile and told her to fill it all the way up. Kit gave her a clean spoon, and she left Kit with the dirty laundry and dishes.

She sat on the pile and stared at the sink. It stared back, the too-large pile, and Kit got up. She went to the bedroom and dropped onto her bed face first.

Chapter Eight

She wandered late at night, not wanting to sit in her apartment with the arrow and the mess. The stars were covered in dark clouds, and the magic paint on the castle was dim. She wove around the stragglers and drunks, following the pavement, and wished she knew where she wanted to go.

Laughter came from a tavern to her left, and her stomach rumbled. A drop of rain hit her forehead. Kit tilted her head back and squinted at the dark sky. People ran for cover, but she stood there for a few seconds, letting the rain remind her that she needed to bathe.

Then she headed for the tavern. Kit knew she should be headed home instead. There was a perfectly good stew waiting for her.

She sat at the end of the room and put her head in her hand. Her mind spun. Kit considered whether or not she was being too impatient. It'd been less than a year. There were still things that needed to be done. Things still needed to change. 'Better' didn't happen overnight.

"Here you are, girl," a frail-looking woman said, setting a plate and a cup in front of Kit. Kit fished out the payment that would suffice and tore into the fatty pork. She crushed potatoes with her spoon as she chewed, then soaked them in the meat's juices. Her mind worked as she stirred things around and ate.

Jassin told her to get an apartment close to the castle before he became a Crown.

Jassin was one of the leaders of the human revolution. He regularly spoke of humans needing to be in power and he held meetings in the home they used to live in. She overheard nearly every one and attended meetings when she was bored.

Jassin mentioned the Niverly slaughter and her family more often than anyone else, even Kit herself.

Jassin gave her a new bow months before she assassinated the prince. He helped her practice with it, testing her aim with moving targets and from things like trees so she could use different angles.

Jassin convinced her to stay when he knew she wanted to leave and start a new life elsewhere.

Jassin handed her the arrow.

She picked apart the pork, ate everything together, and then drank some of the ale before her. Her stomach gradually filled as much as her head.

"We're doomed," she heard from behind her. The man was shushed by someone else. "No one knows where to look—what to look for!" He was whispering, continuing despite what his friend probably wanted.

Like Kit did as a child, she created a story surrounding them. They were looking for something important. Treasure, maybe something golden, and if they didn't get it... Who hunted for treasure? *Pirates!* If they didn't get the treasure, the pirates were going to kill them; that's why they were doomed—

"We still have just under two months to find and crown the New Heir," the second voice whispered. Kit's story halted. New Heir? As in the one the court was talking about the day she killed the prince? They said they needed to find the New Heir before the humans took every chance from them.

The first man, who said they were doomed, said, "the land is dying faster than we can search, you can feel it just as well as I can. Lark is gone, the Plains are next—"

"The Plains are not next. That fire will change the direction—"

"We are all going to die!" He hissed, "if we don't find the Heir the land will die in Olyan and all of us with it."

Kit's brow furrowed. She wanted to ask questions, but as soon as she turned around, they'd probably try to kill her for overhearing them. She stared at her food and took another drink. It didn't seem too appetizing anymore.

"No tracker magic is working," the doomed man—male, because they were Fae—continued, "we are out of time. The best we can do is flee to another king-dom—"

"Not if we can get King's Blood," the second said, his voice lower. Kit didn't want to move at all now. She feared any shift would draw attention to her as she brought an-other bite to her mouth. King's Blood. She had King's Blood on the arrow, Ralyn said so.

The doomed male was probably shaking his head. "There isn't a chance in any blessing we'd be able to get into that castle, let alone find the prince's body."

Kit thought they put him in the crypt and gave him a proper burial. Jassin told her they'd even let a Fae pray over him.

"The kingdom is going to die," said the male, "we won't survive another year."

"The New Heir—"

"We'll never find him!" He shouted, silencing most of the tavern and making Kit flinch. Most people went back to their drinking and conversations. Some stared for longer. Kit ate some more, trying to judge how much time she needed to get up without looking suspicious, and fin-ished her drink in a few swallows.

She gripped the sleeves of her jacket and kept her eyes on the ground as she walked out.

Chapter Nine

LIGHT BLED THROUGH THE thinning leaves of the tree. Kit blinked at them slowly. She'd spent two days in the woods, sleeping in the rock hut she and Aspen had made years ago with bugs to keep her company. It rained again while she was there, so she froze for part of the night, but otherwise, she'd felt something close to content. It seemed like an impossibility until it happened.

The spring itself was a small pool of water that had branched off the Farsho River. There was a shallow and a deep end and plants that brushed her toes when she swam in it. Kit often thought she'd like to live by it. That she'd build a real house and never go back to Calar again.

She sat up, turned the spit where a rabbit was cooking, then laid back down. Her hand was in the spring, and her mind was in the castle. She was mapping her way into the crypt and recalling all the times the Crowns were together. It would be easier to get into the crypt at night. She wanted to see if the body was really there. For all she knew, they lied to her.

Jassin lied again.

Every time she thought about that little fact, it hurt. "Entering!"

Kit shot up to her elbows, and her heart skipped a beat in her chest as Aspen ran forward and jumped into the spring. Water splashed into the air, making the fire hiss as it hit it. Her front was drenched. Kit's jaw dropped as he surfaced and swam over. Aspen was clean-shaven, his swelling was down significantly, and he was smiling.

"What are you doing in the woods without me?" He asked with a tilt of his head. It was an innocent question, but Kit wondered why he hadn't come two days ago. Part of her thought he would've gone looking, but he didn't.

"Escaping," she said. He considered this and she asked, "what have you been doing in the city?"

Aspen rested his arms on the rock she was sitting on. "Working," he answered. "What are you escaping?"

She turned her spit and laid on her back so their heads were closer. Aspen smiled gently at her. "My life," she said.

"Aww, it's not so bad."

Lately, it felt like it. "I suppose," Kit said. He continued staring at her, his eyes moving slowly over her face. Kit sighed and looked at the rabbit. "Aspen, what do you know about the New Heir?" She asked. Kit sat up again and took the rabbit off. She held it in the air, willing it to cool down.

"Isn't that a Fae thing?" He asked. "The heir to the throne is called a new heir or something. But you killed him."

She ripped off a piece for him and handed it over, then sucked on her fingers. "There's another one," she said, "somewhere out there is another heir."

He asked, "are you going to hunt this one down, too?" There was a glint of excitement in his eyes. "Be King Assassin two times over?"

"No," she said, "no, *gods* Aspen."

"What?" His brow furrowed.

She got up and dropped her rabbit. "What is with you and the King Assassin? Every other conversation, it's like suddenly every part of who I am is centered around me killing someone!"

Aspen got out of the water, shocked, and asked, "where is this coming from?"

She breathed in sharply and put her hands on her head. Kit turned away from him. There was an ache in her chest that she didn't know how to get rid of, and it didn't leave when he touched her elbow. He turned her body and put his hands on her face. She opened her eyes.

"Are you all right?" He whispered, his red brows pulled together with such intense concern. "Kit?"

She shook her head, glancing at his entire face, and shook it again. She let her hands fall until she was holding his wrists. "No," she said, "no, no—" He put his arms around her. "No," she sobbed.

"What happened?" He asked into her hair.

"I don't want to be called that anymore," she said through heavy tears and sobbed again, "I don't want to be that."

He nodded. Aspen said, "all right, I'm sorry. I didn't realize it bothered you so much."

She was silent. She wished he did realize. She wished he knew.

"Can I take you home?"

Kit nodded. She stayed in the same place and wrapped her arms around her chest as he dressed and put out her fire. He took the rabbit to eat on the way. Aspen was silent, and she wondered if he was going over the last ten months trying to find those things that showed King Assassin made her uncomfortable.

"I'll come by tonight," he said when they stopped on the street. She nodded. He kissed her head.

Kit went up, climbing the stairs slowly. Her feet thumped against each step loudly, but she stopped abruptly when she saw a familiar face at her door. Ralyn looked like she was about to leave. She stood in front of the door with one foot turned toward the stairs. A smile appeared on her face. "Kit," she said, "I came to check on you. There wasn't an answer yesterday." Then she added, "or the day before that."

"You checked on me?"

She nodded as if the question was stupid. "You're my friend. I was worried."

Kit smiled. "Would you like to come in?"

"Sure," Ralyn moved so Kit could unlock the door. "Where have you been?"

"In the woods," she answered and went inside. "Oh," Kit said. It was a mess—different from the usual—and many things looked broken.

Ralyn gasped, "great blessings. Did someone break in?"

Great blessings, Kit repeated in her mind as she walked further in. Only Fae praised blessings because they were given to them by nature. Like Crius the Great's wings and every pair of wings after that. "It happens sometimes," Kit said as she pushed her chair back onto its legs. "They never find anything interesting and usually just break things when they figure out they can't get the arrow off the wall."

"I have to say I'm surprised you're reacting so calmly," Ralyn said. She picked up a few candles.

"This is the first this month," she said. Kit checked her pile of clothes and smiled because none looked ripped beyond repair. Her stew was gone, however.

Ralyn repeated, "this month?"

"It happens," Kit said and started cleaning up. This gave her a reason to actually wash things. "How is everything with you?"

Ralyn laughed a little. She started picking up glass. "I've been a night guard these past few days, which is exhausting."

"Why are you awake now?" Kit looked out the window at the bright day.

"Where is your broom?"

Kit paused. "I think in my closet."

She went in that direction. "I can't sleep during the day," she answered from the other room. "I get a few hours when the sun is still low, but otherwise, I'm awake."

When Kit decided to stop, most of the clothes were organized. "Have you tried a sleeping drought?" Kit asked as she walked into the kitchen. The dishes were in terrible condition, and one of her cabinets was bent oddly.

"I have," Ralyn said as she returned with the broken broom and a pan. "So, what were you doing in the woods for two days?"

"Escaping," she answered as she had for Aspen.

She asked, "is there something here you need to escape from or did you simply need a break from the city?"

"Both, I think," Kit said. She picked up a broken plate. "Things have been stressful lately."

"Is there anything you need?"

"A different identity would be nice," she muttered. Kit made a pile of broken dishes on the island and started washing things that weren't too far gone. Ralyn began sweeping, and Kit wondered if she'd heard her. She hadn't replied. Kit quit the dishes quickly, opting for tea instead, and when Ralyn finished sweeping, they sat together. She blinked slowly, looking as if she longed for sleep. Was that a Fae thing? Not being able to sleep during the day?

Rayln asked, "why are you staring?"

She blinked. "I was wondering about your sleep dilemma," she answered, and Ralyn nodded. She heaved a great sigh. "What if you mimicked the night? If you slept in a room that was pitch black?"

"I have mixed results," she said, rubbing her right eye. "I think the walk home wakes me up more than anything."

Kit considered this. "Would you like to come here?" She asked. Ralyn's brow furrowed and she cast a wary look her way. "I have a sheet I can put on the window, and you can even stuff one under the door; that way, you're closer to the castle and can sleep right away."

Ralyn smiled just a little. "You want me to come here in the middle of the night and sneak into your bedroom?"

"I'm usually awake anyway," she shrugged. "I sleep in my bed, then that chair." She pointed to the one Ralyn was lounging on. "I get a couple hours in that if I can, then I'm up when it's light."

She looked at Kit for a long while. "You have trouble sleeping?"

Kit stood and went to the fireplace, removing a brick to reach a spare key. It was the third in her set. Kit had one, Aspen had the second, and now Ralyn. "Here," she handed it to her. She took it gingerly.

"Why do you have trouble sleeping?" She asked with her eyes on the old key.

"I have a decent amount of nightmares," she said. Her eyebrows raised and fell. Kit sat back down in the lumpy chair with a huff. The silence that followed tried to haunt Kit, but she let it pass over her. She did not consider Ralyn's pity. She didn't want it. Kit just sipped her Fae tea in her uncomfortable chair and wondered if she should take a nap. Her eyes shifted to the fireplace instead, then back to the Fae trying to get her eyes to stay closed. "Ralyn, can I ask you a question?" Ralyn only hummed. "What's so special about King's Blood?"

Her eyes opened. Ralyn sat up slightly, looking at the arrow. She blew out a breath and shrugged ever so slightly as if she were working through what to say. "It's magic," she said, "and you can do quite a few things with it. Why?"

"How can blood be magic?" She asked.

"His blood specifically?" She nodded to it. Ralyn said, "because for all of time there have only been Fae Kings, so the blood of every king flowed in the prince's veins. It's powerful. I heard once that every blessing given by nature has also been given to the Kings... so it's magic."

Kit looked at the arrow again. "Do you think that's why people try to take it?"

"Possibly," she laid back with her eyes on the arrow. "Many say you can do anything with King's Blood."

"I used to wish I had magic," she said softly. Kit turned and laid on the chair, her eyes on the ceiling. "I used to think a lot of things would be different."

She asked, "you stopped wishing?"

"What's the point?" Kit countered, shifting to a more comfortable position. "All wishes are dreams, and all dreams turn into nightmares eventually."

Chapter Ten

When the door opened that night, Kit was in her favorite chair. She'd been awake for a while, and Ralyn was just coming in. Her feet were dragging, but she looked at Kit and squinted in the light of one candle. "Goodnight," Kit whispered, and she smiled a little. She said nothing as she shuffled into Kit's bedroom. Her uniform clunked to the ground behind the closed door and a sheet was stuffed underneath the crack.

When she got up again, Kit was in the same place, this time with a cup of tea.

"Good morning," she said.

Ralyn rubbed her face. "Is it morning?"

"Mid-afternoon," Kit corrected, "I made breakfast and the kettle's still warm if you'd like tea."

Ralyn smiled brightly at the window. "I actually feel rested," she said. She went to the plate Kit had set out for her. It was just boiled eggs and toast covered in wildberry jam, but Ralyn looked at it as if it were a feast. She went for the eggs first, stuffing one into her mouth. She made herself tea while she chewed, then sat in the lumpy chair.

"You are so nice," she said with her hand over her mouth so she didn't spit any food in Kit's direction.

Kit laughed a little. "What were you expecting?"

"For you to live in the castle all... assassin-like."

"I can't stand the castle," Kit said. She sipped her tea. *Entering* was shouted from the hall. Ralyn looked in that direction while Kit laid back further. Aspen came in after a few seconds and said a kind hello to Ralyn. Kit smiled at him. "What are you doing here?"

"We're rebuilding the roof on an inn nearby. I'm hungry and your place is closer than mine," he said. Aspen bent over the chair to kiss her cheek. "May I?"

Kit motioned toward the kitchen, and he went there, scavenging like an animal through her cabinets. Something fell, and she looked up. "Be careful, Aspen. I only have a few good dishes left."

"Maybe you should change the locks on the windows," he suggested.

She grunted once and mumbled, "I asked you to do that two months ago."

He didn't hear her, for which Kit was glad, and Ralyn remained silent in the lumpy chair.

"Are you still thinking about the new heir thing? Because I have a theory," he said as he returned with bread slathered in butter. He sat on the ground, leaned against Kit's chair, and looked up at her. "Would you like to hear my theory?"

"Is it a stupid theory?" She questioned, raising a brow.

He rolled his eyes. "I think there isn't one. I think the Fae made it up to give them hope that someone would defeat the humans and put them back on the throne for good, but it's not real. The prince didn't have any kids, so there is no heir. Give it maybe a year and the rumors will die off if there are any."

We're doomed, the male had said, *we won't last another year.*

"That is a stupid theory," she told him. He chuckled softly and kept eating. "What do you think of his theory, Ralyn?"

She had a bite of toast in her mouth but swallowed thickly and said, "I always thought the New Heir was some legend, not an actual person." They both looked at her and she shifted uncomfortably, saying, "it's a bedtime story."

"You were told Fae bedtime stories?" Aspen asked.

"After my parents died, my brother and I were taken in by an orphanage," she told him, "I roomed with a Fae, and she'd tell them to herself. The New Heir was a legend about a Fae not born of royal blood who would bring peace and close the Rift."

Kit asked, "the Rift closes? Isn't it a natural formation—a canyon?"

"A canyon full of darkness that kills anyone who tries to climb in it," Aspen grunted. "Hey, I was right then," he looked up at Kit. "It's fake. Nothing closes the Rift, and the New Heir isn't real."

"Huh," Kit said. She glanced at the arrow before leaning back and focusing on her tea. She hadn't put enough sugar in it, leaving a bitter taste in her mouth. Almost as bitter as some legend both of her friends agreed was fake. Unless Ralyn was lying.

Chapter Eleven

HER BODY WAS CLEAN, and so was her kitchen. Kit wasn't sure who'd done the last part while she'd been collecting laundry and buying new dishes. She was in the midst of scrubbing dirt off her boots when the door opened. She got up quickly and dropped the boot into the bucket of water. "Jassin!" She gasped, making her way over. "What are you doing here?"

He hugged her tight. "Checking on you," he said, kissing her head, "you haven't visited for a while, so I thought I'd make the trip. I brought your bow as well. And I have a gift."

She took the bow and quiver and set them with the older one. Jassin made his way into her apartment, his gaze sweeping as she sat on the arm of her favorite chair. His eyes fell on the side table he'd made for her.

"Still have that old thing, I see," he said and she nodded. Jassin walked over, standing directly in front of her. He held up a thin black box. "This is for you," Jassin said as he opened it. He bent toward her just a little, smiling coyly.

A dainty iron arrow on a black cord was rested in the box. "Because I love you, Kit."

"I love you, too," she whispered.

Jassin removed the necklace from the box, and Kit moved her hair so he could put it on her. It hung just under her collarbones. He squeezed her shoulders gently before sitting in the chair with a sigh. "I like what you've done with the place," he said as he looked around.

"This is the cleanest it's been in a while," she admitted, "and I wasn't even the one that did most of it."

"I hate cleaning," he said with a shake of his head, "so did your father."

Kit looked at him. She knew that already and figured she'd inherited the trait, but hearing it from someone else felt different. When Kit nodded, he smiled. Jassin had been a friend of her father's for years before she was born. They hadn't grown up together, but Jassin introduced her parents. He'd been one of the first people to hold Kit when she was a baby. He was the uncle who showed up randomly with gifts and old stories, then left for months or sometimes years.

"I miss him," Jassin said quite vulnerably.

"I miss all of them," she said. He nodded. Kit took her necklace out of her pocket and showed it to him. Jassin's hand shook as he reached for it, barely brushing his thumb over the metal.

He laughed sadly, sniffing. "Gods, I can't remember the last time I saw this."

"Years and years ago," she whispered, setting it in his hand. Jassin gripped it tight and moved his arm around her back in a soft embrace. Kit leaned into him. Her eyes closed.

"Tell me what you've been up to," he said. Kit sat up, taking the necklace back and sliding it into her pocket. He had an expectant smile on his face.

"I made a new friend," Kit said with a grin. "Her name is Ralyn, and she stayed here last night."

His brows rose. "Oh, you had a friend stay the night?" He asked. "I'm happy for you, Kit."

She beamed at him. Kit got up and went to the kitchen. "I got new teacups, too," she held them up, and he crossed the small room to hold the plain, cracked cups. "They aren't the best because I can't get anything new, but I think they've got character."

He agreed with a nod but asked, "why can't you buy new ones?"

"Aside from the price of new ones?" She asked with an ironic laugh. Kit went to her kettle and filled it with water. "People break in all the time. I don't want to spend the money just to lose them in a few weeks."

His gaze shifted to the windows. "I'll have new locks installed by the end of the week," he said, "and spells so only who you allow can open them."

Kit smiled. "How's being a Crown going?" She asked. Her back was to him, but she felt his approach as he came closer to her.

He answered, "I've been dealing with much, but I know that it will all get better soon."

She nodded. Kit waited for the water to heat and breathed in deeply. "It'll all get better," she agreed, smiling at him. Jassin nodded. He moved to lean against the island next to her. He put a gentle hand on her back.

"Would you like to talk about the attack on your friend a few days ago?" He asked. Kit had expected him to mention it, but not so outright. She looked away from him. "I worried," he said.

She said, "he didn't do anything to provoke it. They just attacked him." *Did you send them to attack? Did you send Fae to attack Aspen?* Kit checked her kettle and looked at him again. He seemed to be waiting for something, but Kit didn't outright say that she hated Fae. She wouldn't. "And I killed one of them," she said.

"I heard," he said softly, "how are you doing with that?"

"I didn't want to," she said, "but I didn't have a choice. They weren't going to stop."

Jassin stepped forward and pulled her into a hug. "It will get better," he said as she had. She buried her face in his chest, and a strange smell entered her nostrils. Old, maybe, but sort of like the smell of the dungeons. A note of mold and death was hidden in the scent. The crypt? "Things take longer than we want, but they still get better."

He held her until the water was boiling, and she prepared tea. Jassin took almost as much sugar as she did. She stirred both of them as she decided to enter the crypt after the sun went down. She could look inside at night if he smelled like it during the day, and no one would know.

Her mind was stuck on what she might find. Bodies? Didn't they bury them? Or encase them in stone?

"Thank you for the tea," Jassin said when he was finished, "I hope to see you soon. Perhaps we should have lunch in the castle in a few days?"

She smiled. "That sounds wonderful."

"Goodnight, Kitali," he said as he smoothed her hair down. He ran his hand through it, taking some of it over her shoulder.

"Goodnight, Jassin," she replied with another hug, smelling the old rotten crypt again. He kissed her head and left. He was headed back to the castle, to his study or his rooms.

And Kit would go into the crypt.

Chapter Twelve

THE DOOR OPENED TO Ralyn, who had a smile on her face. It was refreshing to see her after Jassin. Kit had never felt exhausted after having tea with him. Ralyn set her bag on the lumpy chair and gathered her uniform for guard duty.

"Are you working tonight?" Kit asked from her favorite chair.

"West Ball again," she said with a nod. Ralyn straightened. "At least I'm posted near a window. It gives me something to look at for the first half of the night."

"And you'll come back after?"

She hesitated. "Is that all right?"

"It's wonderful," she rushed to say, "sorry. Would you like dinner? We can eat before you have to go."

Ralyn said, "actually, I already got us something." She reached into her bag and produced a rolled-up cloth. She set it on the uneven end table by Kit's chair. It revealed cold sausage, cheese, and fresh bread. "And this," she said, going to her bag and returning with a teacup. It was one of Kit's that Ralyn had been using. She held it out and dropped it. Kit gasped, sitting up sharply only to watch the cup bounce on the ground and roll to a stop by her foot. She picked it up. "I had it spelled," Ralyn explained, "so it won't break like all the others."

Kit ran her thumb over the thin edge of the cup. It didn't feel or look any different. "Who spelled it?" She asked.

She shrugged. "Some human in a magic shop."

Kit's face was bright with a smile. She hugged the cup close to her chest. "Thank you, Ralyn," she said. Ralyn waved her off and organized the meal so they both received equal shares.

"Did someone come by today?" She asked.

"Jassin," she nodded. Kit took a bite of the still-warm bread. "He came for tea. Maybe next time you'll get to meet him."

Ralyn pushed the lumpy chair closer to Kit and sat. "Maybe," she said. "So you really know each of the Crowns personally?"

She bit off a bite of meat next and nodded. "Mali likes me because of the King Assassin aspect," her brows raised and fell, "Nolen doesn't like me at all." He was the one who said they needed someone to take the fall. He was prepared for Kit to die. So was Jassin. "But Jassin is different," she said.

"He raised you?"

"No, Jassin found me eight years ago in my house a few days after my family died," she said. Kit began organizing what was on her side of the cloth. "He carried me out and got me cleaned up. He gave me a place to stay." She swallowed. "I owe him my life."

Ralyn just looked at her. The beat of silence left Kit with her guilt. She was about to sneak around and *spy* on the man who saved her life. She would've died in that house if it weren't for Jassin showing up. It was easy to recall—how she'd found her family. The way they'd been left. And Jassin, days later, walking into their home and cursing so loud it frightened the crows feasting on their bodies. Kit had been trying to keep them away. It was Jassin who pulled her out of the pile. It was Jassin who helped her bury them. It was Jassin who brought her to a safe place, who gave her a new home and a place to store her memories. And now?

"Would you do anything for him? Because you owe him?" Ralyn asked, knocking Kit from her thoughts. Kit looked at her.

"I'd die for him whether I owed him or not," she said and sat back. *Does he use that against me?* She tried not to consider that as an option.

"What happened to your family?" She asked softly.

Kit said, "they died in Niverly. And you? You said your parents died, but you have a brother?"

She nodded. A small smile formed on her face. "Witker. He's all I have. Our parents were killed a few years back, so we take care of each other."

"What's Witker like?" Kit asked. She pulled a leg up and wrapped her arm around it.

Ralyn was quiet for a moment. "He's kind of an ass," she said and Kit laughed. "Our mother used to say he took after his father that way. He died before Witker was born."

"Where is he now?"

Ralyn put her head back. "Petaki, I think. Definitely not in Calar. Too many people."

"I agree," Kit said.

"Where would you rather live?" She asked as she stood. Ralyn went around the chair and into the kitchen, lighting the fire for tea.

Kit considered the question. As far away from Calar as she could get? "Masai," she said, "between the rivers. Or Basik, I did a competition there once in the spring and it looked beautiful. Anywhere is better than here, though."

She nodded from the kitchen. "I'm sure it would smell better, too," she said with a laugh.

Kit joined her softly. "I don't know why any Fae wants to live here, especially in the lower districts."

She looked over. "Is the smell worse over there?"

"It's disgusting," she cringed, "and with the heightened senses, it must be so much worse for them."

"So they should all just leave?" Ralyn held her hand over the kettle.

Kit's brow furrowed. "No, I would be the last person to say that every member of a species should be run out of their homes."

"Because of Niverly?"

She stared at the bread in her hand, wiping some of the crumbs away. "We grew flowers," she said, "in Niverly, we grew flowers for dried tea and bouquets and things. So maybe we were run out because of the smell."

"They still grow flowers there," she said. Her voice had quieted slightly. "The Fae that live there now. The tea I bought you is from Niverly."

Kit muttered, "how ironic," and continued eating.

Chapter Thirteen

When Ralyn left for the castle she took extra food with her. She was off to West Ball in full, heavy armor. Kit would be going near West Ball because the crypt entrance was on the castle's west side, but she doubted she'd seen Ralyn if she was right about the rotations.

She stood drinking her Niverly tea as she tossed a pair of black pants onto the bed. Her next toss was her boots, which clunked against the ground rather than her mattress. Kit found a dark shirt and her leather jacket. She couldn't help but feel guilty. It boiled in her gut. She'd once told herself she'd never wear such dark clothes again—not since the prince. Kit hadn't taken out the black pants in months. She'd been an assassin in them. Not a hunter or an archer. An assassin.

Kit washed some of her dishes before going back to the clothes. She pulled on the pants and the shirt first, itching to take it off and go to bed. The fabric was rough against her skin, scraping like the tiles of the domed roof had when she made her attempt to escape the assassination.

She pulled her boots on.

With her hair tied back, she was reminded again of that day. Of the stress. Of the . Of her family and the reason she sought revenge.

What would her mother think of her? Kit tried not to imagine her disappointment as she walked to the castle. The world around her moved in a blur of darkness and candlelit windows. Kit made no conversation with the guard at the gate. He did nothing more than open the door for her. Other guards looked at her, but no one said anything. Her heart beat rapidly as she went to the west part of the castle, then leaned one shoulder against the wall on the corner. There was a large hall she looked down at, one completely stone with various paintings on either side. Down it would be the crypt.

Torches were spaced on either side, and guards seemed close to falling asleep. Kit waited, pulling the sleeves of her jacket further down her hands.

A guard closer to the top of command walked down, speaking to those in the hall. They were about to be rotated east. Some of them straightened, others stretched. East Hall meant they'd be going in the same direction Kit was headed. They'd go left, and she would cut right.

She looked behind her, listening to the yawns in the hall and the commander snapping at them. She told them they'd have a chance to eat soon, which got some of them moving. They went into formation.

Kit stood straight and waited for them to turn before following slowly. She kept to the shadows as best she could, deciding to treat the task like a hunt. She was navigating the area as silently as she could—just like the coronation. It was as simple as sneaking through a window when she killed the prince. She had to climb the castle, sure, and almost slipped on the way up, but it had been simple. She went through a window, waited, and watched, and when the prince began walking down the aisle, she fired.

But something about that had always felt off. Not the sneaking and waiting. The Fae were too busy with themselves and the guards weren't anticipating such a horrific attack. It was her hesitation. She'd hesitated up on the rafter by the window she opened.

Kit's talent was impressive, but when she wasn't sure about the shot, she was never as accurate. She hesitated up there, and she shouldn't have been as accurate as she was.

She'd brushed it off as nerves before, but now, with everything Jassin might've done... What if another human was there, making sure she didn't miss? So that her assassination was successful whether she died or not.

While the guards went left, Kit went right. She hugged the walls and checked every which way as she neared the stairs that led down to the lower level and the crypt.

Once through the door, she took the steps one at a time. Her chest tightened with nerves and she looked down the steps to catch a shine of light from a torch. She kept going and found it hanging on the wall. Her pace slowed further. The stairwell twisted slightly. She struggled to keep out of sight.

A grunt made her stop. Her eyes darted back and forth as someone muttered, "this is disgusting."

Another said, "it is necessary."

Kit tiptoed forward. She peeked around to find no one in her direct line of sight and stepped into the old, smelly crypt. Another torch was lit before her, and she stepped to the right. There were three halls—three rows of dead and buried Fae Kings—and the one on the far right was occupied.

Jassin said, "we need an heir. If we could do this differently, we would."

She moved to another wall and saw their shadows. Light flickered over the dusty place. Kit glanced behind her before shifting as close as she could and looking toward where the Crowns were. She could see Jassin with his arms crossed and Nolen behind him wearing a nightgown and a dressing robe. Boisin was there as well, though he was off to the side with a cringe on his hairy face. They were all looking at something. Kit dared to shift closer.

She wished she hadn't.

Mali was in a nightgown as well, but she wasn't standing. She was squatted on top of a body and rocking with a disgusted look on her face. A shine of magic was beneath her. She was looking down at who she was sitting on, and Kit saw a sheet covering the face of a familiar male figure. She was on the prince—who looked the same as he had the day he died, as if he'd been dead for only a few minutes and not ten months.

Kit almost vomited as she slapped her hand over her mouth and stepped away. She went toward the stairs. Her stomach churned. They were trying to create an heir using the prince Kit had killed. That was his dead body. They were...

She stopped at the top of the stairs and swallowed thickly. Her entire body heaved, but she forced down anything that might come up. Kit opened the crypt door and searched for signs of movement before she exited. Then Kit shut it gently behind her.

There were eight guards in the long hall, four on either side, and Kit walked past them with her back straight. If anyone asked or told Jassin, she would say she wanted to sleep in her castle rooms for the night before her window locks could be spelled, but changed her mind and went home instead.

Until then, Kit struggled to keep her breathing even and her face neutral.

Chapter Fourteen

ALTHOUGH SHE WANTED NOTHING more than to leave, she went up a flight of marble stairs. Kit wanted to flee the castle. She wanted to throw up and curl into her bed without any nightmares. She wanted a hug from Aspen. But most importantly, she wanted answers she couldn't get at home.

She opened the door to Jassin's study, her hands shaking as she tried to light a candle. The room was dim. The hair on her body stood on end. The chairs cast shadows and they creaked in her mind like some haunted place.

Glancing at the door like Jassin would appear, she approached his stacks of papers. None of it made any sense to her and the longer she stared at them the more the words changed and floated away from her. She blinked hard and tried to concentrate. Laws and laws and more laws. Kit searched for anything about the Fae and picked up one document. She held it to the candlelight, and her eyes darted over words about taxing. Fae would have to buy magic licenses to practice any spell casting.

She found another document signed by Jassin and Nolen stating that those who practiced magic without a license would be held accountable for their crime and punished depending on the type of magic they were illegally using.

What were they doing? Why were the Crowns doing this? Even the Fae let humans use magic.

The land, the taxing, the licenses, the heir…

And the Crowns were building prisons for Fae.

She put the pages back. Kit had killed the prince because she wanted revenge for her losses. For Niverly. Because she believed that it would be better and that they would be more equal if humans had control. Jassin had been the one constantly saying that.

This wasn't equal. This was far from equal.

Kit blew out the candle and exited the room, heading to the door. When she reached the gate, she managed to smile at the guard. Few people were on the streets, making her walk home only slightly less strenuous on her mind and body.

She opened the door to her apartment and stared at her things. Kit had only taken money from the Crowns once when she was desperate, but they always offered to pay her. To compensate her for what she'd done. To pay her rent. They got the money from the Fae Kings and were now trying to get more.

But there were only two signatures, so didn't that mean Mali was hesitant about that drastic of a law?

But all three of them were in the crypt...

Kit rushed to the bathing room and heaved into the chamber, the image of Mali on the body—

Her entire being hurt. She'd vomited twice in the last hour and had curled into a ball on her favorite chair with a blanket wrapped around her. Her eyes were pointed at the arrow. The arrow that had King's Blood on it.

Kit had been used to put humans on the throne. They spent ten months covering up dying land in the north, killing those who rioted against their rule, blaming Fae for the fires they started, and working on making life miserable for the Fae. Kit had wanted revenge on an entire species for what they took from her, but now the humans were taking so much more. The Fae thrived on magic. Taking that from them was like removing a piece of who they were.

Was that her fault?

The land was dying, and the only way to save it was to find the New Heir and crown him before the year ended. If the Crowns were attempting to sire an heir using the prince's body, she would have to find the real one. They'd intend to secretly crown their heir so the land stopped dying and they could continue ruling.

If Mali had a male, of course. Females couldn't be rulers.

What if Jassin was just as terrible as she believed the Fae were?

Fae were awful, but they shouldn't lose magic like humans didn't lose it when the Fae were kings. And they'd been ruling since the beginning. Kit had interrupted the flow of King's Blood with an arrow and a broken heart.

She looked at the arrow again. How many times had she wanted to snap the thing in half and burn both pieces? To melt down the arrowhead and throw the ball into the river? King's Blood was magic. The Fae were talking about King's Blood in the tavern. Tracker magic and King's Blood?

Kit could use it to find the heir. She could track him if she had the magic.

She had doomed everyone, but looking at the arrow on the wall, she knew she could save them.

Chapter Fifteen

She didn't sleep. She couldn't stop thinking. Kit was sluggish and pained.

The Niverly tea smelled different now that she knew where it was from. Kit could imagine her father tying up the flowers and spices to dry. He'd smell them every so often. She could hear her mother telling her she used too much sugar. There would be a shortage in Niverly if she kept up with her addiction.

Kit slowly stirred copious amounts of sugar into her tea, smelling the dried flowers and leaves with her eyes closed.

That was why she killed the prince. Because of her family, because she lost them. Because the Fae were cruel and disgusting and they took things away. They took her family. They claimed her home in the name of the prince.

She waited until Ralyn was awake to change, wondering if her reason for murder was a good enough one. She threw her black pants to the back of the closet and dressed in something lighter. When she saw herself in the mirror, it was someone close to death.

She washed her face and breathed into a cloth before finally brushing her hair. She moved her fingers through it the way Jassin did. It was comforting, and it had been for so long. It was her connection to her life before, such an identifying feature on her body.

She braided it back and laced her boots.

"Are you going somewhere?" Ralyn asked. She was in the kitchen, standing over a pot. Kit hadn't made breakfast, and the sight of it made her realize she was starving, but she grabbed her bag and put it over her shoulder.

"I was going to see if the baker had my favorite sweet bread today," she said, "then maybe shop. Can I get you anything?"

She shook her head and looked Kit up and down. "Are you all right?"

"I didn't sleep last night."

"Oh," she said. Ralyn faced her better. Kit itched to leave. "Maybe after you eat something, you can try again. Take a nap."

Kit nodded. "Maybe. I'll see you soon." She said her goodbye and rushed down the stairs, walking across the street on the off chance Ralyn was watching through the window. She purchased the bread and ate small pieces. A Fae spit on her as she passed on the way to the shops.

The place where she often bought her spices was open and empty. It was a small shop with just four walls lined with different ingredients and a rack or two of dried herbs. Kays, the owner, smiled at her and asked if she needed anything. "I'm just looking," Kit said and went to the shelves. She had a recipe in mind, just not for cooking. Kit had been friends with someone who liked to change the color of her hair and she once listed everything she used to do it. Now Kit had all the same things. She went up to the counter and set them down. "Actually," she said, "do you know where I can find a magic seller?"

"A magic seller?" She began wrapping Kit's purchases as she paid what she owed. "There's a woman who sells some spells from inside the apothecary further down the street. Usually things to prevent pregnancy, but I heard she does it all."

Kit nodded. "And the spells work?" One could never be sure with humans—their connection to magic only stretched so far.

"Every time," she said. Kit smiled and left with her things, headed to the apothecary. She bought meat for lunch and a few vegetables from the market. There were more people in the apothecary than she expected. They were packed together in the thin, short aisles looking for medicinal care. Kit moved slowly around the clusters of people and their whispers about *King Assassin*. She found a woman speaking to a man in a hushed voice and went there, waiting patiently while looking at an herb that didn't smell very good.

"Can I help you?" The woman asked when Kit stepped up to her. She had wild, light hair and wore many necklaces. Her clothes looked too big for her and she kept adjusting her sleeves.

Kit said, "I'd like to buy a spell. I was told you could help me."

She looked her up and down. "Of what kind?" She asked.

"A tracking spell," she answered.

"Ah," the old woman nodded. She looked around. "Lose a boy?" Her eyebrows wiggled strangely.

Kit's brow furrowed. "No, I'm going hunting," she decided to say. The woman considered her once before shrugging with a slight frown. "Um, do you have a spell specific to using blood to track?"

"Blood tracking?" The woman's eyes widened ever so slightly. "My, must be some animal." She laughed and said, "I can get it to you, but that isn't the kind of thing I carry around. Meet me outside here tonight. Late. Blood tracking spells take time... That's powerful magic. Be prepared to pay in full."

"Full being how much?"

"Fifty gold pieces would do."

She felt herself pale slightly but nodded anyway. The woman noticed Kit's stiffness but moved on to the next person looking for a spell. Kit walked away. She did not have fifty gold pieces. She had expected a decent price, maybe thirty, and was willing to pay that much—but fifty? She had that a few days ago before she was robbed, but not now.

Kit looked at the castle as she walked home, then thought of who was inside. The man who said he'd do anything for her—the person who offered to pay for anything she needed.

Chapter Sixteen

⟵————⟴

KIT TOOK A DEEP breath before walking through the castle doors. Her soup sloshed in the lidded bowl, and she tapped a spoon against it as she walked. She looked around like the prince would come out of a door or a hall. He'd be nude and screaming that Kit killed him, that she did this. Like some nightmare she had yet to have.

Her feet took the marble stairs slowly. She kept her heartbeat steady. It was just Jassin. Jassin, who loved her and cared for her. Jassin, who watched someone he worked with... Kit stopped, holding her stomach. *I will not vomit,* she told herself, *I will not vomit.*

This time, she knocked on his door and opened it before anyone could answer. "Jassin?" She asked, but the room was empty. Candles were lit, which led her to believe he was just there or would be back soon. Kit sat in a chair and leaned back. She put her feet up on the edge of the desk.

He was touching her arm when she opened her eyes. Kit groaned and grabbed her neck. "Worst chair to fall asleep in," he told her with a small laugh. "You must be tired."

"I made you soup," she mumbled as she rubbed her eyes. "It's a bribe soup. Pure bribery."

"Well, I always take soup, even for a bribe," he said. Kit looked at him. He was wearing a dark tunic and a gold necklace. She thought about the one she had around her neck that he gave her. Had that been a bribe? "What do you need?" He leaned on the desk and nudged her feet.

She said, "fifty gold pieces."

He raised a brow at her. Jassin took a bite of the soup and stirred it around. "And the reason you need that much gold?"

"I thought I had enough set aside to buy some things for my apartment to replace what I broke *and* pay rent *and* feed two people plus Aspen," she picked at a little divot in the desk, "but I don't, and I was wondering because you said you'd always support me... if I could bribe you into giving it to me. I can pay you back if—"

"Absolutely not," he said. Kit blinked in shock. "There will be no paying back," he said. Jassin set the soup on the desk and went to a table covered in books at the back of the room. He returned with a leather bag of coins and put it in front of her. "That, I believe, is close to eighty."

"I asked for fifty," she said, putting her feet on the floor and dumping some of the gold. Her own profile shined up at her, as well as the new seal and the faces of the Crowns. She picked up the pieces, her mouth open. "I only need fifty."

He nodded and continued eating, "yes well now you can pay for all the things you need and buy something for yourself as well. You're too hard on yourself, Kit; you should spoil yourself every once in a while."

"I don't need to spoil myself when you do it for me," she replied as she put the pieces back and tied the bag. He smiled. "And the soup wasn't even that good," she added.

"You know I love your cooking," he said. Kit rolled her eyes. "How long have you been here? It's almost sunset," he motioned outside the room.

Her brows raised. "A while, then. At least a few hours because I was waiting for you."

"No wonder the soup is cold."

She sneered, and Jassin laughed, setting the now empty bowl aside. He put the lid on top and the spoon next to it. Kit breathed in deeply and leaned back. "Jassin, how are you?" She asked. "I feel like I only ask about being a Crown, never about you."

"Stressed," he said after a moment. Jassin laced his fingers in front of him. "And you?"

"Tired," she answered. He nodded knowingly. "I haven't been sleeping very well lately. I don't know what it is."

He asked, "would you like a sleeping drought?"

She shook her head. "You know I don't like those. I don't like feeling like I can't control what's happening."

"If it helps you sleep..."

"But it's making me sleep," she said. He was quiet. Kit looked away from him. "I don't like not being in control of myself. Even if it's just a sleep aid."

Jassin nodded and reached forward to take her hand. "Why don't you go home, try to sleep early. I'll have the bowl cleaned and sent over tomorrow with someone who will change your locks."

She breathed in and stood, wrapping her arms around him. He didn't smell like the crypt, and she thanked the gods for it. She might've vomited. Kit squeezed her eyes shut and relaxed against him. "Thank you," she mumbled into his shirt, and he squeezed her. Jassin smoothed her hair down, and she opened her eyes, slowly pulling away from him. He kissed the side of her head and she took her bag, leaving him and the castle beginning to hate her hair. His attachment to it, its connection to her mother. All of it.

Chapter Seventeen

WHEN KIT GOT HOME she counted out fifty gold coins and put them into an old pouch. She even sprinkled a little dirt from her old shoes so they didn't look as new as castle gold, then put the rest of her money into a leather bag. This, another shirt, two knives, supplies for arrows, and laces for her boots went into the bag she'd been carrying for years. She put dried meat, cheese, some fruit, and bread into it, then sat in her chair with her stuff in the closet.

Time did not pass quickly. Kit's legs shook as she waited for the sun to set. It was as if some god she wasn't aware of was forcing the day to go by slower and slower. As if they'd tied a lasso to the sun and was pulling it back, fighting its need to set.

Eventually it did, because no god could challenge nature in such a way. The gods were unlimited in their power, but nature was unyielding.

She stood and picked up the old bag of new coins, stuffing them into her shirt and pulling on her jacket. It had been a few hours, and she wanted to get it over with.

The woman was against the wall, nearly hidden in shadow. She would've been if she wasn't on the corner in the light of a shop about to close. "I almost thought you wouldn't show," she said to Kit when she stopped. "Blood magic is something different."

"Why?" She asked, "is it dangerous?"

She held out a scroll for her to see, a smirk on her face. "Only if you do the wrong thing."

Kit nodded slowly and brought out her coin.

"It's blood to find blood, King Assassin, but I'm sure you'll be fine with that little accuracy talent of yours," the woman said. Kit looked her up and down. She held the scroll out and traded the coin for it. "It'll work," she said, then disappeared down the street. Kit went in the opposite direction. She held the scroll inside the sleeve of her jacket repeating *it will work*. The spell was on the paper—Kit just had to say the words. It didn't matter if she didn't have a lick of magic inside her as long as she had the confidence. She itched to open the scroll but kept going just in case someone was looking at her.

Ralyn was already at the castle and had been for some time, so Kit lit candles and sat in front of her fireplace. She chewed on her lip as she flattened the scroll before her.

Take the blood in hand. Give the name.

Blood to find blood.

That was all. Kit ran her hand over the paper, then looked at the back of it. This large scroll for... twelve words? Twelve words! Fifty gold pieces for *twelve words*.

She lifted the arrow off the wall and shivered at the feeling of the shaft between her fingers. She twirled it once and sat in front of the expensive piece of nothing. In the light, she couldn't see the blood. She still knew it was there. In her hands. "Take the blood in hand," she said, "New Heir. Blood to find blood."

Her eyes moved. Nothing happened.

"Take the blood in hand," she repeated. Kit looked at the arrow. She put it in her left hand and repeated the words. Again, nothing happened. With her lips thin, she turned the arrow and tapped it against her palm. She stared at it. Blood to find blood. Her brow furrowed. What if it didn't work with dried blood? "Take the blood in hand," she said. Kit stifled a yawn. "In," she said. She blinked hard. Kit straightened and pressed the arrowhead down to break open her skin, hissing as it went, and repeated, "take the blood in hand. New Heir." She pulled the arrowhead out of her hand and rolled her fingers into a fist. "Blood to find blood."

Blood dripped onto the page and her candles went out. The smoke twirled in the air as if someone blew out the fire. Pain crawled up her arm, sparking through her elbow and shoulder. Blood was suddenly *pouring* out of her hand. She gasped and stumbled into the kitchen to grab a rag. Kit wrapped it tightly around her hand and breathed heavily. It was a struggle not to scream.

Gods, gods, gods. She went for the paper again, sweating, but the words didn't change. Kit's blood soaked into the parchment and disappeared. Her eyes blurred, and she looked at her hand. It was on fire. It had to be on fire.

⟵———⟶

She woke with a start, instantly up to her hands and knees. A horrible strike of pain ran down the entire left half of her body that sent her back to the floor. She groaned deeply and shifted her hand out from beneath her. The rag had been soaked through with blood and there was a small puddle of it on the floor below her.

It was still dark, but Ralyn could come back soon. Kit couldn't move. Heavy anxiety told her she'd done something wrong. It prickled at her lower back. Beads of sweat ran down her face.

"Get up," she told herself. She swallowed, a knot quickly developing in her throat. "Come on…"

Her leg moved, which nearly had her laughing with joy, and she got her right arm under her. Kit pushed upward with her left hand cradled against her chest. The room spun in the dark. She got to her knees and grabbed the paper. *What did I do?* Kit balled it up and tossed it into the fireplace, struggling with a match to get rid of the evidence. The spelled burned a bright green in the fireplace.

She gripped the arrow next, her head tilted to the hooks it usually rested on. She'd have to stand to get it there. Could she? The left half of her body said no. She thought it was best to listen to that half.

But no, she had to. She had to put the arrow back before Ralyn got home. Kit wiped her blood off of the arrowhead and got against the wall. She counted down before lifting herself onto one leg. Her upper body and face were pressed against the bricks as she dragged her arm up. Her mouth fell open. Kit stared at the two hooks that held the taunting, haunted arrow. She hit one of them, groaning as she shifted her body to reach the other. They seemed to move, dancing on the wall, and she squeezed her eyes shut to clear her head. Kit got up to her toes and set it on the hooks.

She dropped down to the ground. In the fireplace, the spell was gone. While she managed to get a few candles back, she knocked over most of them and tossed one weakly toward the table it was supposed to go on. She put one on Jassin's table and rested her head against the cushion of her chair.

"Kit? Kit, what are you doing on the floor?" Ralyn asked and she opened her eyes, looking around. "Kit?"

Her brow furrowed. "I fell asleep," she said.

"On the floor?" She tilted her head. Kit nodded. "You must be so sick," she said. Ralyn put the back of her hand against Kit's face. "You're burning."

"I'm all right," Kit breathed.

Ralyn shook her head. "Let's get you to bed—"

"No, I don't want to," she said quickly. For some reason, she was desperate. Ralyn wouldn't hurt her, but she didn't want to go to her room. She didn't want to go in that direction; she wanted to go south.

South.

It worked.

"I'm all right," Kit said as she sat up. There was no pain in her left side. "Did you just get back?"

"What happened to your hand?" Ralyn took it in her own. Kit winced. The rag was covered in blood, as was her hand, but the cut itself was the most interesting part. It was golden. "Did you do this to yourself?"

Kit stared at it. "What?"

"How did you get this? Blessings, I think you need stitches," she said as she looked it over. "Do you have a kit for that?"

"In the bathing room," she said. Ralyn left. Had she not seen the gold, or was she ignoring it? No, she wouldn't have been able to hide her initial reaction to a glowing cut in her hand.

"Here, come to the sink," Ralyn said. She lifted Kit and caught her as she swooned, helping her clean the cut. She then had her sit so she could stitch it. "What were you doing?" She asked.

Kit looked at the few candles still scattered around. From another's perspective, she could've just knocked them over accidentally. "I meant to be in my chair," she said. Ralyn glanced at her, and Kit winced as the needle moved.

"Well, you're going to stay in this chair until you aren't feverish," she decided. "If I have to stay awake and keep you here, I will."

Kit smiled and put her head back. "You sound like my mother."

"She had the right idea, then," Ralyn replied. Kit looked at the golden line. It was closing but still very obviously shining. "Have you felt ill recently?"

"I vomited a few times last night," Kit told her, "and I didn't sleep at all. That might have something to do with it."

She nodded. "Well, I'll make you tea—"

"Lots of sugar."

Ralyn smiled as she wrapped Kit's hand in cloth. "Lots of sugar, I know." She got up. "You'll have your tea and sleep in this chair, all right? And tomorrow, you'll eat something that you can hopefully keep down."

"All right, Mother," she mumbled and closed her eyes. Ralyn moved her legs over the arm of the chair. She cast a blanket over her and went into the kitchen.

Chapter Eighteen

KIT REALIZED SHE NEEDED to buy a map early the following day. Ralyn wasn't awake, but she wasn't trying to move despite how much she itched to go south. Her hand throbbed and her head was reaching the same point, so she laid still and thought she nodded off a few more times waiting for Ralyn to come out. She wanted to take her bag and go south. She needed a map. And a horse. She hoped to use Treyla, the castle horse she loved so much. Every time she and Aspen went out together, Kit rode Treyla.

Would Treyla enjoy it? Kit imagined they'd have a good time together out in the world. They'd spend time on the roads and in the woods...

She hadn't thought it through completely. She needed more supplies if she was going to stay in the woods.

Kit could tell the castle guards she was going on a long hunt as well. That way, everyone would know that was where she went. She'd have to have Ralyn tell Aspen because he'd insist on coming with her.

So she needed a bedroll, maybe a tent, flint, steel... and other things for hunting.

At least she knew what she'd be doing all day.

"Did you sleep well?" Ralyn asked when she came out of the bedroom, fully clothed and scratching the back of her head.

"I feel much better, yes," she nodded. Ralyn looked at her for a moment before going to the kitchen. Kit got up and relieved herself while she cooked. As soon as she came out, Ralyn put a cup of tea in her hand and placed the back of her hand against her temple.

"You aren't as warm as last night," she muttered.

"I feel better," Kit insisted. Ralyn tilted her head at her, then went back to the kitchen. Kit sat in her chair and cast a glance at the arrow. It was in the same place. Like it had never been moved at all. The spell was only ash in the fireplace, the puddle of blood was cleaned off the floor, and the candles had been picked up. Kit looked at her hand and wondered if it was still golden. Then why Ralyn hadn't noticed.

"Breakfast," Ralyn said. She set a plate on the edge of Jassin's table and caught it when it started to slip off. She put the plate in Kit's lap. "Eat," she said, "sick people need to eat, it's one of the rules."

Kit looked at her and nodded slowly. *She's a Fae.* Of all the evidence Kit had against Ralyn, this was what sealed the deal. Fae didn't fall ill unless they were poisoned. Ralyn wouldn't know how to care for a sick person, hence the rules. She went back to the kitchen, and Kit bit into an apple slice.

"I'm planning on going on a long hunt," Kit said as casually as she could, eating slowly. "I've been thinking about it for a while. Another escape."

Ralyn looked over. "You shouldn't go anywhere if you aren't feeling well." She crossed her arms. Kit was again reminded of her mother.

She said, "I feel better. I think I just needed some sleep." Kit stood and brought her plate to the sink. "Thank you for breakfast and for stitching my hand."

"Kit, you looked terrible yesterday. I don't think you should go on a hunt. You could get hurt."

"I'll be fine," she assured her, "if anything, it'll be good for me. I don't have to breathe smelly Calar air."

She shook her head. "It's not a good idea."

"Then I'll regret it and come back," Kit shrugged and went to her bedroom. She tried to judge whether or not she needed to bathe. And then whether she needed to buy another bag. Or a saddlebag. She needed to get food for Treyla as well.

"Or you could realize that you could fall unconscious in the woods and be unable to help yourself," Ralyn called through the doorway as Kit began to fill the tub with water. She looked at her sickly reflection, which would be why Ralyn's concern shone through so brightly. But Kit felt fine. It was just the spell that made her weak—it had been called dangerous for a reason.

As the water rose, she found clean clothes. She decided to keep the bandage on while she bathed, hating to admit that she was almost afraid of the golden mark. She scrubbed every part of her body with her right hand, dragging the soap through her hair and scratching it into her scalp. She was a prune by the time she was finished, and she dried off meticulously.

Ralyn was waiting on her chair when she came out braiding her wet hair over her shoulder. "Kit—"

"I need to do this," she interrupted, "I need this. I could care less if I was dying or if I had the stamina of a Fae—I *need* this. I'm tired and feel like the entire world is pushing down on me and trapping me in a box. I need to be somewhere else. And I'm going to be somewhere else. You cannot stop me."

She sat back. "Fine," Ralyn said, "how long will you be gone?"

"I don't know," she shrugged. "You can use the rooms for as long as you want. Move in, even. I need to go get some things." Ralyn nodded. It felt awkward to return to her bedroom to take things out of her bag to make room for more supplies, then even more when she had to leave without a real goodbye.

Chapter Nineteen

HOURS AGO, SHE HAD decided to wait until sunset to leave so fewer people would see her. Kit's hair was in two braids, both falling below her ribcage. The more she stared at them through her bathing room mirror, the more she questioned what she was doing. She had never been overly attached to her hair, but this suddenly felt drastic.

She picked up her shears and held them beneath the mark she'd put in her braid. Her breathing quickened. Kit continued to tell herself all the reasons she was changing the way she looked—it was her most familiar feature, she'd been told once that people had portraits of her in their homes, Jassin, and not to mention the fact that brown hair wasn't a common color in the area she lived—yet her hand still shook.

Kit grimaced, her eyes squeezed shut as the sound of the shears cutting through her hair rang in her ears. When the hair fell away, she looked at it. Her eyes went wide. She stared at the difference between the braid on the left and the one on the right. *Oh my gods.*

She set her hair in the sink and went for the second braid. No going back now. "All right," she breathed in sharply. A small noise came from her throat as the second braid fell away. She breathed out slowly. "It's fine," she told herself. Kit ran her fingers through it. It was now at her shoulders and choppy at the bottom.

Would it be justified if she cried?

She took another set of shears, trimmed the bottoms, and then looked at her bowl of premixed ingredients for lightening hair. In a world without magic, changing her hair color in just one sitting was impossible. Kit's bowl of chamomile, lemon, and honey would do little without the cosmetic powder she'd sprinkled into it. She stirred it around a few times, watching it sparkle. It had primarily been used for color-changing paints, but it worked just fine on hair.

"It will be all right," she told her reflection and began painting paste onto the short layers of her hair. Kit wasn't brave enough to leave it on for too long, but even after she'd washed and dried it, the color was lighter than she thought it would be. Not quite the common fair color, but not quite the near-black she was so used to. "Well..." she said. Kit tied it behind her head and looked at the small bunch of hair sticking out. "Lovely," she decided and left.

Kit gathered her supplies and dressed, pulling a cloak over her jacket and covering her head with the hood. She felt like a completely different person, especially with how little people paid her any mind—even with the arrows.

The guard at the gate looked at her curiously, however. "Going hunting?" he asked.

"Stealing a horse," Kit replied. He laughed a little and let her through. She adjusted her bow on her shoulder and picked up her pace. The last thing she needed was to run into a Crown on her way to the stables. Kit finally stopped in front of Treyla and pulled her stall door open. She smiled as a wash of ease ran over her. Treyla was a giant horse, one that towered over Kit, with thick brown hair and white around her large hooves. She wasn't used for riding very often—mostly for pulling carts and carriages—but Kit absolutely loved taking her out for walks.

"What are you doing?"

She spun around quickly. "Aspen?" Kit asked.

"Yes, Aspen," he said, his arms crossed. "I went to your apartment because I wanted to talk to you, and Ralyn told me you were going on a hunt while ill—"

"I'm not ill," she said, "and I want to go—"

"No," he shook his head and walked toward her. Aspen pulled the bow off her shoulder. Kit gasped and grabbed for it. He held it out of her reach. Her hood fell back when she tried to grab it again. "What in the name of great gods did you do to your hair?" He dropped the bow with his mouth open.

Kit swallowed. "I wanted something different. Why does it—" She cleared her throat. "Does it look bad?"

"Yes!"

Her heart fell. Kit had thought it was fine, but if he didn't like it... "Well it doesn't matter," she decided. "I don't need to have nice hair to go on a hunt."

"You are not going on a hunt, you're delusional." He reached for her bag and she pulled it away. "Kitali!"

"I don't see what's wrong with me wanting to have time for myself," she said and went toward Treyla's saddle. "And I probably won't even be gone very long."

"Right, because you aren't leaving," Aspen snapped, yanking her hand off the saddle.

Her eyes went wide. "Aspen, what's wrong with you—"

"You aren't leaving," he said. He grabbed her arm and pulled her away from the horse. "Especially not when you're sick."

She jerked out of his grip and stepped back. "You do not get to tell me what to do, and you do not grab me like that. I am an adult, I feel perfectly fine, and I can make my own choices. I am leaving—"

He shoved her against a post between two horse pens, gripping her upper arms. "I don't think you understand how terrible you look right now."

"Let go," Kit squirmed, "Aspen, let go of me!" Treyla neighed and hit her front hooves against the ground. "Aspen!"

"Kit, you need to come inside."

"No I don't!"

He sighed. "Do I need to tell Jassin what you're doing?"

"I'm going hunting, Aspen!" She shoved him, and Treyla stomped forward a step. "And Jassin is not my father. He doesn't control me!"

"You aren't in the right state of mind—"

Kit kneed him between the legs and he gasped, putting his head on her shoulder. She shoved him again and Treyla hit Aspen with her snout. She pawed the ground like she might charge him and he stumbled back, holding where she'd kneed. Kit grabbed the heavy saddle, reins, and her bow. She bolted out of the stables with Treyla trotting next to her and didn't stop despite how much her chest hurt and the heavy weight of everything she was carrying. Treyla slowed once they entered the woods and Kit finally stopped. She fumbled with everything in her hands and adjusted how she was carrying them.

Aspen wasn't following. She stared at the castle, then looked at the impossibly dark woods, and reached for Treyla. She huffed, her heart beating quickly under Kit's hand. "Thank you," she whispered. She squinted as she walked through the woods, shuffling her feet to keep from tripping, and they walked for another few hours to get to the spring.

Thunder boomed across the sky as she pushed her things into the hut hoping they didn't get completely soaked. She produced carrots for Treyla, who munched gratefully.

"Are you going to be all right in the rain?" She asked. Treyla huffed a little, and her brows knit together. The first drop fell. "Maybe you can put your head under the cover," she suggested, looking at the hut. Treyla shook her head and nudged Kit toward it.

She wondered if the Fae bred magic horses instead of regular ones. Ones that understood.

Treyla nudged her again, and she took the quiver off her back, setting it next to her bow as she attempted to settle down. She looked at the cloth wrapped around her hand, and Treyla laid her head in front of the hut. "Thank you for helping me," she whispered. If horses could smile, she was. Kit laid down, questioning whether or not she should've given Treyla a blanket, and fell asleep with her hand on the horse's neck.

She shot up gasping hours later, holding her throat as she got up to her knees. Panic filled her. She coughed and crawled out of the hut toward the spring to gulp down the cold water inside. The nightmare moved through her body with each swallow. She ran her hand over her face and head.

Kit groaned and sat back. Treyla stared at her from the place she'd been grazing in.

"I had a nightmare," she told her, "it happens a lot." She stood awkwardly and wiped her hands on her pants. "Are you ready to go south?" She perked up—or tried to—and went to the horse. "I'm looking for something."

She snorted.

"Right," Kit agreed. She looked over at the saddle. Kit had always needed help because Treyla was such a big horse. Getting the saddle up on her looked impossible, but Kit had no choice. She lifted it, and Treyla moved to her side. "I can do this," she grunted, heaving it over Treyla's back. She adjusted it to where she thought was the proper place and tilted her head.

Her mind moved over every step they usually took and found a cinch. Kit mumbled the steps and did her best. She mimicked what others did, now worried that she would do it too tight or loose. Every move she made, she questioned.

"Did I do it?" She asked Treyla. "I think I did it." A sort of nod from the horse was all the confirmation she needed. Kit picked up the bridle next. "Let me know if I do this part wrong," she told her.

She blinked at Kit without any other reaction as Kit put on the bridle and slung the reins over Treyla's head—another blink.

"Good?" Kit asked. Treyla bobbed her head. "I will take that as a yes," Kit decided, "now to situate everything else."

Chapter Twenty

THE RAIN HADN'T BEEN something she anticipated. Or how much of it. Treyla and Kit were almost constantly soaked, and Kit was freezing. Her fingers felt close to falling off when the fifth day came around, but they shouldn't have been far off from Petaki. Calar was at her back. That was all that mattered. It was days behind her, and so were Aspen, Jassin, and Ralyn.

"I wish we could see the mountains," she said to Treyla as she led her around dense trees. Kit was walking to avoid cramps in her thighs and putting too much weight on Treyla for prolonged amounts of time. Rain fell hard on both of them, and she wrapped her cloak even further around her. "Wouldn't that be nice?" Treyla didn't respond, but it made Kit feel better to say anything at all. To know that her voice still worked. "I remember going to a competition once in Icar," she sniffed and watched her breath become a cloud before her. "The mountains were beautiful there, especially in the early morning. My mother used to paint them."

She trailed off. Kit sniffed again.

"Watch your step here," she said, stepping over a fallen tree. Treyla did the same. The rain began to let up slightly, but Kit didn't have hope of it staying that way. For five days, all they had was rain. She truly had picked the wrong time to go hunting—maybe she really would get sick. "My mother made her own paint," she said. She wasn't sure why. "I couldn't tell you how, but she did. And it smelled funny. I thought it would smell better with everything she used, but it didn't. Father would grow roses for her, and even then..." She breathed in.

The mountains would be on her right. With Calar nestled into the extended range of mountains and hills, Petaki was in the middle. It was the second largest human-occupied place in Olyan.

"Maybe we should find a road," she mumbled as she stopped. Kit ran her hand over the wet hair on Treyla's neck and the horse pushed her slightly, then pulled on the reins in her hand as if to say *let me lead*. Kit must not have been doing a good enough job. "You're so much better at this than I am," she told her. Treyla snorted.

She climbed onto the saddle and pulled her hood off. Her hand went into her pocket, where she ran her thumb over her necklace and tried not to think too hard.

Treyla easily wove through the trees, taking them both through the light rain toward the road. Kit lifted her face to the sky. Tiny droplets peppered her cheeks and flattened her hair to her head.

"We didn't own a horse," she told Treyla. She leaned forward and ran her fingers through the light brown strands of her hair. "Every time I went to a competition I had to pay my neighbor some of my winnings to use his. Her name was Filia. She was spotted and smaller than you and liked to run. Taking her long distances was so much fun—unless my father went with. He used to go to most of them, especially when I was young."

Kit took a piece of hair and separated it into three.

"They were both so supportive," she said. Many people in her village were once she started making money. Pain reached her throat as she thought of them. Kit often got so caught up in her family that she blocked out everyone else. All of her neighbors, her parent's friends, and her friends. The Niverly attack had taken almost everyone. The humans called it a slaughter. The Fae called it a tragedy. "When I told them I wanted to be an archer, they didn't laugh like the boys did," she said, "they all said that a girl born to grow and dry flowers wasn't meant to shoot an arrow, but my parents... they said they'd see what they could do."

The braid hung with the other strands of her hair and stuck to her neck.

"It was my mother who bought me the bow, though," she said. The memory floated to the surface of her mind. Her mother came home with an oddly shaped package telling her to get to the kitchen. Kit had thought she was in trouble for something. *Open it,* her mother had said sweetly. Kit did. And in the yard in the shade of the house away from the neighbors, her father painted an old rotted haybale for her to aim at.

She had been six. Six and her parents had given her a weapon she would later use to murder a prince and doom a kingdom to die.

The rain let up to a drizzle, then nothing, but there were still no mountains. A man was riding toward her. Kit moved to the right, itching for the bow behind her back. He looked older than her with a nice sword attached to the saddle of his dark brown horse. A black hood covered half of his face. Kit tried not to stare as she passed, but he lifted the hood and smiled in her direction. A scar on the bridge of his nose shined with leftover rainwater.

"Afternoon," he said. Kit smiled. "Headed to Petaki?"

"I'm traveling in that direction," she answered. He stopped his horse, and her stomach lurched. Kit kept going, and Treyla quickened her pace just slightly.

The man asked, "did you just leave Calar?"

She looked back at him, then urged Treyla to move even faster. She obliged, tense, and they went around a bend where three men stood and blocked the way.

"Saw you in the woods," said one. He wore no cloak and had fair hair plastered to his large head. His ears were slightly pointed, indicating he could be Half-Fae. They were outcasts of both species. "Do you talk to your horse?"

Kit fidgeted and looked behind her. The man rode casually forward. "Let me pass," she said with a tremble. The

Half-Fae laughed at her, and another joined. This man was enormous—so large that his stomach ripped his shirt and a straining button held up his pants.

"For your horse and supplies," said the third man. He was leaning against a tree, sharpening a dagger. He might've been the strangest looking man out of the four of them, with long hair, long arms, and red blotches all over his face.

"No," Kit shook her head. Her hand went behind her back and wrapped around her bow. "No, let me pass." She received silence after this. Treyla shifted to the side and pawed at the wet dirt beneath her hooves.

The man on the horse was much closer now. Kit got a good picture of how big Treyla was now that he was near. His horse had to have been a foot shorter. "Do you know how to use that?" He asked.

"Yes," she spat, "and I am not afraid to. Let me pass."

He moved forward, and she lifted the bow, an arrow already notched. Kit wasn't aiming for him. She pointed the arrow at the fat one. Treyla shifted, itching to run, and Kit knew she would as soon as the arrow flew. The Half-Fae flinched forward.

"I won't miss," she said, glancing at the one with the dagger. The man on the horse grabbed her elbow, and she let the arrow loose. Treyla reared, and Kit screamed as she was pulled in two directions. Her hand flailed out, smacking the man as Treyla burst into a run. Kit grasped Treyla's hair to keep from falling. She drew another arrow and looked back at the man riding toward her. She let it fly and his cry of pain echoed on the empty road.

Fire erupted in her shoulder. Kit reached around and grabbed her cloak. Her fingers met hot liquid and her vision blurred. She groaned as she looked at the blood on her fingers, then back toward the men.

As far as she could recall, they only had one horse between them, which meant they were traveling primarily on foot, and she'd injured two. So she was ahead and moving faster.

Kit reached around again. The cut went further than her shoulder. Blood ran down her arm as well—she was bleeding in two places. "Slow down, slow down," she breathed. Treyla slowed. Her breathing was heavy, and she looked back fearfully. Kit grit her teeth and untied her cloak. She pulled her jacket off slowly, holding it in front of her. Her shirt stuck to her body, warm and slick with blood soaking into it. "I'm all right," she told Treyla as she turned her arm. "It just hurts, don't worry—" Treyla shot forward quickly. Kit grabbed the saddle and her bow, losing her cloak to the ground.

She concluded that Treyla was not a regular horse when she didn't stop for the rest of the day. Not once, no matter how much Kit tried to get her to. She took them both to Petaki without a break as if she knew what those men intended and what an injury out in the woods could do.

Chapter Twenty-One

Treyla wasn't pleased when Kit had to leave her in the stables. The man held her reins and she followed with her hand wrapped around her body. Treyla reared and huffed, trying to twist away from the stable hands. "Treyla, it's all right," Kit told her. She huffed again. She backed into the pen, and Kit pulled the bridle off. "He won't hurt you and I'll be back tomorrow," she said.

"Is she Fae-trained?" He asked quietly while Treyla tried to nip at him for coming close to Kit.

She looked at him. "What does that mean?"

"That's what people call it when the Fae breed 'em," he explained, "they're magic, Fae-trained horses. Intelligent, quick." The man nodded to Treyla, "loyal, that's why she don't wanna leave you. Were you injured recently?"

"Yes, why?"

"She won't wanna leave you until she's sure you're healed," he said. They got the saddle off, and Treyla kept her eyes on Kit the whole time. "Fae-trained horses are very protective of their riders."

Kit smiled. She pulled her bag off the saddle and tried not to wince as she carried it, the bow and quiver, and went around to Treyla's front. "I'll have something good for you tomorrow," she said, "and I'll be right across the street."

She snorted.

"I'll be back tomorrow," she repeated, and she went through the gate. She shut Treyla in. Kit paid the man for the night and went across the street to a small inn. With the night around her Kit couldn't see most of Petaki, and with the rain, it wasn't as active as she was sure it usually was. It was a significant trading post and the final stop before Calar, yet very few people were around.

She pushed the door open and went past a small dining hall. Her stomach ached. She reached into her pocket and squeezed her necklace. The woman at the counter looked at her as she wiped a glass. "Can I help you?" She asked.

Kit stepped closer. "I'd like a room for the night and something to eat brought up if you don't mind," she said. A higher price than expected rang in her ears, but Kit just fished out the coin to avoid an argument. "And could you point me to someone that can see to injuries?"

The innkeeper's eyes moved over her. "Are you well?" She asked.

"Yes, I just had trouble on the road," she said, "a man threw a knife at me. I'd like to be sure I don't need stitches and that it doesn't get infected." Kit waited for her nod and the directions to her room. "Thank you," she said when the key was in her hand. A healer would be up to see her soon. She repeated that fact as she went up the stairs. She passed a Fae on the way, and her heart fluttered. He didn't notice. He didn't care. Kit smiled.

Her room was small and not the comfort she expected when she paid the price she did. It was rather empty, with just a small bed and a little table with one chair next to a fireplace. Kit crossed to it, setting her bag down. She put her bow and quiver on the floor and went to the fireplace to poke the burning logs with the tool.

Kit shivered when a knock came to the door. She wiped her hands, set the tool down, and went over. The Fae she'd passed on the stairs smiled at her. "Hope you don't mind," he said with a wave toward his ears, "I'm all you got."

She nodded shortly and stepped aside. The Fae had fair hair that was tied back with a string. He walked with a hunch in his back as if he wanted to make himself smaller and less intimidating. Despite that, Kit couldn't help but wonder if she should close her door.

It clicked shut.

"I was attacked on the way here," she told him, "these men tried to steal my horse and one of them threw a knife at me."

The Fae nodded. "Where is the injury?"

"My right arm and shoulder."

He nodded again. "Would you be comfortable removing your shirt? I can work around it if not," he said. He put a small bag on the table. Kit took a deep breath and tried to mimic how calm the male was. He didn't seem to want to hurt her at all—he was in her room for the opposite, after all. She pulled her jacket off as she went over and he pulled the chair out for her.

Kit took her shirt off and sat with her back to him. She tugged at the wrap around her chest as if it would disappear.

"Well, it looks like you could use some stitches on your shoulder," he said. "Let's clean it up, have a good look. I tell you," he chuckled slightly as he opened the bag on the table. Kit glanced at him. "I was worried coming up here with what direction you came from. Every human I meet from Calar tends not to have the best... eh, *opinion* about the ears. Most don't want me touching them."

"Is that difficult for you?" She asked as he searched for something. "Humans not wanting you to heal them because you're a Fae?"

He laughed ironically and went to her back. Something cold touched her skin. "I find," he said as he wiped around the wound, "that the largest difference between our species is when we're injured. A Fae will face a human healer and shut their eyes to get it over with because our survival is much more important than our fear."

"And a human?"

"I mean you no offense," he said, "but it's the opposite. You'd all rather kill a Fae and die than be touched by one."

Kit considered this. She knew humans were stubborn. A Fae once told her that humans were good for just two things—breeding and being too stubborn to die. After the prince died humans flocked to Calar to breed and be stubborn. They pushed out plenty of the Fae. It created an even bigger rift between them. "What's your name?" She asked.

"Knot, miss," he said. He continued gently cleaning her back and arm.

"I am not offended, Knot," she said. He stilled. "And I appreciate you braving the human from Calar."

His hands began moving again. "Are you from Calar truly? You don't sound like them. I think humans from Calar and around here have a heavier accent."

"I was raised in Niverly," she said.

Knot breathed in and out slowly. His breath brushed Kit's neck. "Then I am truly shocked you're letting me touch you at all," he said. She was silent. "You know," he went to his bag again, "I've had tea from Niverly recently. It's Niverly that grows the best kinds, yes?" Kit nodded. "And your family grew for the tea trade?"

"All kinds of flowers and some spices," she nodded again.

"I'm going to stitch you up now," he warned softly. He returned to her back. "I have to say—" She hissed when he pinched. "Apologies, miss." She nodded stiffly and gripped the side of the chair. "As I was saying," he continued, "there's something artificial about how the Fae growers make their tea leaves. Many say they use magic to cheat things into growing faster or larger..." He stitched for a moment. "I preferred it when the humans were growing.

Don't tell anyone I said so, but it tasted better when you lot were doing it."

A smile crossed her face. "My father watered most of his flowers by hand," she said, "it was his second favorite thing. Tending to his gardens."

"What was his first?"

She answered, "my mother."

Knot asked, "are they still here?"

"No, I lost them," Kit looked down. "I moved to Calar a little while later. Haven't left since."

"Until now," he said. The fire popped and he stitched in silence. Kit tried not to focus on the feeling of the thread dragging through her skin. She counted her breath and thought of other things. Of Fae, of her old home. "All right," Knot said softly. He bandaged her arm and shoulder, then gave her a small cream for the pain.

She watched him pack. "How much do people usually pay you?" Kit asked.

He looked at her. "You'd like to pay me?"

Her brow furrowed. "Am I not supposed to?"

"No, no, you can," he nodded, "I just haven't been paid by a human in weeks. They usually assume the inn employs me."

"You offered me your services despite your reservations," she said, grabbing her leather purse. "So how much should I give you for it?"

He stared at her with his mouth open, then shut it quickly. "A few coppers?"

She looked in the bag and fished out coppers and a silver. "Thank you very much," she said. Kit put the coin in his open hand and tied her purse shut. He went toward the door slowly. "Actually, can I ask you something before you go?"

He still had his palm out in shock, staring at the silver coin. "Yes, miss?" He asked almost faintly.

"Do you know anything about Fae-trained horses?"

"Fae-trained?" He blinked. Knot stuffed the coin into his pocket. "Well, I can tell you only humans call them Fae-trained. It's how they sell them."

Kit nodded. "Are they expensive?"

"Terribly so," he said, "but for more than one reason. Most people won't purchase a horse that's already attached to a rider, so they have to break them."

"How do you break a horse?"

He shrugged, "take its memories. Do you have one?"

"In the stables across the road," she said, motioning in that direction.

"With Bill? Good man, he'll keep that quiet. 'Fae-trained' isn't something you want advertised."

She nodded again. "What do the Fae call them?"

"Contrens," he told her, "old Fae word—means loyal to no fault."

"Huh," she breathed. Kit asked, "how do you train a horse to be like that? Could you do it with any horse?"

Knot laughed. "I assume you just found out why your horse is so loyal to you? Well no, you cannot do it with every horse. It's usually only the females; they take on a defensive mothering instinct much easier than males. Fae breeders spell pregnant horses, and the birthed foal will be stronger, more intelligent, and loyal, but the females get trained to have riders. The males are either put with a female for breeding or sold off. Wealthy Fae like to try their luck at breaking them in."

"That's terrible."

"It is," he agreed. "I'll tell you what, though, you must be someone special to that horse if it's chosen you. They only pick the best."

Kit felt her face burn and he said goodbye.

Chapter Twenty-Two

Kit had more oats and food for herself early the next morning. They were heavy in her bag. The morning brought mist from the mountains and the skies were still a cloudy grey, but they seemed thinner than they had been. Kit wiped under her nose as she looked up at them. She hoped it wouldn't rain anymore.

She listened to music coming from further down the street as she went toward the stables. Bill was shoveling straw when she walked up to him. "Good morning," she said. He wiped his hands on his apron and smiled. "How is Treyla?"

"Stressed as she was last night," he said, leading her through. Kit smiled brightly at Treyla. "She's been fussing all night," Bill said.

"Treyla," Kit called. Her horse's head turned sharply. She whinnied and went over, sniffing her head and shoulders. "I'm all right now," she said. She looked at Bill. "Has she been difficult?"

"No, just noisy," he said, leaning on the stall. "Might've been worse if you just left her like some Fae do. Those are the screamers. Treyla here calmed a bit when you told her you'd be back. Don't think she slept, though."

Kit nodded and went into the pen. She got the saddle on easier than ever with the help of Bill, who told her he wouldn't have been allowed as close as he was hours ago. Kit situated her bags and gave Treyla a carrot on the way out of the stables. She thanked Bill again. He just waved and went back to shoveling. "Are you ready?" She asked Treyla. "I learned what you are, you know. A contren, huh? And you know what?" Kit pat her neck. "You're something special to me, too."

Treyla nickered, and Kit smiled as they moved around people who parted for the big horse. There were more Fae around than the night before. A blanket of tension covered the town, one that could engulf them in seconds. Humans and Fae moved around each other. They shot glares in different directions, but it was nothing like Calar. Petaki had a *normal* amount of tension. Calar was a place Jassin once compared to a castle made of cards—one wrong move and it all came crashing down.

Kit walked until the street thinned, then mounted Treyla to move faster. She moved her bow and quiver across her back and started off. Still south, which meant they'd be on the road for another uncomfortable week before the next town. Her stomach churned with sudden worry. If the window to find the New Heir closed in less than two months, she wasn't sure if she could find the heir and crown him in time—or how to crown him at all.

They reached the edge of town when something slammed into the back of her head. Kit went forward and lost complete control of her body. There was shouting around her, and Treyla was screaming. She slipped to the side slowly, and the shuffling of horse hooves rocked her body back and forth. Treyla reared onto her hind legs. Kit was thrown backward. She hit the ground hard, and her bow snapped beneath her. The breath left her chest.

She coughed and opened her eyes. To her left, people were trying to grab Treyla's reins. She was kicking and stomping. Kit groaned and a face appeared above her. She looked up at it, unable to make out a single detail. The head tilted, and Kit coughed again.

He kicked her in the face and her neck snapped to the side.

An intense pain flared in the back of her skull. Another thrummed above her left eye. She winced and tried to lift her head or open her eyes—the latter being preferable—but couldn't move. Her jaw dropped slowly. Kit wondered if her face was working at all. The crack of dried blood made her wince.

She grunted and stretched her fingers. She couldn't lift her arms. Her eyes opened slowly, and Kit blinked a few times. The blur faded in her right eye, not her left. She lifted her head slowly. Kit was in an empty room. Each wall was wood, and a window was behind her, covered in a black sheet. She, a torch on the left wall, and the chair she was tied to were the only things in the room.

Kit swallowed thickly and pulled on the rope around her wrists. She kept blinking, inwardly begging the blur to go away so she could see clearly.

The door opened. Her head snapped toward it. Kit watched a male walk into the room. "Human," he said hatefully.

"Fae," she replied. A smile shifted the stern expression on his sharp jaw. He shut the door. Kit's stomach formed uncomfortable knots. The Fae was tall and had a build stronger than anyone she'd ever seen. Kit had lived around Fae for years, but she'd never seen anyone like this before. He was broad around the waist and shoulders. A stag came to mind, one with thick shoulders and strong muscles. He stood across from her, observing her now that she was awake.

Kit was too human. She was very easily distracted. Not just by the thought that he could probably snap her neck with his big hands, but that he was undoubtedly one of the most beautiful people she'd ever seen. It was such a horrible thought, and she was sure he knew she'd had it. The smile on his face widened as she looked him over—from his full lips to his dark, shining hair to the bright green of his eyes.

"King Assassin," he bowed his head. She said nothing. "You don't look like someone who could kill a king," the male said. He came closer. "Did you enjoy it?" He asked. He placed his hands on her arms and leaned forward. His weight felt crushing. "Did you enjoy killing our young prince?"

She looked away.

The male grabbed her jaw and yanked her forward. "Did you, King Assassin?"

"No," she grit out. He shoved her back into the chair and straightened.

"I find that very hard to believe," he said after taking a single step back. His eyes moved over her hungrily. Dread settled with the knots in her stomach as he tilted his head. "What are you afraid of, human?" He asked softly. "What keeps our King Assassin up at night?"

Her eyes darted around.

He stepped toward her once again, this time to the side. "I'd like to know." Kit twisted her wrists, and he stopped on her left. "Not your dreams. I want to see your nightmares." She jerked away. He flicked her temple, and the flames in the torch flickered. Kit watched smoke float on the ground and against the wall in front of her. The Fae put his hands on her shoulders as it shifted to something else, curling into the view of a village covered in ash.

It was like she was there, in Niverly, walking through the street and gagging at the smell. People looked at her. They cried. Bodies littered the ground.

"What are you doing?" Kit asked. He jerked her back into the chair, and a house appeared in the smoke. Half of the roof was caved inward, and the flowers that once grew in front of the two windows were nothing but ash in their pots. "Stop it—" The door opened, and the perspective shifted forward as if she were running inside, then onto a beam. Her bow was in her hand, and people were below her. They sat on rows and rows of pews facing a small carpeted stage, though each head turned back to the great oak doors. Two guards opened them.

"Why are you having nightmares about the coronation?" He asked, curious and unconcerned. His grip tightened on her shoulders and Kit squirmed.

The prince came through the door. An arrow was notched. Kit could practically feel the feather against her cheek as she waited. A thumping sounded around her. Just like it had happened then, she hesitated. Her bow dipped slightly before she corrected and fired. But the Crown Prince caught the arrow—only he didn't look like the prince anymore. At least not the living one.

Kit sobbed as her dream self crawled back and turned around, headed for the window she'd entered from. He was there again, in nothing but a wrap around the lower half of his body. He screeched and tried to grab her.

"You did this!" He shouted, and she fell off the beam.

She jerked around in the chair and sobbed harder. "Please stop, please—"

Her dream self landed in the crypt and her mother appeared over her. She pulled Kit up. *You did this,* she said. Her voice was not the one Kit tried so desperately to remember. Her mother told her it was her fault, that she was to blame for everything. Her mother's face was there, saying the same thing, no matter where she looked.

Dream Kit ran through a door.

"You have very elaborate nightmares, human," the Fae said, "this makes it so much easier to—"

"You played your part perfectly, Kitali," Jassin said. The dream ended up in his study, where he stood over the table looking at a paper. "And they're all going to suffer because of it."

"What part?" Her dream self asked. "Jassin?"

He straightened. "Honestly, I didn't think you'd fall for it. But you truly are just a sad, lonely girl in desperate need of someone to love you again." He came close and ran his hand through her hair. "And it was so easy to pretend to love you. But you've outgrown your usefulness. You've become quite a problem, actually."

Suddenly, her dream self was being shoved and pulled every which way. It was by Jassin and the Crowns and Aspen. Everyone was telling her how much of a problem she was, how sad she was, and how pathetic she was. They pushed her until she fell into a stone box and was shut inside. She turned over and banged on the lid.

"What if I was going to be the king who made things better? What if I was going to heal the Rift?" The prince asked. He was on her right. His voice was sincere, nothing like the gravely, horrifying one that haunted her. "All you've done is make things worse. And for all you know, you'll fail to fix your mistake and have truly doomed everyone. Just because your feelings were hurt."

The Fae flicked her head again, and the smoke disappeared. Kit was staring at the wall, her mouth open and tears running down her face. He walked around the chair and stood before her, blocking her view. "Wasn't that interesting," he said, "what mistake?" She sobbed and began to hyperventilate in the chair. The Fae put his hands where they had been and pressed down. "Breathe, human," he said. His face was close enough for her to feel his breath on her cheeks. She sobbed again. The Fae hooked a finger under her chin and repeated, "breathe."

"Why did you do that?" She asked, and he straightened. His thumb brushed over her chin gently. "Why would you do that?" Her head throbbed in every place.

"I enjoy inflicting nightmares on weak-minded humans," he said. Kit didn't care about the *weak-minded humans* comment. It was true; people simply denied it. She focused on the *nightmares* part. It must've been some kind of magic. It was cruel and terrifying, and— "It makes it much easier to get answers from you."

She shook her head and his hand left her. Her skin chilled. "I shouldn't have killed him," she said. He tilted his head. "I shouldn't have assassinated the prince. It was the worst mistake of my life, and I need to fix it before the year ends."

"You're looking for the New Heir," he realized.

Kit said, "I can find him." The Fae stared down at her.

Chapter Twenty-Three

HE LAUGHED AT HER suddenly. And he laughed some more. The door opened, and another male said, "Witker, if I have to reverse the mental damage of another human—" He stopped abruptly. Knot stood there with a stool and his little medical bag. "What's she doing here?" He asked.

"This is King Assassin," the male—Witker—said. This was Witker? Ralyn's *brother*, Witker? "I'm torturing her."

Knot looked at her. "King Assassin," he said. Kit winced. "What are your wounds?"

"I threw a rock at the back of her head," Witker answered, "and obviously her forehead."

"How are your stitches?" The healer asked as he walked toward her. He set the stool down.

Kit shrugged an arm. "They aren't really my main concern," she said.

"And what is?"

"Everything is blurry in my left eye."

Witker leaned against the wall casually. "Let's keep it that way. Can't shoot with a dead eye."

"I'd be happy to test that theory," she snapped, and he chuckled. Knot set his bag in her lap and began to go through it.

He cleaned and assessed the wound on her forehead first, and Kit sat still, her wrists starting to hurt and her mind on everything she'd seen on the wall. "Looks like you've got some blood in there..." he said as he squinted at her eye. "It may fade with time."

"Was that one of the Crowns?" Witker asked with his arms crossed.

She said, "Crown Jassin."

"And he loves you?"

"I don't know," she admitted faintly. Kit said, "I'd like to think so, but I learned a lot in a very short time, so for all I know, he never did."

Witker mocked, "how terrible for you. The Crown doesn't love you? Would you like our sympathies?"

Anger flared hotly within her. "As if you'd be able to provide anything more than murder."

His eyes moved away for a few seconds and a smirk crept up on his face. Knot said, "she came from Niverly," and he nodded once. Witker didn't look at her again. "You do not need stitches for this, miss, but I'll bandage it once I'm finished," he said, shifting to her back.

Her eyes widened and she looked at Witker. "Where's Treyla?"

"Who?"

"My horse!"

His brow furrowed. "Right, she's tied up in the stables. Won't let anyone near her. I had to threaten your life to get her to stop fighting."

"She's contren," Knot muttered from behind Kit. "All right, you'll need stitches back here."

Witker asked, "so you regret killing our prince?"

She looked at him for a moment. He was waiting for her to say no, maybe so he could hurt her. "I hesitated," she said.

He repeated, "you hesitated?" He still wouldn't meet her eyes completely.

"I think I would've missed," Kit elaborated. Knot stopped moving behind her. "It's my talent. I'm never far off and never miss a shot completely, but I hesitated when I lifted the arrow, and I shouldn't have hit his heart."

He got off the wall. "What do you mean?"

"I mean that Jassin and the Crowns wanted to guarantee I was successful whether I was executed or not," she said, "so they had to make sure I didn't miss. I think I would've hit his shoulder. I don't think I would've killed him unless they spelled the arrow."

Once again, the door opened. Knot said, "hello Ralyn," and Kit looked at her. She finally had her hair back—revealing two pointed ears. Ralyn's arms were crossed defensively. She glanced at Witker and Knot, but her eyes settled on Kit. "Took some time off?" Knot asked.

She nodded. Ralyn took a deep breath. "I like your hair," she said.

"Really?" Kit asked with a flutter in her chest. "Aspen said it looked bad before I left."

"It suits you," she said. Ralyn rocked her feet and motioned to herself, "you aren't surprised?"

"No, I guessed pretty early on," Kit said, wincing at the stitching behind her head. She heard him sniff. He leaned toward her, his nose on her neck, and Kit tensed. Knot lifted the string of her arrow necklace.

"Tracker magic," he said.

"What?" She turned her head.

Witker cursed and went forward. He yanked the necklace away and hissed in pain. A bit of smoke flew from his hand and he waved it through the air. Witker held the necklace by the string and smelled the dainty arrow hanging off the cord. "Ralyn, will you get rid of this, please? Don't touch the iron."

"Sure," she said quickly. Ralyn grabbed the necklace and left.

Jassin spelled my necklace to track me? Kit stared at the door, her brows pinched together. Her heart fell. Witker began to pace, and she chose to watch him instead. Knot was finished with her stitches by the time he stopped and just left. The door shut behind him. Kit breathed in deeply as her head was bandaged. "Do you think he'll kill me?"

"Most likely," Knot said. He collected his bag and his stool, then left her there too. Her vision blurred with tears. She looked around and twisted her wrists, blinking quickly. Treyla was in the stable somewhere; they would be free if Kit could get to her. She could ride bareback, but she doubted she'd have to if they couldn't get close enough to get the saddle off. She just had to get out of the chair and to the window.

She jerked around and the chair creaked beneath her. Kit did it a few times, even bouncing up and down while trying to make as little noise as possible. They might have heard her and laughed at her attempt to escape, but Kit kept going nonetheless. She grit her teeth and moved until the chair went *snap* and she slid to the side.

Kit pulled the armrest off the chair and untied her wrists. The rope had cut into her skin and turned them raw. Her jacket was gone. She dug through her pockets until she found her father's necklace, then went to the window.

She pushed the sheet to the side and looked at the darkness surrounding the house. Kit was on a second story. Jumping was possible, though problematic. She glanced back at the door. There was no way she'd be able to navigate a house of Fae, so she opened the window and put her legs over. Kit sat on the sill. She'd jumped from enough trees to know how to keep from breaking something, but it still seemed like the most dangerous thing to ever do when she looked down.

The clouds cleared a fraction over the moon—enough to tell she was in a farmhouse. The land expanded more on the right side, and she was on the corner. Animals were tucked in for the night and a dog was barking somewhere in the distance.

She breathed out and stretched her ankles. "I can do this," Kit whispered and jumped down. She landed hard, one leg slipping into a hole in the ground. She dropped and grabbed her ankle, covering her mouth to keep from screaming. Kit sobbed once and gasped. She trembled.

Someone shouted in the house—a call for dinner—and Kit tripped forward, rushing to move toward the woods ahead of her. She limped forward and her head turned.

The stables.

Treyla.

"Kit?" A voice hissed from the dark. She froze and they repeated, "Kit?"

She swayed and looked at the woods. "Aspen?" Kit asked. He ran forward and pulled her into a tight, breath-taking hug. "What are you doing here?" She asked as he grabbed her in random places as if he wasn't sure if she was real.

He took her hand and started dragging her toward the woods. "I'll explain when it's safer, come on," he said.

"Wait, my horse—"

"I already have one for you," he said, yanking her into the tree patch.

Kit tried to stop. Her ankle protested how quickly he was moving. "Aspen, I have to risk it—"

He turned back quickly and punched her in the face. Kit hit the ground hard and grasped her forehead. "I'm sorry about this," he said faintly. Kit removed her hand and looked up at him. He blew something bright and shiny in her face, then held her still while human magic put her to sleep.

Chapter Twenty-Four

THE SHEETS WERE TOO soft to be hers. She smoothed her hand over the silk bedding and breathed in against a wave of pain that crashed through her entire body. Kit reached up and touched her head. Soft bandages prevented her from touching something swollen.

"Kit?"

She tried to open her eyes, groaning as she rolled onto her back. "Aspen?" She squinted. His head was tilted to the side and he sat on the bed, hovering. She blinked a few times to get a better look at him, but one eye stayed blurry. "What happened to your face?" She asked.

He laughed hoarsely. "That's your first question?"

"You have a scar," she said. Kit reached out and paused, looking at a bandage wrapped around her wrist. Her left wrist had the same bandage, and another was wrapped around her hand. "What happened?"

Aspen's expression softened. He took her right hand gently. "We have some stuff to talk about," he said, "the Crowns thought it would be better to have someone you're comfortable with explain it to you. I have tea from the healers—"

"Explain what to me?" She sat up on one elbow. The pain in her head grew, both in the front and the back.

"You were…" He breathed in. "You were abducted a few weeks ago, do you remember?" Kit stopped moving. "We were at the spring when it happened. This group of Fae, they attacked us and they took you."

Kit could hardly remember the last time she was at the spring. In her mind, it had to have been weeks ago. She'd taken Treyla, and Aspen had a mare. But they'd gone home afterward. "What are you talking about? We haven't been to the spring in forever."

"The healer said that you might not remember anything," he told her.

She sat up the rest of the way.

He continued, "they were saying it was revenge for what you did. I got hit hard, and they dragged you away. We found you in a farmhouse last night. You were completely out of it… Do you not remember?"

Her head throbbed. She looked away from him. Kit was in her rooms at the castle, not at home, where she'd much rather be. It was a lifeless room she slept in sometimes, not the messy place she knew. "A farmhouse?" Kit repeated, uncomfortable. She shifted backward and looked down at her body. Someone had changed her into a nightgown. "There was a Fae," she mumbled weakly.

"Don't try too hard," Aspen said. He moved closer, and she flinched back. "Kit?"

"They took my memories?" She asked. He nodded. Kit shook her head, "how does... How do you do that? Is that m-magic or—" She inhaled sharply. "Or torture? How—"

"We're going to figure it out," he said. Kit sobbed. Aspen crawled toward her, taking her in his arms tight. "We'll figure it out, Kit, all right?" Tears stung her eyes, and her head throbbed.

Kit pushed him away. She shoved the heavy blankets down and pulled the nightgown skirt up.

"It wasn't like that," Aspen said quickly. "Kit, look at me," he took her hands away as she searched for bruising or pain. "Kit, it wasn't like that. It was all in your head, all right?" He pushed the blankets back into place and she trembled. "It was all in your head."

"I don't remember anything in my head," she said, "there's nothing, I don't remember anything."

He said, "it'll be all right."

The door opened, and Jassin came in winded and with red cheeks. "Kitali, thank the gods," he said as he rushed across the large room. "Thank you gods." He crashed against her and Aspen, squeezing harder than Kit had ever been squeezed. "We were so scared you wouldn't come back to us after they broke you."

Broke you. Kit winced. Jassin was inspecting her, holding her face as he looked at her. Tears were in his eyes as well as hers. "What happened?" She asked him weakly.

"It'll be all right, Kit," he said like Aspen did. Kit wasn't sure what would be all right if she couldn't remember what happened. She was just sitting in a too-soft bed with two men who knew more than she did. "We're hunting them down," he told her.

She looked away from both of them.

"Can we get you anything?" Aspen asked.

"I don't know," she said slowly. "I don't..." Kit looked at Jassin. "How long do I have to be here?" His brows pinched together. "I want to go. I don't want to be here."

He said, "we can't let you go home yet. You're safe here."

"I don't want to go home, I want to go somewhere else," she said. Kit wasn't sure why. Hadn't she wished she was home and not in the castle rooms? A worried look crossed Jassin's face. He looked at Aspen for a moment as if it was their decision. "Jassin," she said, "when can I go?"

Jassin said, "as soon as we find who hurt you."

She nodded and sat back.

He asked, "where do you want to go?"

"South," she said. Kit blinked rapidly. "I think there's something there," she said, her voice faint. "But I don't know what."

He nodded. "All right," Jassin said, "well I'm going to get you something to eat, all right?" He squeezed her forearm. The pressure reminded her of something, though she wasn't sure what. Kit nodded slowly. "Aspen is going to stay with you."

"What happened to my clothes?" She asked, "I had a necklace in my pants—"

Jassin reached into his pocket and pulled out her necklace, easing it into her hand. She squeezed it and he said, "I remember that. Your father always had it on him, didn't he?" Kit nodded. She leaned into Aspen carefully. "I miss him," Jassin said. She looked at him. "All of them."

"Me too," she whispered. He leaned in and kissed her hairline before leaving. Kit ran her thumb over the smooth metal necklace. "Aspen?" She asked. He hummed. "Do you think they'll come back? My memories."

He rubbed her arm. "Maybe," he said.

Kit closed her eyes. She had a nightmare about watching a nightmare and a green-eyed male.

Chapter Twenty-Five

A FEATHER QUILL BRUSHED against Kit's face as she stared at some parchment in her lap. Aspen was doodling on it while she stared at the words she knew for sure. *Farmhouse. Fae. Broken. Memories.* It was a pathetic attempt to jog what she could despite everyone telling her to give it time.

"Will you say something?" He asked. Aspen had been on his stomach, using her lap as a table for the past few minutes. They'd gone from the bed to the uncomfortable ornate couch back and forth for two days because no one would let her leave the room. This was the first time she'd tried to remember anything since she woke up.

"What would you like me to say?" She asked softly. Kit looked away from the words. He sat up and crossed his legs, setting his quill down.

He looked her over. "Say you'll be all right," he said.

She tried to smile. She'd had days to process and calm slowly, but Kit had little heart left. "I'll be all right," she said. He looked on the verge of tears. Aspen reached out, taking her chin in his hand. His thumb brushed over her skin gently. "I just wish I knew something," she said, "anything."

"Me too," he said. He was looking at her lips. Kit hesitated, her head turning back to her parchment. His hand dropped against her arm. "The most I know is that you'd managed to escape. You jumped out of a window and hurt your ankle..." She looked at the wrap on her propped ankle. "I found you. Gods, it was the happiest day of my life when I found you."

Kit nodded. She looked at him again. "And the Fae? Were they there? Did you see anyone?"

He shook his head. His fingers brushed over her arm. "My only focus was you."

She leaned over and put her head on his shoulder. Kit lifted the parchment. "Is this us?" She asked as she turned his drawing to the side. Aspen was no artist the way he was a singer, but she didn't think it was meant to be anything profound—just two figures in the woods, one with a quiver.

"All that time you were gone, I kept thinking it was my fault. I wasn't strong enough, and I couldn't protect you," he said. She put the paper down. "And then I didn't know whether or not you were alive... Gods, I felt like the worst person who never said the right thing and couldn't be there when it mattered."

"You're here now," she said, "and I'm alive. We just need to get my memories back."

"A healer will be by tomorrow, I think," he said. Kit focused on Aspen's hand brushing her arm. She tried to picture what he wanted to say—the right thing he never said. It might've had something to do with her name. Something to do with King Assassin. She then thought it could have been something completely different. The sort of thing friends weren't supposed to say to each other because friendships could be ruined. "Jassin sent for the best," Aspen told her.

Kit said, "so they can fix my injuries and my head?"

"Hopefully," he said. He didn't sound as enthusiastic as she wanted. Didn't he want her memories to come back? Didn't he want her to remember him finding her? To be a hero at the farmhouse?

Her head began to hurt. Kit lifted it off his shoulder. "Would you like to go for a walk?" She asked. "Maybe we can see Treyla."

His face fell. "Oh, Kit," he said. Her brow slowly furrowed. "Jassin was supposed to tell you."

She straightened. "Tell me what?" Kit moved away from him, watching him prepare to say something terrible. "Is Treyla all right? Did she get hurt?"

Aspen shook his head. "Kit," he said softly, and a knot formed in her throat. *She's fine. She has to be fine—* "She's dead," he said.

"No, but..." Kit breathed in, "but the stables. S-she was in the stables."

"She was with us," Aspen said.

She got off the couch. "What do you mean?" Kit asked, "she can't be dead—"

"Kit," he whispered.

She sobbed and limped backward. "You're lying," she said, "you're lying. She's not dead." Her voice cracked. He got up and went toward her, holding her arms. She tried fighting his embrace but fell against him with just the smallest pull of his hands.

"It'll be all right," he said. Aspen rubbed her back, making her shoulder ache with an injury a Fae had inflicted.

Kit shook her head.

"Hey," he rubbed her arm, and pain moved through her again. "Why don't we have a practice day, huh?" He pulled back and held her face with one hand. "It'll take your mind off things, don't you think?"

She sniffed. He wiped beneath her eye. He told her to wait where she was, and Kit didn't move. She stared at what was ahead of her—a balcony. She never really liked these rooms. The main one, the bedroom, was as big as her apartment and simply too perfect. There was a study Kit had filled with books people gave her things she didn't have a place for at home, which was not a lot of things. Mostly furniture. An *antechamber* that just seemed too high-class for her to ever use was by the door.

She wanted to go home. She wanted to be in her bed, not the smooth, soft one. She wanted her chair, not the flowery couch.

Aspen returned as Kit contemplated the reasons a Fae would kill a horse. She couldn't think of any. She couldn't think at all. Everything felt so wrong. "Here," Aspen said and handed her a bow.

"What happened to the one Jassin gave me?" She asked as she held it. He led her to the balcony and opened the doors. Kit looked out toward the trees. From where she was, she knew what path they'd take to get to the spring.

"They snapped it," Aspen told her. He put a quiver over her shoulder and a bag of pouches on the ground. He lifted one and tossed it into the air, so she smiled. "Ready?" He asked. Kit tried to put on a better mood like she would an itchy jacket. Aspen accepted it too easily.

She notched an arrow and pulled back. He chucked the pouch. Her arrow flew and grazed the little bag, making her smile disappear. Kit paused and closed her right eye, then her left.

"Everything all right?" He asked with another bag in hand.

Red dust was supposed to burst from the pouches when she shot them. Kit hadn't hit the one he threw enough for it to break. "My left eye is blurry," she said.

He reached over and touched where the bandage had once been. "You must've gotten hit pretty hard," he said.

"Stomped on more like," she muttered. Kit took a deep breath and took out another arrow. "I can do it. Can you throw higher?"

Aspen threw them higher and lower, some straight across, but her accuracy was faulty. Out of the sixteen he threw, Kit only burst ten. One went right above their heads and showered dust over them. When the pouches were gone, Aspen said a regretful goodbye. Kit wasn't sure why, but he took the bow and arrows with him.

She went to a little side table pressed against the wall by the door. A jar of honeysuckle was on it next to another couple of books. She reached into the pocket she'd nailed into place on the underside of the table and took out a short blade. Kit smiled at the object and set it down. If she couldn't keep her arrows, at least she had that.

Chapter Twenty-Six

THE HEALER HAD HER ankle propped on a pillow on the arm of the flowery couch and Kit held a book above her head. This one caught her eye because the cover was red, and that was all. She didn't care to read the title. The words danced over the pages. Over the past ten months—more now, maybe—she'd perfected the amount of time it took to read a page. Judging by the comments, including 'you read that fast' and 'you've been on that page for a while,' she concluded that it differed depending on the person.

A reader wanted the book to be finished quickly. Kit hated having readers recommend books to her. They asked the most questions, and she had to skim the book to pretend she knew what was happening.

Someone like Aspen wasn't paying attention, but if she flipped a page too quickly, he'd notice and joke that he wasn't actually reading.

When it came to older folk—Jassin's forty and up—taking a decent pace was key. With the woman currently prodding at her ankle, she stayed slow. The healer lifted her leg and she winced, putting the book on her chest and lifting her head. "It's all right," she said. The woman was odd, but Aspen told her she was the best.

"Do you have ways to heal it quicker?" Kit asked. Healing and medicinal remedies were fascinating. Her neighbor grew plants for some apothecaries before he died, and they paid handsomely for them.

"I do," she nodded and went to her bag. Kit put her head back down. "Would you recommend that book to anyone?" She asked as she searched for something.

Kit said, "no, it's rather dull. If you'd like a good book there is a stack in the study and the top five books are the ones I've most enjoyed." It was a statement she felt she was constantly repeating.

"My daughter loves to read," the healer said, and something cold covered Kit's foot. She looked down and watched a sock move up her calf. "She'd be overjoyed to hear that King Assassin also enjoyed stories. Do you have a favorite?"

"I've never been able to choose between them," she said, "what does the sock do?"

"It's cooling," she explained, "this is just what I use to get the bones ready for healing."

Make them cold? "Did I break something, then?"

"Just a simple sprain, not to worry," she said. She put her hands on her hips and looked at the sock. "Let's see about your head. I have this for the scrapes and bruises," she said, handing Kit a tin. "They'll be gone in a few days if you keep up with it. Twice daily for three days, morning and night." Kit nodded. "The stitches on your shoulder and the back of your head are fine to stay where they are for the time being, I don't think we should mess with them much. As for your memory, that is a magic issue that will need a magic solution. Those things take time."

"But you think you can fix me?" Kit asked hopefully.

She sat on the small space next to her and took her hand. "I can do my best, but there is a difference between Fae and human magic. I may only be able to retrieve some memories, but that would be if we were lucky. You will also have to be asleep for this. Accessing memories is easier while dreaming or using nightmares. I would prefer it if your other wounds were healed before I begin. Is that all right?"

"I'll do whatever I have to to get them back," she nodded. "Take your time. I don't want to rush anything."

"You are a kind girl," she said with a smile. She went back to Kit's ankle and removed the cold sock. She put something on her fingertips and placed them on either side of her leg. After a short pause, she pushed. Kit screamed. A guard came in and the healer stopped. Kit crawled away from her. "I apologize. I didn't intend to hurt you. Usually it's only a pinch."

The guard looked at Kit. She nodded to him and looked at her ankle. She laid back down. The healer put her ankle back on the pillow. She looked at it momentarily before rubbing her fingers together and putting them back where they had been. Kit held her breath and gripped the couch cushion. There was no need to pretend to read now—no one could concentrate on meaningless words with this lady touching them.

Her face turned red as she strained against a wave of curses she wanted to scream at her. Her head fell back against the pillow when she stopped.

Aspen came to visit after she left. "How are you?" He asked easily. He poked her toe, which was still raised on the pillow. Kit feared putting weight on it despite being told she could walk. Instead, she rubbed the terrible-smelling cream onto the cut on her forehead.

"It was painful," she mumbled, "but she's going to see about my head once I'm healed everywhere else. So I just have to do that." Aspen sat on the couch, lifting her head and moving a pillow to do it. She looked at him as he ran his fingers through her too-short hair. Kit was in denial about it. She refused to look in the mirror again after seeing the strange *light* shade the Fae must've changed. Her dark roots were peeking through. "Do you think it'll work?"

"I think you'll be all right either way," he said. It wasn't the answer she was hoping for at all. Still, she found comfort in it. Aspen brushed his knuckle over her cheek. "But I hope it will," he said.

"Me too," she said, then sat up and turned to face him. Aspen smiled. "What?" She asked.

He shook his head. "You look more like you, that's all," he said, "I'm glad. My Kit's shining through."

"Oh, your Kit?" She raised a teasing brow.

He chuckled, and her heart fluttered around her chest. "Would you like another practice day?" He asked.

She shook her head. "Just sit with me," she decided, "for a little while." Aspen nodded and put his arm around her. Kit sighed.

Chapter Twenty-Seven

THE RED BOOK ON the ground stared up at her. Kit groaned and grabbed it, chucking it toward her study with a grunt. It smacked against the door. She dropped heavily onto the couch, now facing the bed. She folded her arms and put her chin down. After a moment of sitting there, she twisted around and got up. Aspen kept coming and going, leaving her bored in a room no one wanted her to leave, and Jassin only came in for lunch to stare at her with such a guilty look that she hardly looked forward to seeing him anymore. She grabbed a piece of chalk from a drawer in the study, then an old slingshot.

Kit drew a target on the fireplace wall and sat with her food tray, leaning against the couch.

She balled up old toast from breakfast and shot it against the target. This wasn't enough, so she moved on to strawberries. The fruit splat against the stone and she huffed, still unsatisfied. Kit turned her head. She looked at the vase of honeysuckle and got up, taking it into the bathing room. Aside from water, it was full of pebbles. Kit threw out the flowers and dumped the water.

When she came out, someone was in her bedroom. She stopped in front of the couch. The male was in front of the open balcony doors, surveying her room. When his eyes finally landed on Kit, he smirked ever so slightly. "Human," he said.

"Fae," she replied, setting the vase on the couch. She reached into it and gathered a handful of pebbles. It wasn't a weapon, but she could take an eye out if she tried. "How did you get in here?"

He said, "my sister works here, I know my way around the guards."

So there was a Fae in the castle?

"How you managed to get yourself abducted twice, I don't know, but I'll admit this is a nicer room." The Fae stepped toward her, and she flinched back. The pebbles were heavy in her hand—

The knife on your table.

"What?" She stepped back. *Get to the knife.*

He didn't answer. "I thought about what you said, and as much as I hate to admit it, I think you may have been right about the New Heir. I've decided to help you find him."

"What are you talking about? What New Heir?" She shook her head, backing up further.

The Fae paused. "Are you serious?" He stepped toward her, moving around the couch. Kit shot a pebble at him and turned. She went for the knife as fast as she could, but his strong arms still wrapped around her. "You hit my forehead," he grunted. The rest of the pebbles fell from her hand. The Fae pulled her tight against his chest, tenser than she was. She slammed her head into his chin and he let go.

Kit threw herself at the knife and turned sharply. The tip of the blade sliced a thin line in his throat when he appeared in front of her again. She pressed it against his windpipe. "Who are you?" She asked.

"What?"

Her hand shook. "Who are you?" She repeated. Kit struggled to keep her composure as his green eyes bore down on her.

His brow furrowed. He leaned forward and peered at her. "You don't remember me, do you?" He asked. A drop of blood slid down his throat. He leaned even closer, and Kit stepped back, hitting the desk. The Fae grabbed her wrist and took the knife from her as if she wasn't gripping it until her knuckles were white against the handle. He twisted her arm back, held it against the table, and leaned into her.

When she moved back, he held her jaw. His eyes were full of concentration. Kit was still. His grip was firm, but there wasn't anything violent about the way he was holding her. He just looked confused.

"What did they do to you?" He asked softly, his breath brushing her skin.

Kit punched him with her free hand and went for the door.

His arm hooked around her waist and his hand clamped over her mouth. She screamed, clawing at his skin and jerking against his chest. "Sorry about this," he said softly, moving his arm. He flicked the side of her head before continuing, "but the best way to jog a memory is through nightmares."

Everything turned dark in front of her and he pinned her arms down. Jassin's voice came through the dark, echoing in her head as the Fae shifted to the side. He slid down the wall, taking her with him.

Somehow, a version of her she didn't quite recognize was in front of her. She was in a chair, her hands tied. Her arms were bleeding, and she was screaming, but no one could hear her. Aspen stood with Jassin right in front of her, but neither of them did a thing to help her.

"Come on," the Fae said from behind her, "have a nightmare about me."

She was walking into a house in the nightmare in front of her. Her home. To the left was the workspace for her parents, empty. On the right was the dining room. Behind the wall would be the sitting room. An old couch would face a fireplace. But the rooms were empty. There was no one there. There was no one in the kitchen and no plates on the shelves. No chairs or tables or drying flowers making the whole place smell sweet.

A veil was on the wall. It was a dainty thing, one that her mother wore the day she married her father. As per tradition, it was torn partially in half. A blue thread had been laced through it to mend the tear and it was hung above the fireplace the day her parents moved into their home.

Kit knew this nightmare. She had it often. In front of her was the body of her mother, her hair unkempt, and her clothes ripped. Blood stained her back, but the wound had been inflicted from the front. She pulled the veil from the hooks and turned to her. It was the same dead face she had seen eight years ago. The same dead eyes looked right at Kit, and she tore the veil in half.

As soon as the veil hit the floor, it all burst. The home she knew crumbled around her. The furniture was back, but it was tossed and burned.

"Is that your mother?" The Fae asked, and she jerked so much he had to pin her legs down with his own. She cursed and screamed.

A new nightmare appeared—this one was different. Kit couldn't recall the torch. It was familiar, and all of her nightmares were rooted in some reality, but Kit couldn't place it. It glowed harshly against a curved wall. She went down curved stairs and stopped in a hall.

A crypt.

Her ears rang, and her head started to throb.

"Oh, have we reached an erased memory?"

She whined in pain, the back of her head feeling like it might burst open. Her temples were being hit with hammers. She was dizzy, and her stomach rolled with nausea like the waves of an ocean.

"It is necessary," a voice in the nightmare said.

Jassin's voice said, "we need an heir," and her dream self looked around the corner.

"What in the name of blessings—" the Fae started, and maybe Kit's head really broke open. Everything was black because her eyes were closed. She knew she was screaming because both of the Fae's hands were over her mouth. He had a leg around her waist and was shushing her. Kit wanted to curse him. To shout and scream terrible words for trying to stop her from expressing her pain.

She was on top of him. Mali was on top of him. She was on top of him—

Kit went limp.

The Fae breathed heavily against her back. His grip loosened slightly. "Do you remember me now?" He asked.

Her brows twitched. Kit turned her head and looked up at him. She gagged and he let go. Kit ran to the bathing room and landed on her hands and knees in front of the chamber to vomit up her breakfast. Witker followed, pushing the door so it creaked but didn't shut.

Water splashed off to the side. "Here," Witker said. She turned her head, finding a cloth in her face. "Would you mind explaining what that nightmare was?"

"Part of a memory," she mumbled as she took the cloth. Kit wiped her face. She even pressed her tongue against it and gagged again. She let the waves in her stomach settle before saying, "the land is dying because there isn't a Fae on the throne. Turns out the New Heir needs to be crowned before the end of the year, or everyone will die."

Witker slowly lowered himself down to her level, staring. "The end of the year marks one heirless cycle since you killed the prince," he said. Kit nodded. "So the Crowns are trying to make their own heir. But it won't work. They're human. Nature won't accept it—it could even know how they've violated the Crown Prince."

Kit sniffed. "My eyes have been violated," she muttered and sat back.

Witker straightened. "Someone's coming."

Chapter Twenty-Eight

HE STOOD AND MOVED against the wall as a knock came from her door. Kit groaned and got up, throwing the cloth aside as Jassin entered the room.

He smiled, but concern took over. "Are you all right?"

She cringed. She didn't have to look happy to see him if he thought she was ill. "I have started my monthly bleed," she lied. She was due to start—by her faulty calculations—in a week or two. Just thinking about it made her stomach cramp. "Everything hurts. I just vomited and there's so much blood—"

"All right, all right," he held her shoulders. "I understand. There is no need to go into such detail." Jassin laughed awkwardly. "Do you need anything?"

"To be left alone to die," she said and started to pull away from him.

He raised a brow, "is that you being serious?"

"No, it's me being sarcastic. I hate being a woman," she said, "with all the cramps and the urges—"

"Kit," he said, "why don't I send for something for you to eat?"

"I might vomit again," she admitted. Jassin looked her over and pulled her into a hug. This was the man who took her memories, not the Fae, and yet all Kit wanted to do was fall into him. The comfort of his embrace. He and Aspen, two liars who once brought her so much peace.

She wondered how and when it happened. When Jassin decided to use her. Had it been when he found her in Niverly? Maybe the first year they were in Calar? When did he begin to see her as a tool to be molded?

Jassin kissed her head. When he stepped back he held her cheeks, a soft and concerned smile on his face.

She asked, "how much do you love me?"

He thought this over, looking away with his grey brows slightly creased. "I don't think there are words to express that."

"What if I want words?"

Jassin brushed his thumb over her cheeks. "Everything I do is for you. To keep you safe, to keep you with me. I'd stop the world for you, Kitali. Like I would've for your father before the Fae took him from us."

She took a deep breath. Every word stung. "I love you," she said.

He smiled gently. "Can I have something sent for you?"

She shook her head. "I'm just going to lay in the sun while the inside of me tears itself apart—"

"You're doing this on purpose," he laughed, nudging her.

"Maybe a little," she smiled.

He looked at her so fondly. "I love you, Kit. I'll come by tomorrow."

She tried for a nod. He left her standing there. It took a moment for Witker to come out of the bathing room. She was still staring at the door. "Do you think he was telling the truth?" He asked.

"Where is my horse?" She turned to him.

He made a face, confused. "Where I told you she was last time."

Kit nodded. Her eyes went to her hand. There was still a bandage on it. "How long until the year is over?" She asked, unwrapping it.

"A little over a month," he answered. Witker was looking at her hand now. He went up to her and took it, then brought her hand to his face and breathed in. "Did you put blood in your hand?"

"King's Blood," she nodded and pulled, but he grabbed her wrist with the other hand. "Hey," she said. His nose was pressed against her palm and he breathed in deeper with his eyes closed until she finally hit him on the side of the head and he let go. Witker looked just the slightest bit outraged. "Don't do that."

He sneered. "It's magic," he said.

"I know that. It's tracker magic," she said and waved it in front of him. He followed it with his eyes. "And the New Heir is south."

"Let's go then," Witker grabbed her hand again, dragging her into the bathing room. He opened a wardrobe and found it empty.

She tilted her head at him. "I don't live here, Fae. I don't even have a pair of shoes. You'd think they would bring me clothes, but it's just a pair of night clothes at a time."

He looked down at her and cringed. Kit wore a matching yellow top and pants, both covered in flowers. "How unfortunate, human," he replied, "you'll have to do without them."

He pulled her to the balcony. "Did you climb up here?" She asked, looking down.

"No, actually," he said. He tilted her head upward. Kit hit his hand, spotting little ledges and footholds on the wall going up, then over to one of the towers. "Come on, human," he said. Her jaw dropped. Witker grabbed her waist and lifted her onto the stone railing. The wall before her was aged enough for there to be spots for things like birds and sliders to live, as well as stones that stuck out in good enough places for them to scale the wall. She stuck her hand in one of the holes, her eyes wide. "Climb, I'll catch you if you fall."

"You will?" She squeaked. Her hands were slick with sweat.

He was at her back, now moving her hand to another hold. "Promise. I can't save the kingdom without you. I won't let you die."

She breathed in and pulled herself up, digging her toes into the bird-hole. "This is going to hurt very badly," she said, and he chuckled from below. "I won't be able to feel my fingers after this," she continued, lifting herself higher.

"You'll be all right," he held her calf and pushed upward.

"For someone that hates humans, you touch a lot," she told him, daring to look down at the drop that would surely kill her.

Witker said, "I like to think of it as leading pigs around a pen. Sometimes you have to nudge them to get them moving."

She stopped. "Are you calling me a pig?"

"I'm calling your entire species pigs," he corrected. It didn't make her feel much better. "Disgusting, loud, annoying, murderous pigs."

"Oh, I'm the murderer?" She looked down at him this time.

He shrugged. "You murdered the prince. Keep moving—"

"I'm not talking about the prince, *Fae*. Last time I checked, it wasn't the humans murdering entire villages to further their land in the name of that prince." Her fingers ached, and she knew she should move them, but she wanted to look at his face. "I lost everything and everyone to the Fae, so I killed the person I thought was responsible. I'm trying to fix my mistake. You're the one calling me a pig because we defend ourselves from your kind."

Witker was silent, and she kept going. "I've lost things to humans, too," he said. She slowed with her lips forming a thin line. "Yours isn't the only species that loses."

"No, it's not, and I'm not going to deny that," she said and grunted as she went to the next ledge of stone. "But your species gets to go home. That house you saw in my nightmares? That was mine. My entire life was taken from me. Even the veil was gone."

"What is the veil?"

Her arms screamed. "A wedding tradition," she answered.

"It was torn," he continued, "that's part of it, right? Your father mended it with blue thread. I think we have a similar tradition. The males go into the woods and select a green branch and form a piece of it into a semicircle when we come of age." She reached the middle of the climb and let out a breath. "And we carry them in our pockets—"

"We have to go back," she gasped.

"What?"

"I forgot something. We have to go back down," she said, kicking his knuckles. He jerked away. "Go down!"

He glared up at her. "All right. Blessings, human, calm yourself."

She wanted him to go faster than he was, but he wouldn't, and she didn't want to yell at him again. As soon as she was back on the balcony Kit ran into the bedroom. She jumped onto the bed and began rifling through the sheets before spotting the worn-down necklace on the side table. Kit snatched it, hesitating for only a moment before she put it around her neck and went back out to the balcony railing.

He was silent for most of the climb up, but curiosity got the better of him. "What did you insist we go back for?"

"Jewelry," she answered, smirking at the wall. She thought she could hear the appalled expression as she put her toes in the last hold and looked to the side. Her stomach lurched. "You'll catch me?"

"I promised," he said, "just let me get next to you."

Her eyes widened. "How are you going to do that?"

"You're going to move."

She looked up at the sky, grinding her teeth as he told her where and how, and he seemed to be patient as she tried to slow her breathing and concentrate. "Gods, gods, gods," she prayed.

"You're doing well," he told her. It didn't help. "Take your time."

"Hey!" Someone shouted from below. "Stop!"

She looked down at a guard, then another. Witker said, "you can't take your time. You need to move." It was true, and his hitting her leg got her to go again. One of the guards started to climb. "You can do it. Just keep moving."

"Why do you carry the semicircle thing around?" She asked.

"What?"

"Talk to me, Fae. Why do you carry the circle branches around?" She looked at him desperately. He was right next to her, his eyes wide. What would happen if they were caught? Would he be executed? Would they take her memories again?

Witker said, "they're half a wedding band."

"A wedding band?" She continued moving along the wall. He followed.

"It's a ring that signifies marriage, like your veil tradition," he explained as she looked at the guard. He was in armor, so he was heavier but making progress. "We carry it until we meet the Fae we wish to marry and give it to them. If they accept, they make the other half. Usually, it's completed through magic, but some have used string that will never break or even vines. They wear it for the rest of their lives."

Her hand slipped, and he grabbed her arm. Kit gasped for breath. "What about the males? Do you get a ring?"

"That is up to the bride. Males who marry males are guaranteed. If a male asks a female, she doesn't have to give him a ring. She can, but the importance is the one he gives." He let go of her arm and she kept moving. "Two females usually make their rings, and sometimes they don't, but we know they are wed."

"How?"

"Scent," he answered.

She looked back at the guard, her entire body shaking. "So they smell... married?"

Witker laughed. "No, it's a form of magic. They become one as their scents twist together. Everyone has a scent; when you marry, you gain another."

"What do I smell like?" She asked when she reached where she had to climb up to get to the tower window.

"Magic, sweat, sadness, oranges for some reason," he said.

She breathed a laugh. "They put some in my bath this morning. That and lavender, can you smell that?"

"No, the oranges are overpowering."

"Do you like it?" She glanced down at him. "Do you like the way a disgusting, murderous pig-human smells?"

He scowled, and she kept climbing. She lifted herself over the windowsill into the tower. The door was barred, but banging was coming from the other side. Witker hopped over and grabbed something off the floor. A shackle clinked around her wrist. "I'll take them off, I swear," he said, but Kit still fought him, glaring as he lifted her hands above her head, then lifted her chin so she could look at a dark rope. The chain was over it, and she couldn't lower her arms.

"Why do you keep doing that? Leave my chin alone," she said and took a step back. The door burst open. Witker moved behind her, putting a knife to her throat and pulling her head back by her hair. Jassin was the first one in, a sword in hand. Witker put an arm around Kit. She kept her eyes on Jassin.

"Let her go," he said.

Witker removed the knife, sliding it across her cheek. He said something in Travesta and yanked backward. His hands left her completely, but she was falling out of the window. Kit screamed. "Lift your legs!" Witker shouted in her ear, and she did as she was told. "We're going to hit a tree!" Her eyes widened, and her feet brushed leaves. "It's going to hurt!"

Chapter Twenty-Nine

WITKER KEPT HER BACK from being shredded, but he didn't stop the jarring pain from slamming into a tree. He groaned and tears watered her eyes while he dropped from the rope and left her to slide back against the bark. She hung there and coughed.

"Dropping you now," he said breathlessly, swinging a sword above his head to cut the rope. She fell, landing on her hands and knees. "Come on, human."

"I am never doing that again," she gasped, and he lifted her up. "You are a terrible, terrible Fae."

He rolled his eyes. "I'm saving your life." Witker dragged her, rushing, and the sound of more guards came from behind them. He practically threw her onto the horse and climbed on after her. "You know your horse tried to kill me when I went near her," he said. He turned the speckled brown horse and kicked into a run.

"They told me you killed her," she said, "and cut my hair."

"I wouldn't have done as good of a job if I cut your hair," he said simply, though Kit smiled to herself.

They were moving quickly, every bounce bringing her closer to the Fae that abducted and tortured her. Her back pressed against his chest, and his arms caged her in.

When he finally slowed, he pulled keys from his pocket and reached around to her wrists. She tensed, feeling his head against hers and his chin over her shoulder. "It was clever, what you said to Crown Jassin."

"About my bleeding?" She watched his hands go to the second shackle. The horse was walking now, breathing heavily under them, and it was nearly nightfall. She was forced to squint to see, though she doubted the Fae had to do much more than blink a few times to adjust to the night that was closing in around them. "How is that clever? It makes men uncomfortable—everyone knows that."

"It doesn't make Fae uncomfortable," he told her as he removed the chains. He put them in the saddlebag. She rubbed her wrists. "It's normal for males to treat females with the utmost respect and patience in those times." She felt herself begin to blush. "We tend to whatever needs they may have."

She turned her head slightly and he stopped the horse to climb down, taking the reins. Kit stared at the back of his head, cold. "Why did you pretend to take me against my will?" She asked, and he stopped to tie the horse to a tree. They were in a small clearing with running water in the distance and plenty of coverage around them.

"Can you hunt in the dark?" He asked.

"Sometimes," she nodded. He jerked his head, and she swung her leg over. Just like that, his hands were on her again. She grit her teeth. "I can walk, truly. Even in the dark and without your magic Fae eyes."

He snorted. "There are thorns on the ground."

When he set her down, she turned. "Answer my question."

Witker went to the horse to feed it and unpack the saddle. "If this goes wrong you can go back. Take them down from the inside."

"If this goes wrong we're all going to die," she said, "so what's the point?"

"Maybe I enjoyed abducting you, and I wanted to do it a second time?" He tossed a bedroll at her and she was glad she caught it. Dropping it would've been far too embarrassing. "If I could've left you hanging from that rope longer, I would've."

She looked away quickly. Kit situated her roll and he approached her with a bow and a quiver of arrows. "How do you know I won't shoot you?"

"You are a human looking for a Fae in a world where we still hold some power in the south. You need me to stay alive." She looked him up and down cautiously before she took the bow and arrows from him. Kit wasn't aware of Fae holding any power in the south—though she knew that there were plenty of uprisings and riots still happening in the east. Perhaps it was the same south of Calar. "There's an animal in that direction," Witker told her.

He pointed behind her and she sighed. Of course she was hunting. Of course she was back to killing. She slung the quiver over her shoulder. "Whatever I'm killing, you're eating."

"I'm not picky," he replied. She felt an urge to hit him as she went into the woods, stepping lightly. Kit drew an arrow and twirled it around her fingers as she listened to something moving above her. She went deeper into the trees. There, she stopped and closed her eyes. Her mind was on Jassin, which she hated. She tried to push it away, but she wondered what he thought. About the Fae, about whatever words he'd spoken.

She closed her eyes and got onto her knees, concentrating on what she could hear. There was a light breeze and it smelled sweet, so she turned in that direction. Her guess was berries, and with the thorns Witker had mentioned, it seemed accurate. She kept her eyes closed and crawled forward, silent over the soft grass—silent to her, anyway.

She'd shot things with her eyes closed before. It was never a moving target, and she usually saw it beforehand, but she'd done it successfully. Kit decided this was the same as her old archery competitions. Something simple, where she was blindfolded and shooting at painted round targets to win gold.

Leaves rustled in front of her, and she froze, holding the string of her bow. Her eyes opened, hardly adjusted to the dark, and she blinked a few times. Something was in front of her. It looked to be a decent size and was most likely a mammal. She breathed in through her nose and drew the string back, begging for this shot to kill it.

When the arrow flew away from her there was a cry of pain and a growl before it silenced. She still waited and pulled out a second arrow, starting to stand. Kit only got a few steps before her foot landed directly on a thorn. She grit her teeth and grabbed the arrow with the animal attached, then limped back the way she'd come from.

"Why are you limping?" Witker asked.

"Possum," she said and held it up. "I'm not skinning it."

He took the kill and repeated, "why are you limping?"

She sat on her bedroll, turning her foot to look at the wound. "I stepped on a thorn," she answered, pulling it from her foot. She tossed it into the fire. "Why couldn't you kill dinner?"

"I'm a farmer, not a hunter," he shrugged, but he was in the process of skinning the possum like he knew exactly what he was doing. "And I wanted to see how good you were in the dark, King Assassin."

Her eyes moved away from her foot, which was bleeding, and she mulled over her new situation. Her best friend had drugged her and helped steal her memories, then lied about everything he possibly could. All of it halted when the Fae who wanted to kill her came into her room and used nightmares to jog her stolen memories. Now, they were in the woods about to eat a possum before making a potentially long journey to find the heir to a kingdom.

"What did you say to Jassin before you pulled me out of the window?" She looked at him.

Witker glanced at her, then returned to the meat in front of him. "That I was going to take the thing he loves the way he took what I loved. And that I was going to keep you as a pet until you died."

Her eyes remained on him. "Would you have killed me before?"

"Most likely," he shrugged, "eventually." This time, she looked away. Of course he would've. He was a Fae that was using her. He might still kill her. "Did they fix your eye?" He asked after a few minutes.

She laid back. "Everyone agreed that it should fade in time—I just have to wait until the blood clears," she said. Kit stared at the sky through the thin trees around them. "But I can still hit moving targets, just so you know. In case you feel like moving."

He laughed a little, then tossed something at her. She picked up a roll of cloth. "For your foot," he explained.

This made her sit up. "Thanks," she muttered, wrapping some of it around her newest injury. She tossed the rest back and tied it off. He was staring when she looked up. "What?"

He shook his head and went back to the possum.

Chapter Thirty

"Human!"

Kit jumped. Her eyes flew open. "What?" She asked as she sat up. Witker was standing over her bedroll. She had abandoned it in the middle of the night. He looked at her, also wide-eyed. "What?" She repeated.

"What are you doing over there?" He snapped hotly, baring his teeth at her.

Her heart skipped a beat as she stood. "I don't sleep in the same place twice," she told him, walking over to the bedroll. The wound on her foot stung as she stood there looking up at him. "Happy?"

"You can't disappear like that," Witker warned.

"I didn't disappear," she replied, "I was against a tree. When I wake up from a nightmare I can't go back to sleep in the same place, so I moved. It's not that big of a deal."

She got off the bedroll and bent to collect it, but he grabbed her arms and lifted her back up, holding her tight. "You are the only person with access to the New Heir's location," he said as if she didn't know it. "If I lose you, I lose the kingdom, and everyone dies."

"I'm not a set of keys, Fae, you aren't going to lose me," she jerked away and grabbed the bedroll. He stared as she did, looking until she glared up at him. Kit pushed short hair behind her ear and tied off the roll so it didn't come undone. Witker took it from her.

"So where is he?" He asked as he attached the supplies to the saddle. She shrugged. "You don't *know*?" He looked at her funny.

"It's just a feeling," she said, crossing her arms. She watched him stomp out the fire, then come up to her. "I just know what direction I need to go in." He stood in front of her, perfectly still, as if waiting for something. She looked him over, then glanced down at her feet. "Now what?" She asked because she wasn't standing on anything or in the way. Witker said nothing; he just put his hands on her hips and lifted her into the air. She groaned grabbed his shoulders.

"Let me guess," he said plainly, "you can walk?"

He set her on his horse. She turned to sit on the saddle. "I very much can," she said, and he pulled on the reins, leading them where he intended to go. "We have to go south," she insisted, accidentally urging the horse to go faster. Witker looked back at her. "Sorry."

"Blood magic is serious and quite dangerous," he said, looking away, "it seems you got overenthusiastic. Your urge to move quickly and not patiently could get you killed."

"Well I did what I had to," she said. He grunted. Kit looked around to distract herself. The sun was rising, showing off the leafless trees. It seemed they'd all fallen in the short time she was in the castle. Winter had approached hard. It would begin to snow soon.

Witker didn't speak for an hour or two, so she didn't either. It was aggravating because she hated having to spend time with a Fae while also sitting in silence with him. Finally, he said, "it'll be cold tonight." She waited for him to say something else. It was cold the night before as well. When Kit woke up from her nightmare she was freezing, though she wouldn't admit that to a Fae. She figured they had some extra layer of heat humans didn't know about. He'd been sleeping soundlessly when she was moving to the tree. "And we'll most likely spend another few days out here before we reach Petaki."

She could tell he was leading to something, but whatever it was didn't keep her interest. She said, "we don't have enough time, do we?"

He paused, looking back at her. Witker said, "we just have to move quickly."

"Then why are you walking?"

He looked at the horse, then at her. "We'll take a break for a few minutes and eat something, then we'll get to the road and ride as much as we can, even into the night if we have to. When we reach Petaki, we can trade this one for yours. She'll sense your urgency and move faster."

She felt her brows furrow, braving her newest question. "How? I thought they were bred to care more and that was all."

"They have better stamina," he said as he led to the right. She assumed they were headed to the river she could hear distantly. "Contrens were bred to be better horses. More loyal, faster, stronger. And because she's chosen you, she'll be in tune with your needs. She'll respond to you."

Kit nodded, then asked, "did you manage to get her saddle off? You said you couldn't go near her, so has she had it on the entire time?"

"We managed to remove both the saddle and bridle," he answered, "nearly lost a finger doing it." Witker went quiet after that, and Kit followed suit. She was shivering when they reached the river, sniffing as she climbed down to the cold river stones. The horse, a stallion Witker hadn't named, began to drink. Witker grunted for her to watch him while he left to relieve himself. She knelt beside the horse and cupped water with both hands, bringing it to her mouth. The river they stopped at wasn't vast, but it must've been active with animals. She spotted deer tracks in fresh mud. Kit followed them absentmindedly, catching sight of footprints more fresh than the tracks.

She stood, holding the reins loosely in her hand as she searched the trees for movement. The blur in her left eye almost made her want to close it and look with the right, but she focused on using both. Her head turned, and she stepped closer to the water, reaching back for Witker's bow. The tracks stopped suddenly, facing the stream as if the person had decided to stand there. Nothing indicated they'd jumped back to the grass or into the water.

When she leaned around the stallion, she could see no footprints.

A wary feeling settled in her stomach. She picked up an arrow, once again scanning the trees. "Wit—" she started, then rushed movement appeared in the trees to her left. A cord wrapped around her neck, yanking her backward. She gagged, and her bow fell from her hand as she reached back. Her mouth opened. She thrashed.

Kit threw her arm back over her shoulder, connecting the arrowhead with flesh. Whoever was behind her cried out, loosening their grip enough for her to twist and stab again. There was no one there. Someone was gagging, but no one was there. Kit pulled the arrow out and heard bare feet slapping on mud.

Her throat burned. She reached for her bow. Water splashed behind her. She turned quickly, loosing the arrow blindly, and watched it connect with something. Someone, maybe, but all she saw was an arrow suspended in the air.

"Witker!" Kit screamed, and someone grabbed her shirt, throwing her into the water. The horse neighed loudly and reared as she was turned onto her back. Her head was pushed down and a weight slammed on her torso. Kit gagged and scratched at whoever was holding her. She clawed at hands desperately.

The body flew back, and her head surfaced. She coughed, spitting up water as she went for her bow again. She could see Witker out of the corner of her eye fighting off someone that she hoped, for her sanity, he couldn't see either.

She crawled over rocks and mud, standing with the help of the saddle, and grabbed another arrow. Kit notched while looking wildly around. Water splashed upstream. She swallowed and drew back, aiming for what she thought would be the center of whoever it was, and fired. Her arrow hit her target, and she grabbed another one.

"Get on the horse!" Witker shouted. He ran toward her as she climbed on, steering him toward the woods. Witker jumped after her and smacked the horse's hindquarters to get him moving quickly.

Chapter Thirty-One

WITKER DIDN'T LET THE horse stop until halfway through the night when it couldn't go any further. Kit had the good sense not to question him. "Get off," he ordered roughly. He climbed down and held the horse steady so she could drop down to the soft, cold ground. "Let's move."

"I can't see anything," she reminded him while he pulled her along. "Witker—" Her foot hit a fallen tree branch, and she tripped, cursing.

"Damn human eyes," he muttered. He stopped to lift her over his shoulder. "Keep quiet, I need to think."

She did not want to keep quiet any longer. "No, you need to talk to me," she said, "because I have no idea what happened back there, and you need to explain what that was and why you're all of a sudden in such a shit mood."

He dropped her onto her ass and she groaned quietly, squinting in the dark to see him rushing around, grabbing things and moving things. "I hate killing my own kind," he told her with a tone not as rough as before. "You do it very well, however."

"Sorry," she mumbled and looked away from him. He cleared an area and started digging a place for a fire. It sparked to life, growing and flickering around as he leaned in and blew on it gently. He held his hands over it to warm them. Witker continued working, taking the bridle off the overworked horse, feeding him, and laying his bedroll in front of the fire.

"Come over here," he said.

She got up, stepping over another branch to go to him. Kit reached for her bedroll, but he grabbed her wrist. She tensed. "What are you doing?" She asked as he pulled them down to sit on one bedroll. His large frame cradled into her, his leg wrapped around her. She watched him unlace his boot, pull it off, and remove his sock. Witker stuffed his foot back into the boot, tied it up again, and then grabbed her leg. She squirmed, saying, "I can put it on myself—"

"Stop moving, human," he muttered, pushing her wrist away. He said *human* like it was a curse again before he slid his dirty sock on her foot. "Blessings, you're freezing," he said hatefully. He folded the sock over and moved to his next boot.

She stared pointedly at his actions. His fingers laced his boot expertly. She saw small scars on his hands in the firelight and wondered if they were from combat or work. He held her dirty foot, removed the bandage because it was utterly ruined, and slid the sock to her heel. His hands moved gently, dragging the sock over her ankle. He folded it meticulously.

"Thanks," Kit mumbled, "and I'm sorry about the Fae."

"You kill well," he said as he had before, with the same breathless hate.

She grimaced and leaned forward to add another dry stick to the fire. "Sorry," she said again, not knowing what else she could do.

Witker produced what remained of the possum. He separated it, eating his half in silence while she picked through hers. She more shredded it than ate it, then just stared at the pieces. "Tell me why you're sorry," he ordered. He'd finished his share, now taking from hers.

She swatted his hand away and put food in her mouth. Kit brought her knee up to her chest as she chewed. "I don't like killing people," she told him.

"I wasn't aware you considered my kind to be people," he commented.

She turned, looking at him. "I don't think any less of you," she said. His dark brows creased just slightly on his head. "I am simply terrified of you—justifiably so—but I don't believe you are less than I am."

"You believe we are terrifying monsters, then," he decided with such finality that Kit wanted to smack him for it.

"I believe that the Fae group who killed my family and my friends are terrifying monsters, Witker. That doesn't mean that you are or that all the Fae in the world are," she shook her head and watched his eyes dart over her face. Some realization settled in his expression as he looked at her. "I am only afraid of you because I know you'd kill me if I wasn't useful to you."

Witker nodded once. "Finish eating. We should get a few hours of rest before we need to go."

She nodded, looking away.

The cord wrapped around her throat and she gagged. No one was behind her. The leather seemed to have a mind of its own. Jassin was in front of her, watching as she pleaded for his help. He had to help. She gasped and gagged and tried to crawl to him, but he laughed and backed away—

Kit jumped, shooting to her knees and coughing. Tears burned in her eyes. She put her hand against her throat. Witker stirred on his bedroll with a grunt when she covered her mouth. She faced away from him. "I didn't mean to wake you," she said quietly. It felt wrong to speak, so she was filled with the urge to take it back. To remain silent.

"What were you dreaming about?" He asked. His voice was rough and sleepy. When she looked at him, he was on his back, resting his head on an arm.

"I don't want to talk about it," she said as she wiped her eyes.

He said, "I could find out."

"If you ever violate my mind that way again I'll put an arrow through your heart," she spat. She grabbed her bedroll and walked away from him.

Witker sat up. "You know, maybe the reason your nightmares plague you is because you never talk about them."

"And so I'm supposed to tell them to the male that tied me to a chair and entered my mind to torture me with them because he liked it?" She snapped, sitting with her bedroll against a tree again.

"The second time I did it to save your life," he said and smiled, "nightmares are my specialty."

"Why?" Kit asked, "what kind of magic is it?"

Witker smiled wider as if he was proud of his ability. "The best kind," he said. She looked him up and down before sighing and sinking down the tree. He said, "the core of a person is shown by what they fear—what keeps them up at night."

"But... that doesn't really make sense," she said, looking at him again, "because someone could have a nightmare about... an evil *frog,* and it's just a nightmare. There's nothing special about that."

"You have a very human understanding of nightmares," he grunted. Witker turned to the fire and began coaxing it back to life. Kit squinted up. They wouldn't have slept much longer even if her nightmare hadn't awakened her. The sky was beginning to lighten. The stars were leaving.

She asked, "then what's your Fae understanding of nightmares?"

Half a smirk moved over his cheek, but he didn't answer. He poked their fire until the sticks he'd laid out lit again. Kit got up and dragged her bedroll back over, sitting beside him. Witker glanced at her. He asked, "my Fae under-standing?"

Kit nodded. "I know that Fae are better with magic than humans. You have a better understanding of it. You're better connected to it because it comes from nature and not the gods."

Witker reached into the saddlebag he'd kept at the base of his bedroll. He produced a knife, beginning to whittle his stick. Kit guessed it was so he didn't have to look at her for too long. "It's called *sominum,* the ability to see into a person's heart through their dreams or nightmares. It was first given to Fae in a time of war. The blessing can come to any Fae at any time. I received it after the death of my parents."

"So you can see into a person's heart?"

He nodded. Witker was frowning now, making a sharp point with his stick. "I use it to torment humans," he said, "but it can be used for many things. To comfort, to heal, to return memories. All things can be found in dreams and nightmares."

"What kind of person does that make me?" Kit asked.

Witker answered, "an annoying, murderous one."

"I could've told you that without the nightmares," she replied and got up again. Kit left him to relieve herself.

Chapter Thirty-Two

THE WHISTLING OF WIND through the trees sounded more like water rushing around rocks. Kit lifted her head, watching branches sway on either side of them. Despite most of them looking the same, she couldn't help but catalog everything she saw; from the broken branches to the dying birch that was dipping toward the ground as if it were a man on the verge of collapse. Kit stared at it, spotting another tree just like it further into the woods.

Witker slowed the horse to a stop.

"The result of your murder," he told her harshly.

Kit looked back at him. His jaw was set so hard she was certain he was going to break a tooth. "Is everywhere like this?" She asked.

"Everywhere in Olyan," he answered. The roughness of his voice was mixed with pain. Sympathy for the trees. Witker's eyes moved to them, and he urged his horse to the side. "When you interrupted the flow of Fae Kings..." he said as he climbed down. Kit held onto the horse's reins, shifting in the saddle to watch him walk to the birch tree. "You angered nature. I'm sure you've reaped some consequences of your own, but this is far deeper than I'm sure you know."

Her nightmares. Every time she woke up screaming, thrashing in her bed with the feeling of hands clawing at her trying to drag her into the ground—that was nature? That was its revenge?

"Humans are a destructive sort of species," he muttered to himself. Witker stood in front of the birch tree, wrapping his strong hands around the trunk. His fingers sunk into it partially, as if it were a bit of moss and not a great tree. He let out a soft, mournful sigh. "Perhaps if you hadn't taken the throne so violently, perhaps if you had..." he shook his head slowly. "If you had begun your rule better than you did, nature would not be reacting in such a way."

Kit climbed down from the saddle and led the horse forward. She stood next to Witker, though managed to keep her distance. Anger pulsed off of him. "You mean the fires and the riots?" She asked. He looked at her. Kit shrugged and said, "I overheard Jassin and the other Crowns talking about it. The one in Lark, and there was another one somewhere recently."

"In the Aori Plains," he said with a nod. "It was humans, then? And they blamed us yet again?"

She looked away from him. "Maybe we are a bad species," she whispered. Kit reached out and touched the soft bark. "I was so convinced that things just took time—that we'd make it better if the Fae just stopped fighting. And now everything is dying because of me."

"Not everything," Witker said. He let go of the tree and touched another. A birch that hadn't begun to die. That was still strong despite what was happening to the one just to its right.

"I don't get it," she admitted. "If the land is dying and we have until the end of the year... how come there's still green?" Kit motioned around. "Shouldn't we be seeing so much more death?"

He pulled on the sleeve of Kit's nightshirt and began walking away. Witker moved the horse's reins over his head and they moved down the road. She was forced to follow, her eyes mostly on the ground to avoid stepping on stones or twigs. "It isn't that simple," he said, "though I'm sure your human mind cannot wrap itself around it."

She glared at the back of his head. "I got my information from a Fae, mind you," she said in as harsh of a tone as she could manage. "He was saying that we're doomed and wouldn't last another year."

"We won't last *another year*," he repeated, looking back at her. Kit jogged forward a few paces to move in step with him. Witker said, "this is only the beginning."

"So that's why all of the Fae are leaving Olyan? Because it can only get worse from here?" Kit asked. She looked around again. There were more dying trees, but none as haunting as the drooping birch behind them. Kit's head turned back to where it was and her heart skipped a beat.

"There are people coming," she said. Witker slowly looked behind them as if he didn't have a care in the world, then shoved Kit hard.

She yelped and fell into the tree line, smacking her shin against a stone and landing roughly. "Ow!" She shouted and turned over. Witker had stopped and was reaching for something in the saddlebag. She watched him produce a single silver coin and show it to her. It had the human seal on it. As the group of three Fae riders passed, he flicked the coin toward them. They flicked one back. One of them looked at Kit for some time, his head turning to face her until he couldn't look anymore, and they trotted down the road on their dark horses.

"Come on," Witker said easily.

Kit stood. "What was *that* for?" She asked, stomping over to shove him. Witker didn't move, but Kit stumbled back a step. She let out a breath as her momentum fled her body. Witker raised a brow. "Why did you shove me?" She asked a little breathlessly. His nostrils flared and his eyes moved down. Kit looked at her shin and cursed, only just seeing that a spot of blood had soaked through her soft yellow pants. "Shit," she said.

Witker grunted something she didn't understand before grabbing her hips and lifting her up. Kit groaned deeply. He set her side-saddle on the horse and once again went into the saddlebag. "I shoved you because you are a human," he answered.

"Ralyn was right, you are an ass," she said. Witker produced the roll of cloth once again. She grabbed it, but he smacked her fingers and pushed her pant leg up.

"Ralyn is often right about many things," he replied.

She ground her teeth together. Witker wiped the dirt off of her shin before he wrapped the length of cloth around her leg twice. It was a small cut—not something she would've worried about had she been wearing real pants. Witker ripped the cloth and tied it in a tight knot that made her jump. He looked up at her as he lowered her pant leg back down. "Fine, so what was with the coin?" She asked.

Witker nudged her left leg and she swung it over the saddle with a roll of her eyes. He climbed on after her. "A Fae trade," he told her. Witker put the silver coin in her hand. It was the same silver and the same human seal. The wings of Crius the Great, only instead of a sword, there was an arrow striking the space between them. "When two suspicious parties find each other on the road they'll toss each other a silver coin, as if to say that no one will speak of their passing."

Kit turned the coin over once. "What was suspicious about them?" She asked.

"They were anything from a band of murderers to rapers. Wouldn't you rather pay them than risk getting into even more trouble than you're used to?" He asked calmly.

Her eyes slowly lifted. Kit couldn't see the three Fae on their black horses. They'd moved on too quickly. Witker took the coin from her and slid it into the saddlebag.

Chapter Thirty-Three

HE WATCHED HER FIX an arrowhead like he was studying for a test. Kit wiped rainwater from her brow, looking over the log they were crouched behind. The deer was in her sight while Witker shifted beside her, thankfully not making any noise while doing it. She shivered once. He'd given her his jacket when it started raining. Apparently her nightshirt wasn't very thick. It had nothing to do with her being cold.

She closed her eyes, trying not to picture herself on a beam high in the air waiting for a boy to come into a nice room wearing ceremonial clothes—

"It's not the throne room," Witker whispered with his hand flat on her back. "It's a deer, not a prince. Not a Fae."

Her eyes opened, and she wondered if he could see into her mind. If it went with the sominum. She glanced at him, only seeing some assurance. He'd been strange the past few days and even stranger now that they were this close to Petaki. Off and on. He hated her; he didn't. He wanted to talk; he snapped for silence. It was as if he was at war with himself and holding her at a distance because of it. She tried not to care, comparing the Witker in front of her to the one from her newest nightmare—the one of him killing her. His emotions weren't as erratic in them. He just began trusting her, got her to trust him, and then killed her as soon as she was no longer useful.

She drew the arrow back. Witker's hand remained where it was. It grounded her, keeping her out of the castle in her mind. Kit rose, straightening, and made a clicking noise to get the deer to turn his head. He did, and she let her arrow fly into its eye.

"Impressive," Witker said. His hand left her back.

A smile appeared on her face, and when she stood she could see Witker was wearing one, too. She picked up the sticks he'd woven flat and tight so they could drag the deer without much trouble. Her feet sunk into the ground as she went and laid the stick line next to the deer.

"Are you sure the butcher will take the whole thing?" She asked, standing at the head.

He nodded. "Positive. He won't sell to you, though."

"Fae?"

"Yes," he grunted, bending to grab the legs. Kit grabbed the front ones and they lifted the deer, both trying to kick the sticks underneath it. "Blessings, this thing is heavy."

She shifted her bare feet, grinding her teeth as she found purchase on the wet ground so she wouldn't slip. "I hope we get paid well," she huffed. They dropped the deer, and she picked up the antlers. "These alone should be worth twenty silver."

"We won't get that here," Witker told her. "Should we cut them off?" She nodded and he went over to get the rope he had on hand. He had rope, but he didn't have blankets. She'd been sharing his warmth for days. They'd taken to putting the second bedroll over them for added protection from the elements and spent the last two nights holding it over their heads in the pouring rain.

They began dragging the deer back to the horse, both silent. Kit slipped halfway through the walk, and her knee hit a rock. Wikter said nothing about it.

"I'll go in and sell the buck," he said as he tied the deer to the horse, "and you wait. Don't take money from anyone."

Her brow furrowed. "Why would anyone give me money?" His eyes moved over her. She looked down. Kit was drenched and covered in mud in ratty, torn clothes. Nothing on her was clean, and she looked terrible. "Fine, I won't take anything from anyone."

This made him smile, and he motioned for her to get on the horse. Witker led, stopping once they could see Petaki. He looked up at her. "Bow and arrows," he waved his hand, "just wait outside and stay on the horse—"

"I'll be fine," she told him as she handed the bow and quiver over. "That deer is worth more than you'll be offered at first," she said, leaned on the horse, and he started smiling softly at her. She continued, "don't accept lower than seventy gold—I'm serious, that is a perfect stag. I could sell that thing for one-fifty even without the antlers."

He nodded. "No less than seventy," he said. Witker took his knife out and sawed off the antlers, handing them to her before walking them to the butcher's shop. She rubbed dirt off of the antlers absently, watching him go. The street was nearly empty because of the rain, but gazes were still cast over her. Humans and Fae walked into a few of the shops that lined the road. Some stumbled out of one tavern and into another. Kit waited patiently, using the rain to clean the antlers off, pretending she wasn't a girl in nightclothes, barefoot, with an oversized jacket over her shoulders.

"I know you," a familiar voice said from behind her. She turned her head, seeing the man that attacked her on the road so long ago. Water dropped into the scar on his nose again as he said, "you shot me and my friend."

What was she supposed to do in this situation? Kit looked around for help, but suddenly, everyone in town wanted to escape the rain. "I did," she swallowed and looked at the man, "and... I apologize."

"Don't apologize to me, apologize to him," he seethed, "I'll take you to his grave." The man stalked toward her just as Witker exited the shop. He grabbed her, his skinny hand wrapping around her calf. Witker stalked over with a dejected sigh and wrapped his large hand around the back of the man's neck. He held the money bag out for her. Kit took it.

"Let go of her," he said to the man. He did, grunting in pain.

"She killed my friend," he said, "I deserve my justice. It's owed to me by the gods. Her life is mine."

Kit didn't know a single god that would agree to that. Witker nodded, though. "You're right, but the same applies to me, and it might be biased, but..." His hand moved around to the man's throat, and he lifted him off the ground. The man squirmed and kicked his legs. "I think I'm more important than you. Don't you agree? My justice is more important?"

The man said yes, of course, but it came out *"yrrsss"* in a gagging, hissing way. Witker dropped him. He coughed and glared as he crawled away. The man bumped into the butcher on his way to get the kill Witker claimed as his own.

Witker looked at her. "You're always in trouble, aren't you?"

"As of late," Kit rolled her eyes and he untied the deer for the butcher to deal with. He climbed onto the horse behind her. "Thank you," she said and turned her head. "I wasn't sure what to do."

"You're welcome," he replied, and they went silent. Kit looked at the things she'd seen before, then the path she'd started taking when Witker threw a rock at her head. He said, "this is where I threw a rock at your head."

"Amazing, I was just thinking of that," she said dryly.

He added, "one of my best throws to date."

"Mhmm," she rolled her eyes.

Witker leaned forward, his chest hitting her back and bending her forward slightly. "How badly did it hurt?"

"I'd be happy to replicate it for you, just let me find a rock." She started to get off the horse while he was walking, and Witker pulled her back. Kit smiled to herself as the walk continued. "Witker?" She asked and he hummed, silent otherwise. "Won't Jassin and the others come back to the house?"

He said, "no, there's a glamour around it now."

Kit's brow furrowed. She didn't know what a *glamour* was. It must've been another Fae magic they kept hidden from humans. There had to be a few of them. Perhaps a glamour was a way of hiding something. A secret. Maybe one she'd never learn.

They didn't speak again for the rest of the ride. Kit discovered that the farmhouse wasn't very far from where she'd been hit. It was a giant house—much bigger than she thought it was before. The wood panels were a faded red and splattered with mud and disrepair and the roof slanted in a steep drop toward the ground. Each window was clean, though there were more splatters of mud on the sills that lacked living plants inside them. She perked up when he steered them toward it. "Where are the stables?" She asked.

"We're on our way there. Stay calm," he put his arm around her so she couldn't move even if she was jumping slightly. "Human, you need to stop," he warned when she could actually see the stables—and Treyla. "She's just a horse."

"She is not, now get *off*," she shoved his arm and jumped down, grinning as she ran toward Treyla's stall. The horse saw her and stomped her front hooves, almost jumping like Kit had been. "Did you miss me?" She asked her, pulling the gate open. She wrapped her arms around Treyla. "I missed you," she said, "they told me you were dead. I missed you so much."

Kit backed up, and Treyla nudged her, sniffing all over. Kit hugged her muzzle briefly before taking her out of the stables to walk around. She stayed right next to her.

"I suppose this is a difference between us," Witker said as he walked over, leading the tired horse into another stall. He removed the bridle as Treyla snorted and pawed at the ground. "She'd be just a horse to me," he said, "contren or no, but humans..." He took off his horse's saddle and walked over with an apple. "I suppose you connect with animals more, despite us being closer to nature."

Treyla went for him, rearing back, ready to hit him with her hooves. Kit cursed and stepped in front of Witker, pushing him back. Treyla moved to the side and stomped. "It's all right," Kit said, "he's fine now." Treyla didn't seem to agree. "Witker is helping me. He's going to help me, it's all right."

"We're fine now," Witker told her, holding out the apple. Kit took it and stepped toward Treyla. She put her hand on her nose, giving the apple over. "I'm going to get a room ready for you. A bath, too," he said. Kit nodded and waved goodbye, staying with her Fae-trained horse.

Chapter Thirty-Four

IT WAS DARK WHEN she finished taking Treyla for a long walk. Kit went through the front door to a much better interior. The front was open and bright with clean wood floors, and a large staircase led up to the second floor. Kit could hear people arguing above her. She looked left at a large sitting room with a fireplace, a white decorated mantle, and two soft couches. She went further into the house. "Wit—"

"Kit," Ralyn said from the right. Her hair was back again, showing her ears. "Welcome back," she said.

"Thanks, I think," Kit faced her. "I'm looking for Witker, he said he had a room I could bathe in."

She looked at the ceiling. "I think he's busy. Come on, let me feed you," she said. Ralyn walked back to where she'd come from, past a wall of paintings, and into a kitchen. It was large, with each cabinet painted a light shade of blue. Another island was in the kitchen, reminding Kit of home as she put her arms around herself. Ralyn collected teacups and took out sugar, looking at a steaming kettle. "You know this is the first time we've had a human in our kitchen."

"Should I not be in here?" She asked. Ralyn chuckled and shook her head.

She brought out a pot and set it over another fire. "How are you feeling about all of this?" She asked. Kit watched her reach up and pull on her ear. "Me, Witker, the house..."

"Did you know it was me in the castle the day we met?" Kit asked as she walked further into the kitchen. An open window over the sink showed a chicken coop that was closed up for the night covered in sleepy darkness. Ralyn shook her head, busy with bowls coming from a cabinet. "Then why were you there?"

"I was going to kill you," she admitted as she took a large spoon out of a cup against the wall. She began stirring whatever was in the pot. "After we began to feel the land decaying, I got angry and blamed you so I went to Calar and got a job at the castle thinking I could get to you and maybe even the Crowns. And then I met you, and you were different from what I'd pictured, so I thought I'd get to know you, maybe get into your house and kill you there."

Kit leaned her back on the counter, the island still separating them. "And then?"

"I kept finding excuses not to," she said, "you just have such a personality, it's hard to describe." Ralyn tapped the spoon against the pot and set it down, facing Kit. "And you were different from who I thought you'd be. You had so much regret and sadness, I just... couldn't."

"Thanks, I guess," she said, her cheeks warm.

Ralyn nodded. She returned to the pot and waited for whatever was inside to warm. Kit looked around. The dining room looked to be through a doorway ahead, but it was dark inside. The walls were decorated with even more paintings, all in the red-pink color scheme. There must've been a theme to them.

"Here," Ralyn said. She slid a bowl of green stew over, and Kit walked to the island. She took the spoon and stirred the stew around. As soon as she lifted it to her mouth, it was snatched from her hand.

"Don't eat that," Witker said. Stew dropped from the spoon and fell onto her foot.

"Gods, you are such an ass," she said, deciding to wipe her foot on the back of his pants. He scowled down at her.

"There are grapes in this. You're allergic," he replied, taking the bowl away. He slid it over the counter and spooned some into his mouth. "Wouldn't want you dying on me."

Her brow furrowed. "How did you know I was allergic to grapes?"

"You said it in your sleep," he told her.

"I don't talk in my sleep."

Ralyn said, "yes you do. Very softly." Kit shook her head. "I didn't notice at first. I thought you were snoring until I actually listened. Last time you slept around me, you were talking about a horse."

She turned to Witker. "Grapes?" She inquired.

"You were talking to someone," he said with a shrug, "that's all I got before you started having a nightmare." Witker went around Ralyn and opened a cabinet. He produced cheese and slices of some meat, sliding them toward Kit. She ate them together while Ralyn took the boiling water off the fire and began prepping tea.

"Is Projo pissed?" She asked.

Her brother nodded. "Quite pissed. He's going to tell everyone to stay out of our way until we go."

They said nothing else, understanding passing between them. Kit ate slowly, watching Ralyn dump sugar into a cup and stir it. Kit reached for it, but Witker swiped it away. He said nothing; he just drank it. She took the next cup.

When Witker finished eating, he began washing used dishes. Kit watched his broad shoulders move and his arms work until Ralyn smacked her arm and pulled her out of the kitchen. "He means well," she said.

"What?"

"He means well," she repeated. They climbed the stairs that creaked just a little. "And you're you, so being nice to you is new for him."

Her lips formed a thin line as they reached the second floor. She figured that to her right was the room she'd been placed in after Witker threw the rock at her. They passed it over a soft rug that lined the hall and went into another room. The bed was on the far wall, a red blanket and two pillows covering it. There was a small table with an unlit candle directly to her right and a short dresser with a few more candles lighting the room. Only one window was in the room, and it looked sealed shut.

"Here's the tub," Ralyn said. Kit looked over and went into the small bathing room. Ralyn turned the handle and water sputtered out. "You can't take a long bath, so if you want to soak, I suggest getting all the washing done beforehand. The stopper doesn't stop all the water from draining."

"Thanks," she nodded.

"A rag for you," she said, handing one over, "and your clothes." She put a hand on a grey towel beside a sleep shirt and pants. Next to that were clothes for the next day. Kit nodded. "I'll see you in the morning if you aren't coming back down."

She said, "I probably won't. Thank you, though." Ralyn left, and Kit set the drain stopper.

Chapter Thirty-Five

After the nightmare, she almost didn't want to get out of bed. The blankets were warm, and the pillow was the softest she'd ever laid her head on. After she settled her mind back down, Kit turned onto her back with her eyes closed, slowly trying to find sleep again. She could feel it, but it wouldn't come—not after sitting up, not after taking a deep breath.

So she sat up once again, leaning over to light the candle on the bedside table. She slid off the bed and held the candle aloft, squinting as she made her way to the door. It made no noise as she eased it open. Kit looked out. Just two candles lit the hall.

She wasn't sure where she was going. She didn't want to disturb anyone, but there was nowhere to move in the bedroom. There were no chairs or lounges she could sleep on for another few hours. Kit tip-toed across the hall and descended the stairs, following the candle and wincing at each soft creak.

No noise came from above her. She kept going. Her feet were silent as she walked practically hunting the couch she'd seen before, and she set the candle on the table beside it. A blanket was cast over the back, so she pulled it down. It was still dark out. The window in front of her showed nothing but night. Kit curled up, watching the dark until her eyes grew heavy.

It wasn't a nightmare that woke her. It was the thumping of shoes on stairs. She jumped, morning light temporarily blinding her as it shined into the room. "Blessings and Kings, human!" Witker shouted, stalking toward her.

"What?" Her eyes went wide as she sat up to her knees.

He grasped her jaw and roughly tilted her head back. "Stop doing that," he hissed, his grip firm.

"Doing what?" She tried to pull away, but he wouldn't let her. He brought her closer. Kit grabbed the back of the couch and glared up at him.

"Moving at night, stop doing that," he said.

She squeezed his wrist and said, "Witker, let go."

"Get it through your weak human mind," he said through grit teeth, so close now that she could feel his breath against her face. Mint wafted toward her. Witker said, "you need to stop moving when you wake up. Stop disappearing from the last spot I saw you in."

He let go and she dropped back onto the couch. Kit rushed after him, finding him in the kitchen as if he'd done nothing. "I am not going to stop doing what makes me comfortable just because you don't like it," she snapped, going around the kitchen island to shove him away from the warming kettle.

Witker brushed her off to reach for teacups in the cabinet above her head. His jaw was set, and he was visibly pissed. Kit felt like a child being given the silent treatment. He grabbed the cups and turned, setting them on the island. "Go get dressed, we'll have breakfast here and go to town—"

"No, not until you get it through your thick Fae head," she moved around him, finally getting him to look her in the eye, "that I am not changing my habits for you."

He sighed. Witker grabbed her upper arms with a tight grip. "You are King Assassin," he said.

"I know that—"

"You are King Assassin in a house full of Fae that were going to help me kill you and feed you to the pigs just a few weeks ago," he snapped, jarring her body as he shook her to make a point. "You can't just go disappearing, do you understand me?"

She said, "maybe not in this house, but in the woods—"

"Fae thieves attacked you—"

"Will you let me finish? *Gods*." She pulled away from him, saying, "I can't fall asleep in the same place twice. It's been this way for *months*, you can't expect me to start staying in one place now."

Witker looked her up and down. She felt herself losing her confidence under his intense stare. She was getting smaller. She, a human wearing borrowed night clothes, couldn't challenge a Fae that towered over her. One that would've killed her the day they met if she hadn't escaped him. She watched a flicker of amusement dance in his eyes before he turned to get the steaming pot of water. "Fine."

"Fine?" She asked abruptly, watching him pour water over the tea. Steam rose to him and he waved it away. Witker set the pot aside. "That's it?"

"That's it," he agreed with a nod that told her he knew something she didn't. He played nonchalant, dumping a generous amount of sugar into the two cups. He stirred both with different spoons. "You can sleep in two places."

She took the tea he offered, wary of her next step. He faced her, his hip resting on the island, and blew steam from his cup before sipping. Witker set it down, probably finding that he hadn't let the tea sit long enough. He looked at her. Her cheeks reddened. "What?"

"Nothing," he shook his head.

"Why are you looking at me like that?" She asked, "and why didn't you argue with me? I feel like you should've argued with me."

Witker shrugged and went to another cabinet. "How do you take your eggs?" He asked casually. She watched him, brow furrowing. Witker went about his tasks—lighting a small fire, setting the pan down, grabbing a few ingredients—like nothing was happening at all.

"You're acting very strange," she told him.

"Actually, you're reading too far into things," he replied, dropping a chunk of butter into the warming pan. They both watched it melt and then Witker cracked four eggs into it. "I'll just make them all the same, then."

She stepped back, setting her tea on the counter. "I'll get dressed," she mumbled, leaving without a goodbye. Looking back, she saw that he was dutifully manning the eggs.

Chapter Thirty-Six

KIT TIGHTENED THE KNOT around her boot, listening to Witker whistle something. He kept up the same tune as she walked into the kitchen. He separated the eggs onto two plates. "You should have an apron," she told him, resting her elbows on the counter and leaning into it. She slid her tea toward herself.

"Should I?" He gave her a plate.

"Do you have salt?" She asked.

He shook his head. "Fae don't use salt." He gave her a piece of toast and a jar of strawberry jam. "We make this ourselves," he told her, tapping the lid of the jar with a knife.

"So strange," she whispered, taking the fork he offered and breaking the yolks of the eggs. He said nothing as he did the same. They ate silently, alternating between the toast, eggs, and tea.

"We'll do some shopping today," he said and drank the last of his tea. He wiped his hands on his pants. "Get supplies and hopefully be headed south by midday. Sound good to you?"

She straightened. "Why didn't you argue with me before?"

"Still on that?"

"Yes, you just gave up."

Witker said, "wouldn't you rather me give up than argue?" He set his things in the sink and rinsed the pan, then started to leave.

"No—well, yes, but—" he laughed at her. She glared for a moment before saying, "it just seems like you gave up for a reason, like you know something I don't. And if we're going to be working together, then," she stepped toward him nervously, "we should be on the same page. About this."

He considered her, his expression neutral until he stepped toward her and closed the space they'd had before. The kitchen felt much smaller than it had a moment ago. "I don't consider us to be working together," he said firmly, brow furrowing slowly. He was angry, visibly so. His shift in mood came on like a strike of lightning. "I'm keeping you alive until we find the New Heir, *King Assassin*, and you're leading me to him. There is no *together*."

She shook her head and stepped back from him. "Choose how you feel about me, *Fae*. I can't keep up with your mood swings and I'm not dealing with them for however long this trip is." She pushed past him and went outside.

Treyla was waiting, happily stomping as she approached and grabbed a brush for her. She whinnied in Kit's direction and leaned into her hand.

"You like me, huh?" She asked. Treyla nodded her head, making Kit laugh. "That's right. You won't be nice and then mean suddenly, will you?" She focused on the brush's direction while Treyla shook her head around. She wouldn't be nice and then mean. She wouldn't hold her for one moment and then jump off a horse to escape her the next.

"Kit!" Ralyn jogged forward, her hands full. "You're leaving today, right?" Kit nodded. She put a cloak and jacket over the gate and leaned against it. Ralyn sniffed in the cold air, going quiet. It wasn't foggy, but clouds hung heavy in the air. The bright morning sun was gone quickly. "I heard my brother being an ass earlier," she said as casually as she could manage.

"I mean you no offense, but there is something seriously wrong with him," she said, continuing to brush Treyla down.

Ralyn nodded. "He's been that way since we were children. It's not just you. Well, it is you because you're you, but this is something different." Kit looked at her, waiting. "I call it dropping," she said, "the thing he does when his mood changes like that. Suddenly he's nice and it's him rising. Usually this is his mood level," Ralyn lifted her hand, showing it flat and moving through the air slowly.

"And then…" Her hand plummeted. "That's his mood. Sometimes it goes up the other way."

"And with me being King Assassin and a human… what? He's just an extra asshole?" She asked, moving to Treyla's other side.

Ralyn laughed, "I suppose so. The smallest things set him off. A tone shift, a smell, something he thinks about. Since you pointed it out, though, he might apologize. That's always good. And when he does, he means it. Trust me."

Kit said, "I do trust you."

"And Witker?"

This made her shrug. "I have so far. I shouldn't expect anything from him. Just whatever we're doing now."

"Shame," she said as she took a step back. "He could use a human friend. Anyway," she shifted, "I got a jacket and a cloak for you."

"Thank you," Kit smiled. At least one Fae didn't hate her or act strangely. Kit turned back to Treyla. So every time he suddenly shifted, he was dropping? In the kitchen, before, his mood had been fine—he was happy, even—and then suddenly, it was different. Perhaps it was the 'working together' line. He had to emphasize it when he shut her down.

Kit went through everything that had happened in the last few days. How he'd been at least somewhat considerate, how he'd get angry and wouldn't explain why or suddenly depressed for no reason—and now, calling her King Assassin as if he was reminding himself of it, not her.

Or she was reading into it, and he just hated her.

That seemed more accurate.

Chapter Thirty-Seven

WITKER WAS ONLY A step away from her as she went into an apothecary. He stayed close for some reason, and she could only assume it was because a Fae ran the shop. She pulled trimmed cloth and an ointment for many wounds off the shelf in front of her. There were three total in the shop, but each of them was stocked and rose to her shoulders. Witker hovered behind her, silently rushing as she moved along and read different labels. They'd gotten everything else—extra socks, gloves, food for them and Treyla, more arrows, and a tent—so now he was pushing for them to go faster. He hadn't seen the point of needing any medicinal care.

She handed him the items and found another ointment, handing it over. He read the label, and his brow furrowed. "What's this for?"

"Cramps," she answered and walked away from him. He paused, acknowledged the evident reason, and moved on. Kit passed a woman headed down the aisle and moved to the far wall. The shop was small, the aisles thin, so she watched Witker squeeze past the woman in fear of touching her. It made Kit smile, then recall what she was doing and quickly look away from him. He came over when she was done picking out which collection of pre-cut rags she'd need. "I'm finished," she said.

He nodded shortly, taking them from her and leading her to the front. His hand was on her back, pushing her forward. The Fae looked at her as Witker set their purchases down. "You didn't steal anything, did you?" He grunted with a sneer on his pale, smooth face.

"No, sir. Everything I picked up I gave to him," she nodded to Witker. He said nothing, but did slap down a few bronze and a couple of silver coins.

The Fae selling to them straightened a bit, his hands on the counter. "I don't believe you."

"Go outside, human," Witker ordered, shoving her slightly.

She looked at him, then the seller, and stepped away. The seller said, "I hold the right to search her." Her eyes went wide, and she looked at Witker again.

"I don't have time for this," Witker said, "just take off the cloak and jacket for the male."

Glaring, she untying the borrowed cloak and threw it at him. He smiled when he caught it, and then the smile grew when she threw the jacket. The woman she'd passed put her items down and left as the seller approached Kit. He grabbed her wrists with his skinny hands and patted down her arms. Kit gritted her teeth when he squeezed her shoulders, even pulling on her hair. A sickly feeling pooled in her stomach when he touched her waist. His hands went up.

"Watch your hands," Witker said as he neared her chest, "I'm being nice and letting you touch the human as it is. You'll have to pay me for those liberties." She shot a glare at Witker, though she was grateful to him for not letting the male grope her. Witker reached behind the counter and took money from the shop owner. He was watching closely while the seller bent down to pat her legs. Shining money was in Witker's hands, then his pockets.

The seller got up and smiled crudely at her, putting his hands in her pants pockets. His gross fingers found her necklace and pulled it out. Kit grabbed on. "That's mine," she said, holding it tight.

"No, it's not. You stole it," he challenged, his Fae strength battling her human one. She felt the chain slide down in her grip slightly. "Let go, or I'll have your hand removed."

Witker stepped toward them and she snatched the short knife she'd seen him sharpening on the walk there. Kit held it to the Fae's throat, gritting her teeth. "Give it back," she said evenly.

"I *will* have your hand now—"

"I'll have your life," she told him. There had been a hint of amusement in his eyes before, but it was fading now. "I will kill you if you don't let go and finalize our purchase right now."

His eyes darted to Witker. "You letting your human do this?"

"I'd like to see where this goes actually," Witker crossed his arms curiously. Kit pressed harder, letting blood be drawn from the Fae's throat. She wouldn't actually kill him, though the seller didn't know that. She'd kick him between his legs and knock his head against the counter, but she wouldn't take his life. "The human is acting like a Fae, how entertaining," Witker muttered.

"Not if you're the one with the knife to the throat," the Fae hissed.

Kit said, "give me back my necklace and I will happily remove it."

"All right," his grip slackened. He put his other hand up. "Fine, you can have it. It's yours."

"Let go of it."

There were seconds between them where she thought she really would have to attack another Fae, but he released his hold on her necklace and backed up. Witker stepped between them, his muscular build offering no chance of passage, and he nodded to the counter. "Let's go, I have places to be."

He took the money and gave the supplies, staring at Kit. He didn't even count the coin. Witker pushed her out, and this time, she was fine with it.

"Would this be the jewelry you went back for when I broke you out of the castle?" He asked. Witker traded her jacket for the knife and led both of them from the shop. They went down a street and she shrugged it on. Treyla eyed the both of them as they stopped at her saddle. Witker stuffed their supplies into any open spaces. "Must be important," he continued, turning to her and wrapping the cloak around her shoulders.

"It belonged to my father," she said as he tied the cloak. She showed it to him. Witker said nothing, he didn't even touch it. Just looked. "I don't wear it around my neck because it doesn't feel right, but I can't be without it."

Witker nodded understandingly, making her wonder if he carried something from his parents. They continued walking in silence. She kept her hand in her pocket the whole time. He eventually stopped and faced her. "What you did was beyond stupid," he said.

She crossed her arms. "I thought it was a human acting like a Fae. If that's true, then aren't all of you stupid?" He bit the inside of his cheek and shook his head with a sigh but didn't say anything. She grinned at his defeat. "So—" she started, stopping abruptly when he put his hands on her waist and lifted her into the air. "I thought we were past this," she said as he turned toward Treyla.

"It's too much fun," he said, setting her down. Witker had a distinct smile on his face, something mischievous and satisfied. She kicked her leg over and adjusted, waiting for Witker. He lifted his foot into the stirrup, and she urged Treyla forward. He tripped, letting go to keep his balance, and Kit laughed. He put his hands on his hips.

"Sorry," she shrugged.

Witker rolled his eyes. It didn't seem like his mood shifted too considerably. His shoulders were still light, and he wasn't scowling. He walked close and gave her a warning look before he mounted Treyla and took a map out of the saddlebag. "Don't do that again," he said, holding the map before her. Treyla began to walk. "Now, where are we going?"

She turned her head and looked over her shoulder. "I just know south. I couldn't—"

He grasped her jaw with his right hand and pulled her head back, facing it down at the map. "Focus."

"I'm going to bite you next time you—"

Witker put his hand over her mouth and pulled her back sharply into his chest, forcing a yelp from her. "Human," he said shortly. She squirmed, and he tensed beneath her. "You used blood magic to find the prince, did you not?" She hesitated, then nodded. "And you were successful, but you aren't focused. You must've done something wrong along the way—and don't get me wrong, a human performing a blood tracking spell like this is impressive," he added before she could say anything. This satisfied her enough to relax against him. His hand stayed where it was on her face. "However, you should be able to focus it and do more than just point in one direction."

She looked at the map as he removed his hand and folded it over. They were reaching a small fork in the road, where horse hooves could be heard from the left. When they were closer, they came into view, and Witker steered them out of the way.

They moved to the right fork where she wanted to go, and when nothing but the sound of wet woods and distant horses was around them, she turned and smacked Witker's arm. "Stop doing that," she said, "stop touching my face."

"Fine, look at the map," he said. She turned, staring at the old paper. He said, "it takes focus, but you should be able to give us an idea of where we need to go."

She took the map and folded it over to make a smaller area, cutting the kingdom in half. "How long do we have until the new year?"

"Thirty days," he answered.

"So not enough time," she concluded.

He said, "only with that human attitude."

Chapter Thirty-Eight

Go go go go go go go go—

Kit inhaled sharply and lifted her head. She blinked the blur from her eyes as she observed what was through the tent opening. It was just a cheap and easily ripped cover, but it did its job keeping them from the elements. Dew had formed on the rim, dripping steadily onto the ground. Kit saw no rain, but their fire was weak. Half of the coals were covered in ash, and rocks were stacked around it to protect it even more, but it seemed the Witker had woken up at some point while she was sleeping to bring some flames back.

He snorted behind her, and she gently lifted his arm off her, sitting up. Kit set his arm down and leaned forward to climb out of the tent, watching air crystalize in front of her while she added more dry sticks to the fire.

"Human," Witker grunted, wrapping an arm around her waist and pulling her down.

"Fae," she replied, pressing her elbow into his ribcage to try to lift off of him. "Let go of me right now. We agreed—"

He flipped the two of them over, rolling her body over his and adjusting on top of the bedroll. "Now you're in a different place," he said sleepily. Witker even moved her cloak over her body before pulling her in.

"I hate you," she told him.

He hummed, nuzzling against her as if she were some doll he slept with as a child. He breathed against her head, sending a wave of warmth over her scalp. "If this doesn't work, we'll try something else tomorrow night," he mumbled, "close your eyes, stop being so stubborn." Witker then reached up and covered her eyes. She pulled his hand off, making him laugh and wrap it around her body. Kit sighed.

She stared at the tent fabric while he breathed softly and fell back asleep just as quickly as he'd woken up. Witker's fingers flexed against her waist. She looked down at them. With his arm around her, they were tucked beneath her. All she saw was his palm. Kit felt his other hand against her hip. She was laying on that one as well.

She wondered if they'd be numb in the morning as she closed her eyes. Witker's soft breaths lulled her back to sleep.

⟵

"I think you owe me something," a distant voice said above her. "*Hu-man*," he sang, again reminding her of a child. "Wake up, I'm hungry," he said, shaking her shoulder once before his hand went to her cheek and turned her head. She groaned, making him laugh at her. "Come on." He resorted to waving her head back and forth.

"Stop," she whined, pushing him while she sat up. She rubbed her face. Witker was straddling her legs with most of his body in the tent.

He said, "you snored last night." She blinked slowly at him. He seemed to be in one of the best moods he'd been in for a while. He was smiling, and his shoulders were lighter. "You also mumbled a conversation with someone. I do believe it was about me."

"Calling you a monumental ass?" She asked roughly. Kit pushed his chest and he backed out of the tent so she could stand. She stretched with her arms behind her head, shuffling to their pile of things.

"Yes, actually," he said.

Kit smiled and collected what she needed, running her fingers through her hair. "I'll be back," she mumbled, hanging her cloak on a tree branch. He prodded at the small fire and set up a spit for something he wanted her to shoot. "What do you want for breakfast?"

He was quiet while she walked into the woods. "Something big enough for lunch later," he answered loudly.

With a heavy eye roll, Kit relieved herself far enough away that she *thought* he wouldn't be able to hear. Then, she straightened her still-clean rag and washed up in the river they camped near every night. She rubbed water over her face and up her arms.

She looked around on her walk back, stepping over things that made heavy noise. "Are you trying to sneak up on me?" Witker asked when she was closer.

"Shut up," she hissed. They weren't deep enough in the woods for anything large to come by. The road had been busy the day before. Kit had counted eight horses and four carriages on their way to Petaki. There had been a caravan that passed them from behind. The group had been coming from Calar and planned to cross the ocean in the east. She anticipated another busy day of traveling, which meant that deer and other game animals would stay deep in the woods to avoid the footfall.

"Why'd you tell me to shut up?" Witker asked as soon as he could see her. He had mushrooms in his hand, which he dumped on his bedroll. The tent was gone, packed up with everything else.

"You really don't hunt," she said as she went toward him. He collected the bow and arrows. "You have to be quiet before you kill something. Can't go shouting and stomping all over the place."

He held the bow out for her. "You're the expert," he said. Kit couldn't tell how he meant it—as a jab or a simple compliment. Either way, a sick feeling floated through her stomach like smoke as she took the quiver and held the bow. "You really don't like this, do you?" He asked. There was a concerned crease in his brow, but it made her more uncomfortable than the comment. He waited for her to answer, and the more he stared, the less she wanted to.

"It's fine," she muttered, "I'll be back." He didn't say anything while she walked away. Her appetite disappeared. What did he know? He could guess all he wanted about whether or not she liked shooting; he could think long and hard, but she didn't have to respond. To him, she was King Assassin. For all she knew, he'd make fun of her feelings.

Only before they reached Petaki he'd put his hand on her back and told her the deer wasn't a Fae, reminding her of where she was. She thought it was to ground her, and it felt that he knew what was on her mind.

Kit climbed a thick tree. Witker was a Fae who would have killed her before he decided she was right. He was doing some strange protection thing, but he said it himself. *King Assassin*. Who he refused to work with.

When her knees started to cramp, she drew an arrow and set her sights on a snowshoe hare that was turning white for the winter. It twitched its nose and hopped once before she killed it and dropped from the tree. Kit carried it back by its ears, pulling the arrow from its eye.

Witker smiled at the hare, and she tossed the dead thing toward him, cleaning off the arrow and shedding the quiver. She set it and the bow down and went to look for the skin of water.

"Can I ask you something?" Witker inquired.

She pulled out the skin. "You technically just did."

She wasn't looking at him, but she was sure he had rolled his eyes. She went to Treyla as she drank, patting her neck. He asked, "was the prince the first person you ever killed?"

Her hand stilled. Kit took the waterskin away from her lips. "I don't want to talk about it," she replied, turning to watch him skin the rabbit. "Can I ask you something?" He looked over without responding. "Why do you hate humans?"

He looked her up and down, his green eyes moving from head to toe. "I don't want to talk about it," he said.

"Then let's not ask each other those kinds of questions," she said shortly. "We don't need those conversations to do whatever this is. If anything, it's distracting." He just nodded, his good mood vanishing for a moment. It only returned when the food began to cook.

Chapter Thirty-Nine

THE TENSION BETWEEN THEM was obviously her fault, but it only worsened when the two males began riding next to them. They'd come from a hunt near Petaki and were both dragging a cart of what looked like seven dead deer and a bunch of quail and rabbits. Apparently, they were going to stay until the first snow when they saw a woodman's follower. They took some rare butterflies as a sign it was time to go. Witker had nodded knowingly.

They hadn't asked about Kit yet, but they would eventually, and she wasn't sure if the lie she was thinking of was the same as whatever Witker had in mind.

After describing the situation with the butterfly and what felt like hours of one-sided conversation, the hunter closest to them—Poer—looked at the drying hare skin hanging off the saddle and the large antlers next to it. He seemed to be entirely oblivious to things, like the antlers and the food in his beard, and it was only more apparent when he asked Witker if he hunted as well.

"Not often and mostly for food," he answered.

"Through the eye, though," Poer pointed to the hare, "impressive. And the antlers as well."

He brushed it off and said, "just lucky."

Kit shifted, breathing out slowly while trying to remain unnoticed. Her stomach was cramping now, growing increasingly uncomfortable. Witker moved his hand around and slid it into her shirt. His warm palm and fingers splayed over her stomach. Kit looked right toward the woods, her jaw dropping as he pulled her against him.

"And the human?" Asked Detin, the second Fae hunter. He had a similar beard, just one without food, and it was better trimmed. It suited him well. He was far more fit than Poer, too, and looked like he was the one that did most of the lugging of animals. "What's it for?"

"Keeps me warm at night," Witker said. His hand moved down below her naval, and Kit stopped breathing. She was completely unsure what to do about it—or what to do about the warmth that spread through her. It wasn't like she could command her body to stop, and it only got worse when his smallest finger snuck into the waistline of her pants. Kit grabbed his wrist quickly and he stopped. "Took her from her human father when he didn't deliver a debt. Now she's mine," he added. This was *nothing* like the lie she had in mind.

It undoubtedly pleased the two Fae.

"Hello," Poer said to her.

Witker shook her, adding pressure to his hand placement. "Say hello," he ordered.

She grunted, "hello," and squeezed his wrist. Poer chuckled. Kit wasn't sure what could come of something like this. She feared their assumptions and how far Witker would have to go to keep up the lie.

"Where are you headed?" Poer asked.

Witker said, "south before the snow hits, hopefully. Not sure of an exact destination yet."

"Basik for us," Detin said. That was just over a week away. Kit and Witker would have to pass it to get to wherever they were going. "I suppose we'll be seeing a lot of each other, then. Shall we continue on together?"

Kit breathed out slowly, a fresh cramp making her feel ready to vomit. Again, she shifted, and Witker pressed his fingers into her stomach. He moved behind her. "We're packing up early in the mornings. We need to move quickly," he said, "but you're welcome to come along." His other arm came around, and he held the waterskin out for her. She took it from him. "We won't be stopping for you."

"Sounds fair," Detin agreed.

She uncorked the water and drank from it slowly. He took it back as soon as she was finished.

"Might be fair to share the human as well," Poer suggested. Kit looked at him, then at Witker.

He chuckled low. "I'm afraid not," he told the Fae, but his eyes were on her. She sat back again, trying to relax and focus on keeping what was inside her stomach in her stomach. "I'm quite taken with her," Witker said.

"Not even a taste?" The Fae asked. He even reached for her and touched her thigh. Kit smacked his hand away, and Witker grabbed her wrist. Poer had a distinct laugh that made Kit want to vomit even more. "You would let your human treat your new companion this way?"

Kit had never in her life experienced something like this. Being considered *less* than someone, as Witker had implied she felt about Fae.

"You deserved that one," Witker told the male. He folded her hand over where his was beneath her shirt. Kit dug her fingernails in.

Their ride lasted for hours, though it felt like days with how much Poer and Detin spoke. It was as if they spent all of their hunt in silence and were now making up for the time. Eventually, they got bored and began to sing. The sun was setting as they joined together and sang a Fae song about some female with large breasts and a male with an even more prominent 'member.' Treyla walked them into the night. Witker had removed his hand from inside her shirt, leaving the spot cold, and wrapped his arm around her when her eyes began to close.

Finally, *finally*, one of them decided they'd had enough riding.

"Come on," Witker said softly, his lips against her ear. They slowed as they looked for a place to settle for the night. "Wake up, human."

"I am awake," she grunted, and Treyla stopped. Witker swung down, and she began to tilt toward him. He pulled her off completely and set her on her feet. "I think my heart stopped for a moment," she told him, "I thought you were going to drop me."

He chuckled, "as entertaining as that could be, I can't have you breaking anything important." Witker then bent and held her chin. His face was closer than it had been before. "I apologize," he whispered.

She took a deep breath. "Are you going to do anything else I should be prepared for? Like that hand thing…"

"You liked the hand thing," he teased softly. Kit felt her face turn red. She did not want to know how he knew that. Not at all. "I'm just going to keep close to you," he said.

Poer called from a clear spot, "have your human start a fire!"

"Don't mind if I bite you," Witker added before he hooked his arm around her legs and carried her over his shoulder. Kit's eyes were wide. She knew that Fae had sharp teeth, but she'd always assumed it was because their diets mainly consisted of meat. She never thought he'd use them on her. "Go on," he said when he set her down.

She turned and sat. No matter what she did, the Fae didn't trust her fire. Poer redid it, looking at her quite often as he did. "How are you liking the woods?" He asked. Witker set their tent up and put the bedroll inside, then the other in front. He grabbed her and pulled her between his legs.

"Fine," Kit said.

"That's all? Do you not speak more than that?" He asked, leaning toward her. Poer began skinning one of the rabbits he killed. He pointed a bloody knife at her, saying, "isn't it that all you humans are talking all the time? You always have something to say, don't you?"

"I don't mind the woods," she elaborated, "I have no problem with it."

Detin said, "and I suppose you have no problem with your new situation. You can like the woods, but your new owner, Witker? What of him?"

Witker looked at her with a raised brow. She said, "he's kinder than I expected." His brow twitched carefully.

"Not at night, I'll bet," Poer chuckled again.

"You're a disgusting—"

Witker covered her mouth roughly and pulled her back against his chest. He sighed. "Human," he said calmly, "that is not the way we speak to my new friends."

Kit grunted and tried to push his hand away from her mouth. Witker pressed even harder. She looked up at him. His expression was far too similar to the one he wore when she first met him. He wore the sneer too well, though it didn't meet his eyes. They were near playful. Kit looked away and his hand relaxed.

"I expect you to apologize for your behavior," he said. Poer and Detin were both grinning—Poer especially.

He removed his hand. "You're a disgusting *pervert*," Kit finished. Poer bared sharp teeth at her, and Witker threw her into the tent. She gasped, landing hard, and looked back at his apologetic face before he shut the thin flaps they always had open. She sighed and laid down. Kit listened to them laugh and eat. She heard suggestions of punishments come from Poer, and then he asked one last time to have an hour with her before Witker shut him down completely.

He crawled into the tent later than he would've if they were alone. Kit tried to sit up only to be pushed onto her back. She could barely see him as he crawled over. "They're asleep," he whispered.

"Or pretending to be," she said, "maybe Poer wants to hear what you do to keep yourself warm at night, huh?"

Witker sighed slowly. "I apologize. I thought they'd leave you be." She said nothing. "Did you get any sleep? I thought I heard you nod off."

He laid down and Kit moved against him, facing him with her head on his arm. He seemed shocked only for a moment. "I had a nightmare about Jassin."

He nodded.

"He locked me in the crypt, let the prince out with my bow, and told him to go hunting. Jassin wanted to see him shoot me like I did him."

"You're all right now," he said, "because you're awake. Dreams can't hurt you. I would know, right?"

Kit nodded. He closed his eyes and moved his arm around her. "I have a question," she said. He opened his eyes again. "About your mood swings."

This time, he pulled his head back to look at her. "What about them?"

"What are they like for you?" She asked softly.

"Didn't we just agree not to ask those questions because they are distracting and unnecessary?" He countered.

She said, "I think this is different. Maybe it's an uncomfortable question, and if you don't want to answer, you don't have to, but—"

"Shh," he put his finger against her lips. Witker's eyes moved. She heard one Fae grunt and stand. He groaned softly before shuffling away. "Just go to sleep. We can talk about it later."

"Sure, in a few days when they're gone and we both forget about—" He cut her off by moving his hand to cover her mouth once again. What she could see in his eyes showed warning, but she chose against paying attention to that. Instead, she bit him. She'd told him he would, and yet he acted surprised. He pulled his hand away, cursing, and waved it through the air above them.

Witker's gaze settled on her, hand above her.

"Go to sleep; we're leaving early," he said, then put his arm around her. Kit moved closer, tucking her cold hands between them.

Chapter Forty

"WE'LL START AHEAD OF YOU," Witker called over his
shoulder while they walked back to the road. It was early
in the morning, as he had said, and he was entirely serious
about it. They called back and said that they'd catch up.

"What do you think happened to their cart?" She asked,
looking back. Poer and Detin were staying back for repairs.
In the middle of the night, it had broken. One of the deer
was missing from their stock, and a wheel broke off.

Witker said, "self-sabotage."

"What do you mean?" She asked, climbing onto Treyla.
The horse seemed as eager to go as Witker was. He'd gotten up and practically dislocated her shoulder waking her,
then rushed them silently.

He explained, "I think one of them did it. Not only is
that wheel completely repairable, but I was up for most of
the night. I would've heard an animal."

She asked, "why were you up most of the night?"

As soon as he was settled behind her, he urged Treyla
into a casual but quick trot. "I was worried about you," he
said.

Oh. Kit gnawed on her lip, and Witker kicked Treyla's hindquarters, forcing her to run down the road. She moved quickly and for longer than expected. They were both silent the whole time, bouncing with the beat of her hooves until she began to slow.

"Are you all right?" He asked. She nodded. "Are you sure?" She nodded again. "And your bleeding?"

Kit cringed. "It's so strange that you want to know."

"It's perfectly natural," he said.

"Yes, it is, but you're a... well, you're not a *man*, but you know what I mean," she motioned behind her and he laughed. "And I'm not used to men—males, whatever—asking about that sort of thing. Aspen always avoided it and Jassin couldn't get away fast enough. It's odd."

Witker said, "it's just a difference between males and men. We don't run from what grounds us to nature and life."

Her face heated. "Fine, then I did start bleeding this morning, and I feel disgusting. How's that?"

He chuckled and reached behind him, fishing out and producing the ointment she had him buy for cramps. "Where do you want it?"

"I can do it," she said quickly, snatching it from his hand. Witker said nothing, he simply moved his arms so she had more room. Kit opened the tin and smelled the salve, cringing but scooping some onto her fingertips. She lifted her shirt and tucked it neatly under the wrap she'd been stuck wearing. She spread the salve on her stomach. "Can I lean back?" She asked, turning her head.

"Sure," he said simply as if she hadn't been doing that the entire time. She leaned back slightly. There was a difference between this time and all those others. Those other times were just for the sake of comfort or because she was falling asleep, not because she wanted to rub smelly ointment onto her stomach. "You can relax, you know. I'm not going to lash out because you're trying to alleviate pain."

She sighed and leaned back further. Kit closed her eyes and rubbed circles into her stomach and sides, then pushed down under the waist of her pants. "Are you going to tell me about your mood swings?" She pried while pressing into her gut.

When she opened her eyes, he looked just as tense as she was beginning to feel. She tilted her head slightly, looking at his set jaw and his eyes pointed ahead. "Why do you care so much?" He asked as she sat up. Kit still tried to look at him over her shoulder.

She lifted her shirt in the back. "Because maybe if I understand your perspective, I can help both of us."

A twitch formed in his jaw. "I don't need help."

"I didn't mean it that way," she told him gently, "I just think that I should better understand how you're feeling and what you need when your mood changes. Maybe we aren't working together, but we are still together. It would benefit us both moving forward."

He shook his head.

"All right," she said, "I won't bring it up again."

"Lean forward." Witker pushed on her hips gently and took the tin from her. He untied her cloak and it dropped between them. "Let me do this." She turned her head front and thought for a moment. She could refuse. Maybe she should've, but she leaned forward and he put his calloused hands on her back. She rested her arms against Treyla and breathed slowly. Witker's hands were slick with the salve when they began massaging it into her back. "I have no control over it," he told her, "I used to drink this special tea my mother made before she died, and I pretended it helped for her benefit, but I've always been this way."

His thumbs brushed circles over her skin while he held her sides. A tingling, warm feeling moved through her. She grew more aware of every touch. "You just get mad or happy easily?" She asked to distract herself from how good it felt to have his hands on her.

Witker's thumbs went into her pants and Kit's jaw dropped. "If you want to simplify it, yes," he said. She became increasingly distracted by the movement of his hands. They pressed deeply. "I can't always tell when it happens. I just," he let out a sigh, his hands stilling in thought. "I just suddenly don't want to be around anyone anymore, or maybe I want to be around whoever is making me happy even more."

"So what should I do when it happens?" She asked.

"When I drop, it's always three questions," he said thoughtfully. Witker's hands moved up her sides, and he slowly pulled her back against his chest. "One, what are you feeling right now?" His fingers pressed under her naval again. Kit slipped forward and grabbed his thigh, trying not to squeeze too hard. "Two, would you like to talk about it? And three, should I give you space? I suppose when I feel good, just... let it happen."

She breathed in again and adjusted closer. It was the ultimate test of breathing practices. "I'll remember that," she said. He hummed as if to say good, and his hands stopped moving. They remained where they were but stopped. "So what are you feeling right now?" She swallowed, her eyes open as she looked up at him.

"Useful," he answered.

Her brow furrowed. "What does that mean?"

Witker shrugged. "It is... nice to be able to do this for you." Kit became very, very aware of where his hands were. "We are made to want to help when females are bleeding. I enjoy being able to tend to your needs and ease your pain."

She slowly took hold of his wrists and eased his hands out of her pants. "I appreciate it," she said. She sat up carefully and kept looking at him. "Thank you."

"And what are you feeling right now?" He tilted his head.

Her eyes moved. "Icky," she decided.

Witker nodded understandingly. "Is there anything I can do to help you?"

"Tell me why you said you were going to bite me last night," she suggested. He rolled his eyes. "Come on," she turned to see him better. "It will make me feel less icky."

A smirk pulled at his lips. "It is a very old Fae tradition before we learned how to mix our scents," he answered, "partners did it, married or not. It once meant to every Fae that the person belonged to someone."

"And now?" She questioned.

"It is merely a sexual symbol," he told her. Witker looked from her eyes to her lips, then her neck. He looked away quickly. Kit stared at his mouth. She could see the tips of his canines when his lips parted softly.

Her brow furrowed slowly. "Do you... drink the blood or—"

Witker laughed. Her face burned as she turned back around. "We only claim each other," he said when he was done laughing. Kit nodded and grabbed her cloak, tying it back around her neck.

Chapter Forty-One

SHE JERKED HER PANTS up her hips and grimaced as she tied them together. Kit groaned and her feet dragged as she walked to the river. She practically dropped to her knees in front of the soft bank and rinsed her hands off. A bit of blood washed down the river and she cringed at it.

Witker knelt next to her and held out the waterskin.

"Ugh, go *away*," Kit grunted and pushed him. She stood, trudging along the flowing river headed south.

"Human," he said sternly.

She whipped around. "So you're allowed to be mad at me, but I'm not allowed to be mad at you?" Kit asked. He opened his mouth. "No—I don't want to hear it," she waved him off and kept walking. "I don't care that you think this is safer, we aren't moving fast enough any-more—"

Witker followed after her. "Human," he said again.

"I just want to eat something I didn't have to kill," she whined, "like a potato! I miss potatoes, this isn't *fair*."

"We have no idea what Poer and Detin could be doing, this is better than risking them happening upon us on the road—human!" He grabbed her arm and spun her around. Kit glared up at him. "I cannot risk what they might want to do to you, do you understand?" Witker shook her arm just slightly, jarring her like he so often did. "I turned you into an object without intending to, and Poer—" he stopped. Kit looked him up and down as she shifted, untwisting her legs and facing him. "I understand you're tired of the woods and this all may feel unnecessary," Witker said, "but this is what I have decided."

She huffed and looked away from him. They'd been in the woods following the river rather than the road for days. Ever since they left Poer and Detin, he'd been taking far too much care to disguise her scent. Once—and only once—he wiped deer scat on her shoes to try to disguise her scent. Kit had washed the boots, then thrown his into the river he insisted they walk by, and he hadn't tried anything like it since. "Fine," she said.

He released her.

"And if it means so much to you," he said with a shrug, "I will kill something for us to eat next."

Kit laughed. "Right," she said. Kit shook her head and began walking again. Treyla was just downstream drinking from a part of the river that was moving much smoother than the rest of it. "The farmer wants to try his luck at hunting," she said with another laugh.

"You don't think I could do it?" He asked her, following closely. They arrived at Treyla at the same time, and Witker grabbed her bow from its place on the saddle and set the waterskin aside. Kit raised her brows as he inspected it. "It doesn't look too hard," he said. He picked an arrow from the quiver and spun it between his fingers.

"All right," she said as she crossed her arms. "Shoot that tree," Kit said, nodding toward the woods behind him. "The ash tree right there, with the knot on it." Witker turned, looking at the same tree she had. She moved next to him. It couldn't have been more than fifteen yards away. The ash tree was about the width of a human torso. An easy target for someone who'd been practicing for a while.

A smile crept up on his face, as well as a hint of blush. "You don't think I can hit the knot?" He asked.

"I don't think you can hit the *tree*," she corrected. "But please," Kit motioned, "try."

Witker scoffed and notched the arrow. Kit watched, pushing down a smile as he adjusted his stance. He breathed in as he pulled back the string, managing to keep both eyes open. There was a bit of a strain in his arm. Kit watched it shake before he loosed the arrow. It whizzed right past the tree.

"I suppose we won't be eating tonight," Kit said. Witker chuckled and gave her the bow. "Go get the arrow." He was still chuckling as he walked into the woods. Kit smiled to herself as she went to the saddle. She put the bow back in place and patted Treyla's side. "We showed him, huh?" She asked the horse. Treyla bobbed her head and Kit laughed. She looked toward the woods, scanning the tree line. "Do you need help?" Kit called.

She was met with silence.

Kit's smile faded just slightly. She grabbed Treyla's reins loosely and led her into the woods. "How far did it go?" She asked. Kit walked around a thick, leafy bush and found the arrow half-buried in the ground just a few feet ahead. "Witker?" Kit looked around for just a few seconds before her eyes went to the ground. She could see his footsteps in the damp earth by the arrow as if he'd walked right past it. "Witker, it's right here!" She called.

The *snap* of a twig being stepped on made her look left. He walked toward her casually, holding something inside his jacket so she couldn't see what it was. "Look what I found," he said giddily. Kit faced him and Witker took an apple from its hiding place. She gasped and snatched it from him. He looked at her with a swell of pride in his chest. "I may not be able to shoot an arrow," he said, "but I'm quite good at picking the best fruit."

She bit into the apple and groaned, leaning back against the tree closest to her with her eyes closed as she chewed. Treyla came over and sniffed her hand, taking the apple right from her. Kit laughed. "Are there more?" She asked. Witker bent to take the arrow out of the ground. He slid it into the quiver on the saddle and took her hand for only a few seconds, pulling her deeper into the woods to a cluster of apple trees.

"I'm sure plenty of deer are going to be very angry with us for taking their food," he said, plucking a few ripe apples off of the tree. He tossed one to Kit while Treyla went for the ones on the ground. She began munching happily. Kit joined right in. Witker walked over and began stuffing them into open spaces in the saddle bag. Kit took another apple from him before he could put it away. "Are you happier now?" He asked.

Kit nodded with her mouth full. She leaned against yet another tree and took a deep, clean breath.

"And physically?" He asked softly. His eyes moved over her and Kit burned with blush. "Are you in pain?" He asked.

She swallowed. "Not really," she said, "the cramps are going away, I think."

Witker nodded, but he seemed to want something from her. Kit took another bite of her apple and he said, "I want to help you." It sounded far too vulnerable for a male like him. She paused her chewing. "I have never felt such an urge before," he admitted, "and I want to do everything I can for you."

Kit asked, "because I'm all... grounded to life and everything?"

He said, "as my father used to say; there should be nothing more respected than a woman's blood. It is the only kind not born from violence. The only kind born from the cycle of life."

"He sounds like he was a very wise male," she said awkwardly. Kit held her second apple out to him. Witker took it from her hand and nodded as he rubbed the fruit against his jacket. Kit wondered only momentarily if he was wiping *her* off of it. "If you've never felt this... helpful urge before," Kit said, "did you not do things like this for Ralyn?"

Witker laughed, "oh, gods." Kit's cheeks warmed. Witker took hold of Treyla's reins and began leading them back to the river. Kit looked back at the apple trees, silently saying goodbye and thanking nature for the treat. "No, this was Ralyn's favorite time of the whole month," he told her, "she got to boss me around and be as mean to me as she wanted to be."

They moved back into the open. Rain clouds churned overhead and Kit squinted up at them. "I bet you hated it," she said faintly.

"Of course not," Witker said with another laugh, "I enjoyed nothing more than being able to care for my sister and my mother. I am not a man, human, I do not shy from such things."

"So if I told you that going back to the road would be best for me and my monthly bleeding," she said, casting her gaze toward him, "would you insist we go back to taking the easy path?"

He said, "I wish I could help in that way, but no." She groaned and looked away from him. Kit spotted another ash tree on the riverbank. Its bark was colorless and no moss or grass was growing around it. "You'll get your potato eventually," he added. Kit rolled her eyes and took another bite of the apple.

Chapter Forty-Two

WITKER RINSED HIS HANDS to the best of his abilities. Kit watched him scrub river water over his thumbs and underneath his nails, breathing evenly despite her anxiety. "You're a farmer," she mumbled, crossing her arms over her stomach. Kit was sitting on a rock with a warm fire next to her, but she was still cold.

"They need to come out," he said patiently. Kit shook her head. She'd rather her skin heal over the stitches than have him get them out. "Come on, human," he said. Witker stood and waved his hands through the air a few times. She shook her head again. He went to the fire, carefully taking his favorite knife out of the small flames and setting it on his bedroll.

Kit kept shaking her head. She knew that he was right—Kit had started complaining of shoulder pain yesterday, and he'd checked her stitches just an hour ago to find out that it was red and blistering. Sweat and a lack of baths were going to get the old wound infected if they did nothing. And still, she shook her head. Witker was insistent that he remove the ones on her shoulder and the ones on the back of her head. He told her he was prepared to hold her down to do it.

"Infections mean death," he said. Kit bit her lip. "Come on," he held his hand out. Kit whined just a little, looking around her. They were still stuck in the woods, where things were beginning to look the exact same and Kit was sure Witker was going to get them lost. Dusk was beginning to settle around them. The last rays of daylight faded and faded the longer Kit shook her head at him.

He sighed and stood. Witker reached forward and grabbed her upper arms, lifting her to her feet. "We can just wait until we reach Basik and find a healer—"

"Human," he said sternly. Witker walked backward and pulled her along. Kit shuffled her feet and shook her head. He eased her onto the bedroll, where a few rolls of cloth and a cream was waiting for them. "I can do this, all right? You have to trust me."

Witker turned her around so her back was bathed in firelight. She was forced to look ahead of her at the river and the trees beyond it. A bat flew toward the trees to catch a bug. It swooped around quickly. "Do you trust me?" Kit asked faintly. Witker pulled her shirt up her body and eased it over her head. "How am I supposed to trust you if you don't trust me?"

"I do trust you," he said gently. Witker wiped a cold, damp cloth around the stitches. Kit bit her lip hard. "I trust you to keep me alive," he told her, "I trust you to keep me fed, and I trust you to find the heir."

She put her hands together and began squeezing her fingers. "I trust you to keep me alive," she said quietly. "And for you to help me find the heir." Kit hadn't had a nightmare about him killing her after they found the heir in a few days. It was a nice change—most of her nightmares currently were about Poer and Detin. In them, she was alone and she was trapped and they were laughing at her. But at least she wasn't dreaming Witker tricking her, then killing her. "I don't know if I trust you for this," she admitted.

"I may be a farmer," he said, "but I know what I'm doing."

Kit kept her eyes on the bat as Witker shifted behind her. She tried not to pay attention to his shadow. She tried not to look at it at all, even as it grew clearer and clearer the darker it became. Kit looked at the bat. It was joined by a second as the warm blade of Witker's knife first touched her old stitches. "What's it like being a farmer?" Kit asked, "is it hard?"

"It's a lot of early mornings," he answered. Kit groaned when he first began cutting out the thin stitches. She tried to keep her noises of pain to a minimum and focused on not worrying Treyla. The horse was eating out of the bag they had her oats in, looking for the last remnants of her dinner. Kit couldn't alarm the contren horse. "But nothing I wouldn't be willing to go back to," he said. "I found it peaceful. It was rewarding, too."

He began to pull the thin thread from her shoulder. Kit whined low and her nails bit into her fingers. "I never really liked all the work that went into making the tea and things," she said, "I liked drying the herbs, but taking care of them before was always boring and I'd forget to water them."

"Is that why you gravitated toward shooting your bow?" He asked, "because it was a more... immediate reward?"

Kit's eyes moved. "I don't know," she admitted. "I started when I was really young and I think my parents thought I'd grow out of it, but I never did. I loved that I was good at something, and I just kept getting better."

He asked, "did people ever think you were cheating because of your ability?"

She shook her head. "I was never accused of it. It got called my *damned accuracy talent* a few times, but no one ever thought I was a cheater. I still missed sometimes, after all."

"Not entire targets, though."

Kit laughed. "No, never entire targets."

"Not even when you were young?" Witker questioned. His hands continued to move, but the ease of the conversation lessened some of the pain. "I can't imagine you were accurate when you were first starting."

"It was all about my confidence in myself," she said, "if I didn't believe I could do it, then I didn't."

"Like with the prince?" He asked.

It didn't feel like any sort of accusation, but it still stung. Kit looked away from the bats in front of her and her eyes drifted downward. She watched firelight glint off of the bits of whitewater that moved around rocks for a moment. "When the coronation day came," she said softly, "I had this horrible nightmare that I was shooting myself. I'd spent weeks before mapping everything, training how to climb buildings like I did trees, and I knew exactly where I was going... but that had all felt like I was just training for a competition. And then that night the nightmare was so real I couldn't believe I was alive when I woke up."

His hands paused.

"And then I did all of the things I knew how to do," she said. Kit swallowed thickly. "I climbed the roofs and I jumped onto this big tree and I climbed the castle *exactly like* I had in the dream."

"Is that why you hesitated?" He asked, "because you thought it was your dream? That you were going to shoot yourself?"

Kit said, "no, I hesitated because he was a child. I kept asking myself *how did I get here?* and I didn't know the answer. I was younger than he was when the Fae attacked Niverly. My excuses for assassinating him, this kid who'd grown up without parents and had finally come of age... they weren't enough."

"But you fired anyway," Witker said.

"I fired anyway," she agreed with a shrug. "And I should've missed."

Witker continued removing her stitches. He didn't speak again, though he did whisper that he was going to take out the ones on her head. Kit wished he'd make a small comment about it, but he didn't. She wished he'd tease her for the throw, but he didn't. Witker took out the stitches and cleaned up her wounds. He rubbed cream on both of them but didn't bandage anything. Kit sat in the same place. When he removed the stitches from her hand, he didn't look at her at all. Kit stared at the shine of golden magic still etched into her skin, and he didn't say a word.

He put the old stitches in a pouch and stuffed them into the saddlebag so they could be thrown away at another time, then looked over at her. Witker was across the fire, kneeling over their bags and looking at her carefully. "My sominum," he said, "it lets me see into the heart of a person."

Kit nodded.

"I do not see an annoying, murderous girl when I look at you," he told her, "I see someone who is guided by her regret over everything else. It's a dangerous thing to fear consequences, human. It leaves you stranded with your nightmares."

She looked him over carefully. "What should I do instead?"

"I can't be the person to tell you that," he said. Witker pulled their tent out of the pile of bags and began to set it up. "Your inward struggle can only be fought by you," Witker added, kneeling to push stakes into the ground. It began to rain as he ducked his head inside to fit one bedroll in. Kit cringed up at the sky before standing to pick up the bedroll she was on. She pushed her shirt down and went to Witker.

"Can you do it to yourself?" She asked, kneeling next to him. Witker jerked himself out of the tent quickly, his gaze snapping to hers. Kit swallowed her nerves and put the second bedroll in the tent. He was still looking at her as she pushed her hair out of her face and straightened. "You said that you see what makes up a person," she said carefully. The rain pelted just a little harder over her shoulders and head. It dripped down his frozen face. "So do you know what kind of person you are?"

He let out a breath that fogged in front of him and got up again, grabbing Kit's jacket and cloak. "Not the right kind," she heard him say. Kit did not reply.

Chapter Forty-Three

THE FIRST DAY IT snowed, they'd just arrived in Basik. They had managed to stay away from Poer and Detin thanks to Treyla and the trip along the river, though Witker was now pretending he wasn't at all nervous about whatever they had planned. Kit wasn't sure if she could do anything to stop him from feeling the anxieties, and she didn't want to act like they weren't valid. At least he wasn't taking them to the extreme. They'd only found the stables and an inn on the opposite side of town.

She stood in front of Treyla and hugged her while Witker removed the saddle and spoke to the stable owner about payment and how long they'd be staying. "Human," he said. She looked over and glared.

"I have a name," she told him.

"Yes, I'm sure you do," he replied as he counted the coins. "Alas, human," Witker faced her and tossed the coin bag at her. "Go rent a room next door. I'll get us dinner and meet you there."

She looked at the coin and took her bag from him. "How will you know which room I'm in?"

"I'll follow the smell," he answered with a simple shrug. Kit nodded once and kissed Treyla goodbye. Snow fell in soft flurries as she crossed the street. It wasn't quite ready to stick yet, but by the looks of the clouds, it could snow for a long time. Kit walked up the few steps into a welcoming front room. Candles floated magically through the room, and a large fireplace crackled on the far wall. A few Fae children were eating in front of it, paying no mind to anyone else. She could see a kid playing with a bird toy, and her mind went to the child Aspen didn't like.

She went up to a man reading a book at the counter. It was something she'd seen Jassin reading once. The man shared a smile when she came forward and put his book down, marking the page with a dried and pressed lavender flower. Before, she had been reminded of Jassin. Now, she was reminded of her father. Of course, the man looked nothing like her father, but she gazed at the flower for a time.

"Can I help you?" He asked.

Kit smiled again. "I'd like a room for two please," she said and fished out coin as quietly as possible.

The man went to a wall of keys. "One bed or two?"

"One is fine," she said. Kit set the allotted coin on the counter for him and took another look at the dried lavender. She looked over at the children again. The one with the toy shouted for his pa to look, and the man at the counter did, a key in his hand. The two of them looked quite similar, both with the same noses, smiles, and dark umber-colored skin. They must not have been from Basik originally. The child threw the bird, and it flew around the floating candles.

"Very impressive," the man said. He gave Kit the key and directed her upstairs. She went up three floors and unlocked the door to their room, wondering what Witker would do if she walked floor by floor. Would he go up each one, following her scent like a dog, or would he find her in the room first?

It was a larger room than the one she had in Petaki, but she assumed that was because it was meant for two people. She walked over a small brown rug and set her bag by one of the chairs tucked into a round table. Kit ran her hands through her greasy hair and sat. The bed was to her right, covered in pillows, and a fireplace was next to it on the same wall as the table.

Witker came inside. "Only one bed, huh?" He asked. He didn't seem pleased. He walked in with two trays of food and two bags on his back, setting each down as he looked from the bed to her with a critical expression.

"It's less money," Kit said. He rolled his eyes. Witker moved the bags and pulled out the second chair. "We've been sleeping together this entire time. What's wrong with doing it on a bed?"

She watched him sigh slightly. "Nothing, I suppose." His expression turned indifferent, and he turned away from her. "I'll get some wood for the fireplace; you should start eating so we can get to bed early." He began to leave, adding, "and take off that shirt, it wreaks."

"I could say the same for you—wait," she got up and moved in front of him before he could get to the door. She put her hand up. "Did I say something wrong? What are you feeling right now—did I do something wrong with the bed?"

"I just don't see it the same way as you," he decided, his eyes moving slowly around like he was thinking. "I feel annoyed. And I don't want to talk about it. I'm going to walk it off by getting firewood so you sleep comfortably tonight."

She put her hand down, hesitating. "All right. I'm sorry, I should've asked about the bed. I didn't think about any Fae custom or whatever—"

Witker pushed past her and went to the door, shutting it gently behind him. Kit groaned to herself and swiped her fingers over her eyes before taking the shirt off as he told her to. She adjusted the wrap around her breasts, figuring that smelled as well. Kit would have to request they buy a bar of soap for the next leg of the trip through the woods so they could wash themselves and their clothes. She tossed the shirt on the dresser by the door and set her foot on one of the chairs to unlace her boot.

The food in front of her looked delicious. He'd found mashed potatoes just for her, and the scoop on one plate was much higher than on the other. A small pile of salt was on a napkin next to it. Kit smiled and removed both shoes.

The door opened when she got her socks off. She turned, starting to thank him for the salt, but stopped. "Poer," she said cautiously, "what are you doing here?"

"Come to say hello," he said in an amicable, casual manner. Kit stepped away from the table. "Sorry, did you want me to knock?"

"I would've appreciated it, yes," she said, covering her stomach with her arms. Her chest boiled with anxiety, and he glanced at it like he could see panic overflowing inside her. "Where's Detin, is he not with you?"

Poer said, "he is. Downstairs with Witker." He walked closer to her. "I have a question for you, Kitali," he said. She moved to the side again, slowly cornering herself between the bed and the fireplace. *Kitali*. "Does he know that you're using him?"

"What?" She breathed. She took another step back. She had to stop doing that; she needed to move to the side, but all logical, tactical thoughts quickly left her mind. He was going to hurt her. That was the only thing she could think about. Poer dragged his fingers through one of the plates of mashed potatoes and sucked it off. "Poer, I don't know—"

"There's a bounty on your head, King Assassin," he said, "you're worth quite a bit alive. Dead, not so much." Poer pulled a long, sharp knife she assumed was for carving meat from behind his back. "Would you like to come quietly?"

Her feet moved before her mind could catch up. Kit bolted toward the door, acting like she, a human, could be in any way faster than a Fae. He grabbed her throat and threw her toward the wall. The wind was knocked from her chest completely, and Kit started gasping. "I'm not—"

His hand went around her throat again, this time to lift her against the wall. "You're looking for the New Heir, aren't you? Trying to kill him too?"

She gagged, digging her nails under his hand, and he threw her across the room. She hit the dresser and cracked a few drawers before she dropped back onto the floor. Kit coughed and tried to get up. He flipped her over, and for a moment, she saw the damage she would probably have to pay for. She'd broken the dresser with her body. Two drawers were cracked inward, and the handles had fallen off. It felt like one of them was still in her back.

"Now," Poer said. He got on top of her, and Kit resorted to the damsel aspect of 'working' with Witker. He'd come to save the day once again. She just had to scream. She opened her mouth, not even caring to form his name, but got out nothing more than a yelp before he slapped his hand over her mouth. Her head banged against the floor, and she reached up to hit him. "Witker is distracted for now, so it's just you and me."

His knife sliced into her arm. He grabbed her wrist and pinned it under his knee. Kit kept screaming, knowing that there was a likelihood that any Fae on the floor could hear her—maybe a neighbor or someone across the staircase. She hit her foot against the floor.

"I understand why he wouldn't let me touch you now," he told her. He pinned her other hand. Kit jerked around as uncontrollably as she could manage. Tears poured down her face. "But he's not here, is he? And you're such a little human," he said. Poer shifted his hand and covered her nose as well. She gasped and screamed. "I wonder how much you could withstand." The pressure on her face increased. Kit strained, shifting her hand back and forth, trying to pull it out from under his knee. "So many people would pay for this opportunity, did you know that? To be here able to do *anything* to you."

Her head throbbed. He set the carving knife down by her head and moved his fingers along her collarbone. Kit sobbed and grew lightheaded. Poer pulled on the wrap around her breasts and it loosened behind her back. The image of her mother flashed through her mind—the way her skirts had been ripped. The blood. Kit screamed and squirmed, but that only loosened the wrap more.

"How much torture can you take before you break, King Assassin?"

"Not much," Witker said from the doorway. The sound of something heavy hitting the floor came from behind Poer, then the crash of firewood. "She starts crying and gives away everything in about five minutes, then it's just a blubbering weak human in the shell of an assassin. It's disappointing."

Poer was looking back, his hand shifting on her face. "You—" He started before Kit moved and opened her mouth, catching his smallest finger between her back teeth. She bit down as hard as she could. He screamed and cursed, and she kept biting. Poer shifted enough for her to get her right hand out from under his knee. She grabbed the knife by her head and swung at him. It sliced across his chest. He stumbled back. Kit sobbed and flung herself forward, stabbing down so hard that her arm shook. The knife sunk low, but she jerked it out and stabbed him again. And again. And again. Each time, it created a gaping hole in his chest. Poer made gasping sounds. He spit blood. Kit didn't stop.

Witker grabbed her arm and pulled her off. "He's dead," he said, "he's dead, you can stop."

Kit sobbed, dropping the knife. She turned away and spit out whatever part of his finger was in her mouth, and then she threw up.

Chapter Forty-Four

‹———‹

"Up you go," Witker grunted, "come on, human, let's wash your mouth out." He lifted her off the floor and out of her puddle of vomit, dragging her into the bathing room. Kit held onto his arm, on her knees while he hovered over her and turned on the water flow in the tub. "Where are you hurt?" He asked as he wiped blood off her hands and face.

"I bit his finger off," she said numbly.

He paused. "Well, not all the way off, but you crunched up the bone very nicely. It was hanging on just by the threads of skin that didn't end up in your mouth—" Kit vomited again, this time into the tub. Witker sighed. "You held your own very well, up to the end," he said before feeling the temperature of the water. He lifted her to it. "Can't take a bath just yet, so we'll do this…" He put her mouth under, then turned her body and had her shoulders dig into the tub while he scrubbed vomit and blood from her hair. "Human?" He asked, looking down at her.

"Fae," she mumbled.

Witker smiled gently. "What are you feeling right now?"

Her eyes moved. "Shock?"

"Seems plausible," he agreed and turned the water off. "We'll request a different room."

"Two beds?" She asked as he lifted her. Not over his shoulder. This time, he held her.

He said, "I doubt it."

"My body hurts," she told him.

"Where?" He asked as he carried her out of the bathing room. Her head was wet, her hair sticking to her face as he set her on the bed. She looked to the right at the two bodies on the ground—Poer, with blood all around him, and Detin, who Witker had carried up the stairs with a broken neck. Witker took her chin in his hand and dragged her head back to face front. "Where?"

"My back and my head mostly," she said, feeling ready to sleep suddenly. She breathed out and leaned forward, putting her head against his chest. "Thank you for coming to save me," she whispered. The adrenaline moved through her body slowly, fading with each breath she took, until all that was left was a cluster of horrible thoughts that invaded the space around her heart.

He prodded at the back of her head, pressing down. "I have to keep you alive," he said with little emotion.

She straightened, and his hand fell away. He said nothing else. He just looked at her and kept looking at her as she got up and walked away from him. *I have to keep you alive,* he simplified. She grabbed her shirt off the broken dresser and walked to her bag, stuffing it inside and putting on her second one. "Are we going to get a new room now?" She asked as apathetically as she could manage. Maybe Fae and human feelings were more different than she thought—or he was dropping and she couldn't tell—but her feelings were, admittedly, hurt. She could've died or *worse* and would have if he never showed up, but it was just *part of the job* or the inconvenient side of having to take care of a human or *just a means to an end*. Fine. She snatched her socks and shoes off the floor.

"Yes, we need to speak to the owner—"

"Fine," she said, walking out with her things.

Witker followed after her with the other bags and asked, "did I do something wrong as I helped save your life or is this some human version of a monthly bleed mood swing?"

She rolled her eyes, having finished with that four days ago. "Way to simplify it," she replied, skipping down the stairs. "I get it, Fae, it's perfectly clear that we aren't friends, you don't want to be friends, and you don't even want to call this *working together* because gods forbid you work with a human—or maybe it's just me you refuse to work with—but I get it. You just keep doing small things that imply you might care, then snap later; it's perfectly fine."

"This is a human mood swing," she heard him mutter before they reached the main floor.

Kit went up to the counter and put the key down. The nice man smiled again, though concern grew in his expression. "I'm sorry," she began, "someone just tried to kill me in one of your rooms." His eyes went wide, and his mouth opened. "In the process," she continued, "he broke the dresser with my body. There are now two dead people up there, and I vomited a bit. We can pay for the damage but would also appreciate a different room."

The owner leaned forward, looking around, and Kit did too. No one was paying attention to them. "Was it a human or a Fae that attempted to kill you?"

"A Fae," she answered, seeing the owner's son again. He had a slight point to his ears. Kit turned back to him. "The Fae's partner attacked my... friend," she gestured to Witker, and the man looked between them. Witker remained silent. Hovering.

"And are you aware of the reason for this attack?" He asked.

She strained her neck momentarily and spotted a female over his shoulder. She walked to the group of children and... to the Half-Fae. Kit swallowed. "They found us on the road from Petaki and rode with us for a night. One of them, Poer, overheard a personal conversation." The seller nodded along. Kit flattened her hands on the counter. "About marriage."

Witker wasn't touching her, and she couldn't see him, but she knew deep down that he was tense beyond movement.

The seller gave an instant look of genuine sympathy. "Oh, that must've been difficult. And they followed you here?"

She nodded. "We just... Well, Witker and I knew we'd never be able to make a life in Petaki, so we went on the road, but..."

"Dear," he sighed, "I am sorry this happened. Of course you can have another room, no need to pay for that old dresser." Witker came closer. "You must believe there is hope for people like us," the seller said. Her heart squeezed tight with guilt. The genuine caring on his face hurt so badly. Kit nodded, though, and his smile widened. "Then you must have dinner with us," he said. She opened her mouth to refuse, but he called, "Milz, can you close up for the night?" The female went to put a sign by the door. "Come, come meet my new friends."

"Damia," Kit lied, "and this is Witker."

"I am Leo, and this is my wife, Milz," he said. "On the rug holding the bird is our son, Trent." Trent perked up upon hearing his name. He looked over. Trent couldn't have been older than eight. "It's been hard for us, but we must always hope for something better. Blessings be with us, yes?"

Kit nodded, looking away from the boy.

"Milz, could you put two more plates at our table tonight?" Leo asked his wife. Kit could see her stomach bulging from her dress, possibly indicating another pregnancy. "Come around," Leo waved, and Witker put his hand flat on Kit's back, pushing her toward wherever Milz was headed. She took a deep breath, reminding herself that she needed to apologize as soon as they were alone.

He would be angry. He'd scold her. He'd give examples of what she should've said. He'd tell her he should've done the talking rather than her, a stupid human.

Chapter Forty-Five

⟵————⟶

"Damia," Milz said, setting a chair down, "you have a lovely name."

"Thank you," Kit managed, blushing because it was not hers, but her mother's. They'd walked to what looked like a room that wasn't part of the inn. A small fire burned in the fireplace behind Leo's chair with stockings hanging from the nails. It was a short room filled with a table and chairs. Another door led to the kitchen, and stairs were headed up somewhere. "You as well; I've never heard it before."

She beamed at Kit. "I chose it myself, can you believe it?" Milz led her to sit on her left, making her place as she went along. She seemed nervous. She kept twitching. Kit hoped she didn't think this was a trick. It was a lie, but not a trick to hurt them. "When we were young and just falling in love," she looked at Leo with a big smile. Kit looked at him. "We were on the run from our parents and everyone that wanted to tell us we couldn't be together. I don't even remember my old name."

"Neither do I," Leo said and reached for her hand. Kit sat back in her chair, looking at the family. Leo was at the head of the table with his son on his right and his wife on his left. She'd taken the seat next to Milz, and Witker was across from her. He didn't look comfortable.

Milz then took Kit's hand, gasping, "oh, where's the ring?"

Witker choked on air. He put his fist to his mouth, coughing as he looked away. Trent stood on his chair and patted his back. "Thank you," Witker coughed, then cleared his throat. "Thank you, Trent."

"You are very welcome," he said, then plopped back down to wait for his father to scoop quartered potatoes and carrots onto his plate. He seemed giddy for it.

"I've just been waiting for the right time," Witker answered, once again clearing his throat.

Milz made some clicking noise with her tongue and sighed wistfully. "Leo proposed to me in my childhood home the day before we left. He said he wanted it to be my last memory there." Kit smiled at the idea and thanked Leo when he put potatoes on her plate. "Where are you from, dear?" She asked, holding her hand.

"Niverly," Kit answered. She could've lied again and said Calar but couldn't bring herself to. Niverly was where she was from. It felt wrong to deny it. Still, Milz stalled, and Leo accidentally dropped some potatoes off Witker's plate. He recovered quickly, and Witker helped scoop the food into place.

"I am sorry," Milz said softly. "I remember when that happened. That was a tragedy." Kit nodded. "And your family? Is all well with them?"

After a deep breath, she shook her head. "No, they were killed that day." She only glanced at Witker, seeing him look down at his food rather than her.

"Then you must have a great heart," Milz squeezed her hand, "I'm not sure what other human would sit at a table with the likes of us, let alone love a Fae."

"Witker had nothing to do with what happened that day," she said, "and besides, I know that I can't hate every Fae for the actions of a few."

Leo asked, "were you in Niverly when it happened?"

"No, I was in Icar," she answered, accepting a few thin cuts of honeyed ham onto her plate. Milz sighed as if she pitied her, her brows pinched.

"And you got away safely?" She asked.

Kit nodded. "I managed."

Milz clicked her tongue again. "Oh dear. Your family..." She let go of Kit's hand to cover her heart and look at her own. They were silent, Kit's head beginning to fill with the sounds of screaming. Milz finally asked, "well, how did you two meet?"

Witker said, "I threw a rock at her head and knocked her unconscious." Trent laughed, and Kit's eyes widened. Both Leo and Milz joined her expression. "I was very anti-human at the time."

"How interesting," Leo mumbled, his fork and knife poised over his food. Kit's face burned under his gaze, and she focused on cutting her meat. "And then what?"

"I tortured her," he said. Kit kicked him, and he looked at her. "It's all fine now." She glared, making him smile. "She grew on me."

Milz cleared her throat, and Kit shoveled food into her mouth. Trent looked from her to Witker with wide eyes and an open-mouthed smile, gleefully taking in the conversation. "Why didn't you kill her?" He asked, using his fingers to eat a few potatoes.

Witker answered, "there was something in her nightmares that made me realize we weren't so different. After that, I spent time with her, and she changed my mind about things—her, humans, and even a bit about myself."

Kit stared at him, chewing slowly. Witker didn't look at her after he said it, and he hardly looked at her at all for the rest of the dinner. When they were alone in a new room, he immediately went to bathe, and she was forced to sit and wait for him. It was nearly the same room as before, down to the furniture placement, so she had nothing new to look at as she listened to the sound of water coming from behind a closed door. Witker didn't take his time, coming out with a towel wrapped around his body. His skin was slick with water, and his hair was wet. She stared for too long at his muscular form, finding him looking at her when her eyes drifted to his face.

"Sorry," she blushed and stood. She wiped her hands on her pants, unsure what to do next. He scrubbed a hand through his hair and went to his bag, which he'd tossed onto the table before going to the bathing room. Kit took a small step toward him, her mouth open to rush another apology, but nothing would come out. Further blush crept up on her neck, and she left to bathe.

What is wrong with me?

Kit scrubbed her body, hissing softly at the cut on her arm. It wasn't terrible and had stopped bleeding quickly, but the soap still burned. "Stupid," she told herself. She followed Witker's lead and didn't bathe for very long. Instead, she chose to get everything over with and brave the lecture she would receive.

The towel was wrapped tight around her body. She peeked out at him first, finding him sitting in the same place she had been, only he was without a shirt, and his elbows were on his knees, eyes on her, expecting something.

"I should've consulted you first," she said.

"Yes, you should've," he agreed.

She walked out, blushing furiously, and went to her bag. Kit grabbed what she would be wearing. "It was basically the same thing as what you did in the woods," she said, then looked at him. Witker frowned deeply. "You can do the talking from now on," she offered quietly before dressing in the bathing room. She breathed deeply. The lecture hadn't come yet. She wrapped her hair up and went out again. *Maybe it'll come now,* she thought.

"You're bleeding," he said with his eyes on her arm.

"It's nothing," Kit covered the cut, standing awkwardly. She rocked back and forth on her feet. "Are you going to yell at me?" She asked softly. "I feel like you should yell at me."

His dark brows creased partially, his eyes trailing. Kit swallowed nervously. Witker stood and went to the bag first, obviously collecting the roll of cloth he was constantly using on her. She tensed up when he stopped in front of her. He opened one of the creams she'd gotten from the apothecary weeks ago. Witker slathered it on one finger and took her arm, slowly wiping it over the wound. He tossed the cream back to the bags before positioning the cloth, wrapping it carefully around the cut. She kept her eyes ahead. Her breath stalled when he grabbed her chin and tilted her head up. "Do you want me to yell?"

"I thought you'd be mad," she admitted.

Witker's thumb brushed over her bottom lip before he dropped his hand. He lifted her up. "We have an early morning," he said. She held his shoulders, hoping her fingers would pinch painfully into his skin, but he showed no sign of discomfort before he tossed her onto the bed. Kit yelped and sunk into the soft mattress while he blew out candles. The fireplace cast a faint glow through the room.

"Witker," she said as he threw the blankets back. He shoved a pillow between them, looking at it as if it were his only hope. As if they hadn't been sleeping close enough to share morning breath for days. "Will you..." She watched him lay down and face away from her. Kit pulled the towel off her head. "Will you say something more?"

He sighed slowly. "Don't touch me."

Her heart shattered. Kit pulled her lips into her mouth and laid down facing the other direction.

Chapter Forty-Six

She slept through the night.

The *entire* night.

Kit smiled to herself and breathed in deeply, only to find a heavy weight on her chest. Her eyes opened slowly, and Witker grunted, his arm flexing as he stretched. It was tight around her, as was most of his body. At some point in the night, Witker had thrown the pillow off the bed and decided her chest made for a better one. He held her close, covering her more than the blanket did.

He groaned sleepily and shifted his head, slowly waking. Kit snapped her eyes shut and relaxed as much as possible while he slowly removed his arm from around her. Witker breathed in and the bed shifted around her indicating he was about to get up and pretend he never moved close to her at all.

"You're awake, aren't you?" He asked, a hint of shocking amusement in his voice. She opened her eyes. "How long have you been awake?"

She shook her head, "not long." They were far too close. She recalled what he'd said upon discovering only one bed in the room and how he saw it differently. Could this be why? Witker and Kit had always been close; they needed it, but it was different now because they were on a bed. Because he was on top of her. "I slept through the night," she said with a smile.

"I noticed," he told her. Witker sat up and rubbed his face, then climbed out of the bed quickly.

Her eyes trained on his back, which was still bare, and she slowly slid to the other side and stood. She could hear her heart beating rapidly—could he? "Can I ask you something?" She moved around the bed, holding onto the post at the end of it.

Witker said, "I defer to our agreement about not asking personal questions."

She didn't listen. "Do you agree with what they're doing? Milz and Leo, how they're in a relationship." The muscles on his broad shoulders tightened slightly. "I know some Fae would consider Trent to be a... monstrosity. Do you think so?" He was silent, but his head turned partially. She pulled her lips into her mouth and breathed in slowly. "Witker?"

He turned around and walked toward her, making her straighten. Witker grabbed her wrist roughly and slapped something against her palm. He closed her fist and walked into the bathing room. She sat slowly on the bed and ran her thumb over the curved bit of green wood, recalling Witker say they fashioned half a ring from a tree.

Witker returned looking much calmer than he had before.

"Is this supposed to answer my question?" She asked. "Is it your wedding band?" He said nothing. Witker went to their bags and began to dress. "Should I leave you alone, then?"

"No," he said. Witker tossed her clothes and shoes on the bed. "Get dressed. I will only say this once, so do it here, and I won't turn around."

She looked at the shirt. "Seriously?"

"Do you want me to answer or not?" He snapped, taking a deep breath.

"Fine," she said, "then what do you want me to do with your ring thing so I don't lose it?"

Witker answered, "keep it with your necklace for now. I'll tell you when you can give it back to me." Kit nodded and went toward him. He was surprised when she appeared beside him, but her necklace was on the table. She set the half ring down. He jerked his head at her, and she rolled her eyes before returning to the clothes he'd thrown on the bed. She wasn't sure why she was changing at all, seeing as she could very easily leave in what she'd worn to bed, but she pushed her pants down anyway.

"I'm listening," she looked at him.

"You should show the ring to Milz. It will please her," he said. Kit tightened her belt around her waist. "It's not so much of..." She took her shirt off with her back to him as he grappled for words. Kit didn't understand what could be so difficult about answering because it was a simple yes or no. When she looked back, his eyes were on her. Tingles ran up her spine, and she quickly shoved her shirt over her head. "No, I don't think it's wrong. I commend them for braving the world as it is, although I do think it's odd that they chose Basik to settle down. I would've gone west if... if I were to do something like that."

She turned to him when she was covered, clearly seeing he hadn't looked away. A slight cringe was on his face, causing her to wonder if she was what he thought was disgusting. Maybe it wasn't humans and Fae together. Maybe it wasn't even humans. Maybe it was just her.

"Why didn't you say that before?" She asked, hoping he'd realize he was looking at her like she was everything wrong with the world and wipe the expression away.

He didn't. It got worse. His dark brows furrowed even further, and his eyes trailed her as she sat to put on boots. "It's complicated," he replied.

"I don't see what's so complicated about saying you don't see the idea of a Fae and a human falling in love as something evil," she said, "you made it seem like you were going to go on some righteous rant about the mixing of species—"

"*Human*," he snapped.

"What?" Kit straightened. "Can't you just say you'd have no problem with having a relationship with someone like me?"

He was on her in a second, shoving her back onto the bed and covering her mouth when she gasped. "You speak too loudly," he said. She pushed him, but he didn't move at all. A frustrated grunt escaped her while he just sat there, his eyes unfocused and his ears twitching. Witker leaned toward her, his nose brushing hers. She froze. "I would never think to have a relationship with the likes of you," he said, "never in my entire life would I stoop so low, do you understand me?"

She heard footsteps pass by, and her eyes went to the door. The shadow came and went, but Witker didn't get off of her.

"Do you understand me?" He repeated, jarring her head so she looked at him again. He removed his hand from her face and placed it by her head, waiting expectantly. "Say it so you understand, human."

Kit stared at him. Her brows pulled together. "Really?" She whispered. The hard, cold look in his eyes flickered. "Are..." She breathed in slowly. "Are you pretending—"

"No," Witker snapped. His hand turned to a fist next to her head. His green eyes bounced over her face, trying to bring back the hard, cruel look. Kit couldn't read what he wanted from them, even when his gaze lingered on her lips for too long.

She said, "I understand." Kit looked up at him with her eyes beginning to water. Had this hate always been there? Was he pushing it down for the sake of their search? She tried to think back to each small thing that had happened.

Each time he helped her, each time he laughed at her. Perhaps none of it was real. Perhaps *this* was it.

He stayed on top of her for another minute.

"Witker—"

He got off and stalked to their bags. Witker watched as she finished getting ready, but neither of them said anything again. Her heart hammered in her chest as she shoved his half-ring and her necklace into her pocket. She was quick to get away from him.

Chapter Forty-Seven

Kit walked through the woods, knowing that Witker was listening to every step. He'd acted as if everything was fine just an hour after they left, but Kit wasn't letting her mood shift. What he said *hurt*. She wasn't going to let it go just because he felt fine. She didn't. As soon as they stopped to rest, Kit walked away to find a place to cry.

She tried to pretend it didn't matter, but that wasn't true. Kit had struggled for long enough not knowing if she could make friends with a Fae and he destroyed any thought that maybe they were close with a few sentences.

Twigs snapped to her right. Kit stopped. She hadn't brought anything with her—no means to defend herself—but it was just a deer standing there with vines wrapped around his antlers. They were connected to a tree. Kit looked around. The deer huffed and tried to pull away but couldn't.

"Can I help you?" Kit asked. He shuffled his feet around. She walked over slowly, her hands up at her sides, and the stag squirmed harder. The vines snapped, and he ran away. Kit let her hands fall.

She wiped her face again and returned to their designated rest camp. Witker was kicking patches of snow away and setting a bedroll down to sit on for a while. "Who were you talking to?" He asked without looking at her.

"A stag," she answered on her way to Treyla. At least she was happy to see her. "He had his antlers stuck in vines. I was going to help him get them off, but he did it himself."

Witker paused. "A stag was stuck in vines?"

She shrugged, "I'm sure it happens a lot." Kit pet Treyla gently.

He went quiet.

She took a deep breath and looked him over. Witker was sitting, staring at the woods across from him. "Do you think I'm not worthy of friendship?" She asked. Kit stepped away from Treyla to get a better look at his face. "Am I... so disgusting that you can't even imagine being friends with me?"

Witker said nothing at first, and Kit walked toward him. She got to her knees on the bedroll.

"Witker?" She asked.

He took in a shaky breath before he looked at her. "I'm dropping," he said, "and I would like to be left alone."

"No," Kit said, "answer my question."

He didn't.

"I'm trying," she said. His jaw tightened. "So I made a mistake saying we were together with Leo and Milz, but why does that mean you can't be my friend?"

Witker's eyes moved back ahead of him. He released the tension in his jaw. "I have no desire to be your friend, human."

"My name is Kit," she snapped, "it's short for Kitali."

He was silent.

"Say it," she said, "say my name."

He didn't.

"Kitali. I am not some human, I'm not some hunter or archer or—"

"Assassin."

Tears formed in her eyes. "I'm Kitali. I was named after the goddess of soft breezes and spring rains. I am the daughter of flower growers who praised her every day, and they loved me so much." Kit grimaced when he said nothing and pushed on. "They used to sing my name, and when they died, I couldn't hear it anymore, so I shortened it to Kit, but you can call me either. Please—" she inhaled sharply. "Please call me either of them."

Witker got up and started walking away.

"Please, Witker," she said. He stopped, placing his hand against the tree closest to him. "Please call me Kitali, please. I don't want to be some human, and I am no longer King Assassin. I am more than those two things, and you know it."

His head turned only partially. "I do not know your gods, human," he said faintly before he walked away again. Kit couldn't wait for him to leave her sight before she sobbed, sitting back on the bedroll. She covered her mouth and inhaled sharply, shaking.

Chapter Forty-Eight

WITKER WAS GONE FOR hours. Kit waited and waited, eventually choosing to set the camp up because they wouldn't be riding anymore. The sun was too low to go on, so she took off Treyla's saddle and brought her to the river to drink from. Kit washed up, scrubbed her extra clothes with the bar of soap they'd purchased, and tried not to think too hard. Every action was meticulous. She was determined not to think of anything else.

She built a large fire and hunted enough food for both of them, but she only cooked her own. Kit ate with her horse. Treyla didn't mind at all.

"I am worthy of friendship," she whispered to Treyla. The horse huffed and bobbed her head, then sniffed around for more of the oats Kit had been giving her. Kit poured some more and tied the bag off.

The sun set, and Witker was not back.

He's a Fae—no point worrying about a Fae in the woods.

Kit cleaned and organized her pack, then took every arrow out of the quiver. She'd intended to fix a few of them, but Kit set the quiver aside and ran her thumb over each smooth shaft. They had once meant so much to her. Now? "You are the worst thing to ever happen to me," she told them. They reminded her of Witker suddenly—empty and silent. Kit threw all of them away, and they landed at the very feet of the person she wasn't sure she wanted to see anymore. Witker stopped in front of them and looked at her.

"You blame arrows for your problems now?"

"Why are you so mean to me?" She asked faintly. He hesitated. "I didn't do anything, and you keep being mean."

"It's not my intention—"

"Then what is your intention?" Kit stood and faced him. "If not to be mean. I'm not sure you even have one at this point. I think you want to hurt me. You want me to feel like I can't fix what I did. You want me to be just as broken as I was before—it's why you remind me repeatedly that I'm what's wrong with this world."

His brows twitched, but he said nothing.

Kit said, "you only do kind things to confuse me, don't you? With my nightmares, with all the times you were holding me, what you did to help me when I was bleeding—"

He said, "that was real."

"*Why* was it real?" She threw her arms up. "Don't give me any of that Fae and nature shit—why was that real and everything else wasn't?"

"It is about nature—"

"I am a part of nature!" Kit shouted. "I was born, I am breathing, I grew godsdamn flowers!" Her breath hitched, and her voice broke. "Maybe you don't know any of my gods, but every single one of them worships nature just as much as you do. Kitali is a child of nature; *I* am a child of nature."

"You are King Assassin," Witker said, but it came out breathless as if he was reminding himself again.

"No, I'm not," her hands formed fists. "That was a name given to me because of something I did, but if I were King Assassin I wouldn't be here. I never would've taken that arrow off the wall, and I never would've allowed you to hurt me and keep hurting me."

She thought he would argue more. That or walk away again. Maybe he'd leave her altogether. Witker bent and picked up the arrows. He lined them all up and organized them as he walked toward her. Not away. He stopped in front of her. "Are you trying to prove you can be friends with a Fae? Is that what this is? You think that if you can convince someone as hateful as me that you're more than King Assassin you'll be complete?"

A tear fell down her cheek.

"You don't want your nightmares to be real?" His eyes searched hers. "You think they'll go away if the big bad Fae says you're his friend? If you can befriend just one of us you won't be the monster everyone thinks you are?"

"No," she said, her voice cracking. "I do have a Fae friend. Her name is Ralyn." Witker's anger struggled to remain in his eyes at the mention of his sister. His lips parted as he mustered up some more of the hate he so obviously had for her.

"Then why are you so determined to befriend *me*?" He asked.

"Why are you so determined to do the opposite?" Kit replied. He didn't answer. She breathed in. "I don't know what happened to you to make you hate humans so much," she said, "and I'm sorry for it. But *I* am not who hurt you. You don't have to be cruel to me."

"You don't know anything," he said with a shake of his head, "you have no idea."

Kit just looked at him. The anger flickered and the hate that made his brows turn down into such a disgusting scowl began to leave. She thought of Ralyn again, how she said that something as simple as a *thought* could change his mood. Could it change his opinion as well? "You don't have to keep hating me, Witker," she whispered. His brows smoothed over but his lips formed a thin line. A decision rolled over him, tensing his shoulders like he was preparing for a brisk rain to fall from the sky.

Witker reached up and she flinched. He put his hand against her face. "I am sorry for hurting you," he said, "I do it a lot to many people without meaning to. I get angry with myself and make it worse. You're just..."

She stepped back. His hand stayed in the air. "Just King Assassin?" She finished.

"You're too much for me."

Kit's brows pulled together. She couldn't tell if that was worse. "What?"

"I am at war with my mind, and you have become collateral damage..." he said. The arrows clattered to the ground, and he stepped forward. Both of his hands rested on her cheeks. He pulled on her. Kit shuffled forward fearfully. The placement of his hands felt far more intimate than any other time he touched her face. "But understand this," he said, "you are not only King Assassin and you are not only a human. You are more than both of those things, and I know that. I know what you are. I've seen your heart."

"What am I?" She asked. Kit desperately wanted to hear him say her name. She was finished with *King Assassin.*

"You are intelligent and stubborn. You are skilled," he said, "you are worthy of more than me." Witker's eyes dropped down, and his voice turned to a whisper. "You are intoxicating, and I can't have that. I have to hate it."

She reached up and held his wrists. "You don't have to hate me."

"Yes, I do," he whispered, "and you should hate me too."

Kit shook her head, and his hands dropped to her neck. She felt his fingers flex into her shoulders.

"I'm just going to hurt you more," he told her.

This has absolutely nothing to do with me, she realized. He was projecting. He *did* like her. Maybe too much. "Witker," she said, "I'm not going to hate you."

He grimaced. "Please do," he said.

"No."

"Please," he begged. Kit squeezed his wrists and shook her head. He let out a soft breath and mumbled something she didn't understand before he fell against her. His face was against her neck. His mouth was. Kit grabbed onto his jacket before she fell over. Her eyes closed, and her body flooded with many different warnings. "Kitali," he breathed. His canines scratched against her neck.

She wasn't sure what she expected when he bit her. Pain, sure, but not pleasure. She didn't expect the grip he had on her—on her back and her neck. She didn't expect the way he pressed against her. The way her knees would go weak. Kit moaned, and the bite turned into a kiss.

He covered her mouth with his. It only took a few seconds to tear himself away. Kit stumbled, her head spinning, and blinked quickly. He breathed heavily. She reached up and touched her neck. Just a few drops of blood rubbed against her fingers.

"Human blood is toxic," he told her. She looked at her fingers.

"Oh," Kit mumbled, "sorry." She moved to wipe her blood onto her pants, but he grabbed her wrist. "What are you doing?" She asked.

He said, "I'd rather die than let you do that."

She asked, "then what do you want me to do?" He just shook his head. Kit looked at his mouth, at the little bit of her blood on the edge of his lip. She reached forward, and his grip loosened. She touched his bottom lip and swallowed. Witker slid them into his mouth and sucked softly, groaning as if he couldn't decide whether or not it hurt. "Are you all right?" She asked. He nodded. "Does it hurt?" He nodded again. "Then why are you doing it?"

He took her fingers out of his mouth. "Because it feels just as good," he answered. Witker put his mouth back on her neck and sucked harder. Another wave of pleasure spread through her. It ran downward from the top of her head, washing everything else away. Kit pulled on his jacket, and he tore hers off. It was thrown to the side; she didn't know where, and he bit her harder than the first time. Her jaw dropped, and her lashes fluttered. Kit understood the feeling of something being drawn forward by pleasure—she'd finished before, and she knew what it felt like, but she never imagined the feeling of her blood leaving her body would create the same reaction. "Kitali," he moaned and licked up her throat.

"Say it again," she insisted.

"Kitali," Witker whispered. He kissed her, and his mouth formed her name once again. "Kitali," he said, "Kitali, Kitali—" She pressed her lips to his and pushed on the lapels of his jacket. He threw it in the same direction hers had gone.

She stumbled a little, and he backed her up, hitting a tree with a jarring thunk. Her back scraped the bark. "Please," she breathed.

"Please what?" He asked in a low, rough voice. His mouth roamed her neck. He would suck and kiss and nibble and breathe, and she wasn't sure which one felt better.

"Tell me what you want, Kitali," he said. His hands went into her shirt. He gripped her bare waist.

She held his jaw and kissed him slowly. Kit pushed his head back a little and looked at him. He had a drunken look on his face that made her hesitant. "When you said human blood is toxic, what did you mean?" She asked. His eyes left hers, and he looked at her neck. "Witker, what does it mean?" She shook his head just a little.

He blinked quickly as if he was breaking free of a spell. Witker let go of her and stepped back. She sunk down the tree partially. "I'm sorry," he said.

"For what?"

Witker wiped his mouth. "This was a mistake," he said, "I shouldn't have touched you."

"What?" She stepped toward him, and he stepped backward.

"You should cover that," he said and turned away from her.

Chapter Forty-Nine

Kit stared ahead of her, numb. Her fingers tingled, but she was certain that was the only part of herself that was real by that point. Witker was not there when she woke up from her nightmare and dawn was approaching.

There she had been, holding her arrow and aiming down at the prince wondering if this was the right thing, and fired anyway. There the arrow went, soaring down from the beam and into her own heart.

And Witker wasn't there. She sat in the opening to the tent hardly able to see the soft, warm flames in front of her. His avoidance cut like a knife. Cut like cold wind in the snow. Kit reached forward slowly, leaning and leaning until her fingers were close enough to the hot stones around their fire. She held them over it.

"You're awake," his voice said from somewhere behind her. Kit blinked slowly. "Did you have a nightmare?" Witker asked. He knelt next to her and grabbed her wrists, pulling her backward until she sat up again. He held onto her chin and turned her head, looking her over with soft eyes. Snow was in his hair, though it was melting quickly.

Kit watched a drop of water roll down his temple. "Kitali?" He asked.

She looked at his mouth.

"What was it about?" Witker pressed, though he didn't try for long. He straightened suddenly, and his hand fell away from her face. Kit blinked a few times, wetting her eyes and facing front again. She attempted to call back some feeling in her body. Witker looked around as she moved her fingers and squeezed her hands into fists. Chatter came from in front of her. Witker stood and produced his knife. It glinted in the firelight. Kit stared ahead, watching a dark figure move between the trees in a stumbling, unbalanced manner.

"Who is it?" She asked.

"The Rift, the Rift, the Rift," a faint, pitched voice said. It came closer with the figure still stumbling around. It hit a tree and snow dropped onto it, knocking it down. "The Rift, the Rift, the Rift," it said again.

Witker knelt next to Kit with his eyes on the figure. It was slowly standing up. He reached back and grabbed Kit's bow, then an arrow from the quiver. "Just in case," he whispered as he gave them to her. Kit's numb fingers wrapped around the bow. He stood again. "Show yourself," Witker said.

"Are you the Rift?" The figure asked. it stumbled forward again. Kit could see now that it was a man—or had once been. He was wearing a thick coat and had a strange look on his face, as if drunken joy was permanently etched into his tan features. The man's eyes drifted from one place to the next as he crawled forward. "This isn't the Rift," he said, his eyes on the fire. "This is warm."

Kit's brow furrowed. "Are you all right?" She asked.

His head snapped upward. "The Rift!" He shouted, making her jump. It kickstarted the warming of her body. Witker shifted to stand in front of her. "Oh, what a beautiful voice you have, speak again, speak again."

"Witker, what's wrong with him?" She asked faintly. The man giggled and rolled onto his side in a fit of crazed laughter.

Witker said, "you know what happens to people who go into the Rift, don't you?" He glanced down at her.

The man straightened again. The drunken look on his face was gone. "The Rift," he said softly, "what a dark place. You'll never find a darker place, full of war and heartbreak and death." His wild eyes slowly turned back to Kit. "I saw you in the Rift," he said, "I saw you."

"What?"

"On a beam," he said faintly, "and in a town. I saw you in two places in the Rift."

Kit asked, "why would anyone go into the Rift?"

Witker put his knife away and grabbed their waterskin, then the leftover squirrel he'd been saving. He went around the fire and gave both to the man. "Some Fae believe they have the power to heal it," he answered, carefully helping the man drink. His head tipped back and his dark hair fell away from his face, revealing a pointed ear to Kit.

"It's an old legend, that one blessed by nature would heal the Rift. Fae with great power will sometimes go in and face the haunted darkness. They either never come back or end up like this."

"I thought the New Heir healed the Rift," she said, "that's what Ralyn told me, that he'd bring peace and close the Rift."

"The New Heir is blessed by nature," Witker said. He corked the waterskin and opened the bag of food for the male. "The legend is faulty, Kitali, you shouldn't think too hard about it. It's just something people cling to now that humans are on the throne. But when the Rift first split the earth, it was believed that only someone blessed could fix it."

"How?"

He shrugged. The male began to eat slowly. "It's just a story," Witker said. He came back over to her and took the bow and arrow away. She raised her brows for him to go on. He sighed as he settled by her side. "It is believed that the Rift appeared when humans and Fae first battled each other. That the blood spilled ripped open a part of Olyan, and every time humans and Fae fight it gets bigger. With each death, it comes closer and closer to swallowing us whole. *Until*," he said, "someone blessed comes along and heals it."

"Do you think it'll be the New Heir or someone else?" She asked.

"I think that it won't happen in our lifetimes," he answered. "We can hope for better, but after Niverly and the humans taking the Fae Throne... it doesn't seem likely things will get better."

"It grows as we speak," whispered the Fae across the fire. "The more hatred that's spread, the closer it comes."

Kit looked at Witker. "I think the heir will fix it."

His eyes moved over her curiously. "Why?"

"Because I choose to believe that we can be better," she answered. Kit smiled. "Look at us. I'm the girl that killed a prince, you're the male that almost killed me, and we're on our way to make it better already."

He smiled faintly. "We're working together," he said.

"Oh, we aren't *working together*," Kit replied, nudging him with her shoulder. "You're keeping me alive—"

"We're working together," he said again. Kit stopped as quickly as her heart jumped in her chest. She looked at him again, trying to find more meaning behind the words than he presented. Her eyes moved to his lips. "If that's all right with you," Witker added.

Kit was no longer numb. Not in any place on her body. In fact, she was boiling. She leaned forward without thinking, but it seemed that Witker had a similar idea. His nose brushed hers gently, tilting her head upward so he could access her mouth. The kiss was fleeting. It lasted little more than a second before he tore himself away and wiped his mouth on his sleeve. Kit burned with a furious blush. "Sorry," Kit whispered.

The male across the fire got up and continued mumbling *the Rift, the Rift, the Rift* as he walked away.

"Should we stop him?" She asked, looking at Witker.

"No, he'll go until he dies or finds what he's looking for," he answered.

She turned her head the other way to watch the man turn into a muttering figure and disappear into the winter trees. It was as if he'd never been there at all. "What's he looking for?"

"No one knows," Witker told her, "we just know that they're looking for something, and no one ever finds it. We can hope they find it, though."

"That's so sad," Kit mumbled.

He nudged her and she faced him again. "When the New Heir heals the Rift it'll never happen again," he said certainly. Kit nodded once, though she did look back at the male. Even if the New Heir did heal the Rift, he'd still die in the cold before anything could be fixed. "Come on, we should get going," Witker said. He stood and took her hands, lifting her up. Kit fell against him, grasping his jacket. His hands went to her waist.

She remained stuck there. Witker stared down at her, drawing her closer with just the press of his fingers splayed over her hips. Kit breathed out as he reached up to move her jacket aside. The bite mark was scabbing over. Kit could feel the scrape of it as he ran his finger along where his teeth had sunk into her.

He shoved her off and walked away again.

Chapter Fifty

WITKER WANTED HER. HE liked her. But for some reason, he didn't want her to like him. Kit was struck with this new dilemma like lightning. He distanced himself as much as possible for days and days—nine of them. He spent more time walking next to Treyla than riding with her, he went for walks when they rested rather than sitting with her, and for days, he didn't sleep with her. It was almost back to the way it was before, when they first started. The way he looked at her... it was almost the same.

It wasn't until it started really snowing that he came close to her. Kit had been shivering in her tent with her cloak wrapped around her body, unable to sleep because she was too cold when he crawled inside. "It's all right," he said, "come here." He slowly moved over her, finding the right place to lie down.

"Why are you so much warmer than me?" She asked, facing him. Kit put her hands in his shirt, and he draped himself over her. A blanket of warmth came with his body.

"Our temperatures adjust to fit nature," he told her. She groaned. "That's one of our Fae secrets. Don't tell anyone, all right?"

Kit hummed. She sniffed. "I'm so jealous," she mumbled, "I always hated the cold." Her shivering continued. Witker rubbed her arm. "If it were up to me I'd live so far south... that it never ever snowed on me."

"And when the summers are blisteringly hot?" He asked teasingly, "what then?"

She groaned. "Maybe I'll have two houses or something."

He chuckled and pulled her closer. Witker moved his leg around hers.

"Can I ask you something?" She sniffled.

"I'm afraid to answer that."

"If I wasn't King Assassin, would you feel differently about me?" She asked, killing any teasing mood he'd been in before. She could almost feel it leave him. "If I was just Kitali and we weren't looking for an heir or any of it... would you not deny how you feel about me?"

"No," he said.

"But I thought you said you were fine with humans and Fae, just not me," she contradicted, "so did you lie to me?"

"No, Kitali," he said. His hand moved upward. He brushed her hair back.

She lifted her head. "Then why are you acting like it's bad for me to want you?"

Witker said, "go to sleep."

"No," she said. Kit moved partially out from beneath him. "Talk to me. I'm trying to understand you."

"You don't need to understand me, remember?" He said, "we aren't supposed to have these conversations."

She shoved him. He fell onto his side, and she shoved him again. "You don't get to snap at me, and you don't get to drop. Do you understand me?" She asked. He wrapped his hands around her wrists before she could shove him a third time. "You have feelings for me, I know you do, and you know I have feelings for you. None of those feelings are hate—"

"I want you to hate me."

"Why?" Her eyes went wide.

"Because of Niverly."

She blinked quickly. "Why would I hate you because of Niverly?" Kit shook her head, "that has nothing to do with this—"

He asked, "why do you hate Fae?"

"I don't—"

"Why do you hate Fae?" He repeated.

"I don't hate Fae, stop it!" Her voice cracked. "Get over yourself," she said and tore her hands away. She crawled out of the tent and into the snow. "I don't hate you, Witker, I'm not *going* to, and I refuse to hate you just because you want me to. I will not make you feel better about your feelings just because you're afraid to have them."

Witker got out of the tent. He stood in front of her.

"I was there."

Her heart lodged in her throat. She strained as she attempted to swallow it. Kit never imagined three words that weren't *I love you* would make her freeze this way. "You were where?" She asked breathlessly.

He'd paled in the flickering firelight. Snow collected in his hair. "I was in Niverly. I was there."

"What?" She stumbled back and tried to keep her footing. He flinched but didn't move. "You were... what? What are you talking about?"

"It was good money," he winced, "going around and ransacking villages. We were paid to do it. My parents did it, I did it." She watched him swallow as he tried to rush into an explanation of something he didn't want to say. "But when it came to Niverly, we were paid extra to kill."

She stepped back further. "You were paid," she said, unable to hear herself over a roaring picking up in the back of her head. His voice was clear, though. "You were paid... what? You couldn't have been paid—"

"By people like Jassin," Witker said. She shook her head slowly. "Do you hate me now?"

"No, no, you weren't," tears built in her eyes. She inhaled sharply. "You—"

"I killed people in Niverly. Do you hate me now?"

Her entire body ached. It was as if he'd flicked her temple, and all of the nightmares came to the surface, only they were under her skin, *bruising* her and demanding to be felt. "You selfish," she whispered, "awful... selfish Fae." He nodded as if this was precisely what he wanted. Her lip shook, and warm tears fell on her cold face. "You didn't want me to like you, so you chose now to tell me... just because you wanted your life to be easier?"

"Yes," he said, "so now you can hate me. Because your parents are dead, and I could've been the one who killed them."

She shook her head, turned, and left him standing in the snow.

Chapter Fifty-One

Kit stumbled in the dark, completely blind and defenseless, but she would not go back to him and would not answer his call. It had started when he realized she wasn't just walking away to cool off. She was *leaving* him. He and Treyla were following her, but didn't care. She just wanted to be away from him. She wanted him to be gone.

What sort of person did that? What kind of person resorted to admitting to something like that to get someone to hate them?

She tripped and fell against a tree but hardly felt her shoulder connect with it. Numbness had set it. It felt familiar. She was reminded of the numb feeling that took over when she'd been going home. To see the burned buildings and the home she used to live in, knowing the likelihood they were still alive was slim to none.

"Kitali," Witker grabbed her. His hands were so warm, he was so warm, but she still shoved him and kept walking. "You're going to freeze," he told her, "I want you to hate me, not to die."

She squirmed away and broke through the tree line, coming up on a bridge over a river that needed to be crossed. A sign on the post said Niverly, and she stopped breathing. She heard Witker curse softly before he pulled her back into the woods. "No," she said, "No, stop." She pushed him. Kit gasped, "stop, please."

He held her against a tree. "You know you can't just walk in there—"

"I had a brother," she said. He stopped, his hands going slack on her body. "I had a baby brother when I went to Icar for an archery competition, and when I came back, he was dead." Tears dropped down her face. "They choked him to death with a banner he made to congratulate me for winning."

Witker let go of her completely.

"Did you kill my brother?" She sobbed.

He shook his head. "No, I didn't kill children."

"My mother," Kit said. A violent wave ran through her body as she said, "was *raped*." She could hardly see Witker in the dark. He'd gone so still she could've mistaken him for one of the trees that surrounded her. "They went into our home and they r-raped her—did you do that?" She gasped for breath and he shook his head. Kit sobbed, "what did you do? What did you do?"

He whispered, "Kitali, I—"

"I killed your prince," she said, "for them. For my brother, f-for my mother, for my father, and for my friends. And you..."

Witker looked down. "I'm sorry, Kitali," he said, "but you can't go to Niverly—"

"The heir is in there," she interrupted.

His head turned toward the village, then whipped back to her. "You're sure?"

"I wouldn't cross that bridge if I wasn't sure."

He took a deep breath. "Then let's wait until tomorrow."

"No, I have to—"

He pushed her back before she could try to get off the tree. "You are not going to walk into that village in the middle of the night looking for the heir. Do you understand me?" Witker pushed her a second time when she tried to go again. "Kitali," he gripped her arms. "As a Fae to a human," he said, "you are not going into that village tonight. Please do not make me—"

She tried again, and he grabbed her around the waist, tossed her over his shoulder, and began walking back into the woods. "No, go back," she reached back and smacked the back of his head. "Witker, go back!"

He walked until they were back in camp and then dropped her. She coughed, and her chest protested any movement. "I apologize in advance for this," he said to her and bent over.

"What?"

Witker stuffed a rag into her mouth. She screamed and smacked his arms. He completely ignored her digging her nails into his skin to tie the gag around her head. "I want to go as much as you do," he told her. Witker held her wrists tightly. "But not a single human lives in that village anymore," he said, "you know why?"

She continued screaming and squirming while he took the rope he had saved from Treyla's saddlebag.

He shoved her onto her stomach. "Because they kill any human that goes in," he told her. The rope dug into her skin. Witker lifted her again, only a little kinder than before. "If you think having another Fae with you will be enough, you're wrong. Especially at night."

She did not care.

"I know you don't care—Treyla, she's fine," he said, and her eyes widened. She started screaming louder, pleading with the horse. "Don't listen to her. She's going to get herself killed, and I'm stopping that from happening."

She jerked and kicked. Witker did absolutely nothing. He just put her back in the tent.

"Tomorrow, Kitali," he said, "you will thank me when you don't end up dead." She grunted and tried to kick him. "Hate me now?" Her knee landed between his legs, and he gasped the way any man or male would, grabbing onto her as he bent over in pain. "I will," he swallowed, "forgive you for that."

She tried to do it again, and he tied her ankles together.

Chapter Fifty-Two

SHE HATED HIM. DEEPLY. She just wouldn't say it.

Witker slowly packed the saddle, looking back at her occasionally to smile at his handiwork. She glared at him as much as she could. She was beyond tired, having been up with him most of the night trying to escape and get to Niverly. She almost didn't care that it was where the heir was; she just needed to get there.

Going back would hurt, but she was so close now. She could feel him.

"All right," Witker knelt in front of her, facing her now that she was sitting up. He had nothing else to do but untie her, which he obviously didn't want to do. "Kitali," he said seriously, "the Fae claimed Niverly in a way you may not fully comprehend. Every part of it is theirs. Do you understand that?" She looked away from him and he grabbed her jaw, making her face him again. His hand stayed, and his eyes softened. "You need to stay with me—right next to me the whole time. Any of them could snap and kill you. I know how much you want to find the heir, but you need to listen to me. Please."

She shook her head. She did not need to listen to him; she needed to go.

"You can't find the heir if you're dead," he said plainly. She winced, and he reached around her. He untied the gag, taking it out of her mouth regretfully. "Do you understand?"

She ground her teeth.

"The kingdom depends on you listening to me," he said. Witker held her chin. "Please," he added softly, "I can't lose you right now."

"But you can lose me after I find the heir?" She asked. Just like in her old nightmares.

He shook his head with a smirk. "I can't get rid of you now," he said, "It's just a matter of waiting for you to get tired of me pushing you away." He untied her legs and moved around her back. Once she was untied, she got up quickly, only for him to yank her back down. She ended up in his lap. "Kitali," he said.

She sighed. Kit looked at him. "Why do you hate humans?"

His eyes moved over her face. "Some Fae are blessed, did you know that?" He asked, and she nodded. "I was. I was born with wings." Her eyes widened and she looked at his shoulders as if they'd sprout beneath his jacket.

"Humans took them?"

He nodded. "They took my wings and killed my parents. So I hate them. I thought you'd understand that because of what happened to yours."

"I empathize," she said, "but no, I don't hate an entire species because a group of them attacked my village." Kitali's eyes moved around slowly. She added, "I thought I did once, and that's why I killed the Crown Prince... but I think I just needed someone to be angry at so I didn't have to acknowledge my pain."

Witker looked at her lips, his bright eyes trained on them.

"I thought you wanted me to hate you," she said.

"I do."

"Then stop looking at me like that."

His eyes found hers. Witker let go of her and she stood. His gaze burned into her like a brand. Her entire body was on fire. She went into the woods to relieve herself, and the same burning gaze seared into her when she returned. Witker was feeding Treyla out of his hand when she stopped in front of the snow-covered sticks that used to be their fire.

Kit wrapped her arms around herself. "How many people did you kill?" She asked him.

Witker didn't look up when he answered, "eight. People running away, no one younger than thirty."

"How old were you?" She asked next. Kit had been fifteen, but Witker couldn't have been much older.

"Seventeen," he said, "my parents were killed a year later."

She nodded. He still hadn't looked at her. "How much did they pay you?"

He let out a slow breath. She saw him close his eyes. "Kitali," he breathed, "you shouldn't ask that. You don't want to know that." Kit swallowed and took a step closer to him. Witker looked at her. Nothing but pain shined in his eyes, but understanding swam through it. He understood that she needed him to answer. He couldn't spare her feelings. He said, "thirty gold pieces."

Kit felt her lip shake. "Thirty?" She asked faintly.

"I'm sorry," he said, "between me and my parents, it was enough to feed us and Ralyn for months. We were starving before and..." He trailed off, not making any more excuses than that. Witker packed the oats into the saddlebag silently.

"I won thirty gold pieces in the competition," she said. His face fell. "It was the most I'd ever gotten... and you were paid the same amount to murder innocent people."

Witker just nodded. She slid her hand into her pocket and took out his half-ring. Kit handed it to him. He stared at it in his open palm.

Kit grabbed Treyla's reins and pulled her away. She was stubborn enough not to hate him but also hurt enough to. It was a war in her head, just as he had told her he was experiencing. She knew what Witker wanted—he wanted it to be easy. He wanted her to hate him so she didn't have to face his feelings for King Assassin. He wanted her to hate him so he didn't have to process his guilt over what he did. Thirty pieces. Thirty pieces for eight lives.

He walked next to her. "We're still doing this together," he said.

"Do you think it'll look the same?" She found herself asking.

He said, "no, they'll have changed things to suit them better."

She swallowed painfully. "Like?"

"Colors, space," he said. Witker pulled her hand, forcing her to slow down just a little. She felt his ring against her palm. "They've expanded as well. It may look nothing like the place you knew."

"I wonder if I should feel good or bad about that."

"Both," he suggested. She took a deep breath and said nothing else. A knot was building in her throat, and a sour feeling spread through her body. It only got worse when they stopped at the tree line. "Kitali," he said. She managed to look at him. "I can't touch you when we're there, so you're going to hold onto Treyla, and you aren't going to let go."

"You shouldn't be allowed to order me around," she said.

He replied, "you'd be dead without me."

"That's not the point."

Witker chuckled and moved on. "Find the heir, and we'll talk to him together."

"Fine."

She held on tight to Treyla's reins as they crossed the bridge. She was a much better anchor than Witker, and

Kit gripped the leather to keep herself close to the horse. Niverly, the place that used to be her home, did look different. It looked duller. Her memory held a bright, lovely place covered in flowers and color. This was not that. This was uniform. It was plain. It was ugly. Her heart ached for the place she grew up.

"Easy," Witker said softly when she skipped a step before heading down a street she remembered. "Easy," he said again.

"It's my house," she said. It was a different color, and the roof was wrong, but those were the shutters, and that was the door. She stopped in front of it. "It's my house," Kit whispered. "Why does it have to be my house? That's not fair."

"Is he here?"

"I don't want to do this," she shook her head and stepped back, fighting the urge to move forward. "I can't do this, I don't want to do this—"

The front door opened, and a boy no older than ten walked out carrying a little toy bow and a quiver of arrows. He stopped upon seeing the human, horse, and Fae. His pale hand remained on the door handle, and a smile spread over his face before he ran back into the house without what he'd been holding. Kit took another step back.

"You have to do this," Witker said, "you want to, remember?"

She shook her head, "not in my house."

"Is that kid the New Heir, or is it someone else?" He questioned.

"No, I can't do this." She dropped Treyla's reins and backed away. "I can't do this, I can't be…" She breathed in shakily, walking away. Witker said her name, he even grabbed her, but she couldn't do it. She couldn't be there. It couldn't be this village and this house. The heir had to be somewhere else. Not there.

The boy appeared in front of her. He held up a piece of parchment while her heart pumped in her head. It was far too loud. She couldn't hear anything else, but she could see. She could see the parchment held a drawing, and the drawing was of her.

"I don't want to do this," she whispered, unable to hear herself.

He grabbed her hand and pulled. Kit walked numbly behind him, going closer and closer to the door, to the entryway she didn't want to cross. She stopped in front of it and shook her head, but Witker pushed her in. Kit held her breath and squeezed her eyes shut, tripping inside. Witker was behind her, his hands on her waist pushing her forward. She was too dizzy. She would not have made it on her own.

"What are you doing in here?" Snapped a female who did not sound like Kit's mother. Still, it didn't help. She still panicked. "Oh," the female said, her voice now devoid of emotion. "Well," she sounded closer now and asked, "why are your eyes closed?"

"She used to live in this house," Witker answered from behind her. "Her family died here in the Niverly attack."

The female grunted, "how ironic."

She grabbed Kit's wrist and smelled her hand, then pulled. Kit whimpered, walking blindly to wherever she intended. She was forced to take a breath when she got too dizzy. Kit was pushed into a soft chair.

"He's out back growing. It's one of his new magics."

She opened one eye ever so slightly.

"Ever since she came looking, they've started getting stronger," the female said, though she didn't sound pleased. Kit closed her eye again. "The boy will get him. He's been insufferable. I'm almost glad you're going to take him."

Kit felt Witker's approach. She could *feel* him, and she hated it. He stood on her left. "It doesn't look like your nightmare, Kitali," he said, but she shook her head. "You have to look at some point." She shook her head again. He sighed.

The door opened. The sound was so familiar that she bent forward and covered her face with her hands. No, she could not do this. She could not open her eyes. She found the New Heir. He was there, so now she could leave. She could go. She did not need to do anything else.

Still, his hands were on her knees. They were petite and boyish. He had to be young. He was the replacement for the one she killed, so he had to be the same age or younger. "Kitali?" He asked, "Kitali, I've been dreaming of you."

Kit sobbed, exhausted, and he pulled her hands off her face. She sniffed and looked at him. It was not the same face as the boy she murdered. His hair was the color of straw, and his eyes were a dark blue, nearly black. Freckles covered his cheeks, and a smile was on his soft lips. He couldn't have been older than sixteen.

"I know how to be crowned," he said with the same smile.

Chapter Fifty-Three

THE TEA TASTED LIKE a Fae grew it, not a human. Kit stared at the cup and shivered. There was no longer an ache to go, but the ache for something else had arrived. It pressed into her and burned. She could not fight it. It would not leave, not even if she ran from the house and disappeared forever.

"You want to kill her?" Witker asked for the third time.

The New Heir, Masine, said again, "it would not be her final death."

"But you would be *killing her*," he said with far more seriousness than he had the last two times. She put her head against his arm and closed her eyes. They'd made it to a table where Masine told them how he wanted to be crowned.

By killing her.

Kit had no desire to look at many things. She feared finding too many similarities between this home and the one she'd known so long ago. It was hard enough that Masine's family kept their dining table in the same place Kit's had. And that they had herbs drying on the far wall.

And that the taupe color in the kitchen was still the same. She was terrified that if she turned her head to the right she'd find a dent in the countertop from when Kit had dropped a pot full of cold water accidentally. Or looked in the corner, where they kept their broom. Or looked at the wall in the room behind her to find that the veil wasn't there.

She just pressed her temple further into Witker's arm and listened. Because of the violent way Kit had prevented the last heir from being crowned, a violent way was needed to crown the next one. A life for a life. Blood for blood. She would be struck in the heart with one of her arrows, and her death would save the kingdom.

Witker wasn't happy, though she didn't know why. He seemed to believe that she wouldn't come back.

"Where is the closest sacred ground?" Kit asked.

"No," Witker said, "no, he needs to tell us how he's going to guarantee you'll come back."

"Nature will bring her back," Masine said firmly.

His mother set a plate of tea cakes on the table. "It wouldn't be so bad if King Assassin remained dead," she said matter of factly. Kit looked at her. She looked like a kind person. A sneer curled on her lip, and Kit tore her eyes away. She reached for a cake.

Witker smacked her hand and shoved the cakes away forcefully. Masine caught the plate before it could slide off the table while Witker said, "get her something she can eat, or get her nothing at all."

The mother walked away.

"Were there grapes in them?" Kit asked, leaning back in her chair with a heavy breath. Masine ate a cake, so they weren't poisoned. He sighed happily.

"No, but there are foods that humans can't eat," Witker told her, "things that could kill you or make you sick, things that could inebriate you or make you unable to say no."

"Like the Fae dance legend," she said, and he nodded. She frowned. Kit looked at Masine. "So nature will bring me back? How?"

"We would be on sacred ground."

"What sacred ground?" Witker snapped. Kit turned her head to him. He looked ready to grab her and leave. He was far more tense than she'd ever seen him, making her wonder what he knew that she didn't. Maybe there was some other Fae legend she didn't know.

"The burial ground," he answered, "where the bodies of those lost in the Niverly attack are. Nature cared for them and blessed the ground so they may be healed after death. It's sacred ground; that's why no one has built on it."

"You want me to die over the graves of my family?" She asked. He nodded. Kit's eyes moved. Behind her was the living room where she found her family. Her mother, lying dead on her stomach with her dress ripped around her legs. Her brother, his face swollen and the color of a bruise. Her father, with his intestines outside of his body. "Fine," she said quietly, "when?"

"No," Witker turned and faced her.

"It's not your decision, Witker," she said, sliding out of the chair. She looked at Masine again. "When?"

He said, "we can do it tomorrow morning. Just before the year ends. Would you like to sleep here—"

"I am not sleeping in this house. I will be in the woods." She walked away quickly, leaving the house faster than she entered. Treyla was still there, waiting, so she mounted and turned her around. "Come on," Kit urged her forward. Treyla stomped once before she moved into a calm walk.

Kit's eyes drifted slowly. To her right was once the building she did most of her schooling in. Where she learned to write, to read in her poor, unmanageable way. Her neighbor had been her tutor. Now it was replaced with a long neutral-toned building where she could hear some sort of commotion coming from. Perhaps that was where they processed their tea. Fae growers and their magical growth remedies...

A shout came from her left before something wrapped tight around her neck and yanked her to the side. Kit choked out a yelp before she hit the ground. She coughed and reached up slowly. Tears blurred her eyes, but the texture of rope was familiar.

Kit was yanked again. Treyla screamed as she was dragged away. The horse trotted after her, hot breath blowing from her nostrils.

Her ability to move came back gradually. Kit reached behind her, grabbing a taut rope as the laughter of Fae echoed in her ears. She slid to a stop in a patch of snow. Three Fae looked down on her—two males and one female. "What..." Kit started hoarsely. "What are you doing?"

A laugh burst from one Fae that made her jump. He grabbed the rope behind her head and lifted. Kit gasped and dug her fingers underneath it. He moved close to her. Kit couldn't bring herself to think he was beautiful. There was something *odd* about him that she couldn't place. His mouth was wider than she thought possible, and his pale skin had a strange glass-like shine to it. Her skin crawled. "What are *you* doing here, little human?" He asked, "don't you know your kind doesn't come here?"

"I was with... Masine—"

"Oh, you were with Masine?" He nodded with another, sicker laugh. "The growing boy?"

"I—"

He laughed sharply and another hand came up to wrap around her jaw, jerking her head roughly to the side. The female was there. Her cheeks were bright and pink. She smiled with sharp, deadly teeth. "I hate to admit it," she said, though she wasn't speaking to Kit, "but this one is a pretty human, look at that face."

They did. Three Fae looked at her, assessing as if she were a painting and they needed to judge the brush strokes.

"We never get pretty humans coming here," the female said. Kit grabbed her wrist. The female squeezed her jaw hard. "It's usually ugly ones trying to get into our growing buildings, but you... you were here for *Masine*." She laughed. Kit tried to pull her hand off. She kicked her feet weakly. "What did you want with Masine?"

"T-the heir," she gasped, "he's the heir—"

The female released her jaw and Kit fell back.

"I know who this is," said the third male. Kit's eyes went wide. She crawled backward. "Our King Assassin." He grinned.

Kit pulled the rope off of her neck and turned quickly, running between two stone houses. Arms wrapped around her tight and swung her around. She smacked against the wall of the house on her left and hit the ground again.

"Oh, what I wouldn't give," the third male said. He lifted her to her feet. "To see what you look like *dead*, King Assassin."

She screamed and his hand smacked against her mouth, bashing her head against the stones behind her. Kit grunted and her eyes blurred momentarily.

"Haverd, do you have any of those berries?" The male asked. Kit blinked hard. She watched the transfer of something between hands—from the odd-looking male named Haverd to the one holding Kit against the wall. They looked similar, though the one holding her looked less odd. His ears were sharper, too, and he had a broader waist. He shoved a berry between her lips. "If you don't swallow this I'm going to spill your insides onto the earth right here," he said.

Kit breathed heavily. She knew very little of the old Fae dance legend. She knew it used to happen a lot in Calar. She knew that humans would be brought into the castle and given something, then they would spin and dance until they died in West Ball.

She wasn't sure if that was what this berry did, though, or if it was as Witker told her—something that would make her unable to say no, something that might kill her, or something that would inebriate her.

Haverd handed the male a knife and Kit swallowed. Her throat burned as they laughed and someone shouted her name. Vines flew through her vision. A Fae screamed. Kit felt like she was spinning in circles as she slid down the wall.

Witker appeared in front of her. Her brow furrowed. Where had the other Fae gone? "What did they give you?" Witker asked desperately, "Kitali, tell me what you ate so I can fix it!" He grabbed her face roughly and shook her head. "Kitali!"

She blinked hard and grunted, "a berry?"

"A berry, oh thank blessings," he gasped. His head fell against hers. "A berry, just a berry, it's all right—you're all right."

"What does a berry do?" She mumbled. Kit was hot all over. The same burning that was in her throat began to move into her stomach.

"Here," someone said. Kit couldn't turn her head. Witker was holding her too tightly. He grabbed something from someone. Kit's eyes blurred before she blinked a few times.

"Look at me, Kitali," Witker said softly, "look at me, hey..." She moved her eyes to him and he smiled gently. "You're going to feel sick for a few minutes, all right?" He said, "and then you're going to feel really good."

"I feel sick now," she told him.

Witker nodded. "Here, drink this," he said, showing her a flask. He touched it to her lips and Kit opened her mouth, taking the cold, sweet drink down her throat. It eased some of the burning and made her close her eyes. Kit sighed. "Good, very good."

"Why would the Fae want me to feel good?" She asked quietly, "I thought they wanted to kill me."

He brushed his thumb over her cheek. Kit leaned into his hand. "Because in a few minutes you're going to do whatever I tell you."

She said, "that sounds fine."

Witker said, "it wouldn't have been fine if they were the ones telling you what to do, Kitali." She blinked slowly, unable to tell what he meant through the fog in her mind.

Chapter Fifty-Four

KIT FELT THAT SHE should be doing something. She was idle, like a worker on their first day of the job waiting to be told what to do. Kit blinked slowly and turned her head. Witker was building a fire. He had his back hunched and his hands were moving.

They were back in the woods. Kit wasn't sure what she should be doing in the woods. Not even Treyla seemed to know what she was doing—the horse kept walking around and sniffing the ground, probably as bored as Kit was.

Witker had carried her out of Niverly and laid her on her back. Kit had been in the same place ever since. The sick feeling faded after a few minutes of her lying in one position, and she was only slightly afraid that it would return if she moved.

"Witker?" Kit asked.

He hummed and looked over at her. There was something far too gentle about how he looked at her.

"What am I supposed to be doing?" She asked him.

"We're waiting for the berry to pass through your system," he answered, "you just lay there, all right?"

She turned her head back to where it had been before. Kit looked at the branches above her, counting each one until her eyes began to blur over. "Witker?" She asked and turned her head. He looked back at her again. "How long does it take for the berry to pass through my system?"

He smiled. "Are you bored?" Witker asked. She nodded. "All right, come here," he said. Kit sat up and crawled over, sitting at his side. "The berries are called *Svee*. We use them as a medicine. To me, it would relieve pain and help me get to sleep. We learned that it could make a human do whatever we want them to a long time ago, and ever since we've been abusing it."

"Like the dances in West Ball?"

Witker nodded. He shifted away from the fire and Kit followed him, keeping to his side. "For those they used wine made from the berries," he explained, "when fermented, the berries take on a more potent effect. It lasts longer and is stronger. I could tell you to dance and you would, but you also wouldn't be able to stop."

She asked, "are you going to tell me to dance?"

"No, Kitali, I'm going to wait for the berry to pass through your system so we can talk about what Masine wants."

Kit's eyes moved. "Why can't we talk about that now?"

"Because you're inebriated," he answered.

She went quiet. *Inebriated* was a horrible word that she hated deeply, but she wasn't certain what else to call it. She'd been drugged, but was there a word for what she was feeling now? "Would you like to know something about me?" She asked and he nodded, giving her his attention. Witker didn't look annoyed with her at all, as she expected he would. An inebriated human had to be an annoying one. "I like being in control of myself."

His eyes moved over her. "And you aren't now," he said, "does that bother you?"

Kit said, "when I was a child there was this game I played once with my friends... a trust sort of game. You play in teams of four, and one person on each team is blindfolded. There are tasks to complete that the blindfolded person has to trust their team to help them."

He nodded slowly. "Did they do something bad to you?"

"They tied rocks to my shoes and pushed me into the river," she told him. Witker blinked rapidly and looked toward where the river would be. It rushed quickly next to Niverly, twisting around a small bend before it filled into the lake by Mossarai. "I almost drowned," Kit said, "because I gave up control of myself. Afterward, I stopped doing things that would make me lose control. I even stopped taking any sort of sleep aid because I didn't want something to *make* me go to sleep."

"I'm sorry that happened to you, Kitali," he said.

Kit looked at his mouth for a few seconds before she asked, "what would the Fae have done?"

He took a deep breath. Witker looked away from her, reaching forward to prod at the fire. Kit watched his hands.

"I imagine they would've done whatever they wanted to you," he said.

"They called me pretty," Kit told him, "before they found out I was King Assassin... they called me pretty."

Witker moved his arm around her gently. Kit leaned into him. She felt better *doing* something than she did lying down. It still felt wrong that she wasn't doing more. "Would you like something to do?" He asked her and she nodded quickly. Kit smiled as she looked at him. The dizzy feeling made him look brighter and prettier. "Tell me something good about you."

"I'm a very good archer," she told him.

"I know that, tell me something different," Witker said. Kit's brow furrowed. "You aren't made up of just one thing, Kitali, you aren't *just* an archer."

"I like it when you call me Kitali," she whispered. "It sounds like music when you say it." Witker looked at her carefully. Kit looked at his mouth again. "I don't want to hate you, Witker," she said, "I'm tired of hating people."

He shook his head slowly. "You're too good for me," he said, "there's something about you that's... too much."

"I'm not made up of just one thing," Kitali said softly, "I'm not *just* King Assassin. Your sister was the first person who told me that, you know. She was the first person ever to tell me that I'm more than that."

He said, "Ralyn's good at seeing people for who they are. She looked past King Assassin faster than anyone in the whole kingdom, huh?"

"Maybe you should think like her," she suggested, "and look past it. Past King Assassin, past Niverly, past human or Fae… and just see me."

"I do see you," Witker said, "and when I look at you I see someone who deserves better than me."

Kit shook her head. "You know my mother used to say that I should be with someone who makes me feel safe at night. *I* don't even make me feel safe the way you do."

He clicked his tongue against the roof of his mouth and looked away again. "You're too inebriated for this conversation," he told her with a shake of his head.

"I thought I'd be acting different than this," she admitted, "I feel almost the same, everything is just really pretty and bright and I want to do everything you tell me to."

Witker nodded. He said, "you only ate one berry. If they'd given you more you'd be acting more impulsively and you'd be… *drunker* I suppose is a good word."

She asked, "how impulsive?"

"You'd actually be trying to kiss me instead of just staring at my mouth," he said, "you'd be begging me to bite you, too, so we should be very glad they only gave you one berry."

Her face flushed a bright red and she turned away from him. Kit pulled her legs up against her chest. "That felt strange," she admitted, "very, very strange. I didn't have control then, either, but I didn't want it, it was the strangest thing to ever happen to me."

"I could think of stranger things," he muttered. Witker reached for her hand and touched the healed cut where king's blood had once been. The gold was gone, replaced with a simple, smooth scar. "This, for example."

Kit shook her head. "No… I think the biting might've been stranger."

It took another few hours for the berry to stop making the world pretty. Kit hated watching it fade. She was reminded of home—of how Niverly had been bright and alive and pretty, and now it was neutral and not hers. The more she blinked the less she wanted to look at anything at all, until she was staring at a plain fire without any desire.

Witker handed her the flask again. She took it, running her thumb over the smooth metal. "What is it?" She asked.

"Tea that Masine made for you," he answered, "it'll help you feel more like yourself again."

She drank slowly.

"How are you feeling now?"

Kit gave him the flask back and looked at him. She could only hold his gaze for a few seconds before she turned her head away. "I haven't been *inebriated* in a long time," she mumbled. He let out a single soft chuckle. "The last time I got horribly drunk I defaced my statue and woke up the next morning covered in paint."

Witker laughed louder. "You have… a statue?"

"It's so ugly," she said, "but it looks just like me. That's the worst thing, because it's so obviously me that anyone in Calar who saw me would know exactly who I was."

"I'd like to see it," he said.

She smiled a little and looked at him. "Maybe when all this is over you can come back to Calar with me and I'll show you."

He had been smiling, but it faded. Witker looked away from her.

Kit took a deep breath. "My Niverly was so much better than that one," she whispered. His hand moved against her back, grounding her like it had before they reached Petaki. "It was warmer and brighter and smelled sweet all the time."

"I am truly sorry, Kitali," he said. She looked at him again. Witker did not look away this time. His eyes watered and he repeated, "truly sorry." She inhaled sharply and crashed against him, wrapping her arms tight around his middle so she could hide her sobs in the heat of his skin and never be judged for them. Witker held her closer then ever. He said nothing but sorry for the rest of the night.

Chapter Fifty-Five

THE NEXT MORNING, WITKER'S hand was inside her shirt, but it was more than that. His head was once again on her chest, but it was more than that, too. It was that her stomach was exposed. It was that she could feel his fingers in the waistline of her pants behind her. It was that he was holding her, and they were both completely awake. He didn't pull away. Kit looked at him carefully, her head at an odd angle.

"What are you doing?" She asked, her throat raw.

"Listening to your heart beating," he answered quietly, "it's strong for someone who wants to die."

Her brow furrowed. "I don't *want* to die. I just wouldn't mind if I did."

He lifted his head. "That's the same thing when you're willingly stepping onto a graveyard to be shot in the chest with one of your own arrows."

Kit wished they could return to the day before, when things were softer and he wasn't angry for reasons he had yet to explain.

"What kind of wings were you blessed with?" She asked, quietly redirecting the conversation as she reached around him as if she could feel them. "Why didn't I see a scar? I've seen you without a shirt so many times."

Witker said, "they're glamoured."

"They're still there?" She moved her hand up and down his spine to search for them. There was that word again—glamour. It truly must've meant something hidden, because she couldn't find wings anywhere on his back. He smiled softly. "Can I see them?" She sat up, pushing him off in the process. "Please? I've never seen a Fae with wings before, I always wondered—"

"They aren't that exciting," he said.

Her eyes widened. "Are you serious? Witker, they're *wings*."

"I can't use them," he argued, "I can hardly move them. I don't feel them half the time."

She bit her lip and pleaded silently. Witker scoffed as he rolled his shoulders and straightened. She wondered if he was somehow shrugging off whatever glamour was like she would a coat. She watched him remove his jacket and shirt, then turn around. She gasped, *"dragonfly,"* like a child. "They're amazing," she said. Kit touched his lower back and felt a slight shiver underneath her fingertips.

There were four places where his wings should've been. Each of them lay on his upper back between his shoulder blades, like a dragonfly's four wings.

"How would they support you?" She asked, "would they be strong enough?"

"If they were still there," he said, "they would've grown with me." They were only remnants of dragonfly wings. Scars slashed across his back, and they were torn to pieces. "You can touch them," he said, "I don't mind."

The wings were flat against his back, limp without use. They looked like they should've fallen off years ago but were just as stubborn as Witker and refused to. She reached for the closest one, pinching the thin wing between her fingers. She pulled on it just slightly and it trembled. She let go. "They're amazing," she said.

"I was thirteen when they cut them," he told her, "I was jumping off this waterfall and gliding when they grabbed me. They were drunk and rude and..." He sighed. "They took what they cut off. I used to wonder what they did with them."

Kit pulled on his shoulder, and he turned slightly. "I wish I could've seen them when they were whole," she said. He just nodded. "So this is why you hate humans?" She looked at his back. "The loss of your blessing."

"And my parents, but yes," he said. Witker took a deep breath, and a shiver moved through him. Suddenly, the wings disappeared. "And you hate Fae because of the loss of your family. Or—you don't hate them. You refuse to because you're stubborn."

"I don't see the point in holding that much hate inside me. It seems too heavy," she said. Her voice softened considerably. "But you keep trying to make me hate you."

He looked at her lips.

"That silly war in your head," she continued. Kit shifted closer. "I don't want to be in the middle of it." She lifted her hand and held his chin. "Witker, you can have feelings for me. It'll be all right if you do."

He began to shake his head but stopped himself. "And Niverly?"

"You should never have used it as some sick way to hurt me, and I expect a great apology for it."

Witker didn't nod or shake his head, either. He just said, "I want you to live, Kitali, and I'd like to be part of the life you create for yourself."

She leaned forward and kissed him, unable to stop herself. Many things hurt, but at least this one thing didn't send her into some depth of despair the way everything else did. She could sit there and not worry about anything else because Witker was grasping the back of her neck and pulling her closer. He was breathing in deeply. He was shifting.

Kit straddled him, gripping his shoulders. He pulled on her lower back. "I'll live," she told him, and he untied her cloak and took her jacket off. Witker kissed her jaw. "I promise," she whispered. He flipped her over. Sometime between the crying and going to sleep, Witker had gotten out a bedroll. They'd never set up the tent and hadn't taken

Treyla's saddle off because he wouldn't let go of her for long enough.

He was on top of her. Witker kissed her deeply, pressing her head back into the bedroll. "Don't do it," he said, "please don't do it."

"Why not?" She asked. He kissed her throat. She swallowed and moved her fingers through his hair. Witker breathed a soft, pleading moan against her skin. He brushed his lips over the scabs from his bite mark. "Witker," she breathed.

"Please," he whispered. She pulled his head closer, and Witker broke open the scabs with just one quick movement. He moaned her name and sucked hard, biting down when not enough blood broke the healing skin. Kit grew dizzy and light. She scraped her fingers down his chest and gripped his hips.

Kit had never considered that something supposedly violent could feel so good. He was biting her, and yet she wanted him to do worse. She wanted him to find new places to touch, to kiss. Kit found herself begging for it like the first time, when he told her to say what she wanted. He didn't ask this time, he just did it. Witker let go of her neck with blood on his lips and a groan in his throat. He covered her mouth in it and pushed her shirt up her body.

"Don't leave me," he said when it was off. Kit shivered in the cold air. "Promise me," he said, "say you won't leave here, and I'll do whatever you want."

He pulled on her hips and kissed her bare chest. Witker left blood in the wake of his mouth. He moved down, repeating how much he wanted her to promise him something. Kit was too dizzy to focus. She was too warm. He licked and sucked on the underside of her breast, and she put her hands over her head.

"You have to stay," he said.

Witker had his mouth around her tight nipple when she opened her eyes. "I have to go," she said. Morning light shined through the trees.

He lifted himself up and kissed her again, holding her down with his body. "Please, Kitali," he prayed into her mouth, "please stay."

She shook her head, "he has to be crowned before the year ends tomorrow, I have to—"

Witker looked down at her. Tears were in his eyes. "Kitali," he whispered. His lips shook, and she tried to look past the pleasure coating he'd placed upon her with a single bite.

"What's going to happen?" She asked.

He seemed to struggle to get the words out. Witker reached up and brushed his thumb over her cheek. "You're going to die," he told her with a crack in his voice, "and nature will decide whether you should come back."

"Masine said I would," she told him.

"That isn't how it works," he said. Witker swallowed and kissed her again, far gentler than before. It stained her mouth when he lifted his head. "Nature will decide if you're worthy of returning to this world. It will use your nightmares to do it."

She paled as she sat up. He let her, holding her face while he sat on her legs.

"The kind of person you are is reflected by the things that keep you up at night," he told her, caressing her as if his hands would be able to keep her together. "If you go, if you do this, you will relive them."

"You think nature won't bring me back because of my nightmares?"

He shook his head. "I think you won't. I think it'll be too much for you. You're too haunted, Kitali, and haunted people don't come back."

Her heart was in her throat. The frigid air suddenly didn't affect her. She was on fire, burning with an intense heat. "Can you give me a reason to come back?"

Witker's eyes moved over her. He swallowed. "When you were angry with me after Poer attacked you and you dismissed me, I was upset. I didn't want you to say what you said because it wasn't true. I do care, and I did... The next morning, when you asked if I thought humans and Fae could be in relationships, it was the first time I thought about you that way. I'd been ignoring it before, the feeling of wanting you."

She nodded slowly. "You thought about loving me."

"I did," he said softly, "and I wanted to get rid of it, so I thought getting you to hate me would make it stop."

"But I don't hate you."

Witker pulled her in for another kiss. She felt the clash of their teeth and his intense desperation. "Please don't go," he said.

Kit grimaced. "I have to do this. And I will come back."

He stood suddenly and stumbled away from her. "I can't stand back and watch you die, Kitali," he said faintly. He wouldn't look at her anymore. "If you go, I will not follow you."

"Witker..."

"Say you won't go."

She didn't. Seconds moved between them. They ended with him leaving her half-naked on the cold ground, no longer warm in any way.

Chapter Fifty-Six

MASINE WAS A SIXTEEN-YEAR-OLD about to become a king. It seemed to settle on his shoulders now that they were standing in a graveyard. He had a nervous look to him while Kit stared at the wasteland before her. The land was overgrown and in patches. The curved stones were already cracked and faded. Still, she knew where her family was buried. Where she and Jassin said their goodbyes. He stood with her over their graves. He held her and protected her and...

How would her father feel about this?

She reached into her pocket and took out the necklace, squeezing it tight enough for it to pinch her fingers. Her father would hate Jassin for what he did. He would have to. He would not be her father if he didn't. Her soft, kind father who grew flowers and danced with her mother to songs only they knew. He would not tolerate Jassin's betrayal.

Her hand opened. She looked at the necklace. The image that had once been stamped on it was unrecogniz- able—years of her father touching it as he prayed, then Kit doing the same, had erased it. But she knew. *Kitali*. The god she was named after.

"Ready?" Masine stood in front of her. It was just him and his mother, no one else. There was no crowd like there had been last time. No beams or windows to crawl through. No seats, no nice clothes. She wasn't in black, and she wasn't the one holding the bow. The arrow was hers, but she wouldn't be firing it.

"If I don't come back," Kit said, "can you bury this with me and my family?"

He looked at the graves as if he knew exactly where they were. Maybe he did. He knew all about her, why not where she buried her family? Masine turned back to her and closed her hand around the necklace. "You'll come back," he said, patting her knuckles, "I know it."

She looked at the necklace again. It wouldn't be so bad if she didn't, as long as she didn't get trapped in her nightmares. "What If I don't want to?" She asked him. His brows pinched together. "I didn't care if I died the first time, why should I care now?"

"Because there are still things you need to do with your life," he answered.

"Like what?"

He shrugged. "Live it. You must kill Jassin, you must make a home for yourself, you must... find peace in Witker and let him find peace in you."

"Why would I do any of that?" She asked, once again squeezing the necklace.

Masine said, "you stopped living the moment your family died. You turned your mind into a river of nightmares and have only just now begun to stop swimming in it. Besides, you and Witker both deserve to find peace in each other."

Kit blushed furiously. She squinted in the sun as she looked for him. Part of her thought that he'd be there for her despite what he said. Or he'd show up at the last minute.

"And you need to kill Jassin because when you sought revenge for the loss of your family, you killed the prince thinking he was the one responsible—but it was Jassin's gold that paid for those deaths," he said. Kit looked at him quickly. "Five hundred gold pieces were spent for two hundred seventy two lives."

"He what?" She asked, her throat pained.

Masine nodded. "Those are reasons to come back from your nightmares. Just come back."

Her body hummed with denial, but she nodded to make him happy. This sixteen-year-old soon to be king. He went to his mother, who was secretly delighted as she plucked the string of Kit's bow, both because she got to be the one to kill her and because her son was about to inherit a throne. Any mother would be happy with either thing.

She looked again at her necklace, running her thumb over it and considering putting it on. It might've been fitting to die with it around her neck. Or would that mean she was accepting her death?

Kit thought of what Masine had said. She *should* take her revenge on the person who truly deserved it. She *should* make a home for herself. Not one in Niverly, not one in Calar. Somewhere with a river and a pretty view. And she should kiss Witker senseless. If he ever showed up again.

But was it worth her nightmares? If she faced all of them and died, she'd never have to face them again. But if she lived, she'd have to keep facing them. Maybe she'd make new nightmares. And Witker, who had seen them and practically lived with them for weeks, thought she couldn't do it. He thought she wouldn't come back. He didn't believe in her.

"Shall we?" Masine asked. "This is what you came to do, Kitali." She looked at him. He stood in front of her again, already looking older and wiser. He was turning into a king. Wasn't he? And he needed her to complete the transition. So why not?

She nodded. Kit slid her necklace into her pocket. She wouldn't put it on—she was not accepting her death.

"Wait..." he put a finger up, his eyes moving.

"For what?" She asked. Part of her hoped it was Witker. He'd come running out of the woods somewhere to support her.

An arrow struck her from the side. She jerked with the force of it, pain sharp in her heart.

Her heart.

She gagged, gasping once as her eyes moved to where it had come from. Treyla was screaming. Masine caught Kit when her knees gave out and lowered her to the ground. Everything was heavy. Everything hurt. Her breathing was shallow. Kit was reminded of Witker's kiss after he bit her, how her own blood filled her mouth. Before, she hadn't really tasted it. Something had blocked her ability to think it was disgusting. But now she spit it from her mouth and coughed. It splattered over Masine's face.

"It's all right," Masine said as he grasped her hand. He laid her on her back. The arrow shaft stuck out of her chest, the feathered end waving in the cold wind. "It's all right," he repeated, "you'll come back."

Jassin dismounted and drew another arrow.

Chapter Fifty-Seven

⟵———⟨

She stood weakly in the room Witker put her in. The chair was behind her as if waiting for her to sit down. The ropes hung idle, yet they shook like snakes ready to strike. She waited for it. She waited for them to wrap around her, to force her into the chair so Witker could come in and torment her with images of the horrors her subconscious created.

The door opened, so she looked there, and Witker came in, but he wasn't alone and his face was stricken with pain and grief. He didn't even look at her. He was shoved into a chair, shirtless and bleeding and two men tied him to it. They disappeared as soon as the job was done. "Witker?" Kit asked. He lifted his head to her and looked nothing but hateful.

"King Assassin," he grunted hoarsely.

Her brow furrowed. His eyes fell to her hand. She held a knife. "Wait," she said, trying to drop it, "wait, I don't want to hurt you."

Vines crept up the walls, bright and alive as if the ceiling above was the sun and they were stretching to it. Witker didn't look at them, just at Kit. "What's one more Fae?" He asked.

"No, I don't want—"

He screamed in pain, tears falling from his eyes. She looked at the dragonfly wings in her other hand. Witker kept screaming, his voice cracking horribly. She tried dropping the wings and the knife, but nothing moved.

The vines opened the door, and her head turned. The stairs going down to the crypt were beyond the wooden door. She didn't want to go down there. She knew what was down there. "Witker," Kit looked at him, trying to step to him, but she could only go to the side. "Witker, I'm sorry. I'm so sorry—" he screamed again, and she ran. The wings and knife disappeared, and the door snapped shut behind her. She stared at the steps. "It's a nightmare," she whispered. Her voice echoed back to her. "It can't hurt me because it's just a nightmare."

But I'm dead. I died. Jassin shot me with an arrow—

She walked down the stairs, hearing his voice. The firelight flickered over the walls, and she moved along them, not stopping in the hiding spots she had before. She was right in the open, expecting Jassin to be there with the other Crowns, but he wasn't. No one was. It was just an empty hall.

"It's just a nightmare," she said. It echoed from the left. She turned her head, and the prince she killed stood there. He was in his ceremonial clothes with an arrow sticking out of his chest, his face stricken with pain.

"Do you even know my name?" He asked.

She did not. Kit never learned it. "I'm sorry," she said.

"You're a failure," he said. She shook her head. "A thief. You stole safety from the kingdom. You stole security. Isn't it fitting that you die like me?" He stepped toward her. Kit was frozen. "With an *arrow* in your heart—" he ripped her arrow from his chest. Blood poured down his front as he stabbed her in the very same place she'd struck him. Kit screamed and stumbled, her body slamming into someone else. The prince disappeared. The arrow was gone. She turned and found Jassin there. He tilted his head sympathetically.

"You look so much like your mother," he said. His hand moved through her hair. It was as long as it used to be. "She would be so disappointed in you."

"No she wouldn't—"

He smacked her. Aspen hit her. Crowns and a crowd stood around her, hitting and kicking and pushing her toward a coffin.

She closed her eyes once inside, lying on her stomach and listening to the whispers of people who were so disappointed in her. She was a failure. She was cruel. She was not worthy of life. It just kept going, around and around, spinning in her head while a dead prince wrapped her in vines. Nature was questioning whether or not she deserved to come back. It wondered if she was worthy of living, as everyone else said she wasn't. She was a disappointment.

She was wretched. What sort of person deserved to live after what she'd done?

Kit fell through the bottom of the coffin and landed on the beam with a thunk, clinging to it so she didn't fall off. Her bow was in her hand, so familiar against her palm. She took a deep breath, her actions the same as they had been so long ago. She knelt and drew her arrow, aiming down at the prince. Her hesitation was there. She shivered, pushing it away before firing, but the arrow landed in her own chest. Kit fell off the beam.

The whole world moved around her, shifting as she passed through the smoke of nightmares. Kit hit the ground, and Witker looked down at her. Trees were around them, and a soft grass pillow was beneath them.

"Did you think it was real?" He asked.

"Yes," she answered before he stabbed her in the chest and thanked her for finding the heir.

She closed her eyes, drowning in nightmares, and opened them on the same ground in Witker's arms. She had not had this nightmare before. She didn't know it, so she kept her eyes closed. Crickets sang around them, and his chest rose and fell against her face. "Are you sure you want to die?" He asked softly. She pressed her face against his shirt. He was so warm. If she kept her eyes closed, would he stay like this? Or would a new nightmare take over?

"Stay," she whispered, "don't leave again."

"I never planned on asking for the wedding band," he said.

She opened her eyes. "What do you mean?"

"I wasn't planning on asking for it back," he told her. Kit lifted her head, looking at him. He was not bruised or hurt. He was calm, and his features were smooth and sure. "You could've kept it."

"Is this a nightmare?" She asked quietly.

"Do you think it is?"

She wasn't sure. How could this be a nightmare? "Is this a dream?" She asked. He did not attempt to answer. Nothing came from his mouth, and nothing showed on his face. She shifted backward, looking at him with all the attention she could manage to give him. His arms stayed around her, securing her body to his. "I don't understand," she said, "shouldn't I be having a nightmare?"

He said nothing.

"Are you nature?" She asked, "or what nature wants me to see?"

Witker sat up and kissed her. Her lashes fluttered, and she breathed in. He turned them over, now lying over her. His mouth moved perfectly against hers.

A smell filled her nostrils, and she grunted, trying to pull back, but he grasped the back of her head. Kit pushed on his chest. Her mouth turned dry as chapped lips rubbed against her. Her eyes flew open, and she tried screaming, shoving the body away. The prince's back hit the lid of the coffin. His hands wrapped around her throat and squeezed. It scraped against her skin. Kit kicked and squirmed, gagging as the rotten taste filled her mouth.

This was a nightmare.

She hit and hit, kicking and pushing until he finally pulled away. She nearly vomited at the decay on his face. His grip on her throat tightened and twisted into a cloth banner. He pulled on both sides. "Do you think you deserve to be happy after what you did?" He asked. She tried digging her fingers underneath the cloth. "Do you think he would really want to be with the person that killed me?"

Kit reached up and scratched him. His skin peeled off with her nails, and she threw up in her mouth.

"He is disgusted by you," he snapped, pulling harder. Darkness formed at the edges of her vision. "Why do you think he wants you to hate him? You should just die, Kitali."

She shut her eyes and punched the dead prince in the face.

Chapter Fifty-Eight

"STOP IT!" SHE SCREAMED at the trees. Vines curled around her, circling her in the same clearing she'd been in with Witker. "Stop doing this!"

Nature did not respond.

"You see what I am afraid of," she said. Tears dropped down her face. "You saw it, so you can stop now. Stop now!" Her voice cracked, and she sobbed. Kit had relived every nightmare she'd had over the year, and it was enough. "You either wake me up right now or kill me. I don't care, but I am done with this!"

Nothing happened, so she screamed at the top of her lungs and started throwing rocks at trees. Her frustrations boiled down to despair, and she dropped to the ground.

"I'm sorry," she said, "I'm so sorry that I hurt everyone, and I'm sorry I never even learned his name. I'm *sorry*."

Witker walked out of the woods looking the same as he had before. Calm and sure. Kit watched him, waiting for him to turn into a prince who planned to hurt her. He knelt before her and held her chin the way he always did. "You fear your regret," he said, "and that is a good thing to fear. You are afraid of the consequences of your actions, which is reasonable. It is unreasonable to want to die because of it."

She shook her head. "I don't—"

"My dear," he said, "you feel that you should have died with your family. You were a day late going home, and because of that, you weren't killed. And you wish you could have been executed when you assassinated my prince. You would not mind dying. It is why you did not hesitate to do this. You did not consider Witker's feelings and what he was trying to tell you, and you did not allow yourself to second guess your decision."

She blinked quickly, pushing him away and sliding back.

"I forgive you," he said, and only then did she realize nature was speaking through him. "I appreciate your desperation. I appreciate your determination. I have watched you, Kitali, and I only wish you liked your name."

"I do—"

"Then allow others to call you by it."

She pulled her lips into her mouth. "You're going to let me live?" She asked quietly.

He nodded. "Do not waste your life wishing it would end. You must give yourself a reason to keep going. Listen to my prince, Kitali, and say your name."

She nodded quickly.

He stood and walked back into the woods. A dizzy spell churned in her head. Kit shut her eyes again, touching her temple. It was quick to fade, though an ache remained like a heavy winter cloud. She was staring at a ceiling when she opened her eyes. Her entire body hurt, her chest most of all, and she braved a look at it. There was no arrow, and the blood had dried.

"I knew you'd wake," a familiar voice said. She turned her head, looking at him partially upside down. Masine was sitting in a chair with his wrists shackled. "They didn't, but Jassin wanted to keep your body. I didn't tell them you'd come back."

"What's going on?" Kitali groaned as she sat up. She grabbed the side of her head, then her chest. There was a hole in her body. It didn't hurt like there was a hole in her body, but there was a hole all the same.

Masine said, "that will fade, don't worry." He seemed so calm she couldn't help but feel secure with him. "As for what's going on," he said, "we're being taken back to the castle. It's been two days, but don't worry about that."

"Why wouldn't I worry about that?" She asked as she attempted to stand. She was stiff as if she'd actually been dead. Looking at her hands, it seemed accurate. Her skin was a strange, lifeless color.

"Because Witker will come for you," he answered.

She stumbled to the side and caught herself on a chair. They were in a room that only had a table and chairs, nothing else. No bed and no fireplace. "He won't come for you?" She asked, shakily sitting down. She breathed heavily with shallow breaths. Air blew out of the hole in her chest.

"I am not as high of a priority as you at the moment," he said, "I am not the one he left."

Her throat bobbed as she attempted to swallow with a dry mouth. "Why are you acting like nothing is going on?"

"Because we are going to my castle," Masine answered. She looked him up and down. He was no longer acting like a sixteen-year-old. He didn't look like one, either. His back was too straight. He had an intense gleam in his eyes that made him hard to look at. "I will have control once I am there. They don't know that, of course."

"They don't know a lot, then," she said. He nodded. "I don't know something," Kitali added, and Masine tilted his head. "What was his name? The prince I killed... I never learned his name. Do you know it?"

Masine smiled gently. "His name was Crius. He was named after Crius the Great." Kitali nodded slowly and he added, "he is at peace, Kitali."

Her eyes watered, and the door opened behind her. She turned partially. Jassin stood in the doorway with his mouth open. He stared at Kitali, his brows pinched together. "Kit," he breathed. She thought of what nature told her about using her full name. Still, she didn't correct him. She didn't want that from Jassin. "You..." He walked in slowly, looking as weak as she felt. The door shut behind him. "You're alive."

Masine said, "I told her she'd come back."

Kitali glanced at him, unsure what to do. Nature told her to listen to Masine, and Masine wanted her to kill

Jassin. Was she supposed to do it now? He didn't appear to have any weapons, and she definitely didn't. She wouldn't stand a chance against him physically.

He stepped toward her slowly, looking at her as if she were a ghost. Maybe she looked like it. Jassin's mouth remained open in shock as he grasped her face, tilting it up so he could look at her. "How are you?" He asked painfully. She didn't say anything to him. He ran his thumbs over her cheeks. "Gods, look at you," he said, but something else was behind the words. He said it not as a man looking at the girl he loved, grateful she was back, but as if she were something fascinating. As if he wanted to dissect the magic that brought her back. He said, "Boisin," and the door opened. "Put Kit in another room." He let go of her.

Boisin walked over, wordlessly grabbing Kit's arm. She looked at Masine as she was yanked out of the chair. He smiled gently and nodded once. Jassin walked out, and they followed. She could hardly stand on her own, which meant she was dragged out, and her shoes scraped over the wood floor. "In with the Fae?" Boisin asked. His voice was deep and scratchy, matching his large beard and scruffed face.

"No, put her in my room. Don't forget the shackles." He walked away, visibly confused, while she was dragged again.

Chapter Fifty-Nine

KITALI FELL ASLEEP WHERE she had been placed. On the floor. Boisin was the one who woke her up, jostling her roughly. She whined, thinking of Witker and his insistence that they move early in the mornings. Her heart began to ache, knowing the man in front of her was not the male she wanted to see. He dragged her out of Jassin's room and practically threw her down the stairs. Kitali caught herself only to be shoved again, this time outside the inn where they were stopped. She blinked in the light of the morning. Treyla walked over to her, bobbing her head like she was happy to see her.

"You won't be riding her," Jassin said from her side. Kitali looked at him. He had the same fascination in his eyes now. So did everyone else—everyone but Masine, who was quite content sitting in a cage connected to the saddle of another horse. "You can ride with me," he said, but it wasn't an offer. He grabbed her arm and pulled her to a brown steed. "We can talk."

"I don't want to talk to you," Kitali said. Boisin nudged her back and held the horse steady. She did not mount him. "You killed me." She kept her eyes on Jassin. His expression turned pained. It was near regret but not quite there. "And you killed my family," she said. He blinked in shock. "You paid to have them killed. The attack on Niverly was you."

He rolled his eyes. "I suppose a Fae told you that?" Jassin nudged her, too, and Boisin went so far as to force her foot into the stirrup. She shifted to keep her balance, and he grabbed her other leg. Her stomach lurched, and she lifted herself onto the horse before they could grab her anymore. Jassin mounted after her.

He pushed her to adjust them both. Kitali remained tense, unsure of what to do with the way he was grabbing her. Jassin held the reins, caging her in. "You came back from the dead," he said, urging them to move. She stared ahead. Kitali wasn't sure where she was, just that they were headed to the main road that would take them to Calar. Dread soaked through her like a wet cloth. She swallowed thickly, and he said, "I'm glad you did."

"Are you?" She asked without thinking.

"I didn't want to lose you," he said, "I wasn't lying when I said everything I did was for you."

She shook her head. "I find that hard to believe."

"I loved you like a daughter—"

"Did you kill me like one, too?" She turned her head partially. He was silent. "How did you even find me?" Kitali asked.

He took her father's necklace out of his pocket. He kept it out of reach when she tried to take it back, shaking his head. Jassin put it back in his pocket and Kitali faced front again. She never thought about him putting any tracking magic on the necklace—and Witker never smelled it. So they'd followed her the whole time, waiting for her to find the heir. He knew exactly where she was at every step. She never truly stood a chance.

⚊⚊⚊⚊

Woods surrounded them. Everything was frozen and white with snow. Her breath fogged in front of her face, and her fingers began to ache with the beginnings of frostbite. Still, she wasn't focused on that. She was searching for movement while trying not to turn her head. Jassin moved a pouch of whatever he'd been eating into her line of sight, which she refused, as she had for the hours they'd been riding.

"You can't starve yourself," he finally said, "I won't allow it."

"You can't shove food down my throat," she replied, "I'd die again if it meant I'd be free of you."

He took the pouch away. "Would you come back?" He asked.

"No," she said, "that's the point."

Jassin said, "your parents would be so disappointed in you."

She turned, gripping the saddle to look right at him. "Don't talk about them like you aren't the reason they died," she snapped, "don't act like you cared about them at all—or about me. I don't *believe* you."

"You will believe me," he said. Kitali hesitated. "We just have to start over."

She shook her head. "No," she said, "no, you can't—"

"I will."

She turned back around. Desperation clawed into her body. He was going to steal her memories again. "No," she said because she knew it would work. She knew that if he did, she would be his Kit again. She would be Aspen's Kit. She would be King Assassin. She shook her head and tried to launch herself off the horse. He grabbed her roughly. Kitali sobbed when he pulled her to his chest with an arm pinning her down. "Please don't, I don't want to, please—"

"It's not up to you," he said simply. She thrashed and kicked the horse, so he reared in agitation. Kitali slipped out of his grip and fell. His hand just missed her as she bolted toward the woods. An arrow flew behind her, and a scream burst from her chest as it sank into her calf. The entire time, Treyla screamed and fought, too.

She hit the ground and started crawling, dragging her leg behind her.

They grabbed her. "No!" She screamed, "Stop it!" It was as if she was nothing more than a crying toddler—easily lifted and carried back. Jassin kept an indifferent look on his face as he grabbed her jacket. They put her back onto the saddle, and she kicked someone in the face.

The arrow snapped, remaining in her leg. Tears fell down her face.

"Don't worry, Kit," Jassin said, "everything will be fine soon enough."

Chapter Sixty

BLOOD DRIPPED STEADILY DOWN her leg. She felt every roll, every new drop. Sparks of pain caused her muscles to twitch. Kitali held her breath and moved her shackled wrists around her calf. Just lifting it hurt. She breathed hotly, her entire body trembling as she moved her fingers around what was left of the shaft. Masine was next to her, waiting with lines of cloth. He'd been given them to use on her, but she couldn't let him remove the arrowhead.

"It'll be all right," he told her. She had to believe him. What other alternative was there? And his mother nodded from the other side of the fire, so she had to believe her, too. Kitali dug her fingers in, gasping and choking on air.

She yanked the arrowhead out with a crying scream.

Masine wrapped the cloth around her leg. She only shook, staring at the flickering flames in front of her. They taunted her. She was freezing, and they were doing nothing to warm her. Snow fell softly from the sky. Jassin and a few others were under the cover of a tent they were not allowed inside. She could feel his eyes on her, unable to believe she once considered him family. She had thought he had saved her, and he was why she needed saving.

Masine tightened the cloth. She didn't move. Not when they started cooking, not when they put food in front of her, not when they began organizing shifts, not when they laid down for the night. Kitali didn't move. Hours passed. Her eyes were the first thing when the flash of something behind a tree had her hoping. She stared at the thick evergreen tree with leaves still alive on the branches. She thought she saw cloth between them, but her tired eyes couldn't be sure. It was impossibly dark in the woods, and she didn't have the eyes of a Fae.

She blinked slowly, wetting her eyes after all the dry staring. Masine was asleep next to her, perfectly content with being a captive. His mother, too. Kitali couldn't believe how calm she was. Her son was in danger, her other child had been left home alone, and she was being used as a tool, yet Kitali was the only one fighting. She was the only one panicking. She should've been using them as an example, and she should've been following their leads. Yet she couldn't. She was too human.

Her head turned. Boisin was looking at her. He shook his head. "I have to relieve myself," she told him.

He grunted, "you haven't had enough water today to need to go."

"Just because I haven't had enough water in *your* opinion doesn't mean I don't need to go," she countered.

"Piss yourself," he said.

Kitali said, "I doubt Jassin would be very pleased with that. He doesn't seem like the kind of man that would appreciate the smell of piss for hours while we ride."

Boisin considered this, grunting again while he stood. He lumbered over and lifted her up. "I have permission to beat you if you try anything," he said, "apparently Jassin will just make you believe it was a Fae that did it. Do you think he'd be pleased with that?"

He dragged her into the woods and dropped her to the ground at a decent distance. She winced and grabbed the log closest to her. Snow stung with cold against her fingers, and she lifted herself up partially. She looked at him. "Go away," Kitali said. He looked at her with a raised brow. "Can you at least turn around?"

Boisin took three steps backward and turned around with his arms crossed. Kitali sat against the log and breathed in deeply. He didn't move, and she squinted to look around. She did actually have to relieve herself, but most of her was hoping Witker was the movement she saw. She wanted him to come out, to kill Boisin and take her away. Masine and his mother could stay for all she cared. They were going exactly where the new king intended. Kitali was going to have her memories taken from her. She needed Witker to show up.

But she couldn't wait that long. Soon, she was finished relieving herself, and he still hadn't shown. She pulled up her pants and sat on the log, looking at Boisin. She imagined him dying, recalling once how much she once hated killing.

He turned to peek at her and she said, "I'm done."

Boisin came to grab her, unceremoniously carrying her back to her spot in front of the fire. She stared at it again. Kitali stared at it the night after that and after that. For weeks, she stared at the fire and refused to speak to Jassin, wondering if Masine had been wrong about Witker. Maybe he had given up on her. Perhaps he wasn't coming.

Calar was in front of them now. The castle was right there. At that point, they had to put her in the cage. They had to gag her, too, because a few people on the road had questioned her, and she'd done far too much pleading for help. Her shackled wrists were moved behind her. Masine didn't try to help in any way. He was quite happy when they could see the castle.

Kitali, on the other hand, was knocked unconscious.

Chapter Sixty-One

YOU'RE WELCOME, A VOICE in her head said. Kitali groaned at it, shifting in the sheets she'd been put in. Her head throbbed as Aspen said her name. It was the same as last time, where he was faking being so thankful that she was alive and safe. She pushed his hand away when he tried to grab her shoulder. Kitali rolled onto her side away from him.

She wasn't sure where she was. It wasn't her room at home; it wasn't her room at the castle. The bed wasn't soft enough. She opened one eye and peeked out, hearing Masine's voice again. *You're welcome,* it echoed, and she knew that he was the only reason her mind lasted the torture of removing memories. Kitali recalled what she'd been told about contren horses—how they were broken to forget their old riders. She imagined this was similar. It had felt like she was breaking.

Jassin was such a terrible person.

Kitali had a bedside table in front of her, and just a foot or two away was a wall. Nothing was on it but the reflection of the firelight in the blisteringly hot room.

"Kit," Aspen said again. He pulled her onto her back, and she pushed him again. It seemed right—hadn't she done something like this before? The first time. She'd squirmed, hadn't she? "Thank the gods," he said, and she blinked quickly.

"A-Aspen?" She asked hoarsely. Her throat was raw—and she knew why this time. The *screaming*. Kitali had screamed so much as her mind was shredded for Jassin's gain. She sat up slowly, pulling herself out of Aspen's grip before he could dig his nails into her. Kitali looked around. No, this was not her room. There was no balcony or couch, just a bed and a roaring fire. Aspen was sitting on it with her, frumping the large green blanket beneath him. She was trapped under it—too hot—and a new, thin nightgown was stuck to her body. "What happened?" She asked faintly.

It will be more difficult to take nearly two months away, Jassin had said. His voice haunted her. *We can't help the pain. It must be done.*

There were tears in Aspen's eyes. "You're here? You're Kit?" He reached out and took hold of her face. Kitali flinched backward. Aspen looked crestfallen. "Kit, I'm so sorry," he whispered, "you went hunting... we only found out too late what happened."

It was a different lie this time. She wondered how much they'd altered their explanation to make it easier to control her. "What happened?" She asked. Pain rolled through her body like waves. She pushed the blanket down and looked at her calf. A fresh bandage was wrapped around it.

Aspen pushed the blanket back up. "These Fae," he said painfully, "they took you. We just got you back."

Her eyes moved. Kitali couldn't find anything to look at. "I don't remember anything," she said softly. The door opened, and Jassin came in quickly, gasping with a pink tint to his face. His mouth was open, and he grinned when he spotted her.

"Thank the gods, Kit," he said with a strange-sounding sob. Jassin came forward and crashed into her. "It's so good to have you back," he said.

She was not back. She was not Kit.

She was Kitali.

"I don't understand," Kitali said. Jassin straightened, moving his hand through her hair. It felt strange to have him touch her like that again—like he cared. She couldn't imagine that he ever truly did. "Aspen said there were Fae, but I don't remember that—what Fae?"

Jassin looked at Aspen and sighed. "Kit," he said gently, taking her hand, "it'll be all right. They took your memories... we don't think they'll ever return. You know how strong Fae magic is. I've been consulting trustworthy sources, but we can't find a way to bring them back."

He got that out of the way quickly. Immediately removing her hope of the memories returning made controlling his narrative much easier. If Kitali thought they'd never return, she wouldn't be so focused on getting them back like she had been last time.

And last time... She'd escaped through her balcony. That would be why there were no windows around her. And there was no way for Witker to find her. If he ever showed.

Kitali looked at her arms, touching the bandages wrapped around where the shackles and rope had been. She was covered in bruises from where Boisin held her down. She touched her neck next, just to feel him. Witker. Gods, why wasn't he there? "What did they do?" Kitali asked. She wasn't sure what to say. There was no script in her head. She couldn't think of the right thing—perhaps it was better to act confused.

"That doesn't matter now," Jassin said. He took her father's necklace out of his pocket and set it in her hand. "The bad part is over. That's what's important."

She stared at the necklace. Something that had once been so important to her, so influential in her day, had been tainted by him. Was the magic still there? If she showed it to a Fae, would they smell it? She ran her thumb over the smooth metal and brought it closer, holding it against her chest. "Go away," she said faintly.

"Kit?" He asked.

"Go away," she repeated just a little stronger. Kitali wasn't sure if she was *allowed* to do that exactly. It wasn't like before, but how could they control how she reacted? "I don't want you here, go away."

Aspen shook his head, "no, you need to talk to us—"

"Aspen, let's give her some space," Jassin interjected. He put his hand on Aspen's back. "It's a lot to take in. Kit, we'll be close by. Please call if you need anything, I have someone posted outside to keep you safe."

She nodded carefully, squeezing the necklace as they left. Kitali waited a minute before putting it on the bedside table and throwing her blankets back. She dropped off the tall bed and crept toward the door, limping along the way. She heard no whispers coming from outside, but she could hear the shifting of someone in armor. Kitali was used to the sound. It was all over the halls of the castle.

She looked around the room. No window. One door. The bathing room was small—hardly room for a tub at all—and there was nowhere for her to get out from in there.

Kitali ran a hand through her short hair and spun in a circle. She'd have to find a way out. She had to bet that Witker wasn't coming—there was no damsel aspect anymore. It was just her. And Kitali would escape.

Chapter Sixty-Two

She allowed herself three days to play the weak, needy Kit. Just three. Kitali laid in bed and slept—or pretended to sleep—and spoke minimally to Aspen and Jassin when they came in. She'd decided that *Kit* was losing hope. She'd gotten depressed upon hearing that her memories would never return. The two of them came to that conclusion as well. Aspen would offer to take her places or do things with her, but she often requested to be alone.

Kitali was forming a plan. She had three days to work it all through—and those three days were up.

Her fist banged on the door. Boisin opened it in shining armor that fit over his large body. He gave her his attention, looking much kinder now than before. There were no threats in his eyes. He was a completely different person. "Yes, Miss?" He asked kindly, his hand on the doorknob.

"I would like fresh clothes and to leave this room," she said firmly. It was a risk, really. Last time, they'd been adamant about not allowing her to leave. Kitali wasn't sure if they'd let her out. This was step one, though, of plan *A*.

Boisin nodded. "I'll have it sent for you. Would you like company? Aspen has been asking to see you."

"No," she snapped and pushed the door shut. Kitali took a deep breath and rubbed her face. She'd been acting antagonistic lately. Lashing out at people hoping they'd be warned to leave her alone. She'd cursed at two servants and bit the head off of Jassin already. The message she was sending was clear—leave Kitali alone.

She just hoped it worked.

Kitali sat on her bed and messed with the bandage around her calf. It had been changed three times, and each time, she felt better. She wasn't sure who was healing it—Jassin, someone else, or Masine. She swore she saw flashes of green vines in her dreams. Kitali knew he was in the castle somewhere, but she also knew that was exactly where he wanted to be, so she couldn't find it in herself to worry. She hoped his mother was all right, but her focus was on herself. Getting out.

Once dressed—still lacking shoes—Kitali walked down the hall. It only took a few feet before she realized Boisin was following her. She looked back and he stopped moving. Kitali took a few steps and he followed suit. "Stop following me," she said sharply.

"I cannot," he said, "I've been ordered to protect you."

"I doubt a Fae is going to come waltzing into the castle after me," Kitali snapped and kept going. She learned she was on the west side of the castle. The opposite of where she wanted to be. She limped down a flight of stairs and groaned at the pain it caused her calf. Even if it was healing, it still ached. Kitali stopped to rub where the bandage was, glancing back to find Boisin there. He flashed an apologetic look—so unlike the man she knew before—and Kitali glared.

She wouldn't be able to lose him. She didn't in any of the halls or as she passed any of the real guards. She didn't when she finally reached the main hall. He was still there, following like a sick dog. A cruel, mean, sick dog.

"Kit!" A familiar, sweet voice called. Her head turned, and she feigned disinterest, but gods, was she glad to see Ralyn's face. She walked forward carefully, trying to act as nonchalant as possible, and Kitali kept her pace. "I'm glad to see you…" She said, looking her over. Ralyn swallowed. She looked a little nervous. Her helmet was on today when it usually wasn't in the afternoons, and it pressed her curly hair down. Kitali wondered what it did to her ears. "You don't remember me, do you?" She asked faintly.

Kitali glanced at her.

"Well," she said, and her voice softened, "Witker's looking for you. He'll save you like last time."

Ralyn went back to her post, and Kitali kept walking. Was Witker truly here? Maybe she wouldn't have to keep being brave—maybe she'd get to be a damsel again. Her eyes moved as she imagined him bursting through the front door and wrapping his arms around her again.

She moved just a little faster and managed to get down the next hall without Boisin being fast enough to stop her.

Kitali went to the stables and jogged forward despite the pain it shot down her calf. "Treyla," she said sweetly. The horse neighed and trotted over. Kitali reached up as Treyla bobbed her head and sniffed her. "Hello," Kitali said.

"I'm sorry, Miss, you can't ride today," Boisin said. Kitali looked at him. He walked forward slowly, and she kept her eyes on him as she unhooked the latch on Treyla's stall. She pulled the door open. "Jassin is trying to keep you safe, Kit," Boisin said.

Kitali stepped around the door and into the stall. Treyla was already wearing her saddle, and even the bridle was on. It looked like the stablehands were prepared to take her out for a ride. Boisin stepped forward and reached for her, but Kitali was suddenly jerked back. She grunted when she landed against someone's chest. His hand pressed against her mouth and a knife touched her throat.

Witker.

Her body hummed warmly as she recognized the press of him.

"Don't make a sound," he said coldly. Kitali looked at Boisin. He was too calm. "Or I'll kill her," he warned.

"No, you won't," Boisin chuckled, "not with that bite mark on her neck."

Her brow furrowed, but she did nothing. Boisin shouted for guards and Witker cursed, yanking her toward the horse. She yelped when he threw her on and smacked Treyla's hindquarters, holding onto the saddle as she bolted from the stables. "Listen to me right now!" Witker shouted, jostling her against him. She gripped his arm tight, eyes wide as she looked back at the castle. Treyla had never run so fast. "My name is Witker. Jassin took your memories, not me."

Kitali looked at him. He sounded beyond desperate and looked horribly tired. Bags were beneath his eyes, and his cheeks were partially sunken. Was he eating? Sleeping?

"He's been manipulating you," Witker told her, "he's hurting you, he's killing the land—or he was, but you fixed it." Treyla broke the tree line, and Kitali looked back. She was stuck in an awkward position, sitting mainly on Witker's right thigh, but she could see the castle shrinking behind him and saw the many guards chasing after them. Witker grabbed her face and held her jaw tightly. "I can get your memories back, all right?" He asked, "please believe me, I need you to believe me."

She squirmed, and he wrestled for her hands, holding her wrists tight. Kitali grunted and started to slide off the saddle before Witker pinned her back against his chest. Her legs flailed and she screamed. Treyla jumped over a log, winding through the trees expertly. They weren't headed toward the spring—Witker's destination took them north into the frigid snowy woods. Witker smacked his hand over her mouth and kept them both on the saddle with one arm.

"Damn it, damn it, damn it," Witker cursed, "come on Treyla!"

Treyla huffed and kept going. As a contren, she'd potentially outlast them. Kitali wasn't sure how many other Fae-trained horses there were in the stables, but she knew that none of them were as desperate as Treyla, and she doubted they were connected to their riders the way Treyla was to Kitali.

Kitali shifted and bit Witker's hand. He yelped and pulled. She let go.

"I'm Witker!" He shouted.

"I know that!" She shouted back.

He let out another desperate breath. "Blessings, human, just stop trying to escape me!"

"I'm not! I'm trying not to fall off!" Kitali snapped, "Witker, I know who you are, all right, just let me sit on the godsdamn saddle!"

Witker tensed and his grip on her loosened from the shock. She slipped further, and her arm swung out, grabbing his shoulder and nearly sending them both down to the snow-covered floor. Witker gripped the inside of her thigh and pulled her into him much closer than he would have if he believed she didn't know who he was. Her legs were finally stable on the saddle.

"You remember me?" He asked, his breath hot on her face as he spoke in her ear.

"Yes, Masine prevented the magic from taking my memories. I was going to escape before you showed up," she said. Kitali turned her head and looked at him. His green eyes were set on her face, and his brows were creased together. "I remember you, Witker," she said, "I know exactly who you are."

Chapter Sixty-Three

⟵————⟞

Treyla outran the other horses. Witker kept them both steady and touched her face the entire time. His thumb caressed her cheek. He memorized what he could as if he was cataloging every piece of her. Her cheeks, her brows, the bridge of her nose, and the shape of her lips. It was all touched by him, whether it was absently or purposefully. Even when he was looking away, he kept her head against his chest and her eyes trained on him.

When they finally stopped, he looked down at her. "My Kitali," he whispered, his voice filled with anticipation, "you remember me."

"I do," she replied. He climbed down and lifted her to him. Kitali wrapped her legs around his waist and moved her arms around his neck. "I was so worried you wouldn't show, and then Ralyn said you were there…" She took her turn touching his face, moving her thumb over his cheeks as he had to her. "Every day on that road, I waited for you. And in the castle, when Masine kept my memory intact, I kept wishing you'd save me."

"And instead, you saved yourself," he said. Kitali smiled just a little. "Let me build you a fire, my Kitali," he said. Witker set her down and grabbed his saddlebag. He pulled a bedroll off as well before going to Treyla's face and kissing her gratefully. Treyla whinnied softly and walked toward a patch of frozen grass. Kitali smiled.

Witker kicked the snow and sticks away and set the bedroll down. She went over and stood on it, her arms crossed. Her feet were bare. She was not in the right clothes again. He smiled down at her and knelt at her feet, taking socks from the saddlebag. "Just like the first time," she said, "but they aren't sweaty and smell like male feet."

He chuckled and held her ankles one at a time, slipping the warm socks over her heels and fitting them over her pants. Witker looked up at her. "My feet do not smell," he said.

She rolled her eyes, "yes, they do."

Witker shook his head and set up a warm, intense fire for her. Kitali sat down and watched him, holding her knees as her eyes trained on his back and shoulders and face. She was overjoyed that she didn't have to repeat her nightmares. She knew him. She did not forget him. Kitali recalled every part of him, every second of their time together.

"You're looking at me strangely," he said as he built their pathetic little tent. It began to snow lightly over them, collecting in Kitali's short hair. She reached for him, and he crawled over. "Why are you looking at me strangely?" He asked.

She said, "I'm waiting for my turn to kiss you." Kitali grabbed the back of his neck and dragged him close. He moaned just before his mouth connected with hers. Witker breathed her in as if he needed to memorize her scent, as if it had left his nose and he needed to be full of it once again.

He pulled away with a smile. "I missed you," he said softly. Kitali agreed and kissed him again. He said, "I came prepared, at least."

He pulled away from her again. Kitali huffed as he walked to Treyla and removed the second saddlebag. He pulled out a blanket and a waterskin. "Everything but shoes," she remarked, taking the water from him. Kitali took a swig and spat half of it back up, straightening and putting a hand against her mouth. Witker laughed at her as she swallowed. "Wine," she said and licked her lips. "When did you have time to get *wine* while I was being tortured?"

Witker's smile disappeared. "What?" He asked faintly, moving to his knees in front of her. Kitali shut her mouth quickly. His eyes searched hers.

"The way they take memories..." She said. His brows pulled together and he shook his head. She looked down.

"Tell me," he insisted gently. Witker moved closer and sat with her. He lifted her chin. "Please, tell me what they did."

She blinked quickly. Kitali took a deep breath and he swiped his thumb over her lip. Witker's other hand wrapped around her ankle. She thought of the day she shot the deer outside Petaki and when she'd been drugged by Fae berries—how he'd grounded her. Was he doing that now? "We got back to the castle, and I woke up somewhere cold and wet, I think maybe the dungeons," she started. He nodded. "I was tied down and on my back. My wrists and my ankles... but they still needed people to hold me down. I might still have the bruises, I don't know."

He looked her over. His green eyes flashed over every part of her.

Kitali said, "I couldn't see anything, but I could hear them." Her throat began to ache as she thought of it. Of the dampness on her skin—not from sweat, but from the moisture and magic in the air. Of the chill, then the searing heat that ran through her entire body. "Jassin was the one performing the spell, but I think he had help. I know Aspen was there. He was confused as to why it was hurting me so badly. Jassin told him that taking two months of memories was much harder than two weeks."

Rage boiled behind Witker's eyes, but he contained it.

"It hurt so badly," she whispered, blinking at the water gathering in her eyes. She grimaced. "And it lasted so long because they had to be *sure*. I could barely breathe or, or move by the end of it and Jassin just kept saying it was fine because I wouldn't remember it. That it was pain now for a lifetime later on."

"I didn't know," he whispered, "I didn't..." he looked around at the blanket, wine, and tent. "Ralyn gave this to me; I went to her, trying to find a way into the castle. We planned for a day, and she gave me the wine and blanket. She said it was the one you used on your chair. Kitali," both his hands came to her face. His thumbs brushed over her cheeks and such intense regret shined in his eyes. "I am so sorry. If I had known how humans take memories I would've come faster. I would've stormed the castle and killed everyone in it to get to you, I swear it."

She smiled sadly, but it faded quickly. "How do Fae take memories?"

"Dreams," he answered, still sounding a little desperate and full of regret. "We take them using dreams. I've seen it done. It is painful, but not as you described. It's hardly a pinch, like how I bring out your nightmares."

"You flick me," she said.

He laughed. "Is that what it feels like?"

She nodded.

Witker sighed slowly. "Kitali, I am so sorry."

"It's all right now," she said, "you came." He did not seem to want her forgiveness so soon. Kitali smiled and said, "I really liked that growling voice you did when you threatened that guard."

His eyes lit up as his mood changed. "Oh, you did?"

She hummed and nodded. "It was nice. You should do it again."

Witker got to his knees and pushed her onto her back. "What shall I say?" He asked, "I don't want to threaten you."

"You'll think of something," she replied, lifting her head to kiss him slowly. He took her hand, lacing her fingers with his against the cold ground and she moved her legs around his waist.

Chapter Sixty-Four

"I'M SORRY I DOUBTED you." He brushed his thumb over her cheek and mumbled, "remind me to never do it again."

Witker pulled her in for another kiss, then another, and Kitali moved her hands into his jacket. "Never do that again," she warned. He nodded easily and gripped her hand tight, the other hand on the ground by her head. He kissed her throat and she closed her eyes. "Witker, what about everyone else?" She breathed.

"There is no one else," he mumbled onto her skin.

"Jassin and Masine..."

He shook his head. Witker said, "they don't matter. Only you matter." She ran her fingers through his hair, her eyes fluttering open and closed as he kissed her chest. Kitali gripped it tight. "Please, Kitali, can I touch you?" He begged, "please, I need to touch you."

"Touch me where?" She asked.

"Everywhere," he answered, "I need you, Kitali."

Kitali nodded only to realize he hadn't seen it, so he didn't move. She swallowed. "You can touch me," she said, and he moaned his thanks. Witker pressed a kiss to her chest just above her heart. He pulled her shirt off slowly. Kitali breathed out, cold as the soft flurries of snow fell onto her bare skin.

"I have never wanted another person more than I want you," he told her as he kissed her stomach. He left a fire in the wake of his mouth. Kitali couldn't recall anything she was meant to do other than be kissed by him. There was no prince or Crown or arrow. Nothing but Witker and his begging to touch her everywhere. "You have become the only thing I need in this world."

She pushed his jacket off his shoulders and he tore it away completely. Witker removed his shirt as well before looking down at her. His eyes roamed her. Despite still wearing pants, Kitali felt completely naked. "Not much?" She asked him, pulling her lips into her mouth.

Witker shook his head and said, "you are the most beautiful creation in the whole world."

He bent and kissed her. "I like it when you express yourself," she mumbled.

"I need to taste you," he said. Kitali nodded. She expected another bite, but Witker had other plans. Very different plans. He untied the lace of her pants and pushed them off her hips. "Kitali," he whispered, then began slowly moving down. Kitali's heart raced. He took her pants off completely, sitting between her spread legs with hungry, lustful eyes.

Witker whispered what she thought was a prayer before he touched her. Just one finger dipped gently into her, and he sighed with his eyes closed.

He was no longer just saying her name. She was not Kit or Kitali or King Assassin. He whispered, "my Kitali," and bent down. First, Witker kissed her thigh. He moaned as if she'd done something special. Kitali watched him briefly, boiling inside as his one finger turned to two. He then nuzzled his face past the curls between her thighs and got the taste he was after.

Kitali's head fell back. She looked up at the canopy of trees, gripping the bedroll beneath her as he licked over her sweetly. It was as if she was a treat he was prepared to die to eat. Witker moaned with his mouth over her. She could no longer concentrate on the leafless trees or the cold ground or even the snow melting on her skin. Not when he caressed her and praised nature for her. She was a blessing to him.

"My Kitali," he said again and sucked so hard she gasped and grabbed his hair. "I'm sorry," he mumbled, "I'll do better."

"Oh my gods," she whispered.

His fingers were deep inside her. Kitali had little concentration. She had too much energy. It had built and built with the tension of a bowstring. Eventually, she'd have to let go.

"Please don't finish yet," he whispered, and she gasped. Her heels dug into the ground. "Please, I need more." As if he could find any other place to put his tongue. Kitali swallowed hard. A wave of something heavy was building in her body. Like the first time she went to the beach for a competition, where she learned that she preferred rivers and streams to the ocean. Kitali recalled chasing after the waves and being shocked by the incredible surge of power that struck her when she went too far in.

This felt like that—like Witker was running at a wave, and she wouldn't be able to stop it from hitting him.

"Witker," she said, "Witker, please."

He hummed, groaning as if he knew he had to give her what she wanted but didn't want to. "All right, my Kitali," he said. He was still running toward the wave. Any second, just another step—

Kitali inhaled sharply, then stopped breathing. Pinpricks struck her body as the wave moved downward from the top of her head. She couldn't feel her legs. Kitali's breath left her shakily, and Witker appeared over her with a smile. His lips were wet and his eyes were still hungry for more. He sucked on his fingers before he kissed her.

"Please let me do it again," he said.

"Oh my gods," she mumbled weakly.

"Can I do it again?" He asked. He peppered her face with kisses. "Please? Just one more time? Or two?"

She groaned.

Kitali looked up at him. He was smiling at her like he was proud of his handiwork. Rendering her immobile was such a great accomplishment. "What about you?" She asked.

Witker rolled his eyes. "I would much rather be doing this," he replied with a kiss to her lips.

"Are you sure?" She asked nervously. "I can—"

"I don't want a single thing from you, my Kitali," he said, "but if you would *like* to do something, please tell me I can taste you again."

She took a deep breath. "One more time," she decided. He grinned and gave her one final kiss before going back to rest between her thighs.

Chapter Sixty-Five

WITKER TOUCHED HER FACE so long after both of his tasteful adventures, making her groan. He folded himself into her, laying the blanket over her body, but it was his warmth that truly kept her from freezing in the light flurries of snow. She hardly felt them at all. "Don't you have things you want to discuss?" He asked. She shook her head, keeping her eyes closed. "I thought you'd want to convince me to help you kill Jassin."

"I don't have to convince you of anything, you're going to do it no matter what," she replied.

"I am," he agreed.

Kitali finally opened her eyes. "Masine is going to be fine in the castle?" She asked and he nodded. "So we don't have to worry about him?"

"Not in the slightest," Witker said, "King Masine has his own plans, we just need to wait and see how we fit into them. For now, it's just us and our plans."

She smiled just a little. Witker touched her brow and her cheek and her lips. "Nature made me see you," she whispered. His expression shifted uncertainly. "I'm not sure if it was a dream or not, because it looked so real... Dream you told me you never planned on asking for the wedding band back." A hint of fear flashed in his eyes. It was there for only a moment, fueled by what might actually be true. "Were you upset when I gave it back?"

His eyes darted back and forth. "A little, I suppose."

"Why?"

Witker shrugged just slightly. "I wouldn't have minded if you kept it for however long..."

"Give it back then," she said. He blinked quickly, obviously taken aback. "You aren't *proposing* or anything," she said, "you're just letting me hold it. I'll keep it safe." She no longer had her necklace with her. She'd left it in her castle room. It and its tracker magic, but Kitali would have no trouble carrying this piece of him.

"Why do you want it?" He asked.

She answered, "because I gave it back when I was angry with you. I hope you don't mind that I'm not angry anymore."

"You aren't angry at all?"

"We need to talk about it some more," she said with a little nod. "I want to know everything soon, but I'm not angry like I was before."

Witker reached into his pocket and produced the half ring. "I apologize," he said.

She took it from him. "Why a ring? And only half of one."

"I am half," he said, touching the green band, "and my partner is the other half." Witker motioned to where someone like Kitali would complete the circle. "We are not whole without each other."

She nodded slowly.

"Why a veil?" He countered. She looked from the ring to him. "Why a tear?"

"Oh," she smiled, "it's about the mending. My mother would begin my veil when I told her I wanted to marry someone to show that even if I took a new name, I would always carry my family with me. She gives it to me and I continue to make it. The pattern is supposed to be something out of your heart and tearing it is a way of asking your partner if they would be there to mend what love may be broken. It's a way of saying we'll always be there for each other."

Witker smiled, too. "Like a ring."

She looked at it.

He asked, "who's going to start your veil if your mother is gone? Are you going to have one at all?"

"I don't know," Kitali admitted while letting out a breath. She spun the semi-circle between her fingers. "Honestly, I used to think I would rather never get married than do it without my mother. She was..." She ran her thumb over the ring and looked at him. "She was so excited about this stuff. It was her dream to make my veil."

Witker's eyes turned sad. "Doing it without her feels like a betrayal," he said, and she nodded after a moment.

"Humans have an aisle you walk down," he said, "you are led by a parent and you have people you love on either side, yes?" She nodded again. "Our parents do not deliver us. We aren't given away. They stand on the dirt with us."

"You stand on dirt?"

"Yes, we stand on fresh earth that our families pile on the ground. We marry barefoot—" Kitali grinned when he said that, and an embarrassed smile spread over his face. He said, "and once the ceremony is over, we take the dirt and spread it over the doorways of our new home. Is that strange?"

She said, "no, I just... I would get married barefoot, too. Under a tree."

"Oh, see? You aren't very different from a Fae," he said, casually leaning on an elbow. "You're stupid like one, and you want to get married like one." A laugh burst from her chest. "Connected to the earth," he said. Witker's expression softened. He said, "I don't have parents to stand on the dirt with me." Her smile faded. "I have Ralyn," he said, "but she is not them."

"Tell me another Fae tradition," she sat up. He straightened with her. Kitali faced him, stretching out her injured leg. "Maybe we can find similar ones. Maybe we aren't so different." Witker smiled at her faintly, and his eyes moved as he searched for one.

Chapter Sixty-Six

"WE ALL HAVE TO excel at something," he said, "the way you excel at archery, that is a very Fae thing. We must find what we're good at and show we can add value to the world."

"What do you excel at?" She asked, ripping off a bite of a squirrel. They'd moved around since the conversation about weddings. Much to Witker's regret, Kitali had dressed and gotten food while he built a spit for the fire. There hadn't been any dropping on his part, and they both sat comfortably on the bedroll while Treyla munched on oats and grass.

He said, "I happen to be very good at berry painting."

"Berry painting," she repeated, thinking of all the paintings that hung around his farmhouse. He nodded. "As opposed to... regular painting?"

"Mashing berries and only using those to paint."

She said, "like watercolor."

He shook his head. "No, the pigment in those paintings comes from minerals in the earth and other plants. I'm talking about picking a berry off a bush, mashing it, and making paint from it."

Kitali laughed at him, then shut her mouth quickly. "How does that prove your value to the world?" She asked while attempting to push down a smile.

"I am using nature to create something cherished," he answered.

"I see," she said, "and that is your value?"

He scoffed. "Better than shooting an arrow at a target to win a ribbon."

"I won money," she corrected, "and I was the best at what I did."

Witker hummed and nodded. "Sure you were."

"I was," she hit his shoulder with her own. Kitali ripped off another bite and gave it to him, then took one for herself. "Remember, that's where I was when you attacked Niverly. Competing in Icar." He nodded. "I was so nervous because it was my first time competing against an age group I wasn't a part of. It was longer distances and challenges... and I won. I was supposed to go home the same day but I went out with the other kids instead. Then the attack happened."

"That one was just a raid, I remember," he nodded.

"Were you there?"

He shook his head.

Kitali said, "I was terrified. The Fae lit houses on fire; they ran around screaming and breaking things and shouting that it was all in the name of the prince. Smoke was everywhere. I couldn't breathe. I panicked." She swallowed thickly, picking at the squirrel. "The moment someone started to run at me, I shot them. It turned out she was a human trying to help me. One of the girls from the competition."

"You killed a human?" He asked.

"The first person I ever killed," she nodded. Kitali looked at him and tried for a smile. "I'm still the best, though. It's what I *excel* at. And you paint with berries."

Witker chuckled. "I get paid for that, too."

"Sure you do," she replied. Witker grunted at her disbelief and took a bigger chunk of meat from the squirrel. She said, "maybe you'll paint me something and I'll see if it's worth paying for."

"You know, I can't say the same for you because I've seen you shoot, and it's not worth paying for."

She pushed him. "Accuracy is worth paying for," Kitali replied.

"So if I tell you to shoot something with perfect accuracy, you will?"

"If you pay me," she said.

He just laughed, and they kept eating. Witker entertained her as if he was afraid of what would happen if they ran out of things to say. She watched him and listened to him. They compared traditions and lives, but by midday, every story began to sound meaningless. They were speaking to fill the air and eating to distract themselves, and eventually, it wasn't enough.

Kitali adjusted the socks on her feet, picking dead leaves off them after walking to relieve herself. Witker had packed, she wasn't sure why. The tent and bedroll were gone, leaving her stuck on the ground while he stuffed the saddle. "Where are we going?" She asked.

"Calar," he answered, "you have to kill Jassin. Can't do that from here."

"Right," she mumbled. He stomped out the fire. "Why are you suddenly moving so quickly?" She asked. He glanced at her as he kicked snow onto the campfire. "Witker?"

He said, "come on," and held his hands out. She looked at them, silently refusing to get up. "Kitali," he said, "there is an urgency I can feel. You can't because you're human... and maybe I should be communicating that..."

"Yes, you should be," she said.

"Fine," he sighed. Witker leaned over and grabbed her hands. He pulled her to her feet. "We have a connection to the land that you do not, and the king has a connection that goes deeper than we will ever know. He sends messages through it. He tells his people to be calm, he tells his people that a change is coming, and he tells *me* that the change must happen now."

Kitali said, "so I have to kill Jassin."

He nodded.

A breath escaped her. Witker picked her up and carried her to Treyla while she wrestled with the idea that a Fae King could send messages through the ground to tell Witker that she needed to kill someone. "How am I supposed to..." She started.

"Accurately," he said.

"That's not funny."

"No, my Kitali, it isn't," he agreed and set her down so she could put one leg over and settle into the saddle. He climbed on after her. "But it needs to be done."

"Just Jassin or all of them?"

They began heading back in the direction they were trying to escape from. "Start with Jassin. He has the most sway with the humans." Kitali nodded, her eyes moving back to where the bow was.

"I liked it better when we were kissing each other," she admitted.

"We can go back to that," he offered. She rolled her eyes, but he held her chin and brought her mouth to his. "See?" He asked and pulled her closer. Kitali slid toward him. His hand pressed into her stomach and wrapped around her. "Is this better?" He asked.

She hummed with a nod and kissed him again.

Chapter Sixty-Seven

C ALAR WAS NEVER SUPPOSED to be her home, and Kitali was glad about it. Coming back was easier when she knew it was just a place she lived once. She had a room, cups, a kitchen, and chairs she loved, but it was not her home. She didn't have one of those. So it was easier that they were in a room they rented. The Fae they paid growled at her and warned Witker that she was King Assassin and a Fae killer. Witker replied that Kitali would never kill him, then brought her into the room and pinned her against the wall, daring her to try. He kissed her like they were two people in a storybook she hated reading and this was the first night before a happy ending. Even if it was day. Even if someone else had to die.

"Is this all right?" He asked. She wrapped her arms around his neck and he gripped her thighs, lifting her up. Kitali put her legs around him with a nod, and he pressed her harder against the wall. His Fae canines scraped against her lip.

A knock came to the door, making him sigh slowly and set her down. Kitali stayed against the wall, breathing a little heavily, and he smiled at her as he went to the door. Ralyn was the person who walked in, still wearing her guard armor, and her nostrils flared. "Witker, you're disgusting," she said and he laughed. Ralyn looked at Kitali closely. "Are you all right?" She asked. Kitali nodded. Still, her eyes turned to a slow squint, and she looked at Witker. "Get out," she said.

"What? No—"

"Get out right now or I'm going to hurt you," she said. Witker scoffed at his sister and left the room. Ralyn stared at the door. "Walk *away*, Witker," she said loudly. Kitali heard him groan, then nothing else. Ralyn's gaze moved back to her.

"What?" Kitali asked quietly, "am I doing something wrong?"

She shook her head slowly and began removing her uniform. Everything was piled onto the small bed that was pressed lengthwise against the wall. Kitali looked around for the first time. It was the smallest room she'd ever been in. It was meant for sleep and only that. A fireplace was on her left, but it was tiny, and the bathing room door was on the right. It was an addition they paid for.

Ralyn stood in front of Kitali, her gaze quite serious. "Did you let him bite you or did he force you?" She asked.

Kitali blushed a deep red. "I let him," she said, "is that bad?"

"Did you like it?" She asked. Ralyn moved Kitali's shirt to the side and looked at the bite mark. "Or did it hurt?"

"It didn't... hurt," Kitali said. She reached up and covered the bite mark. She moved away from Ralyn. "He still hasn't really explained what it is, though," she said. Kitali stood in front of the unlit fireplace, moving to the ground to change how the logs were piled. Ralyn knelt next to her. "He said it was some claiming thing and an old Fae ritual about half of a belonging."

"Wait, biting and belonging are different, what did he do?" She asked quickly, stopping Kitali from messing with the fireplace.

Kitali faced her. "Well the first time he bit me..." She said nervously. Ralyn nodded, urging her on. "And he drank my blood a little. He told me it was toxic, but then he drank more..." Ralyn's eyes slowly widened. "He called me intoxicating, too. Is that a bad thing?"

"All right, uh," she cleared her throat and sat down. "We aren't supposed to drink human blood."

"Because it's toxic?"

"Because it's addictive," she corrected, "and yes, your blood is toxic because there's iron in it, but when we have feelings for the human, it becomes like a drug. If he just bit you and claimed you as his own, it would be completely different; it's like marking your territory. But because he tasted you and liked it—not to mention *you* liking it—"

"What does it mean if I liked it?" Kitali asked.

Ralyn grew uncomfortable, Kitali thought because it was her brother they were talking about. She shifted and messed with her bootlaces. "Well," she said, "it's a good thing. If you liked it and you... crave something like that, it means you're willing to lose something for him and that you would... take something, too."

"Take something?" She repeated, her brows furrowed.

"You would drink his blood," she said. Kitali's eyes widened. "That's the Fae tradition. Mixing blood. He takes yours into him and you take his into you. It's a really old thing we used to do for weddings but don't anymore because it's pretty gross to watch other people do it." She had a cringe on her face. "It's what he was talking about, though. The half of a belonging thing, that's the joining."

Kitali felt nauseous. "I don't want to drink his blood."

"You might later," Ralyn replied.

She shivered. "All right," she said, "then what about the rings? He let me have the half of his wedding band thing, is that bad too?"

"He what?" She stuttered with wide eyes. Kitali reached into her pocket and produced the curved green stick. She stared at it.

"He gave it to me when we were pretending to be a couple, but he never asked for it back. I returned it when he upset me, but he gave it back when I asked for it. Is that a serious thing for a Fae?"

Ralyn held the back of her hand, her mouth open. "He willingly gave this to you?" She asked and Kitlai nodded. "Kit," she breathed.

"Kitali," she corrected.

She wasn't listening. "Oh great blessings," she gasped, "no wonder he smells like he does. Kit, he—"

"Kitali," she said again.

Ralyn paused. "Since when?"

"Nature told me to use my full name."

"When did you speak to nature?"

"When I died," she answered.

"You *died*?" She asked and Kitali nodded. "When?"

Kitali said, "to crown Masine I had to die. I came back, obviously, and I'm fine. I just have to use my full name and some other things."

Ralyn stared at her. She reached out and held her face with one hand. "I am so glad to know you, Kitali," she said.

"I'm glad to know you, too," Kitali replied.

She hugged Kitali tightly. "Yes," she said, "it is a serious thing that he gave you the band. Even more so that he gave it to you when you asked for it back."

"Why?" She asked against her shirt.

"Because we don't just give them away for someone to borrow and play pretend with," she said. Ralyn squeezed her tight before she pulled back. Her eyes were wet with tears. "He intends for you to keep it. He intends for you to complete the circle."

Kitali looked at the half ring. "He didn't say..."

"It's Witker," she wiped her eyes, "he'll never say." Ralyn grinned before she got up and opened the door. "Witker!" She shouted. After a moment he came back into the room looking at his sister and Kitali. "Be kind to the human," she said.

"I am being kind to the human. What did you do?" He went to Kitali, holding his hands out. Kitali took them and stood.

Ralyn said, "just asked a couple questions and answered ones you didn't. Now," she said despite how Witker seemed to think the conversation wasn't over. He looked at Kitali. "Jassin and the Crowns are going to lock themselves in the castle."

"That's fine. I can get into the castle," Kitali said easily. Witker was still staring at her. "I'll just do what I did last time," she said, "sneak in, kill a ruler, and hope for the best."

Neither Fae seemed very pleased with this plan.

Chapter Sixty-Eight

SHE PULLED ON THE black laces of her boots with shaking hands.

"You can hesitate," Witker said from his place leaning against the wall. He had his arms crossed firmly, though it seemed like a protective stance from where she was. "He's human. He'll die even if you don't hit the heart." Kitali nodded carefully, waiting for him to say something else. He'd been staring for some time, especially since Ralyn left. She would try to pick up someone else's shift and get a night watch to be in the castle in case something went wrong. The moon was rising now. The stars were out. Kitali was in all black. "Kitali," he said. She looked at him. "It'll be fine, all right?"

She nodded.

"Say something," he said softly. His arms tightened over his body, a clear sign of his protective stance. He was covering his heart. From her? Maybe. From the idea that it might not be fine.

She stood. "It will be fine," she said and pushed a fallen bit of hair behind her ear. Ralyn had braided it, but it was already coming out. Kitali had to be fast to keep it out of her face. She moved in front of Witker, smiling as sweetly as she could manage. "I'm just assassinating someone," she said.

"You aren't one, though," he said, holding her jaw. "Understand me? You aren't an assassin."

"What am I?" She asked.

He smiled with half his face. "An archer."

"With a human target," she said. He shrugged and pulled her in, kissing her slowly. She sighed and rose to her toes in boots that weren't hers. "Tell me this is the right thing," she whispered, "tell me this makes everything all right."

Both of his hands now cradled her face. She looked up at him, at the seriousness of his expression, at his lips as he said, "this is right. This is exactly right. Everything will be better after this is done."

"And then what?"

"We help Masine fix the rest of the broken things," Witker said certainly, "and we build a life in the world where everything is all right."

She nodded. He kissed her again, then lifted a scarf over the bottom half of her face. He smiled as he covered her nose. Kitali squinted at him, which only made him smile wider, and he picked up the bow and quiver next to him. He held them out. Her hand continued to shake as she took them. The weight threatened to send her to the ground, but she shouldered it.

"Kitali," he whispered, "I'll be right outside the castle. Come out when it's done. Please."

"Don't worry," she said, even if *she* was worried. She was worried because she had no idea what Jassin could be thinking. She was worried because she hardly knew what *she* was thinking. But she didn't say that to Witker. She just held his jaw like he did to her and said, "I'll find you when it's over."

Witker nodded. He kissed her with the scarf over her mouth and seemed ready to leave with her, but she left without him. She walked silently, avoiding people's eyes as easily as she could. Everything was easy, and that was terrifying. Getting to the rooftops was easy, going right up to the castle was easy. She jumped onto the same tree that she had before, and it was easy. The guards standing around didn't even think to look up. Avoiding snow was difficult, but using the gargoyles she once begged Jassin to have taken down made getting up the castle even easier.

The actions were the same as the first time, only now she was crawling in the dark. It almost felt wrong to do that. It almost felt wrong to get to the high throne room windows and open the very same one.

Moonlight shined down at the pews where guests had once been. Where hopeful Fae sat waiting for a new king. Where a young boy on the verge of becoming an adult walked down in his robes with his head high. Where he died. She could see the spot perfectly as she crawled onto the beam.

This had been her plan. Get to the throne room. She didn't have one after that. She didn't even have a clear way down.

The door creaked open, and she crawled back into the shadows. Crown Nolen walked into the throne room with a guard trailing behind him. "It's not haunted, see?" The Crown said in a high-pitched, nervous, yet aggravated tone. "Get the crown."

"Your Grace," the guard said in a fearful voice. He obviously didn't want to get the crown. It was in a glass box at the other end of the room.

"Oh get in here!" Nolen snapped. Kitali drew an arrow, watching a second guard come in nervously. She gripped her sword tight at her side. "One of you pick up the damn thing!"

The guard walked as if her job depended on it. She grabbed the arm of the second guard, and they both went to the box. One took off the glass encasing it and the other very gingerly lifted the pillow the crown was sitting on. He turned, looking expectantly at Nolen.

"Get it to Jassin," he ordered tightly, pointing to the door. They rushed once again and Nolen was left pinching the bridge of his nose with his head down. Kitali glanced around, then at the arrow waiting in her hand. Seconds went by, and her gut twisted. The seconds kept going, seconds where she didn't notch the arrow, seconds where Nolen left muttering about the guards being imbeciles.

Kitali exhaled as soon as the door shut, her heart hammering loudly in her chest. She covered it as she inched back to the window. The cold night welcomed her. She closed her eyes and removed the scarf, gulping down winter air. She kept shaking as she put the arrow away and moved the bow over her shoulder. Tears brimmed her eyes, and her body suddenly filled with the urge to vomit.

Still, she slid the window back into place and began moving up. Her calf throbbed with each stretch of her limbs. Her body strained until she stopped where she could see a courtyard below. Nolen was coming out of a door below her. He walked along the frozen grass.

She couldn't kill him. Not with this many people around. There were too many guards. She needed to wait. To follow him. Suddenly, Kitali was blessed with the imbeciles. This would be a much different situation if the Crowns hadn't been so paranoid.

When Nolen made his way inside, she was forced to guess which direction he'd be going in. Left or right. Left would take him closer to the crypt, but right would take him to the main hall, then the stairs, and up the stairs to Jassin's study. They so often met there.

There was no harm in being wrong, was there? So Kitali went right, climbing and scaling up to where Jassin's office would be. Her arms strained. She had to stop enough times to know that Nolen had most definitely reached whichever destination he intended before she finally got to the window that opened in the line of them along the hall.

Jassin poured pitchers of water down to the tree he planted when he first took control. A little sprout was below her, well cared for in the perfect spot for the sun to shine on it every afternoon.

She stopped over it, pulled her scarf off her face, and took a few deep breaths. Her hand wrapped around her leg. She was stuck in an awkward position, grappling to the sides of the walls in a way that one slip of her foot would send her falling to the ground. Kit was balancing on a sliver of a stone sill. Half of her foot hung off.

Blood had soaked into a spot on her pants. Kit hissed and grit her teeth, squinting to see if any guards were in the hall. There was light coming from the crack under Jassin's door, which seemed like a good sign.

A few more deep breaths rolled through her. "Nature says I have to," she mumbled.

She pushed the window open and climbed through, dizzy when she was back on her feet. She could hear his voice already, and the sound made her shiver. He was stern and annoyed. Kitali recalled he hardly ever spoke to her that way. Another voice came through the crack under the door. She looked in both directions down the hall and stepped toward the door.

"Your mother's life hangs in the balance," Jassin said, "bring back the Rift and she stays whole."

Kitali drew an arrow once again.

"You said you needed the crown; here it is," Nolen said in his sternest tone. "Why heal the Rift anyway? What could you gain from that?"

"I didn't heal it," Masine said calmly, "Kitali did." This made her pause with her fingers poised on the string of her bow. "When she died, it healed the Rift."

"How?" Jassin asked with a smack to the table. "How does a human heal a Rift that's been in Olyan longer than any of us have been alive?"

The Fae just said, "you'll have to ask her." Kitali opened the door and aimed her arrow at Jassin. He was right across from her on the other side of the table, the angry look on his face slowly being wiped away. He seemed hurt. How could he be hurt? "Hello, Kitali," Masine said with a smile. She glanced at him. The Fae was on her left, shackled to a chair with a map in front of him. He was leaned back perfectly at ease while the Crowns surrounded him wanting answers.

"Hello," she said quietly, her voice shaking.

"Do you know the answer to his question?" Masine asked her.

She wasn't sure how she was keeping her arm steady. "I think so," she said. She had thought Masine would heal it—but then again, the legend said it would be someone *blessed by nature*. Hadn't Kitali been blessed when nature brought her back from the dead? Her eyes swept the room. She couldn't see any weapons. Nothing that any of the other two Crowns could use—as if anyone but Jassin had any experience when it came to battle. She did see, how-ever, Crown Mali shift just slightly toward the cord on the wall that would call a servant to the room. Her arrow changed to be pointed at her.

"Kit," Jassin breathed, "what are you doing? Why are you allowing yourself to be manipulated—"

"Don't talk to me about manipulation," she glanced at him, "as if you haven't stolen memories and lied to me twice."

He shook his head. "I was doing what's best for you."

A quiver entered her hand and she almost released the arrow. "What's best for me," she repeated. "Killing my family was what's best for me?" She jerked the arrow so Mali would walk to the side. She and Nolen moved backward, and Kitali put her arrow back on Jassin. "Why Niverly?"

Jassin laughed as if she were a fool. "Kit, you can't pos-sibly believe the words of a Fae."

"As opposed to my own murderer?"

"I raised you. I *saved* you," he said, "I gave you a home and a family when no one else was there for you." She shook her head. "Kit, look at what you're doing. You know what the Fae will do if you allow them to be in control."

She took a deep, painful breath. "No, the Rift closed," she said, "that means things will be better. When you're gone."

"Darling," he breathed, "I don't think you know what you're talking about."

Masine said, "yes she does."

"He says I do," she nodded to the Fae watching as if this were some show.

Nolen's eyes moved behind her, and her hesitation no longer mattered. She let go of her bowstring and the arrow flew away from her just as her arm was yanked backward. Boisin slammed her head into the doorframe. Kitali didn't see the arrow hit Jassin, but she knew he was dead.

Chapter Sixty-Nine

"YOUR EXECUTION WILL BE held in the morning," Nolen told her.

She loosened the ties of her boots on the damp dungeon ground, hardly able to look at him. She wiped blood off her brow and said, "I was going to kill you second."

He scoffed and walked away.

Kitali was back where she had been. She started there, in the smelly dungeon after executing someone important. Maybe she would end here, too.

No, no she wouldn't. She refused. She would not be executed, not when the opportunity to have a better life was just beyond a cell door. She stood and walked to the bars. There was another cell across from her, empty. Next to that was the doorway Nolen left through.

A vine burst between two stones in front of her. It curled up on the ground and stayed there. "I'll figure something out," she told the vine.

"How did I know you'd end up in here?"

"Witker, you beautiful Fae," she gasped when he emerged from the shadows.

She grinned as he walked toward her with his arms crossed. "That's the first time you've called me beautiful," he said. *Out loud*, she thought when he stood in front of her. He reached into the cell and took hold of her chin. "I like it," he said.

"Are you going to get me out of here?" She asked.

"Unless you can figure something else out," Witker said while brushing his thumb over her lip. She shook her head. "Then yes, I will get you out of here." Her grin widened to a painful degree when he held up a set of keys. "I've been waiting for hours."

"It hasn't been that long," she said as she walked along the bars to the door.

He laughed. "You have been climbing that castle for hours, Kitali, and I have been waiting for you to get caught for just as long."

"I'm disappointed you didn't believe in me," she said. The key slid into the lock and he turned it. "I killed him. Jassin."

"I believed you would do that," Witker said, pulling her into his arms. "I just didn't think you'd make it out. Hence me being kept company by rats." She laughed before he kissed her. Witker picked her up again and she wrapped her legs around his waist while he carried her out the way he came in. "Ready to get wet?" He asked.

She pulled back. "What?"

He bent down and lifted a grate off the floor. Water shined below in the minimal firelight. She cursed softly, then louder when he lowered her down. The frigid water soaked into her boots quickly. It rose to her knees and made her shiver instantly. Witker dropped next to her and smiled. "You won't be able to see from here onward," he said before lifting her over his shoulder.

"What happened to the other way you held me?" She asked. Her voice echoed over the stone walls around them.

"Your face is too distracting," he answered. Witker began to wade through water. She smiled as she pressed her elbows into his back. "I don't want to live in Calar, but I don't want to go home," he said, "I hate sharing a house."

She laughed. "What's wrong with sharing a house?" She wasn't sure where he was going with this sudden change in conversation. He might've been asking her to live with him, but she would not allow this to be how he went about it. He would have to ask her outright.

"Sharing," he answered.

"So you want to live alone?" She asked. He turned, began climbing something, and then dropped back down into much deeper water.

Witker said, "no, not alone."

"Then you'd have to share with someone," she said. A smile crept up on her face. "Ralyn made a perfect roommate. She cleaned for me. You could live with her."

He said, "I am not living with my sister."

"Why not?"

Witker dropped her. She splashed into the water, her hands and knees smacking against the stones beneath her as every inch of her body was covered. Gasping, she stood with her eyes shut and hands out at her sides. "Sorry," he said softly, "I should not have done that."

"If you do not get in that water right now," she pointed down, "I am never speaking to you again."

He laughed loudly. The echo of the sweet sound matched the lapping of the water as he submerged himself. "Better?" He asked. Witker took her hand and patted his body with it to show her he'd done what she wanted. "Forgiven?"

"Partially."

"This is what you wanted; why am I not forgiven completely?"

"You *dropped* me in the freezing water and you think that you and your adjust-to-temperature body being *prepared* for how cold it was when you dunked yourself in is going to make up for that?" She looked at him. Witker wasn't even a shadow. All she could see was darkness.

He asked, "when will you live with me?" In such a soft, gentle voice that it melted something in her.

"Not now," she said, "get me out of wherever we are and I'll think about it."

Witker lifted her again. "We lived in the woods and roomed in inns together," he said, "I doubt this will be much different."

"You were mean to me when we stopped at Leo's inn, remember?" She informed him, trying harder to dig her elbows into his back. He grunted. That was all. "So why is it different for you?" Kitali asked, but he did not answer. "Is there something about sleeping with a girl for the first time that's supposed to be special to a Fae? Or maybe just you?"

He remained silent for a minute or two. She put her chin in her hand and listened to the splashing while he walked. Witker didn't say a word. She must've pushed him too far. "I have never slept in the same bed as a woman," he said. She turned her head. "Females, yes, but you..." He trailed off. The splashing ceased eventually and the ground evened out. "I did not want to be so close to you, especially after I thought of you as someone I could love one day."

Kitali smiled. "That's a very good answer," she told him.

He grunted quite bashfully. A hint of light appeared. She turned as much as she could and looked at another grate. Witker set her on her feet carefully and climbed up to push on the metal above them.

"How did you find this?" She asked.

"It's a storm drain Ralyn found," he answered, "she spent weeks cataloging ways into the castle before she got the job as a guard."

She said, "thank you, Ralyn," while he shoved the grate out of the way. Witker lifted her up and she crawled out, sitting next to it while he lifted himself to whatever street they'd ended up on. Once she could see him and he was in no danger of falling back into the storm drain Kitali shoved him and he smiled at her.

Chapter Seventy

THE WALK FELT NEVER-ENDING. Kitali's leg made it slower. She insisted she not be carried anymore despite the pain that crackled like lightning with each step she took. She kept looking around as they went, walking with a big Fae behind her so no one bothered her. With him at her side, not a single person stopped her from throwing a rock at her statue and accidentally clipping off the end of her nose. Witker had laughed and told her now it looked nothing like her at all, then led her away.

"That's where I used to live," she said after a few minutes, pointing up at a building. Witker stopped and looked. She turned back to him, having only intended to point and keep going, but he faced the building keenly. "I don't have a key to go in," she said.

He frowned. "We could break in," Witker suggested.

She asked, "why?"

Witker shrugged, but he had an answer. She could see it. Kitali walked to him and put her arms around his waist. His warm body was drying his wet clothes much faster than hers was. He was still looking up at the building. She hummed enticingly. "I want to see what you were like," he answered.

"I was... messy," she said, "depressed... I lived small."

"There has to be more than that," he mumbled. Witker nodded and breathed in deeply through his nose. Her brow furrowed. "Come on," he decided and started walking. She let go of him. Witker was on his own mission now, going right into the building without her. Kitali laughed.

He held the door open.

"You are..."

"Wonderful?"

She walked toward him. "Out of your mind," she corrected. Kitali went up the stairs and he followed her to the door, which she motioned to, and he kicked it down. "Shit, Witker," she breathed, "by *break in*, you really meant break in."

He took her hand and kissed her knuckles before walking inside. It was a shock that no one else had broken inside. Kitali looked around at her old home, holding onto Witker's hand as he made his way slowly to the center of the apartment. He stopped there.

"This is an extensive book collection," he mumbled, nudging the stack with his boot. None of them fell. Witker began to spin in a slow circle. "Tell me of this place, Kitali," he said softly.

She rolled her eyes. "Well," she said, and he gave her his full attention. "I moved here upon Jassin's recommendation. He helped me pay for the place... and this," she put her hand on the back of her chair, "is my favorite chair." He smiled. "I slept in it more than in my actual bed."

"Why?" Witker sat in the chair, settling into the cushions as if he were testing how comfortable it was, or maybe because he wanted to see why she liked it so much. His hands slid over the soft arms on either side of him and he sighed with a nod.

His eyes went to the arrow on the wall and hers followed. Kitali took a deep breath as she went over to it, slowly taking it off the hooks. He only watched her. Kitali ran her thumb over the smooth shaft in two short sweeps before she snapped the arrow in two. She knelt in front of her fireplace and placed both halves of the arrow with the ashes and coals, adding small bits of kindling around it. Her heart hammered in her chest. When Kitali lit the arrow on fire it burned quickly. The iron arrowhead melted in seconds, and any remnants of King Assassin burned with it.

Kitali stood. Witker smiled and went to her, taking her hand in his. "Tell me of your bed," he said, motioning to her bedroom door.

"I hate sleeping in it," she answered with an easy shrug. Ten months of weight lifted off her shoulders. Kitali pulled him into the kitchen and told him about her broken pot and cups and having to replace things constantly. Witker asked very few questions. He looked at everything she had. His Fae eyes made it easy. He probably saw things that she didn't. He made few comments. Kitali grew self-conscious in her bedroom, where he decided to lie in her bed. She stood at the end of it.

"I see why you hate beds," he said, "this one is terribly uncomfortable." She laughed. "Why does it smell more like my sister than you?"

"Ralyn sleeps in it," she shrugged. He groaned and got up again. "So what do you think? Have you learned any-thing about me?"

He shook his head.

"So what was the point in coming up here?"

"I wanted to see the person you were before so I can know how much you grow when we have our own place," he answered. "This is the person who went by Kit. She kept to herself, did little decorating, and never bought anything new. I can't wait to see how you change."

Kitali smiled so much that her cheeks began to hurt. "Let's go before we get caught or something," she said, holding her hand out. Witker took it, taking a few lasting sweeps of the small place as they went to the door and back down the stairs. "I'm going to have to find a new favorite chair," she said.

"We will," he agreed. "And many books."

She glanced at him. "Do you like to read?" Kitali asked. She licked her lips nervously and they went down the stairs.

"I love reading," Witker answered. She nodded. *Great.* Witker pulled her out of the building and onto the dark street. Kitali looked back at the castle. "How will they announce his death?" He asked.

"Kit?"

Kitali spun around to the man who said her name. Aspen squinted on the dark, nearly empty street and began walking toward her.

"Oh my gods, Kit," he said.

He tried to hug Kitali. Witker pushed him back.

Aspen looked at Witker, then at Kitali. "Who's this?"

"Witker," she answered. Kitali wasn't sure what to do. She hadn't expected to see Aspen again. Truthfully, she could've gone the rest of her life never seeing him again. Not once, but twice did he pretend everything was fine. Twice, he tricked her. Twice, he hurt her. "Witker, this is Aspen."

"Aspen," Witker realized. He straightened. Aspen also tried to make himself taller, but he had nothing on the Fae before him. Witker had him beat in every way. "I have a question for you, Aspen," he said. Aspen kept looking from him to Kitali. Witker moved in front of her. "Were you knowingly aiding Jassin in manipulating and harming Kitali?" Aspen opened his mouth, but Witker snapped his fingers a few times like a male trying to gain the attention of something lesser than him—a dog, maybe. "Make sure you look at me when you answer."

Aspen laughed. It reminded Kitali of when Jassin did it. "Kit, what's going on? Is this man hurting you—"

Witker punched him in the face. Kitali screamed and covered her mouth as Aspen stumbled back with his hand over his nose. She looked around quickly, but the few people who were walking late into the night began to disappear into shadow. "Male," Witker corrected harshly, "and her name is Kitali."

He spit blood from his mouth and straightened. Kitali could see it rolling down his lip. His nose had broken. Aspen said, "I don't care what you are, you get away from her right now."

Witker looked back at Kitali, who still had her hands over her mouth. She was looking at the two of them with wide eyes. He smiled at her as if to say *let me deal with this.* She lowered her hands. "I think we should just go, Witker."

He turned to her. "Just a few good punches?" He asked.

"You're asking my *permission* to hurt Aspen?"

"Granted," Aspen grunted, and Witker pushed Kitali out of the way before he grabbed Aspen's wrist. She hit the ground, her hands scraping over the street, and Witker grabbed the knife Aspen had been holding as if Aspen was simply giving it away.

He held the knife against Aspen's throat. "As long as I have your permission, Kitali," the Fae hissed, his attention trained like a hunter on prey. "Won't you give me permission?"

"Are you kidding?" She gasped and got up. Kitali pulled on Witker's arm and took the knife from him. "He's my friend," she insisted.

Witker bared his teeth at Aspen, who flinched back a step. "Are you her friend?" Witker asked. He continued to try to move Kitali behind him. Did he really feel like Aspen would *hurt* her? Or was this a Fae territory issue? Kitali couldn't tell. She couldn't match him in strength, either, so he successfully pushed her back.

"I am her friend," Aspen said. He spat more blood onto the street.

"Then why does she have so many nightmares about you?"

Aspen's eyes widened disbelievingly. "They're *nightmares*," he said, "I don't have any control over her *nightmares!*"

"Shall I have control over yours?" Witker countered and lashed out again, but it wasn't for a knife this time. It was for his head. He twisted Aspen's arm behind him and jerked him back. Kitali looked around as he touched the side of the human's head and sought his nightmares.

She'd never seen the sominum from a different angle. The smoke—silver instead of black—gathered in the empty street, rising like it was being pushed against an invisible wall. Kitali stared at it, watching a nightmare form. Aspen was grunting and struggling, and Witker had his eyes trained forward. He covered Aspen's mouth when he began to scream.

"What is this?" Kitali asked. She was looking at herself, her hair long and her face a little older. Pregnant. "You have nightmares about me being pregnant?"

"No, my Kitali, it's a dream," Witker told her, "Aspen doesn't have nightmares."

She mumbled, "lucky him," and watched a different version of her walk around with a big belly in an unflattering dress. She was in a house, something big and bright, and other children were running around. "So... what does this say about him?" She asked. Pregnant dream Kit was talking to Jassin. "Why can't you hear anything?"

"It's just what he sees," Witker answered, "some people aren't creative enough for sound—"

"King Asassin," Kit said happily. She walked away from Jassin through a strange, minimally featured room. Kitali couldn't tell where they were in the house. It was as if it didn't matter. The *dream* was of her kissing Aspen and *Aspen* being King Asassin. Kit took a quiver and a bow from him and hung them on a hook against the wall.

"He's jealous of you," Witker said.

"Is that what his heart says..." She asked, her voice fading as the dream switched. The smoke churned as it changed. It was a sex dream now. Kitali—*Kit*—was below him. Her breasts were much more prominent in the dream than they were in real life, and she was moaning about Aspen being her hero and how he was so strong and good.

It churned with a new one. Kitali looked at Aspen. He was squirming, but not as much as she had been each time her nightmares had been in front of her. She wondered if it was because of what was being presented to him. She had only seen things that haunted her. He was seeing dreams. Things he wanted, things he wished for. Aspen didn't get nightmares.

Witker had been right about some people not being creative enough for full-fledged dreams. All they could really tell was that Aspen was the subject. He dreamed about being successful, about being King Assassin, and about wanting her.

"Witker, what does all of this say about *him*?" She asked after they watched him be presented with the arrow. Kit was standing to the side, cheering for him. "I don't get it, so he's jealous?"

The smoke faded. "He's jealous, infatuated with you, and willing to do whatever he has to to get that version of his life," Witker said as he pushed a confused Aspen away. Aspen hit the ground and stared at the spot where the smoke of dreams had been with a distant smile on his face. "Or some small part of it," Witker said.

"So do you think he really was working with Jassin the whole time?" Kitali asked.

"I would guess that Jassin promised you to him," he said.

Her brow furrowed. "What do you mean *promised me*?"

Witker stepped toward her. Aspen was still on the street. "You were both of their end goals," he said gently, "Jassin wanted to keep you as a fractured daughter, submissive and loving him faithfully, and Aspen wanted you. He's infatuated. Obsessed. Jassin most likely promised to help him win your favor."

Kitali blinked quickly and looked at Aspen. "He did all of that... so he could sleep with me?"

"He is a man," Witker shrugged. "They only think of one thing most of the time."

She let out a sad breath. Kitali stepped backward. "You can punch him a few times," she muttered and walked away. Witker laughed happily, but Kitali didn't watch. Her legs were weak, her body was heavy, and she was freezing. She wanted to go. To be free of Calar and arrows and men.

Chapter Seventy-One

SHE PEELED OFF HER jacket with her eyes closed while Witker untied her boots. He mumbled words of encouragement as if she needed to be encouraged to go to bed. Perhaps she was restless. The walk and seeing Aspen had been too much for her. She wasn't sure how she was standing on her own.

"How long am I allowed to sleep?" Kitali asked.

"As long as you want," he answered calmly.

She dropped her jacket to the ground. "I'm still wet," she said, pulling the scarf off her neck.

"Would you like to take off the rest of your clothes?" He asked. Witker pulled her boot off, causing her to lose her balance momentarily. He chuckled, and she held his shoulders so he could remove her second boot. "I would be happy to help," he offered.

"No, don't look," she mumbled as if he hadn't already seen her naked. Her entire body hurt. Once the adrenaline burned from her system, she felt less like an archer-turned-assassin and more like a grain stalk about to be pushed over by a light wind. She pulled her shirt off her body and limped toward the bed. Witker kept laughing. "You're not supposed to be looking," she said.

"I'm not," he replied. She dropped onto the bed and he took her socks off. "Come on, Kitali," he said as he lifted her hips and shifted her limp body so she was completely on the bed. "Do you want your pants off?"

She said, "I can do it."

"Can you?" His hand rested on her bare lower back. *Gods,* she thought when it did. She grunted. Witker said, "I'll do it for you."

"Don't look."

"I won't look," he said. Kitali did not protest to Witker pulling her pants off her hips. She wanted very much to enjoy what he was doing, to imagine it in a different context, yet as the wet fabric dragged down her calves, she could already feel herself falling asleep. She wasn't sure when he got them off or when she fell asleep, but she knew she was dreaming, and she knew it was of him. Not of his hands on her body but of a river and a discarded fishing pole and a cabin that singing was coming from.

The dream was peaceful. It lasted all night. The leaves were green, and the water was clear. It wasn't cold, but it wasn't warm. Kitali wasn't sure who was singing. Maybe it was her. But the cabin was empty like it needed to be filled, like something was beginning and they needed strong hands to lift each thing inside. One thing at a time. A bed, a couch, a table, a vase of wildflowers. A rug, some blankets, and cups. The cabin would fill, and things would move to make room until a veil was on the wall above the fireplace with a bowstring tying each tear together.

She opened her eyes and blinked fast. Witker was asleep below her, also not wearing a shirt. Looking down, she could see he wasn't wearing anything. "Witker," she said. He grunted. His chest rose deeply, making her rise as well. "Witker," she repeated. He opened one eye. "Why are you naked?"

He snorted and rubbed her back. A shiver rolled through her. "It's all right, Kitali," he said sweetly, "I didn't want to sleep in wet clothes. They should be dry by now, though, if you want to stop being naked."

She drew her lower lip into her mouth and shook her head. He smiled, reaching up to brush his thumb over her cheek. "Why are you looking at me like that?" She asked. He seemed calm. As if this was the most comfortable place he could be.

"You're beautiful when you just wake up," he said.

"For a human?" She asked.

He shook his head. "For anyone." Kitali smiled and bent toward him, kissing his cheek. "Let me get some mint leaves. I have a bad taste in my mouth," he told her, groaning as he got out of bed. She turned over, her arms folded over her chest. Kitali watched Witker bend toward the one bag he brought and take out a little pouch with mint leaves he chewed on sometimes. She held her hand out and he gave her one. They both chewed on mint leaves, staring at each other.

"I've never seen you naked before," she said.

Witker faced her completely. Her eyes widened. "What do you think?" He asked, his hands on his hips.

She had seen his sculpted body on multiple occasions. Recently, too. But Kitali had never seen his thighs, his rear, or... "That's," she said quietly. Witker looked down proudly. "Impressive," she decided to say.

"Why thank you," he said before leaving to relieve himself. Kitali pushed the blanket down and looked at her body, suddenly feeling inadequate. She'd never thought she had more or less of something. Not until seeing how much he had and how Aspen pictured her in his dreams.

Kitali covered herself back up. "Witker, I need you to tell me something," she called. He came out of the bathing room with wet hands and a smile. "I need you to tell me I look nice," she said. Kitali was burning hot and far too disappointed in herself.

"Oh, Kitali," he said. Witker crawled onto the bed and straddled her. He gave her a minty kiss. "You are so beautiful," he told her.

"Are you sure?" She asked.

He nodded.

"What if I'm too... human?" She asked. "You know we aren't really matched well. You're all better looking and shaped and things."

Witker looked down. He sat back on her hips and pulled the blanket down. "You're right, we aren't matched well," he said as he looked at her breasts. Kitali burned brighter.

"There is a toughness to females I find very unattractive. You women, though," he said with a sigh and a shake of his head. "You're so much softer and sweeter. And my Kitali is the softest," he bent and kissed her nipple, "sweetest of them all." He kissed the second.

"You prefer it?" She asked.

"Of course," he said. Witker nibbled on her, his sharp canines scraping over sensitive skin. Kitali breathed in deeply, and he left a trail of kisses around her breast and up her throat. "Do you have any other questions?" He whispered.

He kissed her bite mark, and a fire burned in her belly. "Yes," she said. Witker hummed and waited. "Do you want me to drink your blood, too?" She asked.

His eyes met hers as he lifted his head. "Did Ralyn tell you that?"

Kitali bit her lip. "She told me there's this joining thing and you did half of it. I think I should do the other half."

"You don't have to do that, Kitali," he said. Witker caressed her face and shook his head. "I know it's different for a human. You may not like that sort of thing—"

"Let me try, Witker," she insisted.

He cast a wary look at her. Kitali nodded. Witker straightened once again and looked at his finger, then at her. Her brows rose impatiently. She watched him bite the pad of his finger, and blood bloomed from beneath his skin. "Are you sure?" He asked.

Kitali took his hand. The little drop of blood dripped slowly down his finger. Her heart thumped quickly between her thighs. She pulled his hand toward her and opened her mouth, licking the drop up from the base of his finger to the tip. Witker's intense green eyes never left her.

"That doesn't taste like I imagined it would," she told him.

"What does it taste like?" He asked in just a whisper.

She licked her lips. "It's a lot sweeter than mine," she said, "mine tastes kind of like metal—"

Witker kissed her fiercely and she inhaled sharply. "Kitali, my Kitali," he breathed and kept kissing her. "My lovely Kitali," he said.

Kitali laughed a little and he lifted his head. "Was that a good thing to say?"

He grinned at her. "To taste the sweetness in someone's blood is a very good thing, yes," he said, kissing her deeply. Kitali breathed in, rising to her elbows to stay connected to him. Witker moaned into her mouth and his tongue brushed hers. He said, "we were meant to be."

"Because you're sweet to me?" She asked.

He nodded. "You're sweet to me, too."

"And painful," she added.

Witker chuckled. She realized then that she had never liked the sound from another person the way she liked it from Witker. She had found comfort in the laughs of Aspen and Jassin but safety in Witker. The way he laughed at her or with her. And he was grinning more than he ever had as he did it.

Chapter Seventy-Two

Kitali left the bathing room with more energy than usual. She wrung her hands together as she went to Witker and climbed onto the bed.

"Let me look at your leg," he insisted. She turned, her back to him, and he put his hand on her calf. "It had been bleeding before, yes?"

"I think it tore a little when I was climbing the castle," she said. "Do I need stitches?"

He said, "no, the bleeding stopped and it looks fine. I'd like for you to stay off it from now on, though."

Kitali turned around. "Good thing I have a big, strong male that likes to carry me around," she told him, "and I have a room we don't have to leave." He raised a brow at her. Kitali crawled over and knelt between his legs.

"You don't like it when I carry you around," he said as she nudged him onto his back. Witker sighed against the pillows. His hands dragged over her arms.

"Shush," she replied and kissed him slowly. Witker reached for her face, holding onto her cheek and silently begging for more from her. "I want to please you," she told him, "like you pleased me."

"Ah, no, my love," he said, pulling her back when she tried to move down the bed. "I will only find pleasure when you come for me, not the other way around." Witker pulled her into his lap. She straddled him, remaining on her knees with his hand between her thighs.

She breathed in deeply as his thumb brushed over her. "Do you not... want me to..." She searched his face.

"Allow me to explain," he offered. She nodded, wrapping an arm around his shoulders as he touched her. "You humans have the fantastic ability to feel pleasure at nearly anything. A touch," he said, and she shivered. "A kiss..." He pressed his mouth to hers and she moaned, gasping as his thumb twitched over her. "Even your nipples can provide you with pleasure. Men are the same."

She nodded, gripping his hair as he pressed a finger into her. Kitali breathed out. "And you don't?"

"Ours are different. Males especially. Females have similar abilities to come as you do, but males are driven to please," he said. She swallowed with her eyes closed. His finger moved in and out, curling expertly. "You *could* pleasure me, and I would come, but it would sadden me more than it would please me."

"I don't get it," she mumbled weakly.

"If I were to finish and you did not, it would depress me," he said. Witker moved a second finger into her. Kitali moaned, and he sighed, keeping up the same pace as he had before.

He kissed her neck and she asked, "why? Why is it different for males?"

"Just as I want to aid you when you bleed," he answered simply, "my body was built to please you. Pleasing a female you are partnered with... provides more ecstasy than being pleased. I want more than anything in the world to have your come on my hand, in my mouth, on my cock..." He kissed her, and his other hand moved around her back, rocking her forward. Kitali trembled. "Please let me."

She opened her eyes and looked at him. Kitali nodded. She followed the motion he intended, rocking with his hand. Witker stared at her, pleading with her. She could see it in his eyes—he could go for hours just making her happy. He *wanted* to.

"If we weren't partners," she asked, "would it be different? Like what Poer and Detin thought I was before they knew I was Kitali?"

"If we weren't partners and you were just a human, then yes, my pleasure would matter more," he answered, "but it does not. You are more than a human; I feel you are more than a partner. Now, will you let me pleasure you without further interruption?" Kitali smiled and kissed him. Witker moaned and caressed her, deep inside as he lifted her up and laid her on her back. "Please be mine," he said. She pressed against the rough blanket, moving her leg against the wall. "I beg you," Witker breathed, "I beg you to be mine."

"I need you," she whispered, "inside me, please—"

His mouth covered hers and he shook his head. "Not yet," he said and she groaned. "Not yet, my Kitali. I am not finished here."

"Witker," she moaned. Kitali had never finished on someone's hand before. She had little experience on the subject. She knew men, though. She knew that they were quick, that they did as she asked, but when presented with the opportunity to be inside her, they'd take it. Not Witker. He outright refused, as if to stop with his fingers would bring shame to him. He was so focused on ensuring she finished that it did not matter what happened to him.

He laid over her and snatched her hand away when she touched him.

"No, Kitali, just you," he said.

She groaned and smacked the wall. "It doesn't feel fair," she said, and he rolled his thumb the right way. It was as if he was searching for something, and he'd know as soon as he found it. Her lashes fluttered. He kissed her throat and her neck.

"That is because you are a human," he told her. "Trust me, my Kitali, I am more than pleased."

"Promise?"

"Finish for me," he urged and pressed just the slightest bit harder. Kitali moaned, and he did it again. Over and over until each moan brought her closer and closer and closer. Kitali moaned his name. Her nails dug into his shoulder and she shook as she finished. Witker moaned as if he was the one to feel it. "Thank you," he said with a kiss, "thank you."

"You're so strange," she mumbled, releasing her hand from him.

"Please be mine," he said, "I need you."

Kitali smiled at him. "In what way?" She asked. She reached up and traced the edges of his face. Witker breathed in and leaned into her touch. "Are you going to bite me to mark your territory and call it a day? Please me when you want to feel pleasure?"

"That doesn't sound so horrible, does it?" He asked with a teasing laugh. Witker shook his head, "I would like you to be more than that, my Kitali. I would like you to make a home with me. For us to share the world. To partner and one day marry barefoot over dirt beneath a tree."

"With two rings?" She asked.

"If that is what you wish," he agreed.

Kitali hummed and considered. His eyes grew wary. "*If*," she decided and he perked up. Witker was already nodding, and she laughed. "If we do it like in my dream."

He tilted his head. "And what was your dream?"

"Use your sominum, find out," she said.

Witker kissed her cheek and flicked the side of her head, moving onto his back to watch smoke form over their heads.

"And we're having sex after this, just so you know," she whispered.

"If it pleases you," he said.

She rolled her eyes and the dream started.

Chapter Seventy–Three

"I'm back, I'm back," Witker said as he unlocked the door. Kitali looked up. She was on the floor, mostly dressed and coaxing flames to catch on a fresh log. "You were supposed to stay naked," he told her. Witker shut them both in with a little box and two steaming mugs.

She said, "you dressed." Kitali stood and set her tool aside, holding her hands out. Witker walked toward her proudly. She grabbed the little box before going to the bed. It was the last time either of them promised to leave for the rest of the day—Witker had to get something for her to eat after her stomach began to rumble too much. She crossed her bare leg and left the injured one extended.

"I've got cider and warm ale as well," he said, showing them off as if he'd gone hunting for them. The seller was just next door.

"What a find," she said, leaning forward to kiss him. Witker sat as she opened her box and grinned at the cinnamon-covered sweet. "So, where shall we live?" She asked him.

"Nowhere near Niverly or Calar," he muttered and her smile faded. Witker put the drinks on the floor and slid his bag over. He began to search for something and Kitali looked him over. She set the treat aside and took a deep breath.

"Can we talk about Niverly now?" She asked softly. He produced a map. "I want to know what happened."

He cast a wary gaze her way, grimacing. Witker opened the map and both of their eyes found Niverly. It was right there, the words in shining black ink. "Are you sure?" He asked. She nodded. "It's going to hurt you," he said uncomfortably.

"I want to know what happened," she said surely.

Witker looked away. His eyes moved over the empty wall in front of him and he took a deep, long breath in. He looked at her once again. "I was regularly hired by the human resistance to raid villages and things," he told her, "we would go and... break things, hurt people... maybe one or two humans would die, but they were just raids. Until the humans began to believe it wasn't working. They might've been losing support, I'm not sure, but they decided a true attack needed to be made."

"But why Niverly?" She asked.

"The honest answer is tea," he said. Witker winced at her pained expression. "Fae have always had a better connection to nature than humans, but there was something about that area and the growth that was just *better*. We've always been jealous of it. Your tea just tastes better." Kitali nodded. She pulled her legs toward her and wrapped her arms around herself. He sighed. "It was a good place to stage an attack. With Icar being its sister village, some went there for a raid, but most went to Niverly. Myself and my parents included."

She met his eyes and nodded for him to continue.

"We went in," he said, "burned things, tore down buildings... but the killing didn't start until we burned the fields. We pretended to leave afterward, to fake it just being a raid, and when people went out to try to save what they could, we went back in."

Kitali said, "one thing I noticed..." He looked at her. "When people talk about it. The humans call it a slaughter, but the Fae call it a tragedy. Why?"

"It was a slaughter," he told her, "but we refer to it as a tragedy because of the toll it takes upon nature. To kill that many people... it damages the world. It cuts the Rift deeper."

Her brow twitched at the mention of the Rift, which she had apparently healed by dying.

Witker said, "I've never felt more guilty about anything. And it worked—Niverly sparked support that the resistance originally didn't have, and more humans decided to join. With Jassin's emotional connection to it, I'm sure he gained even more support." She nodded. "The humans rallied, and when the time came... Prince Crius finally came of age, and you killed him on his coronation day."

"Did you keep doing the raids?" She asked him.

Witker shook his head. "That was my last one. After my parents were killed, I put all my focus on that farm and painting to take care of Ralyn."

"How did they die? Your parents?"

He set the map aside and crawled over. Witker pulled her legs down slowly, then pushed her onto her back. He moved her flat and settled over her with his head on her chest. "Some of the displaced humans from Niverly came and took their revenge. They came into the house. I can't exactly be mad... it's what we did to them."

"You can be mad," Kitali said. She brushed her hand over his hair. "Just at them, though. Not at everyone."

Witker wrapped his arms tight around her and nodded as a bang came to the door. Kitali jumped. "The Crowns are all dead!" Ralyn shouted from outside. She banged again. "Get out here, we have to celebrate!"

"We said we'd stay here for the rest of the day," Kitali whispered.

"Are you busy?" Ralyn asked with much disgust. "You could at least answer me!"

"Yes!" Witker shouted and lifted himself for a kiss. Kitali grunted, and he made a sloppy sound and a moan. Ralyn gagged. When he stopped, she assumed Ralyn left. Witker smiled at her. "Sorry," he said and laid back down.

She said, "that was perfectly all right. What happens now?"

"Oh, the humans will be pissed, and there will be a big fight that Masine will have to settle," he grunted. His arms went back around her. "Once word spreads that the Rift healed, it should calm everyone down. You and I, however," he squeezed, "are going to find a cabin in the woods and turn your dream into something real. Like something out of a storybook."

She bit her lip and took a deep breath. "Witker, I have to tell you something," she said with a grimace. He lifted his head. "I hate reading."

"What?" He asked and sat up.

"I hate it," she repeated, "so much."

He shook his head with wide eyes. "But you have all those books—"

"I pretend to like reading so people won't bother me," Kitali told him. He covered his mouth. "I'm sorry, I hate reading and have for my entire life."

"Stories are the foundation for our imaginations. They shape our lives," he said.

"Not mine," she said.

Witker looked quite disgusted with her. She lifted herself to her elbows and kissed him to wipe the expression off his face. He groaned and kissed her harder. It was an angry kiss, but she knew he'd get over it as long as she promised he could tell her about whatever book he wanted to read. Kitali could entertain him the way she did not entertain anyone else. In a cabin like a dream that would never turn into a nightmare.

Epilogue

Witker

THE HUMAN RIOTS AFTER the fall of the Crowns were to be expected. Witker found that they were just as violent as the ones he attended. The ones he fought in. He often thought back to them every time word of another riot spread. How he'd broken things and people and had torn lives apart.

He thought of Niverly more often than ever. From his understanding, there had yet to be another one. Humans were not going into Fae towns and killing, but they were destroying buildings and tearing down more monuments than ever.

Kitali's statue included.

She often stood on the pedestal where it had once been and spoke to the people of Calar. She admitted to assassinating Crown Jassin Gillhan and to betraying the humans and finding the New Heir. When some humans finally gave her a chance to explain herself she managed to calm some of them. Witker was still shocked, though, at the humanity of all of the humans in Calar. He had expected the hatred and the riots, but not their understanding. When it was discovered what the Crowns had had planned for the Fae, many saw it the same way Kitali had—as something shameful and wrong.

The Fae, too, loved her anew. Witker thought that Masine had more to do with that than Kitali did. King Masine walked the streets with Kitali on his arm, saying hello to both humans and Fae. He provided food and comfort, he made promises of peace that not many believed.

But the land was healed, and the Rift had yet to open again. That fact was what was holding the kingdom together.

Witker stuffed Kitali's blanket into his bag, having given up on folding things hours ago. The things Kitali decided to keep were all packed by the door, Witker was only going over the final steps. He had his last bag sitting on the tall backed chair Kitali claimed to love so much, and yet she was leaving it.

He listened through the open window of Ralyn's apartment as a Fae declared his loyalty to Masine and cited his past friendships with humans in the hopes that they could heal their relationships.

Ralyn knocked on the open door before she entered. "You're really going?" She asked him. "Now?"

"It's been two months, that was the time we agreed," Witker said. Ralyn walked closer, her arms around her torso. "Would you like to come?" He asked. She shook her head. Witker knew her answer would be no, which was why he asked. Ralyn had already claimed she'd like to stay in Calar, but would visit as much as she could. She was a guard to someone she *wanted* to protect now. She would not give that up to intrude on Witker and Kitali's newfound peace.

She sighed and said, "I just thought you'd extend the date and keep extending it until things were all right here."

"Things are all right," Witker said. The Fae shouting in the street was joined by a human, one who agreed that peace was on the horizon.

"No they aren't, don't be stupid," Ralyn said. She grabbed Witker's bag and set it aside, then sat in Kitali's favorite chair. "Someone set fire to West Ball last night," she told him, "and we put it out quick enough, but all the windows shattered and a few people have burns that need to be healed. Not to mention the pretty ballroom floor is ruined."

Witker scrubbed his hand over the back of his neck. "Does Kitali know?" He asked. Ralyn nodded. "Shit," he said, "she won't want to leave now."

"She does too want to leave now," Kitali said as she came through the door. Witker straightened. "Masine's peace is Masine's to worry about, I want *mine*," she said. Kitali walked to Witker, wrapping her arms around his waist.

"Let's leave now before anyone else can interrupt," Witker said. He lifted her up with one arm and began carrying her toward the door, but Ralyn kicked his hip and cursed at him. He turned to her, setting Kitali back on her feet. "Yes, Ralyn?" He asked as kindly as he could. Witker rubbed his hip and looked down at her.

"I expect letters and updates as soon as you're settled," she said. "And Kitali," she said, making eye contact with the human still wrapped around Witker.

Kitali smiled. "Of course I'll let you know as soon as it happens," she said.

"Good," Ralyn sighed shortly. "Don't forget your bag."

Witker rolled his eyes and left Kitali to grab the last bag he packed. "Enjoy the place to yourself," he grunted, then took Kitali's hand and led her toward the door.

"Bye, Ralyn!" Kitali shouted, then picked up two bags and left the apartment. She did not look back.

Witker carried her dented pot down the stairs and deposited it in the cart of their things. "Did you already say goodbye to Masine?" He asked Kitali. She hummed a yes as she fixed one of Treyla's braids. He asked, "what was Ralyn silently saying to you before we left?"

She smiled coyly and kissed Treyla's muzzle before she went to climb into the cart. Witker latched the cart door shut and climbed on after her. "Ralyn made a bet with me," Kitali told him as they began moving down the road. Calar, in all its disgusting, smelly might, would be behind them soon enough. Witker could not wait to be free of the place. He hadn't expected Kitali to decide to stay for two more months to help Masine's transition to power, and it had beat on him every day like he imagined an ocean beating against a cliff. It was finally coming to an end.

"And what did you bet?" He asked.

"That we wouldn't last a year without being married," she answered.

He nodded slowly. Witker shifted in the small cart seat. "You don't wish to be married in less than a year?" He asked softly.

"Do you?" She countered with a strangely apprehensive gleam in her dark eyes.

Witker looked at her seriously. "Kitali, I would like to be married to you as soon as possible, I would not have it any other way," he said, "but... would you?"

"*She* thinks it'll take longer than a year," Kitali told him. "*I* think it'll be eight months before you're badgering me about your half ring and I'm looking for the right kind of lace for my veil."

He grinned and kissed her furiously. It was something dangerous he decided to do often—to kiss her in public. The idea that a human and a Fae could form this sort of relationship was still unheard of, but Witker dared anyone to tell him he could not kiss his Kitali.

Witker sat back with the thought of his half ring finally whole, resting on her finger where he could look at it every day.

It took eighteen days to reach Masai. Kitali described exactly what she wanted to happen in the first days of their newfound peace in their new home, deciding everything that would be done to every potential room they might have.

When she discovered that the house Witker had bought from an old friend was a small single bedroom with no separation between her kitchen and her living room, she was not deterred. She simply changed a few things in her original plan.

It was a one-story house at the very end of a dirt road that overlooked one of Masai's twin rivers and was surrounded by trees. There were spiders on the porch and a raccoon living in the rafters. It looked to have once been red but was a far more muted orange color now. Age had turned the windowpanes rotted, and the roof would need to be rebuilt in the next few years, but it was something they could share and work on together.

"Look at the *color*," Kitali said before Witker pulled Treyla to a stop in front of the house. "I bet the light in the evening is so pretty coming through the windows," she said, shaking Witker's arm.

She hopped down and unhooked Treyla from the cart. Witker smiled at her, then at the house.

"We should clear out this area in the front for a garden," she said as she motioned to the ground on the left, "and build a bench where we can sit and fish by the river. And we need room for a pen for Treyla, oh and maybe we could get chickens!" Kitali turned to him. "Can we get chickens?"

He climbed down and nodded. "As many as you'd like," he said. Kitali grinned.

"I want to see inside," she said, bouncing in her boots. Kitali clasped his hand and dragged him toward the door, leaving Treyla to graze along the road. Witker slid the key into the lock and she bounced some more, making the porch creak. "You trust the friend you bought it from, don't you?" She asked, "he didn't sell you a broken house?"

"He shouldn't have," Witker said with a shrug. He pushed the door open and they watched it creak, then fall from its hinges and smack against the floor. Kitali laughed sharply before she dragged him inside.

Aside from the door, it didn't seem too far beyond repair. Witker looked around. The house was as small as he imagined, but Kitali somehow made it look grand. She spoke of color and of curtains for the front windows. She told him what they'd hang on the walls, where they would stack dishes and things in the limited kitchen, then they unpacked their cart according to her dream.

Witker placed two pillows on the floor of their bedroom where the blanket was and Kitali laid against them. They did not have a bed, so the two of them were back to bedrolls and keeping the fire going to ensure Kitali didn't freeze at night. She looked up at the ceiling and he looked down at her, slowly moving to her side.

"Will we have to move when we have children?" She asked softly, "because there's no other room?"

"We could always build another room," Witker suggested. He wrapped his arms around her and rested his head on her chest. Kitali ran her fingers through his hair. "Unless you'd like to move," he added, "then we can find a new place."

She sighed. Kitali said, "do you know what Masine called me when I said goodbye?" He shook his head. "The Healer of the Rift," she told him. Kitali laughed softly, making his head fill with the hum from in her chest. Witker closed his eyes.

"I like that much better than King Assassin," he whispered.

"Me too," she agreed softly.

The End.

There are two sides to every coin, two sides to every con-
flict, and two sides to every story.

Sominium
12/28/2026